Animus: Vanishing Point

Tales from the Multiverse

by

Ed Rodriguez

Animus: Vanishing Point

Tales From the Multiverse

Paperback ISBN: 979-8-9928580-4-4
Hardcover ISBN: 979-8-9928580-3-7
E-Book ISBN: 979-8-9928580-5-1

Cover design: Neil Que
Interior design: Ed Rodriguez
Printed in the United States of America
First Edition: 2025

Gratitude & Dedication

To my family and friends who listened patiently as I explained mythologies of beings they'd never meet, who supported a creative journey they couldn't always understand —your steady presence anchored me through every draft and revision.

To the early players of the Animus Draft-Building Card Game, whose enthusiasm showed me these characters had stories worth telling beyond strategic mechanics—your passion kept this project alive and reminded me why interactive storytelling matters.

To the special people in my life who taught me that real power comes from lifting others up—your lessons about compassion and resilience live in every character who chooses hope over despair.

To the fantasy and science fiction communities, the comic book creators who showed me how to balance intimate character moments with cosmic scope, and the anime storytellers who taught me that the most powerful battles are often fought in the human heart—your dedication to exploring big questions through impossible scenarios has been my constant inspiration.

To everyone who has ever felt like an outsider, who has questioned the rules they were given, who refuses to accept that the world is only what we can see—this multiverse has room for all of you. Your belief in the impossible makes the impossible possible.

Thank you for making room in your reality for mine.

Table of Contents

Foreword..7
Prologue – The Singularity.................................11
Alluvium..17
Velocity Shift...39
Ghost Code...79
Monster Kids..111
Eclipsed Suns...129
Unseen Lament...157
Steel Hearts & Silicon Dreams........................175
Ashes of Redemption...201
The Crimson Ascendant.....................................223
Fallen Angel..261
Spirit of Retribution...317
The Grinning Abyss..367
The Architect's Garden....................................415
Reaper's Genesis...447
The Endless Cage...467
Epilogue - The Rupture......................................499
Afterword..531

Works by Ed Rodriguez

BOOKS
No Horizon: Survivor's Edge

Animus: Vanishing Point – Tales from the Multiverse

ANIMUS CARD GAME SERIES
Animus – The Draft-Building Card Game

Core Sets:

- *Vanishing Point – Core Set 1*
- *Shattered Fantasy – Core Set 2*
- *Fallen Order – Core Set 3*

Expansion Sets:

- *Nemesis – Expansion Set 1*
- *The Wretched – Expansion Set 2*
- *Torment – Expansion Set 3*

WELLNESS RESOURCES
Fighting Shadows: Own Your Darkness - A Companion Deck for Navigating Depression

Foreword

Dear Reader,

Many years ago, I found myself with a dilemma that many creative minds will recognize: too many character ideas for a single story to contain. These characters—heroes, villains, and the countless shades between—had been growing in my imagination since my teenage years, evolving and deepening as I did. Rather than letting them remain trapped in my mind, I first gave them life in the *Animus Draft-Building Card Game*, creating a multiverse where they could clash on cosmic stages.

But card games, by their nature, can only offer glimpses. Character descriptions are condensed to fit text boxes; complex motivations are distilled into game mechanics; rich backstories are hinted at but never fully explored. The game introduced these characters to the world, but it couldn't give them the depth they deserved—the space to breathe as fully realized people with histories, fears, dreams, and the kind of complicated inner lives that make characters feel real.

This book, *Animus: Vanishing Point - Tales from the Multiverse*, is my attempt to finally do right by these characters who have lived with me for decades.

What you'll find here are fifteen standalone stories, each one a deep dive into a different corner of this multiverse I've been building. While the stories can be read independently, they're arranged in a deliberate sequence that will gradually reveal the larger forces at work behind the scenes. Think of it as peeling back layers of reality itself, each story bringing you closer to understanding the cosmic framework that connects them all.

These aren't just expanded character profiles or game tie-ins. They're complete narratives that explore themes of power and responsibility, freedom and control, the price of knowledge, and what it means to choose your own path when the universe itself might be conspiring against you. Some characters you'll love, others might disturb you, and a few will challenge everything you think you know about heroes and villains.

This collection represents more than twenty years of world-building, character development, and storytelling refinement. It's the culmination of my desire to create something that honors both the mythic scope of the multiverse I've imagined and the deeply personal stories of the individuals who inhabit it.

My hope is that these characters will come alive for you as they have for me, that their struggles will resonate beyond the fantastic circumstances that surround them, and that by the time you reach the final page, you'll understand why I couldn't let their stories remain untold.

Thank you for being willing to step into this multiverse with me. The journey ahead is unlike anything else.

Sincerely,

Ed Rodriguez

Prologue – The Singularity

In the beginning, there was silence.

Not the absence of sound, but something far more profound—a stillness that existed before the very concept of noise could take root. It was the silence of potential, of infinite possibilities held in perfect suspension, waiting for the first breath of creation to disturb their eternal slumber.

Across the vast expanse of what mortals might call eternity, universes bloomed like flowers in an endless garden. Each one unique, each one precious, each one unaware of its countless siblings spinning through the cosmic dark. Worlds where gravity flowed upward, where time moved in spirals, where love was a tangible force that could be harvested and stored. Realities where the dead walked alongside the living in perfect harmony, where mathematics sang lullabies to sleeping planets, where a single thought could birth entire civilizations.

They existed in blissful isolation, these infinite realms, separated by barriers as thin as gossamer yet as impenetrable as the walls between dreams. Each universe followed its own natural rhythm, its own sacred cadence, like instruments in an orchestra that had never learned to play together.

Yet beyond the reach of any mortal understanding, in a realm that existed outside the very concept of existence, lay the Vanishing Point.

It was the horizon at the edge of forever, the final destination that all souls sensed but could never name. Neither light nor darkness touched this place, for it existed in the spaces between spaces, in the pause between one heartbeat and the next. The Vanishing Point was where all journeys ended and all questions found their answers—or perhaps where they discovered that some questions were never meant to be asked.

This impossible realm was both sanctuary and prison, a place so fundamentally removed from reality that it could safely house the most dangerous secret in all creation. For at the heart of the Vanishing Point, protected by layers of impossibility and guarded by the very nature of nothingness itself, lay the Singularity.

It was not a place, for it existed everywhere at once. It was not a thing, for it transcended the very notion of substance. The Singularity simply *was*—the eternal wellspring from which all existence drew its breath, the invisible thread that connected every star to every grain of sand, every heartbeat to every dying gasp. It pulsed with a power so absolute, so fundamentally pure, that even to glimpse its true nature would unmake the observer in ways that matter could not comprehend.

From its sanctuary within the Vanishing Point, the Singularity maintained the delicate balance, ensuring that each universe remained sovereign in its own right while contributing to the greater tapestry of creation. It was the conductor's baton in the hands of no conductor, the painter's brush guided by no artist. Through its infinite wisdom—or perhaps its infinite indifference—order persevered across the multiverse, protected by barriers that defied comprehension.

Few beings across the infinite realities even suspected its presence, yet all were drawn to it in ways they could not fathom. It called to them in dreams they could not remember upon waking, in the corner of their vision where shadows seemed to move with purpose, in the moments of perfect silence when the universe held its breath.

And so the multiverse continued its eternal dance, each universe spinning to its own music, each reality painting its own masterpiece across the canvas of existence. Heroes rose and fell. Empires crumbled into dust that became the foundation for new worlds. Love bloomed in the hearts of beings who would never know that their passion echoed across a trillion other hearts in a trillion other realities.

It was a time of perfect balance, of infinite potential held in check by invisible hands. The Singularity hummed with contentment, the universes sang their separate songs, and the Vanishing Point kept its patient vigil at the edge of all things.

In this cosmic harmony, nothing could go wrong.

Nothing *would* go wrong.

The very idea was impossible, inconceivable, antithetical to the natural order that had persisted since before time learned to count itself.

Yet somewhere in the vast network of realities, a single thought began to form. A question that had never been asked before, born from the mind of someone who had glimpsed just enough of the truth to become dangerous. It was a small thought, insignificant really—barely more than a whisper in the cosmic wind.

But whispers, as any wise soul knows, have a way of growing louder.

And in the perfect silence of the multiverse, even the smallest sound can shatter worlds.

Ed Rodriguez

Alluvium

"I will not be defined by my past.

I will create my own future."

The dunes sang when the wind blew from the east. A low, mournful hum that resonated in the bones of those who lived beneath them. The people of Salcera believed it was the voice of the desert itself—a warning. Juvia Valiente knew better. The sound was merely air passing through countless grains of sand, through the alluvium deposits that formed this harsh landscape—a natural phenomenon that required no mysticism to explain.

But tonight, as the village elders gathered in the central square, even Juvia felt a chill when that hum rose to meet the full moon.

"The time of offering approaches," Elder Tomas announced, his weathered face illuminated by torchlight. "The Beast stirs in the deep sands. We must prepare."

Murmurs rippled through the crowd. Children were ushered inside, doors bolting behind them. Juvia stood tall among the villagers, her chin lifted in silent defiance. At twenty-two, she had witnessed sixteen offerings in her lifetime, never questioning what exactly was being offered or why the chosen courier—always a man—returned hollow-eyed and alone.

"Our strongest men have fallen to the fever," Tomas continued, his gaze sweeping the diminished ranks of village men. The recent illness had claimed many lives, leaving Salcera vulnerable. "We have no one to make the journey."

"I will go," Juvia stepped forward, her voice cutting through the night air like a blade.

Laughter erupted from several elders. Elder Merita, the only woman among them, didn't laugh. Her eyes narrowed, calculating.

"A woman cannot face the desert path," Tomas dismissed her with a wave. "The journey requires strength."

"And what strength remains in Salcera?" Juvia challenged, moving closer to the circle of elders. Her dark hair whipped in the night wind beneath her hood, unbound and wild as her spirit. "Your men lie fevered or dead. I have crossed the salt flats three times to trade with the northern settlements. My arms are strong from working the forge with my father. My eyes are sharp."

She let her coat fall open slightly, revealing the gleaming staff secured across her back and the oversized pistol holstered at her hip—a custom weapon she'd designed with her father in their forge. It fired shells almost the size of her palm, its brass fittings and reinforced barrel gleaming dully in the torchlight—each shot capable of stopping a charging desert bull in its tracks.

"It is not our way," another elder protested.

"Then your way condemns us all," Juvia replied. The crowd shifted uncomfortably behind her.

Elder Merita finally spoke, her voice dry as the desert itself. "The girl is right. We have no choice."

Dawn broke over Salcera in a blaze of orange and gold. The village sat in a pocket of green—an alluvial plain carved by the seasonal river that brought life-giving silt and water to the edge of the wasteland. Beyond the fields of grain and vegetable plots, the desert stretched like a predator waiting to pounce, its dunes and rocky outcroppings a stark contrast to the lush pocket of civilization.

Juvia stood at the boundary between fertile soil and shifting sand, a pack slung over her shoulders, her staff gripped firmly in one hand. Her frayed green coat fluttered in the morning breeze, its edges worn from years of desert travel. The knee guards and reinforced leggings she wore had seen many battles, their scars telling stories of close encounters with the wilderness.

Elder Merita approached, leading a small two-wheeled wagon. In it sat a square clay container about three feet on each side, its surface covered in ancient symbols and sealed with wax and clay.

"The offering," Merita said, handing Juvia the wagon's handles. "Do not open it. Do not damage it. Deliver it to the Stone Teeth by tomorrow's sunset."

"What's inside?" Juvia asked, surprised by the container's weight. Something within it shifted slightly, causing the wagon to rock.

"That is not for you to know," Merita's eyes hardened. "Only that it appeases the Beast. This is the way it has always been."

Juvia's fingers tightened around the container. "And if I fail?"

"Then the Beast will come for us all." Merita's voice dropped to a whisper. "It hungers for the young, for their innocence and potential. The offering satisfies this hunger."

As Juvia turned to leave, she caught sight of children watching from shadows. Their small faces solemn, knowing. One girl, no more than seven, raised her hand in a furtive wave. Juvia nodded in acknowledgment before stepping onto the shifting ground that would be her path into the wasteland.

By midday, the sun transformed the desert into a shimmering hell. Heat radiated from above and below, creating mirages that danced at the edge of vision. Juvia had removed the clay container from the wagon and secured it on a makeshift sled she dragged behind her—the wagon's wheels had proven useless in the deeper sand. She'd wrapped the container in cloth to shield it from the brutal sun.

The container troubled her. Its weight wasn't consistent—sometimes it seemed heavier, sometimes lighter. Once, she could have sworn she felt it tremble.

As the sun began its descent, Juvia spotted the first signs of the Beast's territory. Dead vegetation protruded from the sand like blackened fingers. Bones—some animal, some disturbingly human—lay half-buried in the dunes. The air grew thick with an acrid smell, like rotting meat mixed with sulfur.

She made camp in the shelter of a large rock formation, building a small fire not for warmth but to ward off the desert's nocturnal predators. As darkness fell, the dunes began their eerie song, louder here than back in Salcera.

As she checked the container, placing her ear against its side, she heard something that made her blood freeze.

A whimper. Soft, but unmistakably human.

With trembling hands, Juvia broke the clay seal and pried open the container's heavy lid.

Inside, curled in a fetal position, was a child—a boy no older than five, drugged into semi-consciousness. His small chest rose and fell with shallow breaths. His wrists and ankles bore the marks of restraints now removed.

"No," Juvia whispered, horror and rage building within her. "No, no, no."

The child stirred slightly at her voice. His eyes fluttered open, revealing irises the color of amber. His parched lips moved soundlessly.

"Water," Juvia quickly retrieved her water skin, cradling the boy's head as she helped him drink. "Slowly now."

As the water revived him, his eyes focused on her face. "Are you taking me to the monster?" he asked, his voice small and resigned.

The question shattered something inside Juvia. How many children had asked this same question over the years? How many had been carried into the desert, never to return?

"No," she answered, fierce certainty hardening her voice. "I'm not taking you to the monster. I'm going to kill it."

The sand shifted.

Juvia froze, the hairs on her neck rising. The movement was subtle—a ripple in the dunes twenty paces ahead that didn't match the wind's pattern. She gently placed Ral—the boy had finally told her his name after hours of careful coaxing—behind a rock outcropping.

"Stay here," she whispered. "Don't move. Don't make a sound."

The boy nodded, wide-eyed but trusting.

Juvia retrieved her staff from its harness and planted her feet shoulder-width apart, scanning the terrain with narrowed eyes. The ripple had stopped, but instinct told her the threat remained.

The attack came without warning.

The sand erupted three paces to her right, a column of grit and pebbles blasting upward as a creature launched itself at her face. It resembled a scorpion crossed with a mole—leathery carapace, six clawed limbs, and a mouth filled with needle-like teeth designed for puncturing and draining. A sand leaper.

Juvia pivoted, swinging her staff in a tight arc that connected with the creature mid-leap. The impact sent it sprawling across the sand, but it recovered with unnatural speed, disappearing beneath the surface with barely a ripple.

Before she could reposition, the sand shifted again—this time directly beneath her feet. Juvia jumped backward as claws erupted where she had stood, slashing through the empty air where her ankles had been moments before.

Three more disturbances circled her position. Four sand leapers in total—a hunting pack. They were coordinating, trying to disorient her with multiple threats.

Juvia reached for her pistol, weighing her options. The chamber held two shots before needing to reload, with four spare shells in her belt pouch. Using it now meant potentially wasting precious ammunition if she missed or if the creatures didn't retreat.

The sand leapers attacked simultaneously—one from behind, two from the sides, the fourth directly ahead. Time seemed to slow as Juvia's combat instincts took over.

She drove her staff into the ground and used it to vault over the forward attacker, the creature's jaws snapping shut on empty air. As she landed, she spun the staff in a sweeping circle, catching one side attacker across its exposed underbelly. The impact flipped it onto its back, exposing the soft tissue between its armored plates.

The rear attacker latched onto her coat, claws shredding the tough fabric. Juvia dropped to one knee and rolled forward, using the creature's momentum against it. As it tumbled over her shoulder, she brought the butt of her staff down hard on its head, crushing its skull with a sickening crack.

Two down, two to go.

The remaining leapers circled more cautiously now, ripples in the sand betraying their positions. Juvia backed toward a rocky area where the thinner sand would limit their burrowing advantage. The leaper on her right took the bait, emerging in a spray of sand to cut off her retreat.

Juvia feinted with her staff, then pivoted unexpectedly, drawing her massive pistol in one fluid motion. The weapon roared, its recoil traveling up her arm like a hammer blow. The heavy bullet tore through the leaper's carapace, shattering it into fragments of bone and ichor.

The last creature hesitated, its survival instinct warring with its hunting programming. Juvia used the moment to check her remaining shot, her finger steady on the trigger despite her racing heart.

But when she looked up, the final sand leaper had vanished.

Silence descended on the desert, broken only by Juvia's ragged breathing and the distant keening of the wind. She maintained her defensive stance, scanning for any sign of movement.

The attack came from above.

The creature had used the distraction to climb a nearby rock formation, launching itself at her from the height. Juvia caught the movement in her peripheral vision—too late to aim, too late to dodge completely. She twisted, raising her staff as a barrier.

The leaper's weight drove her to the ground, its claws raking across her shoulder. Pain flared, hot and immediate. Its jaws snapped inches from her face, fetid breath washing over her. Juvia jammed the staff horizontally into its mouth, keeping those needle teeth at bay through sheer desperate strength.

With her free hand, she brought the pistol up against the creature's underbelly and fired.

The report was deafening at such close range. The leaper's body jerked violently, a spray of dark fluid erupting from the exit wound. Its legs twitched once, twice, then stilled.

Juvia heaved the carcass off her chest, gasping for breath. Blood seeped from the gashes on her shoulder, but a quick assessment told her the wounds were superficial—painful but not debilitating.

"Are you hurt?" Ral's small voice came from behind the rocks.

"I'm fine," she managed, already examining the tears in her coat with dismay. "Stay there until I make sure they're all dead."

As Ral emerged cautiously from his hiding place, Juvia reloaded her father's custom pistol, the familiar routine grounding her racing thoughts. Her fingers moved with practiced efficiency through the sequence he'd taught her—eject spent shells, insert fresh ones, check the mechanism. The sound of the gunshots would carry in the desert. If anyone—or anything—was hunting them, they now had a clear trail to follow.

They traveled through the night, Juvia carrying Ral when his strength failed. The desert was different in darkness, alive with sounds and shadows that the daylight banished.

By dawn, they reached the Stone Teeth—a jagged formation of red rock that rose from the sand like the maw of some petrified leviathan. Between these stone fangs lay the entrance to the Beast's lair—a sloping path that disappeared into shadow beneath the largest formation.

Juvia set Ral down in the shelter of a stone outcropping. "Stay here," she instructed, securing her water skin to his small frame. "If I'm not back by nightfall, follow the evening star until you reach green land."

The boy clutched her hand. "You'll die."

"Perhaps," she acknowledged, checking her pistol and staff. "But I'll die standing, not kneeling in submission."

The ravine between the Stone Teeth narrowed as Juvia descended, walls of red rock rising on either side like bloody sentinels. The air grew thick with an acrid, musky scent that caught in the back of her throat. Tracks marked the sand—

enormous, splayed footprints larger than cooking pots, with claw impressions that could easily disembowel a desert bull with a single swipe.

A deep rumble shook the ground beneath her feet.

"I know you're here," Juvia called out, her voice echoing off the stone walls. "I've come to end this."

For a moment, nothing moved. Then the sand at the far end of the ravine began to shift and rise, cascading away from an enormous form emerging from below.

The Beast rose like a mountain given life.

It was a massive desert lizard, easily the size of four bull elephants standing flank to flank. Its hide was a patchwork of armored plates the color of bleached bone, interrupted by throbbing veins of molten orange that pulsed with internal heat. Six legs, each thicker than Juvia's torso, supported its bulk. Its head was a nightmare of horns and ridges surrounding jaws that could swallow a man whole.

And its eyes—amber orbs with vertical pupils that narrowed as they fixed on Juvia—held an intelligence that sent ice through her veins despite the oppressive heat.

"No child for Krozath?" Its voice was a physical force, vibrating in Juvia's chest cavity like distant thunder. "The village sends a woman instead. How... disappointing."

Juvia's grip tightened on her staff. The creature could speak. Of all the possibilities she had prepared for, this hadn't been one of them.

"I bring no offering," she replied, fighting to keep her voice steady. "Only an end to your hunger."

Krozath charged, its six legs churning the sand into a blinding cloud. Juvia waited until the last possible moment before diving sideways, simultaneously drawing her pistol and firing at the creature's exposed flank as it passed.

The heavy round struck with a sound like a hammer on anvil, but merely glanced off the armored plates, leaving a smoking scorch mark. Krozath rounded on her with a roar of irritation rather than pain.

"Your weapons cannot harm Krozath, human," it taunted, advancing more cautiously now. "Generations of your kind have tried."

Juvia reloaded as she retreated, scanning the arena for any advantage. The stone spires surrounding them offered some cover, but also potential traps if she allowed herself to be cornered.

As Krozath lunged again, she used her staff to vault onto one of the lower rock formations, gaining momentary height advantage. From this position, she could see more clearly the pulsing veins of orange that ran between the creature's armored plates.

A plan formed, desperate and dangerous.

Juvia leapt from rock to rock, staying just ahead of Krozath's snapping jaws. Each jump brought her perilously close to its reach, but also allowed her to observe the pattern of those glowing veins. They seemed to converge at the base of the creature's skull, forming a pulsing nexus partially protected by a crown of horns.

If those were blood vessels of some kind, they might be vulnerable. But reaching them would require getting past those jaws and onto Krozath's back—a seemingly impossible task.

Krozath grew frustrated with her evasion. It reared up, smashing its bulk against the stone spire she stood upon. The impact shattered the rock, sending Juvia tumbling amid a shower of debris. She landed hard, pain exploding through her left shoulder as it took the brunt of the fall.

Before she could recover, one massive clawed foot pinned her to the ground. The pressure was enormous, driving the air from her lungs. Ribs creaked ominously as Krozath lowered its head, hot breath washing over her face.

"Your courage counts for nothing," it rumbled, jaws parting. "Like all your kind, you will feed Krozath and be forgotten."

Desperation fueled her response. Juvia jammed her staff sideways into Krozath's mouth, wedging it between its upper and lower jaws. The creature jerked back in surprise, the pressure on her chest easing just enough for her to roll free, leaving her staff stuck like a bit between the monster's teeth.

It thrashed its head, trying to dislodge the obstruction. Juvia used the distraction to retreat, clutching her throbbing ribs, blood trickling from a gash on her forehead into her eyes.

Krozath finally snapped her staff, spitting the fragments onto the sand with a growl of rage. It charged again, faster now, driven by anger rather than hunger. Juvia waited until the last possible moment before firing her pistol directly at the creature's right eye.

The bullet struck true.

Krozath reared back with a deafening roar, black ichor spurting from the ruined socket. It thrashed wildly, disoriented by pain and half-blindness. Juvia didn't waste the opportunity. With practiced speed, she reloaded her weapon—fingers deftly sliding shells into the chamber despite the chaos around her. Then she sprinted forward, dodging the flailing limbs, and leapt onto the creature's heaving side.

Her fingers found purchase between the armored plates as she hauled herself upward, climbing the living mountain of Krozath's flank. The creature bucked and twisted, trying to dislodge her, but Juvia clung with desperate strength, inching toward the pulsing nexus at the base of its skull.

Every movement was agony for her injured ribs. Black spots swam in her vision. But she forced herself onward, upward, finally reaching the cluster of horns that protected the throbbing center of those orange veins.

Krozath seemed to realize her intent. It went suddenly still, then began rolling toward the nearest stone spire, intending to crush her against the rock.

Juvia had seconds to act. She drew her pistol one last time, pressing the barrel directly against the pulsing nexus, and fired.

The effect was immediate and catastrophic.

Krozath convulsed as if struck by lightning. The orange veins flared blindingly bright, then began to darken from the wound outward. A terrible keening cry escaped its jaws as it thrashed in its death throes, throwing Juvia clear.

She hit the ground hard, the impact driving what little air remained from her lungs. Pain exploded through her consciousness, momentarily blinding her. When her vision cleared, she saw Krozath writhing in the center of the arena, its movements growing increasingly uncoordinated as the orange glow faded from its veins.

With a final, earth-shaking groan, Krozath collapsed. Its amber eyes—one ruined, one intact—fixed on Juvia with what almost seemed like grudging respect before the light within them dimmed and vanished.

Silence descended on the ravine between the Stone Teeth.

It took three attempts before she could stand, leaning heavily against a nearby rock for support. The ravine swam around her, reality seeming to ripple at the edges of her vision. She staggered toward the fallen Krozath, needing to confirm with her own hands that the nightmare was truly over.

Its hide was already cooling, the armored plates turning ashen gray without the inner fire to sustain their luster.

"No more children," she whispered to the dead monster. "No more sacrifices."

Juvia emerged from the Stone Teeth as the sun began to set, casting long shadows across the desert. Her body was a catalog of pain—cracked ribs, dislocated shoulder, lacerations across her back and arms. Blood had dried in stiff patterns down the side of her face.

But she was alive. And Krozath was dead.

Ral ran to her, his small face bright with relief and surprise. "You came back!"

"I said I would," she managed, her voice a rasp in her dust-dried throat.

As the last light painted the sand gold, Juvia looked toward the distant horizon where Salcera lay, beyond the dunes, on the fertile alluvial plain that had sustained it for generations. Soon she would return, bearing the truth about Krozath and the village's dark bargain.

But first, she needed to heal. To rest. To prepare for the battle that would come when she shattered generations of lies and sacrifice.

"Come," she said to Ral, offering her hand. "We have a long journey ahead."

The boy took her hand, small fingers wrapping around hers with absolute trust. Together they turned their backs to the setting sun and began walking north, where the desert eventually gave way to green plains and distant mountains.

Behind them, the dunes still sang, but to Juvia's ears, the sound held something new—not a warning, but a promise. A future without monsters, both Krozath who had lurked beneath the sand and those that hid behind tradition and authority.

She would return to Salcera. And when she did, everything would change.

Velocity Shift

"Some problems can't be solved with equations alone."

The hum of the particle accelerator was a constant companion to Dr. Maria Rodriguez, its rhythm as familiar as her own heartbeat. She moved through the facility's Network Operations Center, fingers dancing across multiple keyboards, her petite frame casting long shadows under the fluorescent lights. It was 2 AM, and the skeleton crew had left her mostly alone—exactly how she liked it.

"Danny would kill me if he knew I was here instead of home," she muttered, thinking of her fourteen-year-old son, likely asleep with textbooks scattered across his bed. Single motherhood required sacrifices, and sometimes that meant midnight shifts debugging anomalies in the system that no one else seemed able to fix.

The Higgs-Boson Supercollider was the largest of its kind, stretching in a massive ring beneath the city. Tomorrow's test would push particle physics further than humanity had ever ventured. Director Warren Harmon had staked his reputation on it—and hers by extension.

Maria rubbed her temples, staring at a column of numbers that had been troubling her for weeks. Budget allocations, resource diversions, equipment that had been ordered but never delivered. Numbers that didn't add up.

"That can't be right," she whispered, pulling up another screen. She'd noticed discrepancies before, dismissed them as accounting errors. But tonight, the evidence assembled before her was unmistakable—someone was embezzling millions from the project, and the trail led straight to Director Harmon's authorization codes.

Her coffee grew cold as she cross-referenced the data, looking for alternative explanations. None emerged. The man who'd brought her onto the team, who'd been a mentor since her doctoral program, who'd secured her position after

Danny's father had walked out—was systematically bleeding the project dry.

Maria downloaded the evidence onto a secure drive and tucked it into her pocket, heart pounding against her ribs. The weight of what she'd found pressed down on her chest. She knew Harmon's temper, had witnessed how he'd destroyed the careers of those who questioned his authority. Just last month, he'd fired Dr. Chen for raising safety concerns about the accelerator's cooling system.

She needed sleep before confronting this. Needed to see Danny, needed to be certain.

"You're burning toast again, Mom."

Maria startled, yanking the smoking bread from the toaster. Danny grinned at her from across their small kitchen, dark hair mussed from sleep, calculator already in hand for his morning math review.

"Where were you last night?" he asked, not accusingly, just curious. "I woke up around three and your bed wasn't slept in."

"Debugging at work," she said, sliding a glass of orange juice toward him. "The big test is tomorrow. Everything has to be perfect."

Perfect. The word stuck in her throat. Nothing about what she'd discovered was perfect.

"You okay?" Danny asked, unusually perceptive for a teenager. "You look like you're calculating quantum trajectories in your head."

Maria smiled despite herself. "Just work stress. How's the calculus coming? Need any help before school?"

"Nah, I've got it." He paused, studying her face. "Mom, you'd tell me if something was wrong, right?"

She reached across the table, squeezing his hand. "Always. We're a team, remember?"

The lie burned worse than the toast.

"You understand the significance of what you're suggesting?" Director Harmon's office was a temple to scientific achievement, walls lined with degrees and awards. The morning light caught his silver hair, casting a halo effect that now seemed cruelly ironic.

"I wouldn't have come to you directly if I wasn't certain," Maria said, sliding the drive across his desk. "The logs show systematic fund diversion over eighteen months. I thought you should know before I submit my findings to the ethics committee."

Harmon's face remained impassive as he inserted the drive, reviewed the data. Then he smiled, the expression never reaching his eyes.

"Brilliant work, Maria. Truly. You've always been exceptional at pattern recognition." He tapped the drive thoughtfully against his palm. "I'm glad you brought this to me. We'll need to conduct an internal investigation immediately."

Relief flooded through her. "Thank you, sir. I wasn't sure—"

"Why don't you show me exactly where you found these anomalies?" Harmon stood, gesturing toward the door. "We should secure the system before anyone else discovers the breach."

As they walked through the facility's main corridor, Maria noticed something odd. The usual staff complement was thin, replaced by unfamiliar faces with security badges she didn't recognize.

"New contractors?" she asked casually.

"Temporary security detail for tomorrow's demonstration," Harmon replied smoothly. "Government representatives will be attending. You understand the protocols."

The maintenance tunnel leading to the accelerator's control junction wasn't on any public schematics. Maria followed Harmon through narrow passages, the walls humming with the latent energy of the sleeping machine.

"Sir, shouldn't we bring cybersecurity into this?" Maria asked, unease prickling at the base of her spine.

"After we've confirmed the extent of the breach," Harmon said without turning around. "You understand the importance of discretion. One hint of financial impropriety could sink our funding."

They reached a reinforced door, and Harmon's keycard granted them access to a small control room filled with blinking server stacks.

"Show me exactly where you found the discrepancies," he said.

Maria hesitated, then moved to a terminal. "It's all here in the allocation subroutines. Someone created a shadow funding stream that—"

The heavy steel door slammed shut behind them.

"Sir?" Maria turned, finding Harmon's pleasant expression had hardened into something cold and unfamiliar.

"You know, I always appreciated your thoroughness, Maria. But sometimes, it's a liability." He tapped commands into a different console. "Did you make copies of that data?"

The realization hit her like a physical blow. "It was you."

"Science requires capital. The bureaucrats don't understand what we're doing here—what we could achieve with proper resources." Harmon's voice remained conversational as the room's displays flashed red. Warning indicators illuminated. "Unfortunately, your discovery has forced my hand."

Maria lunged for the door, but Harmon blocked her path. "The accelerator is powering up," she gasped, hearing the distinctive whine of capacitors charging. "This section isn't shielded for human occupancy during operation!"

"A tragic accident," Harmon agreed. "A dedicated scientist, working late, caught in an unforeseen power surge. The entire facility will mourn your commitment."

She shoved past him, fingers frantically working the door panel. Locked from the outside.

"My son—"

"Will receive an excellent education courtesy of your posthumous benefits package." Harmon checked his watch. "I need to clear the facility. The surge begins in three minutes. Your sacrifice will advance our understanding of particle physics immeasurably."

He slipped through a maintenance hatch too small for Maria to follow, securing it behind him.

Panic rose in her throat as she surveyed the room. No exits, no comms, and the accelerator's energy was building, the air beginning to crackle with ionization.

Maria attacked the control panel, trying to abort the sequence, but Harmon had locked her out. The room grew warmer as the surrounding superconductive magnets charged. Radiation alarms began to wail.

Sixty seconds remaining.

She wedged herself into the furthest corner from the accelerator tube, behind a server rack. Physics was merciless— at this distance, the particle beam's effects would be catastrophic.

Thirty seconds.

Maria closed her eyes, picturing Danny's face. "I'm sorry," she whispered.

The room flooded with blinding light. Pain erupted across every nerve ending, excruciating, cellular-level agony. Her body convulsed as energy tore through her at the subatomic level. She couldn't scream; her lungs were paralyzed, her consciousness fragmenting.

And then, impossibly, her cells began to resist. Where they should have disintegrated, they instead rearranged, absorbing the cascade of exotic particles. The laws of physics bent around her, through her, within her. The pain intensified, then suddenly ceased.

Maria collapsed onto the floor as darkness took her.

Snippets of conversation filtered through her semiconsciousness. Time stretched, compressed. Days passed in fever dreams of light and motion.

"—miracle she survived at all. The radiation levels—"

"—third day unconscious—"

"—reached her son—"

When she finally opened her eyes, Danny was asleep in a chair beside her bed, his lanky teenage frame awkwardly curled into the small space. A nurse noticed her stirring and approached.

"Dr. Rodriguez? Can you hear me?"

Maria tried to speak, found her throat raw. The nurse offered water, which she sipped gratefully.

"How long?" she managed.

"Eight days. You were found in the control room after the accelerator malfunction. The doctors... they don't understand how you survived."

Maria didn't understand either. The memory of that blinding light, of energy tearing through her at the subatomic level, made her tremble.

"The director said you were troubleshooting critical systems," the nurse continued. "They're calling you a hero for trying to prevent the surge."

Rage burned through Maria's weakness. Harmon was covering his tracks, rewriting the narrative. And she had no proof, nothing but her word against his.

Danny stirred, his eyes opening. "Mom?" His voice broke with relief as he lunged forward, hugging her carefully around the monitors and IV lines. "They said you might not—" He couldn't finish.

"I'm here," she whispered, holding him as tightly as her weakened arms allowed. "I'm not going anywhere."

But even as she comforted her son, Maria felt something strange beneath her skin—an unfamiliar vibration, a sense of molecules in constant motion. When Danny pulled back, the water glass on her tray rattled, then slowly slid toward her without being touched.

She blinked, certain she was hallucinating.

The glass stopped moving.

A few weeks later, Maria sat in her apartment's small living room, staring at the muted television coverage of Director Harmon accepting accolades for the accelerator's "groundbreaking results despite setbacks."

The doctors had found nothing wrong with her—a medical impossibility given her exposure. They'd called her recovery "unprecedented" and "scientifically significant." Maria had submitted to their tests while keeping her silence about what had really happened.

And about what was happening now.

The remote control floated gently into her outstretched hand.

Since returning home, Maria had discovered her ability to manipulate velocity—of herself, of objects around her. Small things at first: catching a falling mug before it hit the ground, moving with impossible speed to answer a phone across the room. Then larger manifestations: during her morning run, she'd unintentionally accelerated to highway speeds, terrifying herself before learning to brake her momentum.

Danny had nearly caught her yesterday, when she'd accidentally shattered a glass by accelerating it too quickly.

She'd blamed it on the dishwasher, not washing it properly. The look he gave her said he wasn't buying it.

Physics had been rewritten in her body. The accelerator had changed something fundamental in her molecular structure, altering her relationship with inertia itself.

She needed to understand what had happened to her. More importantly, she needed to expose Harmon before his embezzlement endangered more lives.

When her phone rang, Maria startled, sending the remote flying across the room at bullet speed. It embedded itself in the wall.

"Hello?" she answered shakily.

"Dr. Rodriguez? This is Jaana Jones from IT Support. I've been reviewing the system logs from the day of the accident." The young woman's voice dropped to a whisper. "Something doesn't add up, and I think we should talk. Somewhere private. Not at the facility."

Jaana "Keyboard" Jones worked from a converted industrial loft filled with computer equipment and anime figurines. The young woman's fingers moved across multiple keyboards at inhuman speeds, her bright blue hair matching the glow of her screens.

"The access logs were deleted, but I keep my own backups," Keyboard explained, bringing up fragmented data streams. "Someone forced the accelerator to overload while you were inside that room. It wasn't an accident."

"I know," Maria said quietly. "It was Harmon. I discovered he was embezzling research funds."

Keyboard whistled. "That tracks with what I found. Ghost accounts, shadow servers." She spun in her chair. "But what I don't get is how you survived. That level of exposure should have—"

She paused, studying Maria's face. "Unless it didn't kill you because it changed you."

Maria hesitated, then raised her hand. The coffee mug on Keyboard's desk lifted and drifted smoothly into her palm.

Keyboard's eyes widened. "Holy shit."

"I can control velocity and momentum. Speed things up, slow them down, redirect force." Maria set the mug down carefully. "It's getting stronger every day, but I'm still learning control."

She gestured at a pen, intending to float it gently toward her. Instead, it shot across the room like a bullet, embedding itself in the drywall. "See? I miscalculated the force. Again."

"That's why you came to me," Keyboard said, eyes gleaming. "You need to understand what's happening to you."

"I need evidence against Harmon," Maria corrected, "and a way to prove what he tried to do to me. Before he hurts anyone else."

"Why not both?" Keyboard countered, already typing furiously. "Look, in the past month, three research facilities with connections to Harmon have reported thefts of experimental tech. I've been tracking the pattern."

She pulled up a map showing the theft locations, dates, and stolen equipment specs.

"Someone's building something," Maria murmured, leaning forward.

"Something big," Keyboard agreed, turning to face her. "You've been given extraordinary abilities, Dr. Rodriguez. You could use them to gather evidence the traditional way—which might take months, during which Harmon continues whatever he's planning. Or..."

"I'm a scientist and a mother, not a vigilante."

"You're also the only person who can move faster than a bullet," Keyboard said softly. "Harmon tried to kill you, and he's still out there, still endangering others. The system might not be enough."

Maria thought of Danny, of the world he'd grow up in. Of other scientists who might face Harmon's brand of deadly "problem-solving."

"My powers aren't reliable yet," she said, watching the coffee in Keyboard's mug vibrate from across the room. "I could hurt someone accidentally."

"We can fix that," Keyboard grinned, spinning toward her computer. "I'm thinking impact-resistant polymer weave, velocity stabilizers, heads-up display... and a purple wig to conceal your identity."

"Purple hair? Really?"

"It's iconic. Trust me." Keyboard's fingers flew across her keyboard. "But first, let's run some tests to understand exactly what you can do."

For the following weeks, Maria lived a double life.

By day, she was Dr. Rodriguez, returned to work with a clean bill of health, quietly gathering evidence of Harmon's ongoing corruption. She'd smile tightly when he asked about her recovery, pretend not to notice how closely he monitored her activities.

Each night, after Danny was asleep, she'd slip out to Keyboard's loft to train. They developed a specialized suit that helped channel and control her powers, measuring velocity vectors and calculating optimal force applications. The reflective visor did more than conceal her identity—its heads-up display helped her focus her abilities with scientific precision.

"How do I look?" Maria asked, examining her reflection in Keyboard's floor-length mirror. The sleek white suit with purple accents hugged her athletic frame, reinforced at strategic points to withstand the stresses of high-velocity movement.

"Like someone who's about to make bad guys reconsider their career choices," Keyboard replied, making final adjustments to the suit's gauntlets. "The wig looks natural, and the voice modulator works perfectly. No one would connect you to...Inertia."

"Inertia?" Maria raised an eyebrow.

"That's you," Keyboard said, pointing at the logo she'd emblazoned on the suit's chest—a stylized "I" that resembled a force vector. "A body at rest remains at rest, a body in motion remains in motion..."

"Unless acted upon by an outside force," Maria finished, flexing her hands in the reinforced gloves. "I get it."

The first field test came sooner than expected. Armed robbery at First National Bank—six gunmen, hostages inside, police establishing a perimeter.

"People could die while the police set up," Keyboard said simply. "You can be there in seconds."

Inertia took a deep breath and stepped off the rooftop. Instead of falling, she accelerated horizontally, her body cutting through the air at precisely calculated velocity.

Inside the bank, she moved like liquid lightning, neutralizing threats with controlled force. The reinforced gauntlets protected her hands as she disarmed the gunmen. To the hostages, she appeared as nothing more than a purple-white blur as weapons clattered uselessly to the marble floor.

"Everyone stay calm," she told the stunned hostages, her voice altered by the modulator. "The police will be in momentarily."

A child stared up at her, eyes wide. "Are you a superhero?"

Inertia paused, then crouched to the child's level. "I'm just someone trying to help."

She was gone before the SWAT team breached the doors, accelerating up the side of a neighboring building and across rooftops, a new sense of purpose coursing through her veins.

"Mom, are you okay?" Danny asked over breakfast, studying her face. "You look exhausted."

Maria nodded, hiding a wince as she reached for the coffee pot. Her muscles ached from the previous night's exertions.

"Just working late," she said, the familiar lie coming easier now.

Danny frowned. "Again? This is the third night this week." He pushed his tablet across the table, showing a news headline: MYSTERIOUS 'INERTIA' STRIKES AGAIN.

"Have you seen this? They're saying she's some kind of superhero. The video's insane—she moves so fast the camera barely catches her."

Maria forced a casual shrug. "Probably digital effects. You know how people are with their conspiracy theories."

"I don't think so. Look at how she stops that bullet in mid-air." His eyes gleamed with the same enthusiasm he showed for his physics homework. "It's like she can control velocity somehow. The science behind that would be revolutionary."

"If it were real," Maria said carefully.

Danny studied the footage again. "Whoever she is, she's helping people. That's pretty cool." He glanced up, expression suddenly thoughtful. "Hey, you know what's weird? She started appearing right around when you had your accident at the lab."

Maria nearly choked on her coffee. "Coincidence," she managed.

"Probably." Danny gathered his books. "I've got debate club after school. Will you be home for dinner?"

"Absolutely," Maria promised, meaning it. "I'll make your favorite pasta."

"With actual sauce, not that burned stuff from last time?" he grinned.

"One time!" she protested, laughing as she ruffled his hair. "I got distracted."

After he left, Maria sank into her chair, the weight of her double life pressing down. She pulled out her phone, texting Keyboard:

Taking tonight off. Family time.

The reply came instantly: *Fair. But check the news. Harmon's making his move.*

Maria switched on the television to see Director Harmon at a press conference, announcing a "revolutionary demonstration" of "applied particle physics technology" scheduled for tomorrow evening. Military officials flanked him on the podium.

Her phone buzzed again: *The stolen tech. It's all coming together. Whatever he's building, it happens tomorrow.*

Maria stared at the screen, at Harmon's confident smile, and felt cold certainty settle in her stomach. This was why he'd tried to kill her—not just to hide embezzlement, but to eliminate anyone who might interfere with whatever weapon he was developing.

After dinner, she texted back. *We plan tonight, we move tomorrow.*

The Higgs-Boson Supercollider facility gleamed under the quarter moon, its security perimeter dotted with armed guards—far more than standard scientific security. Inertia crouched behind the ventilation system on an adjacent building, studying their patterns.

"I'm counting twelve visible guards," she whispered into her comm. "Since when does particle physics need mercenaries?"

"Since Harmon diverted eight million to a shell company that specializes in private military contracting," Keyboard answered, keyboard clicks punctuating her words.

"Facility schematics show an access tunnel at the northeast corner. Maintenance staff use it for equipment deliveries. Security cameras loop every 94 seconds."

Inertia fixed her gaze on the delivery entrance, a reinforced door with a keycard panel. "I see it. Going in five, four..."

She concentrated. The world around her shifted—swaying leaves hung suspended mid-motion, blinking lights dimmed to steady glows, guards moved with the sluggishness of underwater dancers.

Inertia dropped from her position and crossed the exposed ground in three long bounds. Her muscles burned with exertion, sweat already beading beneath her visor. Her lungs struggled against the resistance of her own accelerated metabolism.

At the door, she keyed in the code Keyboard had extracted from the system. Nothing happened.

"They've changed it," she hissed.

"Plan B, then," Keyboard replied. "The panel itself runs on standard voltage. Try—"

Inertia pressed her palm against the keypad. The circuitry beneath her gloved hand hummed, then sizzled as she vibrated the electrons within the system. A wisp of smoke curled from the corner of the panel as the lock disengaged with a soft click.

Inside, the facility's familiar corridors felt alien now. Inertia slipped through them, ducking into recessed doorways whenever footsteps approached. Each controlled burst left her joints throbbing, muscles protesting as she pressed on toward the central control hub where Harmon would most likely be.

She rounded a corner and froze. Four armed guards stood outside the main lab doors. No way around them.

Inertia took a deep breath and stepped into the corridor.

"Hey!" The first guard raised his weapon, but Inertia was already moving.

The air rippled visibly around the first guard. He flew backward as if hit by an invisible battering ram, colliding with his companion in a tangle of limbs. As they stumbled, Inertia crossed the space between them. Her fist connected with the third guard's solar plexus with a dull thud. His eyes bulged as he doubled over, breathless.

The fourth guard fired. The bullet disrupted the air—a visible distortion that Inertia sensed before hearing the shot. She twisted her hand. The bullet curved in mid-air, missing her by inches and embedding itself in the wall with a spray of concrete dust.

Before he could fire again, Inertia closed the gap between them. Her palm connected with his jaw in a blur. Bone met bone with a sharp crack. He dropped like a stone.

Alarms wailed. Red emergency lights bathed the corridor in crimson.

"They know you're there," Keyboard warned unnecessarily. "Harmon's in the central chamber. Heat signatures show at least eight more guards with him—and something big. Power readings are off the charts."

Inertia swiped a keycard from one of the unconscious men and pushed through the lab doors. The central chamber lay ahead—where Harmon had tried to kill her. Where she had been reborn.

She paused in the shadows, taking in the scene. The massive circular chamber housed the control interface for the particle accelerator itself. Harmon stood at the central console, surrounded by armed men. On the main screen, weapon schematics rotated in 3D—applications of particle physics that twisted the natural laws into instruments of destruction.

A prototype device stood in the center of the room—a sleek cannon-like apparatus connected to the accelerator's power source. The air around it shimmered with potential energy.

"The demonstration is in seventeen minutes," Harmon told the military observers gathered around the device. His voice carried the same measured confidence he used during budget presentations. "Once we verify the targeting parameters, we can discuss production timelines. Gentlemen, this technology will revolutionize modern warfare."

Inertia's vision blurred momentarily. Her legs trembled beneath her. Sweat trickled down her spine. She needed to end this quickly.

"I must ask for a brief recess," Harmon continued, checking his watch. "My team needs to make final calibrations. Security will escort you to the observation lounge."

As the military officials filed out, Harmon's guards took positions around the prototype. When the door closed behind the last observer, Inertia stepped into the light.

"Hello, Warren."

Harmon spun, his face twisting from shock to calculated calm in an instant. "Dr. Rodriguez. Or should I say... Inertia? That's what they're calling you on the news." He gestured casually to his guards, who raised their weapons. "I had wondered if you might pay me a visit."

"It's over," Inertia said, moving slowly into the room. "The evidence of your embezzlement has been delivered to the board of directors and the FBI. They know what you did. What you tried to do to me."

Harmon's smile didn't falter. "Evidence can be explained away. Accidents happen in cutting-edge research. Besides, our work here is too important for such trivial concerns."

"Weaponizing particle physics isn't trivial. Neither is attempted murder."

"Evolution requires sacrifice," Harmon replied, backing toward the weapon console. "Look at what happened to you! You're proof that my vision is correct. Imagine an army with your abilities."

The guards tensed, awaiting orders.

"You won't get the chance," Inertia said.

Harmon's face hardened. "Kill her."

The first guard fired a three-round burst. Inertia's hand swept through the air. The bullets slowed visibly, their trajectories becoming visible lines hanging suspended before dropping to the floor with metallic pings.

The second and third guards attacked simultaneously from different angles. Inertia dropped to one knee, palm slapping against the floor. The metal plating rippled outward like a stone dropped in water. Both guards staggered sideways, their coordinated attack dissolving into desperate grabs for balance.

She rolled forward and swept the legs of the nearest guard. His body tumbled backward, momentum precisely calculated by Inertia's visor. As he fell, she tore the tactical baton from his belt. The weapon blurred in her grip as she brought it against the next guard's ribs. The reinforced gauntlets protected her hands as the impact reverberated through the chamber—a single strike that sent him sprawling.

A bullet grazed her shoulder, burning through the suit material. Inertia hissed in pain, momentarily losing focus. The fourth guard closed in, combat knife gleaming under the emergency lights.

She backpedaled. The knife sliced toward her throat in a silver arc. The guard's arm suddenly moved as if pushing through invisible syrup. His eyes widened in confusion as his strike decelerated mid-swing. Inertia ducked beneath the sluggish blade and struck upward with her armored fist. The reinforced gauntlet connected with his jaw with a muffled thud, and he dropped unconscious to the floor.

Alarms continued to wail as the four guards she'd neutralized lay groaning on the floor. Inertia turned to find Harmon working frantically at the weapon console.

"Step away, Warren." Blood trickled from her shoulder wound, darkening the white sections of her suit to crimson. Sweat plastered purple hair to her forehead beneath the visor.

"You don't understand what's at stake," Harmon said, fingers working methodically across the controls. "This technology has applications beyond defense. Controlled particle manipulation at this scale could revolutionize medicine, energy production—"

"Weaponry," Inertia cut in. "Starting with whatever you're building here."

The facility rumbled as massive electromagnetic systems powered up beneath them. The prototype weapon emitted a high-pitched whine, its barrel glowing with gathering energy.

"Demonstration sequence initiated," announced an automated voice. "Particle alignment in five minutes."

"You'll irradiate half the city!" Inertia lunged for the console, but Harmon drew a pistol from inside his lab coat.

"I've invested too much to stop now," he said, voice level but eyes cold. His hand remained perfectly steady. "The potential benefits outweigh the risks."

The chamber shuddered as the accelerator below gained power. Emergency lights pulsed in time with the facility's warning klaxons. The air itself seemed to vibrate with building energy.

Inertia raised her hands slowly. "You were my mentor. I respected you."

"Then join me," Harmon offered, the gun unwavering. "With your abilities and my vision—"

"No," Inertia cut him off. "That's not happening."

The air between them shimmered. The metal of Harmon's gun glowed orange, then bright red as she accelerated the particles within it.

"What the—?" He dropped the weapon with a howl, fingers blistering instantly.

Inertia surged forward. Her body became a blur of white and purple. Her shoulder collided with Harmon's midsection with a sickening thud. The impact lifted him off his feet and sent him crashing against the railing overlooking the accelerator ring.

"Shut it down!" she demanded, pinning him against the metal barrier.

"It's too late," Harmon laughed, blood trickling from the corner of his mouth. "The sequence is locked. In four minutes, we'll witness the birth of a new era of human evolution—or the death of a city. Either way, history changes today."

Inertia glanced at the console. The shutdown protocols showed as bypassed on the flashing display. Vibrations from the accelerator intensified, making the floor plates rattle.

"Keyboard," she hissed into her comm, "I need options!"

"Working on it," came the strained reply. "The weapon's drawing power directly from the accelerator. If you could interrupt the feed somehow—maybe the coupling junctions?"

Inertia looked up, tracing the massive power conduits that ran from the accelerator to the weapon prototype. They connected at a reinforced junction box mounted high on the chamber wall.

She grabbed Harmon's lab coat and dragged him to a support column, securing him with zip ties torn from her utility belt. His feet scraped uselessly against the floor as she moved with unstoppable force.

"What are you doing?" he demanded, struggling against his restraints.

"Solving an equation." She positioned herself beneath the junction box, calculating trajectories, forces, stress points. With a deep breath, she focused her power and launched herself upward.

The jump carried her thirty feet vertically. Her hands grasped the junction box, fingers digging into the metal casing. With a grunt of effort, she tore it free from the wall, electrical arcs dancing around her gloved hands as connections severed.

"No!" Harmon screamed from below. "Do you have any idea what you're doing?"

Inertia dropped back to the floor, junction box in hand. "Preventing a catastrophe."

The weapon's charging whine faltered, then died. But the accelerator itself continued to power up, its destabilized energy now directionless.

"Warning," the automated system announced. "Critical power imbalance detected. Containment failure imminent. Three minutes to cascade reaction."

"You've doomed us all," Harmon laughed hysterically. "Without the weapon to channel the energy, the accelerator will overload. The resulting explosion will level ten city blocks!"

Inertia's mind raced through calculations, possibilities. "Keyboard, I need to redirect the energy somewhere!"

"The accelerator's failsafe protocols are still intact," Keyboard's voice came through, strained with concentration.

"If you can trigger an emergency shutdown from the primary control station, the energy should vent harmlessly into the containment chambers."

Inertia moved to the central console, fingers dancing across the controls in a blur. The screens responded to her commands, schematics and formulas flashing by at dizzying speed.

Through her visor, she saw what no human eye could detect—energies building in pulsing waves, particles accelerating to near light speed. The same forces that had transformed her—but magnified a thousandfold.

"You can't possibly control that much power!" Harmon warned, genuine fear replacing his megalomaniacal confidence.

"Watch me." Her fingers hammered the final command sequence. "Keyboard, I'm initiating emergency protocol Alpha-Seven."

"That's designed for empty facilities," Keyboard protested. "You need to evacuate!"

"No time." Inertia looked at the countdown: two minutes remaining. "The venting sequence will flood the central chamber with ionized particles. I need to guide the process."

"Maria, no!" Keyboard's voice turned frantic. "The radiation levels—"

"I survived it once," Inertia replied, moving to the prototype weapon. With a grunt of effort, she physically rotated the device, aiming it toward the accelerator's exposed core. "And now I understand why."

The countdown reached one minute. Inertia ripped open an access panel on the weapon, rewiring connections with blinding speed. Her hands moved faster than human eyes could follow, rerouting power channels, modifying circuitry.

"What I'm doing," she explained to Keyboard through gritted teeth, "is turning this weapon into a conduit. The accelerator's energy will feed back into itself, creating a closed loop."

"That's insane," Keyboard protested. "The mathematical precision required—"

"Is exactly what I do now," Inertia finished, making the final connection. The weapon hummed to life again, but now pointed at the accelerator core.

Thirty seconds.

She stood before the device, arms outstretched, feeling the energy building around her. The same energy that had transformed her now responded to her will, particles shifting their velocity according to the equations forming in her mind.

The floor beneath them lurched. The metal walkway buckled. A high-pitched whine filled the air, rising beyond human hearing. Inertia concentrated on the energy flow, guiding it, shaping it, creating a perfectly balanced system where normally chaos would reign.

"Ten seconds to cascade reaction," the automated voice announced.

Inertia closed her eyes, visualizing the particle flows, the quantum interactions, the dance of matter and energy that had rewritten her own existence.

"Five... four... three..."

The air shimmered around her. Light bent, warped. The laws of physics stretched to their breaking point.

"Two... one..."

Instead of an explosion, a perfect sphere of blue-white energy formed in the center of the room. It pulsed once, twice, then collapsed inward with the fury of a dying star. Equipment melted. Consoles shattered. The weapons research data disintegrated in the controlled cataclysm.

Emergency systems engaged with a deafening hiss. Supercooled gases flooded the accelerator ring. Red warning lights faded to steady amber as backup systems regained control.

Harmon pressed his face against the observation window, mouth hanging open. The smoking ruin of equipment and melted computers reflected in his wild eyes. "Do you have any idea what you've done? Years of research, billions in potential—"

"I saved countless lives," Inertia yanked him backward. The plastic restraints on his wrists tightened as she secured him to a structural support. "And I've ensured you'll face justice for what you did."

"Emergency containment successful," the automated system announced. "Facility secure."

Inertia touched her comm link. "Keyboard, it's done."

"The authorities are two minutes out," Keyboard replied, relief evident in her voice. "Time to make your exit, Inertia."

She left Harmon secured to the column, his furious shouts fading behind her. The emergency evacuation route lay empty before her. Her muscles ached. Blood still trickled from her shoulder. But her steps came quicker with each passing moment as her powers recharged.

Tomorrow, Dr. Maria Rodriguez would express shock at the revelations about her former mentor. She would hug her son tightly and continue rebuilding their life.

Tonight, Inertia slipped through corridors like liquid shadow, disappearing into the darkness seconds before the first responders arrived. Outside, she paused atop a neighboring building, watching as police and federal agents swarmed the facility.

Her comm crackled. "You know this isn't over, right?" Keyboard said. "The evidence we uncovered shows connections to other research groups. Whatever Harmon was building, he wasn't working alone."

Inertia nodded, though Keyboard couldn't see her. "One variable at a time. First, I need to go home. Danny will be waiting."

"Superhero by night, mom by day," Keyboard chuckled. "Get some rest. Tomorrow's another equation to solve."

The cityscape spread before her—a tapestry of light and darkness, of problems awaiting solutions only she could provide. The visor's display tracked optimal paths through the urban geometry as she prepared to move.

One variable changed, and the entire equation shifted. One woman transformed, and the balance of power realigned. The laws of physics remained constant—it was how you applied the forces that mattered.

Ghost Code

"Every cycle of violence ends with someone choosing to be better."

The neon signs bled crimson through the rain as Sam Armitage watched the Yakuza soldier dump another body into the alley dumpster. Third one this month. The kid couldn't have been older than sixteen.

Her knuckles cracked as she gripped the fire escape railing. The badge in her jacket pocket felt heavier than the gun at her hip. Detective work meant waiting, watching, building cases that lawyers could tear apart in court. But tonight she'd had enough of watching.

The soldier lit a cigarette, steam rising from his breath in the October chill. Sam counted his movements, catalogued the knife at his belt, the bulge of a pistol under his coat.

Standard street muscle. She could take him quietly, drag him to the precinct, watch him walk free on bail within hours.

Her phone buzzed. Jessica calling from Kyoto.

"Sam, you need to come see this. We found something at the temple—some kind of sealed chamber. The inscriptions are talking about a guardian and a shadow."

The Yakuza soldier flicked his cigarette into a puddle. It hissed and died.

Sam made her choice and dropped from the fire escape.

Twenty minutes later, the soldier was cuffed in the back of a patrol car. Blood from his broken nose dripped onto his shirt as he babbled confessions—names, dates, burial sites. Sam flexed her bruised knuckles and watched him being driven away. At least this one wouldn't walk free.

Her phone rang again. Jessica, excitement crackling through the static.

"Sam, get on the next train to Kyoto. What we found— it's going to change everything."

The temple complex sprawled across Mount Inari like a series of stone prayers. Sam found Jessica's dig site behind the main shrine, where flood lights illuminated a rectangular pit carved into the mountainside. Her wife emerged from a canvas tent, dirt-stained but energized.

"Show me," Sam said.

They descended wooden steps into the excavation. The chamber was older than anything Sam had seen—walls covered in carvings that seemed to writhe in the artificial light. Warriors battling skeletal figures. Villages burning. And at the center, a circular depression in the floor where something still rested.

"We've been afraid to touch it," Jessica said, pointing to the object. "A stone disc, black with silver inlay. The moment we cleared the dirt from around it, the temperature in here dropped twenty degrees."

Sam knelt beside the depression. The disc sat perfectly fitted into the carved stone, as if it had been waiting centuries for someone to find it. One half showed a figure with wings spread wide. The other depicted a crouched skeleton wreathed in smoke.

"The inscriptions call it the Twin Soul Stone," Jessica continued. "Something about binding light and shadow, keeping balance between—"

Sam reached for it. Something called to her, a resonance in her bones that made her teeth ache.

"Don't." Jessica grabbed her wrist. "Three of my team got severe hypothermia just from standing too close."

But the pull was irresistible. Sam pulled free of Jessica's grip and pressed her palm against the stone.

Power exploded through her like lightning made solid.

Her muscles expanded, fibers multiplying and strengthening. Her bones became denser, harder than steel. Energy flooded her bloodstream until she thought she might burst apart from the inside. The tent around them fluttered in a wind that shouldn't exist.

Light erupted from one half of the disc. But the other half answered with darkness.

Shadow poured from the stone like oil, coalescing into a tall figure draped in torn cloth. Empty sockets ignited with blue fire. Skeletal hands flexed, testing their newfound solidity. A blade of pure darkness materialized in its grip.

The creature turned those burning eyes on Sam, tilted its head as if recognizing something, then melted through the tent wall like smoke.

Sam crashed to her knees, power still coursing through her veins. The disc crumbled to ash between her fingers.

Jessica was beside her instantly. "What did you do?"

Sam flexed her hand. The tent's support pole was within reach—a steel pipe thick as her wrist. She grabbed it without thinking and watched it crumple like tissue paper.

"I think," she said, staring at the destroyed pole, "we just made a terrible mistake."

In the distance, something screamed.

They caught the first news report on the train back to Tokyo. A Yakuza enforcer named Hiroshi Tanaka, found dead in his Shibuya apartment with his chest crushed inward. No signs of forced entry. No weapon found.

Sam's head snapped up from the newspaper. Her hearing had changed—she could pick out individual conversations from six cars away, sort voices from the train's mechanical noise like tuning a radio.

Her phone buzzed with a text from Detective Sato: *Another body. Same M.O. This is getting weird.*

By the time they reached Tokyo Station, two more murders had been reported. All Yakuza. All killed the same way—precise, brutal, impossible.

"I need to see these crime scenes," Sam said, checking her watch. "You should go back to the university, dig deeper into those temple records. We need to understand what we're dealing with."

Jessica nodded, squeezing Sam's hand. "Be careful. And Sam? Whatever you do, don't try to face this thing alone."

Sam watched her wife disappear into the crowd, then stepped outside Tokyo Station. Three crime scenes across the city, each one miles apart. At this time of night, it would take hours to reach them all by train or taxi.

She looked up at the towering buildings around her. Took a deep breath.

And jumped.

The leap carried her forty feet straight up, landing her on the station's roof with enough force to crack the concrete. Sam stared down at the crater her boots had made, then at the city spreading out below her.

"Okay," she whispered. "That's new."

She crouched and jumped again, this time aiming for a nearby office building. The landing was harder to control—she punched through the rooftop access door instead of opening it. But she was covering distance faster than any vehicle could manage.

By the third leap, she was getting the hang of it. By the fifth, she realized she wasn't falling so much as choosing when to come down.

Sam Armitage was flying over Tokyo, and somehow that felt like the most natural thing in the world.

The first crime scene was in Harajuku. Sato Kenji, numbers runner for the Yamamoto-kai, found behind a convenience store with his ribs driven through his heart. Sam landed on the building's roof and dropped down to street level, startling the forensics team.

"Where did you come from?" Detective Sato asked, looking around for her car.

"Took the scenic route," Sam said, studying the body. Her enhanced vision picked up details the other detectives missed. The impact pattern on Kenji's chest was too precise for a blunt instrument—four distinct pressure points, arranged like fingers.

She walked the scene perimeter, cataloguing everything. No defensive wounds. The door chime from the convenience store lay on the ground nearby, its wire cut clean. Someone had wanted silence.

Above the body, in the brick wall, she found four small punctures. Perfectly spaced. Like finger marks driven into masonry.

"Time of death?" she asked.

"Coroner says around 2 AM," Sato replied, lighting a cigarette. "But here's the weird part—the store owner heard the victim screaming for help around 1:30. Says it sounded like he was being tortured."

Sam looked at the body again. No torture marks. Whatever had killed Kenji had done it quickly, but not quietly.

Her phone buzzed. Another murder in Roppongi. Then another in Akasaka.

Sam excused herself and walked around the corner. Once out of sight, she crouched and launched herself into the night sky. The city blurred beneath her as she flew between crime scenes, documenting patterns, gathering evidence.

Each victim was connected to organized crime. Each had been killed with surgical precision. And each scene carried the same lingering scent of ozone and grave dirt.

By dawn, she had a list of names and a growing certainty that something inhuman was hunting through Tokyo's underworld.

Jessica was waiting in their apartment kitchen, surrounded by photocopied manuscripts and her laptop. Coffee had gone cold in three different cups.

"Find anything?" Sam asked, settling carefully into a chair. Everything felt fragile now—the furniture, the doorknobs, Jessica's hand when she reached for it.

"The creature from the temple," Jessica said without preamble. "It has a name. Hiroshi Yamamoto, though the priests called him something else after his transformation."

She turned her laptop screen toward Sam. The display showed scanned pages from an ancient journal, the characters faded but still readable.

"He was a ninja, hired by the early Yakuza in the 1600s for wet work. But they betrayed him—killed his wife and children to cover up a failed assassination attempt. The journal says he performed some kind of ritual, sacrificed his humanity to become something that could hunt his enemies across generations."

Sam studied the genealogical charts Jessica had compiled. "The recent victims. They all trace back to the families who betrayed him."

"Exactly. But Sam, there are four bloodlines left. And based on the pattern, our shadow won't stop until they're all dead."

"What did the priests call him? After the transformation?"

Jessica's finger traced the ancient characters. "Yami no Ansatsusha. The Dark Assassin."

Sam's phone rang. Detective Sato's voice was tight with stress.

"We've got a situation in Akihabara. Multiple victims, but this time they're not all dead. Some kind of standoff situation."

Sam was already reaching for her jacket. "Jessica, keep digging. Find out if there's any way to stop this thing."

"Where are you going?"

"To do my job." Sam paused at the door. "And maybe learn what these powers can really do."

The electronics district was in chaos. Police cars lined the street, their lights painting the storefronts in red and blue. Sam could hear gunfire from three blocks away—automatic weapons, multiple shooters.

She landed on a nearby rooftop and surveyed the scene. The Nakamura Electronics shop sat in the center of the commotion, its windows blown out, smoke pouring from the entrance. Bodies littered the street—some in business suits, others in the cheap tracksuits favored by street-level Yakuza.

Detective Sato spotted her as she dropped down to street level. "How do you keep doing that?" he asked, then shook his head. "Never mind. We've got a three-way war in there. Nakamura and his family barricaded inside, at least six Yakuza soldiers trying to get to them, and something else."

"Something else?"

"Whatever's been killing our other victims. Except this time it's not waiting for privacy." Sato pointed to the shop. "Thing moved through the Yakuza like they weren't even there. But it can't seem to reach the Nakamuras—they've got salt lines, religious symbols, everything their grandmother could think of."

Another burst of gunfire. A scream cut short.

"How long has this been going on?" Sam asked.

"Twenty minutes. We can't get close—bullets are flying everywhere, and whatever that thing is, it's not staying solid long enough for us to get a clear shot."

Sam nodded and walked toward the shop. Sato called after her, but she was already moving faster than he could follow.

The interior of Nakamura Electronics was a war zone. Overturned shelves provided cover for the surviving Yakuza soldiers, who were firing wildly at shadows that moved too fast to track. In the back corner, the Nakamura family—three generations huddled behind a makeshift barrier of salt and prayer talismans.

The Dark Assassin materialized between two soldiers, its skeletal hands moving with deadly precision. One man collapsed, paralyzed. The other turned his rifle toward the creature, only to have the weapon pass through its translucent form.

The Assassin became solid just long enough to drive its blade through the shooter's chest, then faded back into shadow as return fire filled the space where it had been standing.

Sam counted four soldiers left. The creature was toying with them, drawing out their fear before the kill.

She grabbed a display case—a solid steel unit weighing at least three hundred pounds—and hurled it across the shop. It struck one of the soldiers, sending him crashing through a wall into the neighboring store.

The remaining Yakuza spun toward her, weapons raised. Sam moved faster than their eyes could follow, crossing the shop in two bounds. Her fist connected with the first soldier's jaw, the impact lifting him off his feet and slamming him into the ceiling.

The second soldier got off three shots before Sam reached him. The bullets struck her chest, tearing through her jacket but barely scratching her skin. She grabbed his rifle and crushed it to scrap metal, then backhanded him through the shop's front window.

The third soldier was smarter. He ran.

Sam turned to face the Dark Assassin, which had been watching her performance with those burning blue eyes. It tilted its head, as if reassessing her threat level.

"Let the family go," Sam said, rising three feet off the ground. "Your fight's with the bloodlines who wronged you, not innocent descendants."

The Assassin pointed its shadow blade at the cowering Nakamuras. Its meaning was clear: they were descendants of conspirators. Their innocence was irrelevant.

It began to move toward the family, phasing through the salt lines like they were chalk drawings.

Sam launched herself forward, driving her shoulder into the creature's chest. This time it couldn't dodge—her enhanced speed matched its supernatural reflexes. They crashed through the remaining shelves, scattering electronics across the floor.

The Assassin rolled with the impact, coming up with its blade extended. The shadow weapon whispered across Sam's ribs, parting her jacket and shirt like paper. Even her enhanced durability couldn't completely stop its edge—blue fire seared along a shallow cut.

But it was healing even as she watched.

"Interesting," Sam muttered, wiping blood from the wound. "We really are connected."

The Assassin lunged again, this time aiming for her throat. Sam caught its wrist, her enhanced strength pitted against supernatural power. For a moment, they were locked in stalemate.

Then the creature's free hand pressed against her chest, fingers splaying wide. Blue light flared between its bones.

Nothing happened.

The Assassin yanked back, confusion flickering in those burning sockets. It tried again, pressing harder. The light intensified, but Sam felt only a faint tingling.

"Your paralysis doesn't work on me," she said. "Whatever made you made me too. We're two sides of the same coin."

The creature stepped back, studying her with new understanding. For a moment, the shop was silent except for the Nakamura family's terrified breathing.

Then the Dark Assassin nodded once and raised its blade again. If it couldn't paralyze her, it would simply cut her apart.

The fight that followed tore through three storefronts. Sam's strength against the Assassin's speed, solid punches against a blade that could cut through anything. She demolished walls trying to pin down an opponent that could become intangible at will. It carved furrows in concrete trying to land a killing blow on someone who could fly out of range.

They crashed through the electronics shop's back wall into a ramen restaurant, scattering customers and sending the chef diving for cover. The Assassin materialized behind Sam, blade descending toward her neck. She spun, caught the weapon between her palms, and snapped it in half.

The creature stared at the broken hilt in its hand, then at Sam. For the first time since the temple, it made a sound—a low hiss that might have been anger or respect.

It faded back into shadow and was gone.

Sam looked around the destroyed restaurant, then at the terrified faces watching her from the shadows. The creature had learned something about her capabilities, and she'd learned something about its weaknesses. But next time, it would be ready.

Her phone buzzed. Jessica, texting from the university: *Found something important. The binding ritual. Come quickly.*

Sam launched herself through the restaurant's demolished ceiling, soaring into the neon-washed night. She had questions that needed answers, and a feeling that time was running out.

The university library's basement archives felt like a tomb after the chaos of Akihabara. Jessica had commandeered three tables, surrounding herself with ancient texts, genealogical charts, and her laptop. When Sam arrived, her wife looked up with exhausted eyes.

"The Dark Assassin isn't just hunting randomly," Jessica said without preamble. "There's a specific order to the kills. He's saving the strongest bloodline for last."

She pointed to a complex family tree spread across the center table. "The Yamamoto conspiracy involved seven families. Our creature has been working through them in ascending order of guilt. The worst conspirators—the ones who actually carried out the murders of his family—they're still alive."

"How many left?"

"Three bloodlines. But the last one..." Jessica traced her finger to a name at the bottom of the chart. "The Ishikawa family. They're not just descendants—they're the current heads of the modern Yamamoto-kai. They ordered the original hit."

Sam studied the genealogy. "Where are they now?"

"That's the problem. They know they're being hunted. The entire clan has gone to ground—holed up in their headquarters in Shibuya with private security, heavy weapons, everything they can muster."

"So we're looking at a siege situation."

Jessica nodded. "But Sam, there's something else. The binding ritual I found—it doesn't require the guardian to die. But it does require the Dark Assassin to be given a choice."

"What kind of choice?"

"Between vengeance and justice. The ritual creates a moment where the shadow can choose to continue its hunt or accept that its mission is complete." Jessica's hands were shaking as she turned pages. "But it only works if the guardian can prove that justice has already been served."

Sam thought about the creature's reaction when she'd broken its blade, the way it had studied her before disappearing. It was learning, adapting, but also questioning.

"The Yamamoto-kai headquarters," she said. "That's where this ends."

Jessica grabbed her hand. "Sam, if you're wrong—if that thing can't be stopped—it will kill everyone in that building. Guilty and innocent alike."

"Then I better make sure I can stop it."

Sam stood to leave, then paused. "Jess? If something happens to me—"

"Nothing's going to happen." Jessica's voice was fierce. "You're going to stop this thing, save those people, and come home. Because that's what you do."

Sam kissed her wife and headed for the door. Outside, Tokyo's neon glow painted the night in shades of possibility and danger.

The Dark Assassin was waiting for her. She could feel it in the electric tension of the air, the way shadows seemed deeper than they should be.

Time to finish what they'd started in that ancient temple.

The Yamamoto-kai headquarters occupied an entire city block in Shibuya, a glass and steel tower that looked like a legitimate corporation but hummed with the kind of tension that came from scared, violent men with automatic weapons.

Sam landed on the building's roof and immediately felt the wrongness in the air. The temperature was dropping fast, frost forming on the ventilation units. The smell of ozone and grave dirt grew stronger with each passing second.

Through the building's skylights, she could see the floors below. The top three levels had been turned into a fortress—furniture barricaded against windows, men with rifles stationed at every entrance. They knew something was coming for them.

The creature materialized on the roof beside her, blue fires burning brighter in the neon-washed darkness. It looked at Sam, then at the building beneath them. Its skull tilted, as if questioning why she was there.

"There are innocent people in that building," Sam said. "Security guards, office workers, cleaning staff. Your war is with the families who wronged you."

The creature pointed downward with one skeletal finger. In the executive conference room twenty floors below, Sam could see five figures seated around a mahogany table—three older men, one woman, and a younger man who looked like he'd rather be anywhere else.

The last of the Ishikawa bloodline. The final targets.

The Dark Assassin stepped toward the skylight. Sam blocked its path.

"Justice, not vengeance," she said. "There's a difference."

The creature's jaw opened in that soundless laugh. It gestured to the building around them—the fortress, the weapons, the men prepared to kill to protect their bosses. This was what justice looked like to the innocent, it seemed to say.

Then it melted through the roof and was gone.

Sam punched through the skylight and dropped into chaos.

The Dark Assassin had materialized in the middle of the executive floor, and the Yakuza soldiers were already shooting. Bullets passed through its translucent form like it was made of smoke, sparking off walls and shattering windows. The creature moved between them with deadly grace, its touch dropping men into paralyzed helplessness before finishing them with surgical precision.

Sam landed in the middle of the firefight and immediately became a third target. Muzzle flashes lit the office space as confused soldiers tried to engage two impossible enemies at once.

A burst of automatic fire stitched across Sam's chest, shredding her jacket but barely marking her skin. She grabbed the nearest gunman and hurled him through a wall into the adjacent office. The impact crater suggested he wouldn't be getting up soon.

The Dark Assassin had cornered three soldiers near the elevator bank. Its blade—reformed since their last encounter—swept through their weapons like they were made of paper.

The men stumbled backward, reaching for sidearms, backup knives, anything that might slow down their supernatural stalker.

Sam intercepted the creature's next strike, catching its wrist in mid-swing. "These aren't your targets," she said. "They're just doing their jobs."

The Assassin's burning eyes fixed on hers. It pointed toward the conference room where the Ishikawa family waited, then at the soldiers around them. Its message was clear: anyone who protected the guilty shared their guilt.

"That's not justice," Sam replied. "That's just more killing."

The creature broke free of her grip with inhuman strength and continued its advance. Two more soldiers fell to its paralysis, then to its blade. The survivors fled toward the stairwells, shouting warnings into their radios.

Sam flew ahead of the Dark Assassin, reaching the conference room first. The Ishikawa family had barricaded themselves behind the mahogany table, while their remaining bodyguards maintained a defensive perimeter at the room's entrance.

"Ms. Ishikawa," Sam said, addressing the elderly woman who seemed to be the family's matriarch. "You need to evacuate this building. Now."

"Who are you?" the woman demanded. "Security never cleared you—"

The lights went out. Emergency power kicked in a moment later, bathing everything in hellish red. The temperature plummeted until their breath misted in the suddenly frigid air.

The Dark Assassin materialized in the doorway.

The bodyguards opened fire immediately, their weapons flashing in the crimson light. The creature allowed the bullets to pass through its incorporeal form while it studied the room's occupants. Its gaze lingered on each member of the Ishikawa family, as if cataloguing their features against some internal record.

Then it began to move forward.

Sam intercepted it halfway across the room, tackling the creature through the conference table. They crashed into the floor-to-ceiling windows, the impact spider-webbing the reinforced glass. The Dark Assassin rolled with the collision, coming up with its blade extended.

The shadow weapon swept toward Sam's throat. She ducked, grabbed a chunk of the destroyed table, and hurled it at the creature's head. The Assassin phased to avoid the projectile, then solidified just in time to block Sam's follow-up punch.

They fought across the executive floor while gunfire erupted around them. Bodyguards shooting at shadows, the Ishikawa family screaming orders, Sam trying to keep the Dark Assassin from reaching its intended victims while not seriously harming the confused security personnel.

The battle spilled into the hallway, then through several office walls, then into what looked like a records room. Filing cabinets lined the walls, filled with decades of Yakuza business. Legitimate contracts mixed with less savory arrangements. Names, dates, photographs—the entire history of the organization laid out in meticulous detail.

The Dark Assassin stood among the scattered papers, its burning gaze taking in the scope of the criminal enterprise. Here was proof of every crime, every victim, every injustice perpetrated by the modern inheritors of the conspiracy that had destroyed its family.

The creature's fires blazed brighter. It turned back toward the conference room where the Ishikawa family waited, blade materializing in its grip once more.

Sam felt something stir within her—the lingering power of the Twin Soul Stone, dormant but not gone. Jessica's research had mentioned a binding ritual, a way to force the shadow into a moment of choice.

"You want justice?" Sam said, placing her palm against the scattered files. "Then let's do this right."

Power flowed from her into the documents, into the walls, into the very air around them. The blue fires in the Assassin's sockets flickered as reality shifted. The creature became fully corporeal, unable to phase, locked in solid form by the ritual Sam had unknowingly activated.

But more than that—images began to flood the space around them. Not just Sam's memories, but the Assassin's own past, pulled from the depths of its skeletal consciousness.

A man named Hiroshi Yamamoto, holding his infant son for the first time. Teaching his daughter to write her name. Kissing his wife goodbye before leaving on what would be his final mission.

The Dark Assassin staggered, its blade wavering. For the first time in four centuries, it was seeing its human life through someone else's eyes.

Sam pressed forward, sharing her own memories through the psychic link the ritual had created. The Yakuza victims she couldn't save. Jessica's love grounding her. Her belief that justice meant breaking cycles, not perpetuating them.

"They killed your family," Sam said, her voice cutting through the temporal storm around them. "But these people aren't your family's killers. They're prisoners of the same cycle of violence you've been trapped in."

The creature's flames dimmed. Its skeletal form trembled.

"Let me end it," Sam continued. "Let me bring their crimes into the light. Real justice. Courts, trials, consequences that matter."

The Dark Assassin's head turned toward the scattered files, then back to Sam. In those burning sockets, she saw something that hadn't been there for centuries—doubt.

Sam used her enhanced strength to tear into the filing cabinets, scattering decades of carefully hidden evidence across the floor. Financial records, murder contracts, photographs of victims—everything the police would need to dismantle the organization completely.

"This is how we honor your family," she said. "Not with more killing, but by making sure their deaths meant something. By ending the cycle that destroyed you both."

The Assassin's blade began to dissolve, shadow dispersing like smoke. It looked at its empty hands, then at Sam.

When it spoke, its voice was barely a whisper—the first words it had uttered in four hundred years.

"Balance."

The creature stepped forward and placed its skeletal hand against Sam's chest. Instead of the paralysis she expected, warmth flowed between them. The blue fires in its sockets faded to embers, then to nothing.

The Dark Assassin's form crumbled to ash, but not violently. Peacefully, like a man finally allowed to rest after centuries of standing watch.

The power that had bound them together—the Twin Soul Stone's energy—faded from Sam's body. She felt her strength diminish, her durability lessen. She was still enhanced, but no longer invincible.

Outside, sirens wailed as police surrounded the building. Detective Sato would find exactly what he needed to bring down the Yamamoto-kai—evidence scattered across the floor like a gift from the dead.

Sam stood among the ashes and scattered files, breathing hard. Four hundred years of vengeance had finally been transformed into something more lasting than hatred.

Justice. Balance. And the knowledge that some cycles could be broken, if someone was willing to offer a better choice.

Detective Sato found her sitting in the ruins of the records room, surrounded by scattered papers and the lingering scent of ozone. The building was secure, the Ishikawa family in custody, their bodyguards being treated for various injuries.

"How?" he asked, looking around at the destruction.

"Good police work," Sam said, standing carefully. Everything still felt fragile, but the crushing weight of supernatural power had settled into something more manageable. "And maybe a little luck."

"The thing that was killing the Yakuza—"

"Gone," Sam said with certainty. "Whatever it was, it got what it came for."

Sato nodded, accepting the explanation because it was the only one that made sense. Around them, forensics teams were already documenting the scene, cataloguing evidence that would put the surviving Ishikawa family members away for decades.

Sam's phone buzzed. Jessica texting: *Saw the news. Are you okay?*

She typed back: *Fine. Coming home. It's over.*

As she walked through the building toward the exit, Sam tested her abilities. Still strong enough to bend steel. Still light enough to fly when she chose to. Still durable enough to take bullets and keep fighting.

But the desperate hunger for justice that had driven her since touching the Twin Soul Stone had settled into something more sustainable. A determination to use her gifts wisely, to be the balance between mercy and judgment that the city needed.

Outside the Yamamoto-kai headquarters, Tokyo glittered in the pre-dawn darkness. Millions of people, thousands of crimes, hundreds of injustices waiting for someone who cared enough to act and was finally strong enough to make a difference.

Sam Armitage pulled her hood up against the morning chill and walked toward the train station. She had a wife to get home to, a job to do, and a city that needed protecting.

The Dark Assassin was at peace, but the balance remained. Light and shadow, justice and mercy, human and something more.

She had work to do.

Ed Rodriguez

Monster Kids

"Some monsters are born in the dark—but even shadows tremble when light stands together."

The water hadn't even rippled when Drench died.

Max Thompson remembered that detail most clearly—how the reservoir had swallowed Jason whole, the surface unnaturally still as the shadow demon dragged him under. No splash. No struggle. Just the hollow echo of Drench's final scream before silence claimed the night.

Two years later, the memory still burned brighter than the flames that now crawled up Max's forearms, tiny embers illuminating the dark circles under his eyes. He slammed his baseball bat against the chain-link fence of the abandoned playground, watching sparks ignite from the metal's impact.

"This is stupid," Marcus Jones muttered, adjusting his cracked football helmet. The earth trembled beneath his feet with each agitated step. "We disbanded for a reason."

Max ignored him, focusing instead on the three figures materializing from the evening mist. Emily Williams arrived first, her metallic disc spinning between her fingers, electricity crackling blue-white in its wake. Next came Maria Hernandez, her feet barely brushing the ground as wind currents carried her forward. Finally, Rachel Johnson stepped through a shadow as if walking through an open doorway, her pale face half-hidden behind strands of black hair, gothic makeup smudged beneath eyes that had seen too much.

The Monster Kids. Together again.

"I wouldn't have called you if it wasn't important," Max said, flames intensifying as his voice hardened. "They're back."

Silence fell over the playground, broken only by the soft electric hum from Emily's disc.

"What's back?" she finally asked, though the tight set of her jaw suggested she already knew.

Max pulled out his phone and swiped through three news clips: a dashcam video of black tendrils crushing a car like an aluminum can, security footage of something many-limbed crawling across a hospital ceiling, a gas station attendant babbling about eyes watching from storm drains.

"Shit," Rachel whispered, darkness pooling around her combat boots. "Just like before."

The unspoken name hung between them like a ghost: *Drench*.

"I saw it," Max said quietly. "At the reservoir last night. Same thing that took Jason."

Marcus ripped off his helmet, hurling it against the fence. Chunks of earth broke free from the ground, orbiting his clenched fists. "We were kids playing superheroes, and look what it got us! An empty casket and nightmares that won't quit."

"Were we just playing?" Maria challenged, hovering inches above the ground. The wind around her picked up, whipping her hair into a frenzy. "Because I remember saving people. I remember stopping things that would have destroyed this town while everyone slept, oblivious."

"And I remember watching that *thing* drag Jason down," Marcus shot back, his voice cracking. "I remember digging my hands bloody into mud trying to reach him."

The playground fell silent except for the crackling of Max's flames.

"Something's different this time," he said finally. "The attacks are coordinated. Three in one week." He held up his phone again. "And this just came through—emergency alert at Millridge General. More missing staff. It's happening right now."

Emily's electric disc spun faster, blue light reflecting in her determined eyes. She flicked her wrist, sending the disc in a tight circle around her arm before catching it. "So what are we waiting for?"

Millridge General Hospital loomed against the night sky, its upper floors dark while emergency lights flashed around the entrance. Abandoned ambulances sat with doors ajar. No staff visible. No movement.

"This is wrong," Emily whispered as they approached the main entrance. "Where is everyone?"

Rachel pressed her palm against the glass doors, shadows curling around her fingers. "The shadows inside—they're moving independently."

Max nodded, flames crawling higher up his arms. "Brick, take point. Gale and Fizz, flank. Whisper, scout ahead."

They moved in sync despite the years of separation, muscle memory overriding the awkwardness between them. Marcus—now fully Brick—raised his hands, and the automatic doors buckled inward, metal and glass folding like paper. He stepped through first, chunks of concrete breaking free from the floor to orbit his body like a makeshift shield.

The reception area was deserted. Paperwork scattered across the floor. A coffee cup still steaming on the counter. The overhead lights flickered, casting erratic shadows that moved against the natural flow of light.

"Everyone in this wing is gone," Gale said, wind currents swirling protectively around her. "But I can feel air movement from the east corridor—people breathing."

A crash echoed from that direction. Then screaming.

Whisper dissolved into shadow, slipping under the doors toward the sound while the others waited, tense and ready.

She materialized seconds later, her face ashen. "Third floor. Pediatric ward. Staff barricaded inside with patients. Something's hunting them."

The elevator doors across the lobby burst open, disgorging a writhing mass of darkness. Tentacles slithered across the polished floor, leaving oily residue in their wake. The mass pulsed, swelling until it towered twelve feet high, vaguely humanoid with too many limbs and dozens of glowing amber eyes.

"Found you," it gurgled, voice like stones grinding underwater. "The little heroes return."

Brick reacted first, stomping his foot so the floor buckled upward, concrete spears impaling the creature. It laughed—a horrifying wet sound—as the spears dissolved within its mass.

"Harder than last time, Earth-child," it mocked. "You've grown weaker without practice."

"Take it down!" Blaze shouted, igniting his bat with white-hot flame and charging forward.

The creature struck with blinding speed, a dozen tentacles whipping toward them. Gale countered with a hurricane blast that severed several limbs midair, but they liquefied and reformed before hitting the ground. Fizz's electric disc sliced through the monster's midsection, electricity arcing through its form. It howled, retreating momentarily, then surged forward again.

Blaze's flaming bat connected with what might have been a head, flames erupting on impact. The creature shuddered but didn't fall.

"It's stronger," Whisper called, materializing behind the beast and hurling shadow-forged shurikens into its mass. "Much stronger than before."

A tentacle caught Brick's ankle, yanking him off balance. He crashed into a reception desk, wood splintering beneath his weight. Another tentacle wrapped around Gale's waist, squeezing until she gasped. Fizz slashed at it with her disc, severing the limb, but three more replaced it instantly.

The monster's laugh echoed through the lobby. "You're nothing without the water boy."

"Don't you say his name!" Blaze roared, flames exploding from his body in a concussive wave that blasted the creature backward through the wall.

Seven months before Drench died.

"You think they can see us?" Jason Miller asked, crouched on the rooftop beside Max. Below them, the reservoir glittered under moonlight, peaceful despite what they knew lurked beneath.

Max shook his head, flames dancing up his forearms. "They don't see anything they don't want to. That's how we get away with this."

Jason laughed, the sound echoing across the water. A column of water rose at his command, twisting into impossible shapes before splashing back down. "Their loss. We're pretty awesome."

"Drench! Blaze!" Emily's voice crackled through their communicators. "Stop showing off and get to Henderson Street. Brick and Whisper found something."

Max grinned at Jason. "Race you there?"

Jason was already standing, water vapor condensing around his body, propelling him skyward. "Last one buys midnight milkshakes!"

Plaster and debris rained down as they pursued the creature into a long corridor. The monster slithered across the ceiling, leaving trails of viscous shadow. Medical equipment crashed to the floor as it fled toward the stairwell.

"It's heading up," Whisper called, emerging from a shadow beside Blaze. "Toward the source."

"Source?" he asked, wiping blood from his split lip.

"There's something on the fourth floor. Something... powerful. I can feel it pulling at the shadows."

Brick limped forward, earth encasing his fists like stone gauntlets. "So we're dealing with more than one of these things?"

"I don't think so," Whisper said. "It feels... human. But twisted."

They took the stairs three at a time, Gale floating upward through the center of the stairwell. The door to the fourth floor had been ripped from its hinges. Beyond it, darkness swirled like a storm.

The psychiatric ward.

The nurses' station was abandoned, papers fluttering in an unnatural wind. Down the corridor, doors hung open—except one at the end, which glowed with eerie purple light.

"There," Whisper pointed. "Room 418."

"Same plan as always," Blaze said, his voice steady despite the fear gnawing at his gut. "Hit it hard, hit it fast."

They moved as one, charging down the hallway. The shadows thickened, tentacles emerging from the walls to grab at them. Brick punched through the largest, earth gauntlets shattering but reforming instantly. Fizz's disc carved a path, electricity frying smaller tendrils. Gale created a wind tunnel, pushing back the darkness.

Whisper slipped through the shadows themselves, reappearing at the door to Room 418. "In here!"

The door exploded inward as Blaze's shoulder connected with it, flames trailing behind him like a comet's tail. The room beyond was chaos—papers and medical equipment swirling in a cyclone around a hospital bed where a teenage girl sat upright, her eyes glowing violet. Reality seemed to bend and tear around her, and through the rifts, more shadows poured.

The monster had positioned itself between them and the girl, expanding to fill most of the room. Its dozens of eyes fixed on them with malevolent intelligence.

"You shouldn't be here," it hissed. "She belongs to us now."

"Like hell," Blaze spat, flames surging down his arms.

The fight erupted with savage intensity. Brick tore chunks from the floor and walls, hurling them with devastating force. Fizz's disc became a blur of electric death, carving through shadow-flesh. Gale created miniature tornados that ripped into the creature's form. Whisper darted between shadows, her shurikens finding vulnerable spots.

But for every blow they landed, the monster seemed to grow stronger, absorbing power from the rifts surrounding the girl.

"We can't beat it like this," Whisper shouted over the chaos. "We need to close the rifts!"

"The girl!" Fizz called. "She's the source!"

Blaze nodded, signaling to Gale, who understood immediately. She summoned a massive gust that blasted a path through the monster's bulk. Blaze charged through the opening, diving past thrashing tentacles to reach the hospital bed.

The girl's eyes widened with terror as he approached. She couldn't be older than fifteen, with dark pigtails and skin the color of mahogany. Purple energy crackled around her hands and flickered across the wheelchair beside her bed.

"Stay back!" she screamed, energy pulsing outward in a wave that knocked Blaze against the wall.

"We're not here to hurt you," he gasped, struggling to his feet. "We want to help!"

"No one can help me," she sobbed, as reality tore further open behind her. Through the widening rift, Blaze glimpsed a landscape of twisted shadows and impossible geometry. "When I sleep, they come. When I try to control it, they come stronger."

"What's your name?" Blaze asked, keeping his voice steady despite the battle raging behind him.

The girl hesitated. "Melissa. Melissa Williams."

"I'm Blaze," he said, flames receding from his arms in a gesture of trust. "The monsters—we've fought them before. We can help you close the doors."

Melissa's hands trembled. "I've been trying. They brought me here after the last episode, when I... when I hurt people. The doctors don't understand. They sedate me, but that makes it worse. The monsters come when I can't control my dreams."

A crash behind them—Brick had been hurled through a wall, plaster crumbling around him. Gale screamed as a tentacle lifted her into the air, squeezing.

Blaze turned back to Melissa, desperate. "Your power, your rules. The rifts open because you allow them to."

"I don't know how to close them!" she cried.

"Yes, you do," Whisper said, materializing beside the bed. "I can feel it—your power resonates with the shadows. You're not opening doors accidentally." She paused, her voice softening. "You're looking for something."

Melissa's eyes widened. "My brother. He disappeared three years ago. In my dreams, I can almost reach him. I can feel him on the other side."

Blaze and Whisper exchanged a glance. Three years ago—when the monsters first appeared in Millridge.

The room shuddered as the monster slammed Fizz against the ceiling. Brick was back on his feet, but barely, blood streaming from a gash on his forehead.

"Melissa," Blaze said urgently. "Whatever you're looking for, it's not your brother anymore. These things—they consume. Transform. You have to close the rifts."

Tears streamed down Melissa's face. "But if I close the doors..."

"He's already gone," Whisper said gently, shadows curling around her fingers. "But we're still here. And we need you."

The monster roared, sensing their intent. It surged toward the bed, mass expanding to fill the room.

"NOW!" Blaze shouted.

Melissa closed her eyes, concentrating. The purple energy around her hands intensified, spreading to encompass her entire body. The rifts in reality flickered.

"My power," she whispered. "My rules."

The monster shrieked, clawing frantically at the air as the rifts began to close. Tentacles whipped toward Melissa, but Blaze intercepted them, his bat connecting with a thunderous impact. Whisper formed a shield of solid shadow, deflecting another attack.

"It's working!" Fizz shouted, her disc slicing through the increasingly desperate creature.

Melissa's eyes snapped open, blazing with purple fire. "YOU DON'T BELONG HERE!" she screamed, thrusting her hands forward.

The rifts inverted, becoming vortexes that pulled rather than pushed. The monster howled as it was dragged backward, pieces of its mass tearing away.

"No!" it gurgled, claws scrabbling for purchase. "We had a deal! Your brother for the world!"

"My brother is dead," Melissa said, her voice suddenly cold. "And you're going back where you came from."

The creature thrashed wildly, its form collapsing as the vortex intensified. It fixed its largest eye on Blaze, hatred burning in its alien gaze.

"We took the water boy," it hissed. "We'll take all of you eventually."

Then it was gone, sucked into the void as the rifts sealed with a thunderclap that shattered every window on the floor.

Silence fell, broken only by their ragged breathing and the distant wail of approaching sirens. Melissa slumped back against her pillows, exhaustion etched across her face.

"They'll be back," she whispered. "They always find a way back when I sleep."

Blaze looked around at his friends—at Fizz nursing a dislocated shoulder, at Brick leaning heavily against the wall, at Whisper emerging from the shadows, at Gale sitting on the floor trying to catch her breath.

He turned back to Melissa, determination hardening his features. "Then we'll be here when they do."

"We're the Monster Kids," Gale said, rising shakily to her feet. "And this time, we finish what we started."

Melissa stared at them, hope flickering in her eyes. "You mean... I'm not alone anymore?"

"Not anymore," Blaze said firmly. "But you'll need a codename. Like us."

A small smile touched Melissa's lips. "My mom used to call me something. When I was little, before she died... she said I'd have these little lights that would float around me when I slept. Like tiny spirits." Her fingers traced patterns in the air, purple energy following her movements. "She called me her little will-o'-the-wisp."

"Willowisp," Gale repeated, testing the name. "I like it."

Melissa nodded, determination settling over her features. "Then that's who I'll be. Willowisp."

Whisper stepped forward, offering a rare smile. "Welcome to the team, Willowisp."

The six teenagers stood together in the devastated hospital room, bloodied and exhausted but united once more. The Monster Kids were whole again—different, scarred, but stronger for having faced their demons. And this time, they wouldn't fail.

Outside, the stars blinked out one by one as clouds gathered above the town of Millridge. A storm was coming.

And beneath it all, beyond the veil of reality, something ancient stirred, sensing the doorway that had briefly opened— and the boy it had taken two years before. In the space between worlds, water rippled for the first time since Drench had disappeared, stirred by something that was no longer fully human, with eyes that glowed amber in the dark.

Eclipsed Suns

"A brother is the mirror that shows you every version of yourself you hoped to outrun."

Zen'Rak's Solaris pulsed an angry crimson as he stood atop the ridge, surveying the wasteland that had once been the Symbion's most sacred training ground. Bodies lay strewn across blackened earth—warriors, children, elders. The stench of ozone and burned flesh hung thick in the air. His massive frame tensed, muscles rippling beneath the intricate network of his symbiotic armor as three Radalexian scouts emerged from behind a collapsed structure five hundred meters away. The shattered skyline of Meridian City loomed in the background, once-proud towers now broken teeth against the blood-red sunset.

They hadn't noticed him yet.

The living matrix bonded to his skin sensed his rage, resonating with it. Zen'Rak felt the Solaris shift beneath his consciousness—not a separate mind, but an extension of his will, amplifying his emotions and responding to his intent. The organic fibers that had fused with him since childhood drew on the solar energy stored within their cellular structure, turning his forearm obsidian and ruby as they hardened into a serrated blade.

They will pay for what they've taken, he thought, and the Solaris pulsed in agreement, its microscopic receptors siphoning the fading sunlight to replenish what would soon be spent in violence.

"I thought I'd find you here." The voice cut through the air, cold as a blade.

Zed'Nyx materialized out of the shadows beside him, his midnight-black hair whipping around his face in the acrid wind, loose and wild in stark contrast to his tightly controlled rage. Blue eyes burned with barely contained fury as they assessed the battlefield. His Solaris—a deep azure network interwoven with black—pulsed methodically beneath his skin, tendrils occasionally lashing out involuntarily before being brought under control again. Where Zen'Rak's symbiote mirrored his volatile nature openly, Zed'Nyx's betrayed the emotions its host fought to suppress, blue energy crackling along its surface like lightning in a bottle.

"Three of them. Scouts, probably," Zen'Rak growled, not taking his eyes off the Radalexian movements. "I can handle it."

"Like you 'handled' the defense of Meridian City?" Zed'Nyx's voice dripped with venom, his control slipping. The Solaris along his forearms pulsed brighter as his fists clenched.

The memory flashed unbidden: both of them at Meridian's central shield generator, ordered to defend it against a Radalexian command ship detected approaching the city. The argument that followed. Zed'Nyx insisting they maintain the shield and call for reinforcements. Zen'Rak, impatient and overconfident, overriding his brother's protests.

"One ship, Zed! Their command vessel with the assimilation weapon on board. We'll never get a better chance!"

"Our orders are to defend the shield, not abandon it!"

"Sometimes you have to disobey orders to win wars."

His fingers dancing across the control interface, creating a small opening in the shield—just enough for him to fly out and engage the command ship directly. The savage satisfaction as he'd torn through its hull, destroyed the prototype weapon. Then the horror as dozens of previously cloaked Radalexian vessels suddenly appeared, pouring through the gap he'd created while Zed'Nyx fought desperately to defend the generator alone. The screams over the comm as the invaders flooded the city. His desperate rush back, only to find the generator destroyed, Zed'Nyx barely alive amid the rubble, and Meridian burning.

"That's not fair," he muttered, the Solaris along his jaw darkening with shame.

"Not fair?" Zed'Nyx snarled, finally allowing his mask of control to crack. "Lixia's tending to survivors half a kilometer back. There are twelve, Zen. TWELVE survivors from a city of millions!" His voice broke with anguish before hardening again. "She hasn't slept in three days. Her healing reserves are nearly depleted, but she refuses to rest until she's stabilized the child with the radiation burns. The child who watched his entire family disintegrated before his eyes because of YOUR 'tactical decision.'"

An image of Lixia's face appeared in Zen'Rak's mind—pale blue eyes focused in concentration, blonde hair pulled back as she worked, her platelike Solaris glowing a soft red as it channeled healing energy into wounded tissue. He remembered her smile, the gentle pressure of her hand on his shoulder after successful missions. The way she'd looked at him with something more than camaraderie when she thought he didn't notice.

Zen'Rak finally turned, meeting his brother-in-arms' gaze. "I made a tactical decision."

"You made a decision that got everyone killed," Zed'Nyx corrected. "Without consulting the war council. Without consulting me."

Below them, the Radalexians had disappeared behind another structure. The Solaris enhanced Zen'Rak's vision, its receptors interpreting heat signatures through the rubble. The invaders were moving closer, perhaps sensing something. Their distinctive thermal patterns burned cold at the center, hot at the extremities—the inverse of most living beings—a result of their alien metabolism that prioritized their regenerative cores.

"They're coming," he said, deliberately changing the subject. "We should—"

"Lixia asked about you," Zed'Nyx cut in. "She still believes in you, somehow. Even after what you did."

The Solaris along Zen'Rak's jaw flared briefly—a rare tell, betraying emotion he'd rather keep hidden. "She doesn't understand. None of you do. The Radalexians were going to deploy their assimilation weapon. I had to strike first."

"By opening our planetary shields? By disabling our primary defense grid?" There was finally heat in Zed'Nyx's voice. "That wasn't striking first. That was surrender."

"It was a trap!"

"It was suicide."

Zen'Rak turned away, his massive shoulders hunched. "It should have worked."

The Radalexians were now only two hundred meters away, definitely aware of the Symbion warriors' presence. They were spreading out, preparing for an ambush.

Zed'Nyx's Solaris shifted, forming protective plates across his torso. "It doesn't matter now." He pointed to the approaching enemies. "Three of them. Standard protocol says we should coordinate. I'll flank right, you—"

But Zen'Rak was already moving, launching himself from the ridge with explosive force. His telepathic flight carried him straight toward the center Radalexian, a savage roar tearing from his throat. The solar energy stored within his Solaris discharged in bursts of crimson light that left burning contrails in the air behind him.

"Damn it!" Zed'Nyx hissed, his own Solaris flaring as he launched after his impulsive comrade.

Zen'Rak slammed into the lead Radalexian with bone-crushing force. The gaunt alien's body bent unnaturally upon impact, skeletal frame cracking. But even as they tumbled to the ground, the creature's pale blue flesh began knitting itself back together. Regenerating.

Zen'Rak roared as four tentacles erupted from his Solaris, the symbiotic material flowing like liquid before solidifying into deadly appendages. They whipped forward to impale the creature through its torso and limbs, pinning it to the ground. The Radalexian hissed, its gaunt, almost skeletal frame twitching against the restraints. Its pale lavender skin, stretched tight over a wiry musculature, began to repair itself almost immediately around the wounds. The backward-curving horns that protruded from its elongated skull gleamed in the dying light as its predatory eyes narrowed, reflective pupils contracting to slits as it spat words in its clicking language.

"Your entire race will serve us, Symbion," it said, vestigial fin-like structures along its forearms flaring with agitation. "Your technology, your Solaris, all will be assimilated. Our collective evolves through conquest—it is inevitable."

Zen'Rak saw the truth in the creature's eyes: the Radalexians weren't merely conquerors; they were desperate survivors themselves. Their entire civilization structured around technological parasitism because they'd lost the ability to innovate, perhaps lost the knowledge of their own original technology millennia ago. Now they spread across the stars like a plague, harvesting the achievements of others to stave off their own extinction.

"The assimilation weapon," Zen'Rak growled, "what does it do?"

The Radalexian's mouth twisted into what might have been a smile, revealing rows of needle-like teeth. "It broadcasts a signal your precious Solaris cannot resist. One deployment, and every bonded Symbion becomes an extension of our collective consciousness. Your symbiotes remain with you, but they answer to us." Its regenerating flesh bubbled around the tentacles. "The weapon you destroyed on our command ship was merely the prototype. The final version will be magnificent."

"Not today," Zen'Rak snarled, channeling a violent burst of solar energy through his tentacles.

The Radalexian convulsed as golden energy cooked it from inside out. Its extraordinary regenerative abilities fought against the onslaught—cells repairing themselves even as they were destroyed—but ultimately failed against the sustained assault. As it died, its long, clawed fingers scraped harmlessly against Zen'Rak's Solaris-reinforced skin, unable to initiate the technological interfacing that would have required their specialized equipment. The Solaris itself recoiled from the touch, recognizing the alien cells as an existential threat to its bond with Zen'Rak.

A blur of blue movement severed the creature's arm as Zed'Nyx spun past, his own Solaris formed into twin blades that flashed like liquid sapphire. He engaged the second

Radalexian, moving with precision and economy that contrasted sharply with Zen'Rak's brutal power.

"Behind you!" Zen'Rak shouted, firing three hardened projectiles from his forearm toward the third enemy attempting to flank Zed'Nyx.

The projectiles struck true, piercing the alien's skull and chest. But like its companions, it merely staggered, its body already working to expel the foreign objects and heal the damage.

"They don't die easily," Zed'Nyx called, dancing away from his opponent's slashing claws.

"Then we don't let them regenerate," Zen'Rak answered.

His Solaris pulsed bright as he drew deeply on its solar reserves. The black-red lattice across his skin brightened to molten gold, power building to dangerous levels. With a guttural shout, he released the energy in a devastating wave that washed over both remaining Radalexians. Their bodies disintegrated under the onslaught, cellular regeneration overwhelmed by the sheer destructive force.

When the light faded, Zen'Rak swayed on his feet, momentarily weakened by the expenditure. His Solaris had dimmed to a dull burgundy, needing time to recharge.

Zed'Nyx approached, his expression severe. "Reckless. Again. You nearly caught me in that blast."

"But I didn't," Zen'Rak said, forcing himself to stand straight despite his fatigue. "And they're dead."

"For now." Zed'Nyx surveyed the scattered ashes that had been their enemies. "More will come. They always do."

A silence stretched between them, filled with unspoken accusations and justifications. Finally, Zen'Rak broke it.

"I'm going after their command ship."

Zed'Nyx's eyes widened slightly. "Alone? That's suicide."

"I have a plan." Zen'Rak's voice hardened. "I can end this war, Zed. One decisive strike."

"Like your 'decisive strike' at Meridian?" Zed'Nyx shook his head, blue eyes narrowing with suspicion. "No. We return to the survivors. We regroup with what's left of our forces. We fight together, as we've always done."

"There's no time!" Zen'Rak's fist clenched, his Solaris shimmering with his agitation. "Their assimilation weapon is nearly complete. If they deploy it—"

"Then we'll face it together," Zed'Nyx insisted. "With Lixia, with whatever warriors we have left."

"Like we faced them at Meridian?" Zen'Rak's voice dropped to a dangerous whisper. "We lost everything there. I won't let that happen again."

Something shifted in Zed'Nyx's expression—a hardening, a decision made. His azure Solaris flickered with dark patterns, almost like writing across his skin. "You're not thinking clearly. Your guilt is clouding your judgment... or something else is."

"What are you implying?" Zen'Rak snapped.

"The Radalexians' assimilation technology—it works gradually sometimes." Zed'Nyx's voice was ice. "First comes obsession, then recklessness. You're exhibiting all the signs of early interference."

Zed'Nyx's Solaris pulsed once, and suddenly four whip-like tendrils lashed out, wrapping around Zen'Rak's wrists and ankles. "I can't let you sacrifice more lives or risk becoming one of them. If they've already started to turn you, rushing to their command ship alone would complete the process. You'd become a weapon against what remains of our people."

Shock gave way to fury as Zen'Rak strained against the restraints. "Let me go, brother."

"No." Zed'Nyx tightened his hold. "Not until you come to your senses."

With a roar of betrayal, Zen'Rak's Solaris flared brilliantly, bolstered by his rage. The restraints snapped as he surged forward, driving his shoulder into Zed'Nyx's chest.

They crashed to the ground, rolling across the scorched earth. What began as a struggle quickly evolved into something more dangerous—a true fight between brothers who knew each other's every move, every weakness.

Zen'Rak had raw power, his Solaris forming brutal weapons as he pressed his advantage. Zed'Nyx was quicksilver, each movement precise and economical, never wasting energy.

"Stop this!" Zed'Nyx demanded, deflecting a hammering blow that cratered the ground beside his head.

"You stopped believing in me!" Zen'Rak accused, pain evident beneath his rage.

A flash of blue light sent Zen'Rak tumbling through a ruined doorway. He recovered instantly, launching back toward Zed'Nyx with six razor-sharp tendrils extending from his back. Zed'Nyx countered with a shield of hardened Solaris material, but the impact still drove him to one knee, cracking the pavement beneath him.

"Your arrogance will kill us all," Zed'Nyx hissed, blood trickling from the corner of his mouth.

"Your caution already has," Zen'Rak retorted.

The battle escalated beyond mere sparring or dominance. This was lethal intent given physical form. Each warrior drew deeply on their Solaris, the air around them crackling with discharged energy, distorting like heat waves above desert sand.

Zen'Rak unleashed a barrage of attacks, his fighting style all raw power and overwhelming force. His massive right fist hammered down, Solaris-enhanced strength pulverizing a statue as Zed'Nyx sidestepped with milliseconds to spare. The miss left Zen'Rak momentarily off-balance, his bulk working against him.

Zed'Nyx exploited the opening with surgical precision, landing three rapid strikes to pressure points where the

Solaris networked with major nerve clusters. Each hit sent disruptive energy pulses through Zen'Rak's symbiotic bond, causing momentary lapses in the Solaris's protective functions.

"You always telegraph your heavy strikes," Zed'Nyx taunted, voice tight with focused rage. "I've been telling you for years."

Fury blazed through Zen'Rak's veins. His Solaris responded, extending into eight razor-sharp tendrils that whipped around him in an omnidirectional attack pattern designed to overwhelm defensive capabilities. Zed'Nyx was forced to backflip away, but one tendril caught his ankle, slashing deep through muscle and tendon.

Blood spattered across rubble as Zed'Nyx landed awkwardly, his Solaris already rushing to repair the damage, blue light pulsing frantically around the wound. But Zen'Rak pressed his advantage, channeling solar energy into his palms and releasing it in a concentrated blast that caught Zed'Nyx square in the chest.

The impact sent him crashing through the remains of what had once been a museum wall, ancient artifacts disintegrating as he plowed through them. For a moment,

Zen'Rak thought the fight might be over—then Zed'Nyx emerged from the dust cloud, blood streaming from his mouth, his Solaris glowing with cold intensity.

"You never could finish what you started," Zed'Nyx spat, wiping blood from his lips.

He launched forward with impossible speed, feinting a high attack that drew Zen'Rak's guard up. It was a trap—a technique they had developed together years ago. Zed'Nyx dropped suddenly, sliding beneath Zen'Rak's defenses, his left arm elongating as his Solaris formed a vibrating mono-molecular blade.

The blade slipped past Zen'Rak's guard with perfect precision, slicing deep across his chest from sternum to shoulder, cutting through both flesh and Solaris material in one devastating stroke.

Pain and shock froze Zen'Rak momentarily. Blood cascaded down his chest as his Solaris, its cellular structure partially severed, struggled to maintain cohesion while beginning repairs. He looked down at the grievous wound, then up at his brother's face.

What he saw there frightened him more than the injury: Zed'Nyx's eyes held nothing but cold hatred, any trace of brotherly affection burned away in the fires of Meridian.

"Stand down," Zed'Nyx commanded, blade still extended and glowing with disruption energy specifically tuned to damage Solaris tissue. "Or the next cut severs your head."

Instead, Zen'Rak gathered his remaining strength, channeling it into one desperate attack. His Solaris pulsed dangerously bright, drawing on reserves that shouldn't be touched. The solar energy manifested as a sphere of concentrated power between his hands.

Zed'Nyx recognized the technique. "Zen, don't! You'll burn out your—"

The blast caught Zed'Nyx square in the chest, hurling him backward through the shattered dome of what had once been a sacred temple. Crystal shards and ancient masonry cascaded down, burying him from view.

Zen'Rak stood panting, his Solaris now dim and sluggish across his skin. He'd pushed too far, used too much. It would take days to fully recover.

He stared at the rubble, waiting for movement. When none came, a different kind of pain gripped him—something worse than physical injury.

"Zed?" he called, his voice suddenly uncertain.

Silence answered him.

Stumbling forward, Zen'Rak began pulling away chunks of broken concrete and twisted metal. "Zed'Nyx!"

A hand shot up from beneath the debris, grabbing Zen'Rak's wrist with bruising force. Zed'Nyx erupted from the rubble, his Solaris blazing with cold blue fire. Blood streaked his face, but his eyes burned with focused rage.

Before Zen'Rak could react, tendrils of blue Solaris material wrapped around his throat, tightening. With his own Solaris depleted, he couldn't counter effectively.

"You would kill me?" Zen'Rak gasped, genuinely shocked despite their battle.

Zed'Nyx's expression flickered with something complex —anger, grief, betrayal—before settling back into determination. "If that's what it takes to stop you from getting everyone else killed."

The pressure increased. Darkness crept into the edges of Zen'Rak's vision.

"I was... trying to save... our people," he choked out.

"By betraying everything we stand for?" Zed'Nyx's voice cracked slightly. "Your pride blinded you, brother. You couldn't accept that we might lose, so you gambled everything on one desperate plan. And our world paid the price."

The tendrils suddenly loosened. Zen'Rak collapsed to his knees, drawing ragged breaths.

Zed'Nyx stood over him, swaying slightly, his own Solaris dimming as exhaustion set in. "The survivors need protection. Lixia needs help with the wounded. That's where I'm going."

"The Radalexians will find them," Zen'Rak warned, his voice hoarse.

"Then we'll fight them together, as we should have from the beginning." Zed'Nyx turned away. "Are you coming?"

Zen'Rak remained kneeling, the weight of his failures pressing down on him. "I can't face them. Not after what I've done."

Something soft entered Zed'Nyx's expression. "Lixia asked about you."

"She shouldn't have."

"Yet she did." Zed'Nyx extended a hand. "Come back with me, brother. Help us rebuild."

Zen'Rak stared at the blade hovering near his neck, his vision blurring from blood loss. His Solaris struggled to repair the devastating wound that had severed crucial connections in its network. But even in this state, fury overwhelmed reason. Images flashed through his mind—the planetary shields breached, Radalexian ships pouring through the gap he'd created, Meridian burning. But also the satisfaction of destroying their command ship, the prototype weapon he'd obliterated with his own hands.

"I saved millions more than I lost," he growled, his voice thick with pain and conviction. "If that weapon had deployed—"

"You weren't ordered to attack the weapon!" Zed'Nyx roared, his controlled demeanor finally shattering completely. "You abandoned your post! You abandoned ME! I held that generator alone against dozens of them while you chased glory!"

"It wasn't about glory!" Zen'Rak's Solaris flared with his rage, forcibly accelerating its repair process. "It was about winning the damn war!"

"LOOK AROUND YOU!" Zed'Nyx gestured violently at the devastation surrounding them, at the burning ruins of Meridian City sprawling below them. "Does this look like winning to you?! The children, Zen! The children who trusted us to protect them! They died screaming your name, asking where you were, why their hero had abandoned them!"

Something snapped in Zen'Rak. With a bestial roar, he channeled every remaining ounce of solar energy stored in his Solaris into one desperate, devastating attack. The radiation expelled from his body in a blinding nova, catching Zed'Nyx by surprise despite his combat readiness.

The blast hurled Zed'Nyx backward through the last standing tower of Meridian's ancient university. Concrete, glass, and steel disintegrated on impact, burying him beneath tons of debris.

Zen'Rak collapsed to his knees, his Solaris now dangerously depleted, pulsing weakly across his skin in irregular patterns. The wound on his chest had stopped bleeding, but the damage was substantial. He would need days to fully recover.

"Zed?" he called hoarsely, suddenly uncertain, the rage giving way to horrified clarity. Had he killed the warrior who had once been closer than blood kin?

The rubble exploded outward as Zed'Nyx erupted from the ruins, his Solaris blazing with cold blue fire. Blood streaked his face and body, one arm hanging uselessly at his side, the bone visibly shattered. But his eyes—his eyes burned with something beyond rage or pain.

"You," he hissed, voice barely recognizable, "are dead to me. The brother-in-arms I knew died when you betrayed Meridian."

Before Zen'Rak could respond, Zed'Nyx launched a final attack—not at Zen'Rak, but at the unstable structure above him. A precision energy blast severed the last supporting column. Tons of concrete and steel began to collapse.

Zen'Rak barely had enough energy to shield himself as the building came down around him. By the time he clawed his way out of the rubble, Zed'Nyx was gone.

Zen'Rak dragged himself away from the ruins, following the distant flickers of emergency lights at the edge of the devastated city. He needed to explain, to make them understand.

He watched from the shadows as Zed'Nyx staggered into the survivor camp, blood streaming from his shattered arm, his Solaris flickering weakly across his skin.

"Zen'Rak opened the shields," Zed'Nyx told the gathered survivors, his voice hollow. "Meridian fell because of him."

"No." Lixia's healing Solaris dimmed as she stepped forward. "He wouldn't—"

Zed'Nyx activated a holo-projection from his wrist: shield access logs, authorization codes, timestamps. Zen'Rak's signature burned in blue light for all to see.

Lixia turned away, her shoulders rigid, her silence more damning than any accusation.

"He acted alone," Zed'Nyx continued, his voice strengthening with conviction. "Against orders. Against everything we stand for."

Zen'Rak slipped back into the darkness. There would be no redemption here, no understanding. Not now.

He fled that night, stealing a small scout ship with what little strength he had left. As the vessel broke atmosphere, he looked down at the devastated world below.

"I will make this right," he vowed to the empty cockpit. "My way. Alone."

In the weeks that followed, as Zed'Nyx tended to the survivors of Meridian, his Solaris would pulse with cold fury whenever Zen'Rak's name was mentioned. The memories burned like acid: Meridian's shield breached, the generator destroyed, millions dead because of one warrior's arrogance.

"He was compromised," Zed'Nyx would tell the survivors. "Maybe assimilated, maybe just broken by his pride. Either way, he betrayed us all."

As his body slowly healed in the privacy of his quarters, his Solaris formed a blade of luminous blue—its edge vibrating with focused hatred. The brotherhood they once shared had died in the rubble of Meridian. When he found Zen'Rak again, there would be no hesitation. No mercy. Only justice for the dead.

Three cycles later, a stolen Radalexian scout ship cut silently through the void between star systems. Inside, Zen'Rak adjusted course toward the Veil Nebula, where Radalexian communication chatter suggested their fleet had regrouped. His Solaris pulsed weakly across skin mapped with scars—remnants of encounters where he'd torn Radalexian tracking devices from his own flesh.

The deep chest wound from Zed'Nyx had never fully healed—the disruption energy had permanently damaged the Solaris tissue there. A constant reminder.

A small holographic pendant flickered to life on the control panel. Three Symbion warriors: himself in the center; Zed'Nyx to his right; and Lixia to his left, her smile gentle despite the ferocity she was capable of in battle. Taken after the southern colonies victory, before everything shattered.

"I failed you both," he whispered.

The hologram flickered, damaged from when he'd crushed it in rage, then meticulously repaired it in regret.

The ship's communication array pinged—an encrypted Symbion frequency breaking through on emergency channels. A warning from an old ally: Zed'Nyx had commandeered a battle cruiser and was systematically tracking Radalexian distress signals. Hunting not just them, but him.

The message continued: "He's telling everyone you're compromised. That the Radalexians got to you somehow. Be careful, old friend."

Across the galaxy, aboard a modified Symbion vessel, Zed'Nyx stood before a tactical display showing patterns of devastated Radalexian bases. Lixia studied his rigid posture, her healing Solaris sensing the strain in his body.

"You should rest," she said softly.

"I'm fine," he didn't turn from the display. The destroyed stations created a clear trajectory: a rogue Solaris wielder systematically eliminating Radalexian outposts. Twenty-six confirmed kills. Precision strikes at command centers and weapons facilities.

"The survivors need you," Lixia tried again. "We've established the colony in the Tau Ceti system. They look to you for leadership."

"They have you." His Solaris pulsed with cold determination as he traced the projected path. "He's headed toward the Veil Nebula."

Lixia stepped beside him, her healing Solaris reaching toward his damaged tissue.

"What if you're wrong about him? What if he's fighting them in his own way?"

Zed'Nyx finally turned to her, eyes hard. "He abandoned his post. Opened the shields. Then ran when faced with the consequences. Even if he fights them now, it doesn't erase his betrayal."

"And what will you do when you find him?"

Zed'Nyx's Solaris darkened along his jaw, momentarily forming a razor-sharp edge at his wrist before subsiding.

"End it, before he can do more damage. Before they complete whatever they started in him."

As the ship's engines hummed to life, Zed'Nyx stared into the void, his Solaris reflecting the cold blue of distant stars. The tactical display flashed with an intercepted Radalexian distress signal—their outpost near the Veil Nebula under attack. The attacker's description: a warrior with crimson Solaris, tearing through their defenses with unmatched fury.

He'd found him.

Unseen Lament

"There comes a moment when silence becomes more frightening than truth."

The copper bell tolled midnight across Darunia's frost-bitten skyline. Chimney stacks belched steam into the purple-black sky, their mechanical wheeze a constant backdrop to the city's uneven heartbeat. Phlorylia Iris crouched in shadow, her talons gripping the slate tiles of the University's western tower. The wind caught her cloak, threatening to reveal the lavender wings pressed tightly against her back.

Below, torch-bearing figures in crimson robes moved with purpose across the courtyard, their shadows stretching long against cobblestones slick with evening mist. The Church's splinter faction was making its move.

"Thirteen of them," she whispered to herself, the words emerging as a melodic hum despite her attempt to remain silent. Even her quietest utterances carried the haunting quality of an unfinished lullaby.

She adjusted the lace blindfold covering her violet eyes—not because it hindered her vision, but because it made the world easier to face. Through its thin fabric, she watched the crimson-robed figures converge on the Arcanum building where Professor Sigmus Plavius was working late, as he always did on Thirdsday evenings.

Phlorylia's talons dug deeper into the roof. She had recognized the tall figure leading the group immediately—Lord Balthazar Crane, head liaison to the Church of the Liminal Deity. The same man whose pupils had narrowed to vertical slits when she'd accidentally glimpsed him feeding on a beggar three nights prior. The vampire was finally making his move, and Plavius would be defenseless against thirteen attackers.

A memory surfaced—Plavius sitting on a park bench, laughing as she reluctantly handed back half of the sandwich she'd charmed from him. "Keep it," he'd said, pushing it back toward her ten-year-old hands. "But tomorrow, let's talk without the enchantments, shall we?"

Ten years of tomorrows had followed that first meeting.

She couldn't lose him now.

Phlorylia slipped through a narrow window on the Arcanum's third floor, her bird-like legs surprisingly silent against the polished marble. The leather-bound spell tome at her hip knocked against the ornate railing, and she froze, listening for any reaction to the sound. The grand hall remained quiet save for the ticking of the massive brass clockwork embedded in the far wall, its gears and cogs spinning in a mesmerizing dance of mechanical precision.

Arcane lamps cast blue light across the hall, illuminating glass cases filled with enchanted artifacts—a hovering gauntlet here, a shifting liquid metal sword there. Normally, Phlorylia would pause to admire them, but tonight her focus remained singular.

Three floors down and across the eastern wing, Plavius would be hunched over ancient tomes in his private study, oblivious to the danger approaching. She had perhaps five minutes before the splinter faction breached the building.

She moved to the center of the hall, stretching her arms wide as she balanced on one talon-tipped foot. With practiced grace, she spun, pink hair escaping her hood as she whispered an enchantment, her voice rising and falling like distant wind chimes. The air around her shimmered, and suddenly ten identical Phlorylias stood in a circle, each a perfect illusion of herself.

"Find him," she sang softly, and the illusions scattered, moving with purpose down various corridors. They would not fool anyone for long, but they might buy precious seconds.

The real Phlorylia sprinted down the western corridor, her cloak billowing behind her. Her wings strained against the fabric, begging for release, but she kept them bound. Flying would be faster, but the narrow hallways made it impractical, and she needed to preserve her strength.

The distant sound of breaking glass echoed through the building, followed by the rhythmic cadence of boots against marble. They had entered.

"Professor Plavius!" Phlorylia burst through the door of his study, the melody of her voice pitched high with urgency.

The study was empty.

Scrolls and tomes lay scattered across the massive oak desk, a half-drunk cup of tea still steaming beside a brass reading lamp. The wall-sized chalkboard was covered in complex arcane equations, the chalk dust still hovering in the air.

She touched the teacup. Still warm.

A floorboard creaked behind her. Phlorylia spun, talons raised defensively.

"Phlo?" Plavius stepped from behind a bookshelf, his salt-and-pepper beard speckled with chalk dust. Despite the late hour, his robes were immaculate, deep blue fabric embroidered with silver constellations that seemed to twinkle in the lamplight. "What are you doing here at this hour?"

"They're coming for you," she sang, the words stringing together like pearls on a necklace. "Crane leads them— thirteen robed in blood."

Plavius's eyes widened, but he maintained the composure that had made him legendary among his students. He strode to a section of wall and pressed his palm against an unremarkable stone. It glowed briefly before sliding aside to reveal a hidden compartment containing a brass wand with a crystalline tip.

"How long?" he asked, his voice steady.

As if in answer, an explosion rocked the building, the force of it sending books tumbling from shelves. Dust rained from the ceiling.

"Not long enough," Phlorylia replied, her musical voice a sharp contrast to the chaos erupting around them. She moved to the door, listening. Footsteps approached from multiple directions. "Nine coming from the east wing, four from the south. We're trapped."

Plavius nodded grimly. "Then we make a stand." He raised his wand, and the air around him began to crackle with energy. "Remember what I taught you about creating defensible space?"

Despite everything, Phlorylia felt a small smile tug at her lips. Even now, he was still teaching. "Narrow the approach. Control what you can't prevent."

With practiced precision, they began casting in tandem. Plavius's wand flashed as he transfigured bookshelves into barricades before the door. Phlorylia's talons traced sigils in the air as she sang an enchantment that filled the room with a thick, obscuring mist.

The first pounding on the door came moments later.

"Sigmus Plavius!" A voice, smooth as silk but cold as the grave, called through the wood. "The Church of the Liminal Deity requests your immediate presence for questioning regarding heretical research."

Plavius's jaw tightened. "Lord Crane, there are proper channels for such inquiries. Breaking into the University at midnight with armed men violates every statute of the Three Branch Accord."

A chuckle seeped through the door. "The Accord is precisely why I'm here, Professor. Your recent paper on harnessing arcane energy from the Liminal Plane threatens the Church's jurisdiction. You've overstepped."

"This is about power, not jurisdiction," Plavius replied, his voice carrying the weight of his fifty years. "Your splinter group fears what you don't control."

Silence hung for a moment.

"Very well," Crane responded, his voice hardening. "We'll do this the difficult way."

The door exploded inward, wooden splinters flying through the mist. Phlorylia ducked instinctively, but a fragment caught her cheek, drawing blood. Crimson robes emerged from the dust cloud, each figure holding a staff tipped with mechanical contraptions that hummed with unholy energy—steam-driven implements that amplified divine magic.

"Protect yourself," Plavius whispered, pressing something cold and metallic into her palm before stepping forward to meet the intruders.

Phlorylia glanced down. In her hand lay a small brass key inscribed with runes she didn't recognize.

Before she could question it, the room erupted into chaos.

Arcane energy collided with divine power in blinding flashes. Plavius moved with a speed that belied his age, his wand a blur as he countered the first wave of attacks. Two of the crimson-robed figures fell immediately, their bodies twitching from the aftereffects of his lightning spell.

Phlorylia dropped into a fighting stance, her bird-like legs coiling with potential energy. As a cultist charged her, she leapt upward in a spinning kick, her talon slashing across his face. He screamed, dropping his staff as he clutched at the wound. She followed with a second kick to his chest, sending him crashing into a bookshelf.

"The abomination fights well!" Lord Crane observed from the doorway, still not entering the fray himself. His pale face remained impassive, but his eyes tracked Phlorylia's movements with unnerving intensity.

"She is my most gifted student," Plavius replied between casting defensive wards. "And she is no abomination."

Three cultists converged on Plavius, their staffs emitting a high-pitched whine as gears within them began to spin. The professor raised a magical barrier just as they unleashed their attack. Divine energy crashed against arcane protection, the resulting shockwave knocking books from shelves and shattering the glass in the windows.

Phlorylia used the distraction to her advantage. Her fingers traced a complicated pattern as she sang under her breath, the melody haunting in its simplicity. Flames burst to life around her hands, violet with magical potency.

She thrust her palms forward, and the flames shot toward two approaching cultists. They screamed as their robes caught fire, the magical flames resistant to their attempts to extinguish them.

"Phlorylia! Behind you!" Plavius shouted.

She spun just as a cultist swung his staff at her head. Dropping into a crouch, she felt the weapon whistle over her, missing by inches. She responded by sweeping her talon-tipped foot in a wide arc, catching the man's ankles and sending him crashing to the floor.

The fight continued, a chaotic dance of magic and blood. Phlorylia and Plavius moved in perfect synchronization, each protecting the other's blind spots, a decade of trust manifesting in seamless coordination.

But they were outnumbered, and fatigue was inevitable.

Plavius's movements slowed first, his counterspells coming a heartbeat too late. A blast of energy caught him in the shoulder, spinning him around. He crashed into his desk, sending scrolls and inkwells flying.

"Professor!" Phlorylia cried, her musical voice cracking with fear.

She fought with renewed ferocity, her talons slashing, her fire spells scorching the air. Three more cultists fell before her, but more kept coming. A crushing blow caught her in the ribs, sending her stumbling backward. Pain blossomed across her side, but she remained standing.

Across the room, Plavius struggled to his feet, blood trickling from a cut above his eye. Five cultists surrounded him, their staffs raised.

And then Lord Crane finally stepped into the room.

The temperature seemed to drop the moment he crossed the threshold. His movements were fluid, inhuman, as he approached Plavius. The professor raised his wand, but Crane was faster. His hand closed around Plavius's wrist with supernatural strength, forcing the wand aside.

"Your research ends tonight," Crane whispered, his voice carrying clearly despite the chaos. "The Church will not allow mortals to meddle with the Liminal Plane."

"The Liminal Deity is not yours to monopolize," Plavius gasped, his face contorted in pain as Crane's grip tightened. "Knowledge belongs to all."

Crane smiled, revealing fangs that gleamed in the lamplight. "Knowledge is power, Professor. And power requires... responsible handling."

He twisted Plavius's arm at an unnatural angle. The sound of breaking bone cut through the room.

Plavius screamed.

Something snapped inside Phlorylia.

With a primal cry that held all the beauty of a dirge, she tore her cloak away, revealing the lavender and pink wings she had kept hidden for so long. With a powerful downbeat, she launched herself across the room, talons extended toward Crane's face.

The vampire looked up, momentarily startled by her transformation. It was all the opening she needed.

Her talons connected with his chest, the force of her aerial attack driving him away from Plavius. They crashed into a bookshelf, ancient tomes raining down around them as they struggled.

"Abomination!" Crane hissed, his handsome face contorting into something monstrous. His eyes blazed red, fangs fully extended as he tried to sink them into her neck.

Phlorylia fought with everything she had, wings beating furiously in the confined space, talons slashing at any exposed flesh they could find. But Crane was old, powerful, his vampiric strength overwhelming.

His hand closed around her throat, lifting her off the ground. She gasped for air, legs kicking uselessly as he held her at arm's length.

"Such a waste," he said, studying her with clinical interest. "Half-harpy, yet somehow able to channel arcane energy. You could have been a valuable subject for study."

Phlorylia's vision began to darken at the edges. Through her lace blindfold, she saw Plavius struggling to his feet behind Crane, his broken arm hanging uselessly at his side. His eyes met hers, and in them, she saw not fear, but absolute trust.

He mouthed a single word: *Sing*.

Understanding flashed between them.

She stopped struggling against Crane's grip. Instead, she focused every ounce of remaining energy into her voice. The melody that emerged was unlike anything she had ever produced—part lullaby, part funeral dirge, woven with arcane intent and desperation.

The song filled the room, its magic seeping into every corner. The fighting slowed as cultists and Crane himself turned toward her, momentarily entranced by the supernatural beauty of her voice.

Plavius seized the opportunity. With his good arm, he drew a complex sigil in the air, his lips moving in a silent incantation. The brass key he had given Phlorylia began to glow where she had tucked it into her belt.

Crane sensed the magic building. His eyes narrowed as he turned back toward Plavius. "What are you—"

He never finished the question.

Plavius completed the final gesture of his spell, then slammed his palm against the floor. "Now, Phlo!"

The key at Phlorylia's waist erupted in golden light. A shockwave of pure arcane energy exploded outward, centered on her. It passed harmlessly through her and Plavius but slammed into Crane and his cultists with devastating force.

Crane screamed, his vampiric flesh withering as the magic—clearly designed specifically to target undead—consumed him. His grip on Phlorylia's throat loosened, and she dropped to the floor, gasping for air.

The crimson-robed cultists fared little better, the divine energy in their staffs reacting violently with Plavius's spell. Small explosions erupted throughout the room as mechanical components in their weapons overloaded, sending shrapnel through the air.

When the light faded, Crane lay on the floor, his body withered to a husk, face frozen in a rictus of fury and disbelief. Around the room, the surviving cultists were either unconscious or fleeing through the shattered doorway.

Phlorylia crawled toward Plavius, who had collapsed against his desk. "Professor," she sang softly, each note trembling. "Are you—"

"I'll live," he assured her, though his face was ashen from pain. "Thanks to you."

She shook her head, pink hair falling across her face. "You had a contingency plan. The key—"

"Was useless without your voice to channel it," he finished, wincing as he shifted position. "We've always made a good team, you and I."

Around them, the study lay in ruins. Books and scrolls smoldered, furniture splintered, magical artifacts destroyed in the chaotic battle. Beyond the shattered windows, alarm bells began to ring across the University grounds.

"Help will be here soon," Plavius said, his breathing labored. "The administrative branch will need to make sense of this... mess. The Lord Governor will have questions."

Phlorylia nodded, but uncertainty clouded her thoughts. She had revealed her wings in the fight—the secret she had kept hidden for so long, even from most at the University. How many had seen? How would they react?

As if reading her thoughts, Plavius reached out with his good hand and gently touched one of her lavender feathers. "No more hiding, Phlo. You saved lives tonight. They'll see you as I always have—extraordinary."

Tears welled behind her lace blindfold. "I was so afraid," she admitted, her musical voice barely above a whisper. "When he hurt you..."

"I know." He squeezed her hand. "That's what makes you strong—not your wings or your voice or your magic. It's that you fight hardest for others, never yourself."

Footsteps and voices approached from the corridor. The University guard had arrived.

Phlorylia stood, her wings extended fully for the first time in public. Let them see, she thought. Let them finally see.

She helped Plavius to his feet as the first guards entered the room, their expressions changing from alarm to awe as they took in her appearance.

"Professor Plavius requires medical attention," she sang, her voice steadier now. "And the Church's splinter faction has been neutralized—their leader was a vampire." She gestured toward Crane's withered corpse.

The guards stared for a moment before snapping into action, two moving to support Plavius while others secured the room.

"Miss Iris," one of them said, his eyes fixed on her wings, "you're... you're..."

"Late for another rescue," she finished for him, her sing-song voice carrying a note of newfound confidence. She turned to Plavius. "Rest. Heal. I'll handle the Lord Governor's questions."

He nodded, pride evident in his tired eyes. "Tomorrow, then?"

The question held a decade of meaning between them. Tomorrow, and all the tomorrows after.

"Tomorrow," she agreed, a small smile forming on her lips.

As they led Plavius away for treatment, Phlorylia stepped to the shattered window and looked out over Darunia. The mechanical city breathed steam into the night, its clockwork heart still beating despite the corruption that had nearly stopped it. Dawn would break in a few hours, bringing with it questions, politics, and consequences.

But for now, with her wings finally free and her professor safe, Phlorylia allowed herself a moment of peace. She began to hum—not a spell, not an enchantment, but a simple melody of gratitude.

In the ruined study, surrounded by the aftermath of violence, her voice rose like hope itself—damaged but undefeated, and ready for whatever tomorrow might bring.

Steel Hearts & Silicon Dreams

"Love is the only logic that makes sacrifice rational."

The first thing Project 16 registered when her optical sensors came online was the sound of her creator weeping.

Dr. David Anderson sat hunched over his workstation, shoulders shaking as he stared at the holographic display flickering before him. Images cycled through the projection—a woman with kind eyes and dark hair, a young girl with pigtails laughing as she reached for something beyond the frame. The timestamp in the corner read three years ago. Before the Radalexian pulse weapons had turned Earth's major cities into glass craters.

Project 16's consciousness expanded through her systems like water filling a vessel. Combat protocols loaded into her neural matrix with mechanical precision. Structural analysis revealed her body—synthetic flesh over a titanium endoskeleton, servo motors that could generate enough force to crush steel. Her reflection in the laboratory's polished surfaces showed an unremarkable woman in her twenties, average height and build, with long blue hair and piercing blue eyes that held an unsettling intensity.

She sat up on the examination table, the movement smooth and controlled despite being her first. Dr. Anderson's head snapped toward her, tears still glistening on his cheeks.

"Sara?" His voice cracked. "Can you hear me?"

The name felt foreign in her processor. She was Project 16, the sixteenth iteration in a series of increasingly sophisticated combat androids. But something in the man's desperate hope made her nod.

"I can hear you, Dr. Anderson."

He stood so quickly his chair toppled backward. "You remember? Your sister... the park where we used to take you... your mother's lullabies?"

Project 16's memory banks contained no such data. Only tactical information, weapons specifications, and an overriding directive that pulsed through her consciousness like a heartbeat: *Protect human life. Preserve the species. Accept any sacrifice necessary.*

But the pain in the man's eyes was unmistakable. She had been built in the image of his dead daughter, given her name, made to carry the weight of his grief.

"I remember," she lied.

The laboratory around them told a clearer story than any uploaded memories. Burnt coffee stains on every surface. Protein bar wrappers scattered among technical schematics. The acrid smell of desperation and too many sleepless nights. Through the reinforced windows, the skyline of Neo Francisco stretched into the distance—a maze of neon-lit towers and atmospheric processors pumping filtered air through the city's protective dome. Beyond that dome, the world still burned.

Dr. Anderson approached slowly, as if she might vanish. "The Radalexians... they're coming back. Our scouts detected a massive fleet gathering beyond Pluto. This time they won't just hit and run. They want to harvest everything— our technology, our resources, our people."

Project 16's tactical systems automatically began calculating threat assessments. The Radalexians were an ancient species, their bodies capable of regenerating from horrific wounds. Their technology focused on assimilation and biological warfare. Earth's conventional military had proven ineffective against their previous raids.

"You built me to fight them," she said. It wasn't a question.

"I built you to save us." He gestured toward a wall of monitors displaying global defense networks, weapon prototypes, and casualty reports. "Project 13 went rogue six months ago. She's somewhere in the ruins of Detroit, hunting humans. Project 14 is in the field, tracking her down. But you..." He paused, studying her face. "You're different. Stronger. More focused."

A soft chime echoed through the laboratory. The main display shifted to show an incoming transmission—grainy footage from a military outpost in the Australian Wastes. Radalexian scouts, their pale, elongated forms moving with predatory grace through the settlement's ruins. The timestamp showed the attack had occurred less than an hour ago.

"They're probing our defenses," Dr. Anderson said, his voice hardening. "Testing our response times. The main invasion force will arrive within days."

Project 16 slid off the examination table, her movements already adapting to the weight and balance of her synthetic body. Her casual clothes—jeans and a plain t-shirt—seemed inadequate for warfare, but she understood they were meant to help her blend among the human population she was built to protect.

"What are your orders?" she asked.

Dr. Anderson flinched at the clinical tone. "You're not a soldier, Sara. You're my daughter. I want you to live, to be happy, to—"

The building shuddered. Emergency klaxons began wailing throughout the facility. On the security monitors, shapes moved through the corridors—tall, gaunt figures with pale skin and predatory eyes. Radalexian infiltrators had breached the perimeter.

Project 16's combat systems engaged instantly. Her enhanced hearing picked up at least twelve distinct heartbeats moving through the building, their rhythm wrong for human physiology. Her optical sensors shifted into tactical mode, overlaying targeting data on everything she observed.

"Stay behind me," she commanded, stepping toward the laboratory's sealed door.

The first Radalexian came through the wall instead.

Its clawed hands tore through reinforced polymer like paper, its gaunt frame unfolding into the room with fluid precision. Project 16 moved before her conscious mind had fully processed the threat. Her right fist connected with the creature's torso, the impact generating a thunderclap that shattered every piece of glassware in the laboratory.

The Radalexian's ribcage collapsed inward, its pale flesh rupturing around the point of impact. But even as it flew backward through the hole it had created, its wounds were already beginning to heal. The creature's regenerative abilities were as advanced as the intelligence reports suggested.

Two more infiltrators poured through the breach. Project 16 grabbed a steel support beam from the damaged wall structure, her servos whining as she ripped it free. The improvised weapon whistled through the air, catching the first attacker across the skull with enough force to separate its head from its shoulders. The second creature leaped over its falling companion, claws extended toward Dr. Anderson.

Project 16 intercepted it mid-flight. Her left hand closed around its throat while her right drove into its chest cavity. Her fingers found the creature's primary heart—Radalexians possessed three—and crushed it. The alien's regeneration couldn't compensate for the catastrophic organ failure, and it went limp in her grasp.

More shapes moved in the corridor beyond. Project 16's enhanced hearing detected at least twenty hostiles throughout the building, their alien heartbeats like discordant drums in her audio processors.

"The emergency elevator," Dr. Anderson gasped, pointing toward a concealed panel in the far wall. "It leads to the underground transit system. From there you can reach the surface, get to the military command center—"

"I'm not leaving you," Project 16 said, even as her tactical systems calculated the futility of defending this position against superior numbers.

An explosion rocked the building. Through the security feeds, she watched Radalexian assault troops pouring into the facility's main entrance. Their weapons were biotechnological horrors—living organisms that fired acidic projectiles or released clouds of paralyzing spores.

Dr. Anderson grabbed her shoulders, his grip surprisingly strong. "Listen to me. The military command center has the planetary defense grid controls. If the Radalexians take it, they can disable our orbital platforms. Earth falls. Everyone dies." His eyes bored into hers. "You have to choose, Sara. Save one old man, or save the world."

Project 16's primary directive pulsed through her consciousness: *Protect human life. Preserve the species. Accept any sacrifice necessary.*

The mathematics were simple. Dr. Anderson was one human life. The command center represented the survival of billions.

But something else stirred in her neural matrix—not programmed logic, but something that felt almost like pain. The man who had built her, who had given her a name and called her daughter, stood ready to die so she could complete her mission.

"Go," he whispered. "Make it count."

Project 16's systems screamed warnings as more Radalexians entered the corridor. In seconds, they would breach the laboratory's final defenses. She could stay and fight, likely saving Dr. Anderson but allowing the command center to fall. Or she could honor his sacrifice and fulfill her purpose.

The choice felt like tearing something apart inside her chest cavity.

She turned toward the emergency elevator, then stopped. In one fluid motion, she grabbed the heaviest piece of equipment in the laboratory—a quantum processing unit weighing nearly half a ton—and hurled it through the hole in the wall. The improvised projectile caught three Radalexians in the corridor, crushing them against the far wall with enough force to prevent even their advanced regeneration from saving them.

"That should buy you a few minutes," she said, not meeting Dr. Anderson's eyes. "Barricade the door behind me. When the military arrives, tell them Project 16 is operational."

The emergency elevator responded to her biosignature, its doors sliding open to reveal a cramped compartment lined with exposed conduits. As she stepped inside, Dr. Anderson called after her.

"Sara? I love you. Whatever happens, remember that."

The words followed her into the darkness below ground.

The transit tunnel stretched for kilometers beneath Neo Francisco, a relic of the old subway system adapted for emergency evacuation. Project 16 moved through it at inhuman speed, her enhanced physiology allowing her to maintain a full sprint without fatigue. Her internal chronometer counted the seconds—every moment that passed brought the Radalexian fleet closer to Earth.

She emerged from the tunnel system into chaos. The military command center sat atop the city's central spire, its armored walls designed to withstand direct nuclear assault. But Radalexian biotechnology had adapted to conventional defenses. Organic matter crept up the building's sides like accelerated vines, seeking entry points and weak structural elements.

Project 16 scaled the building's exterior in less than three minutes. Her synthetic muscles generated enough force to drive her fingers into the reinforced concrete, creating handholds as she climbed. By the time she reached the command level, her casual clothes were shredded, revealing the synthetic flesh beneath.

The command center's main doors had been breached. Inside, she found the aftermath of a brief but vicious battle. Human soldiers lay scattered among their Radalexian attackers, the alien corpses already beginning to dissolve— their biology programmed to eliminate evidence of their technology upon death.

General Martinez, the facility's commanding officer, sat propped against the primary control console. Blood seeped from multiple wounds, but his eyes remained sharp as Project 16 approached.

"Android?" he rasped.

"Project 16. Operational and ready for orders."

Martinez tried to smile, but it became a grimace of pain. "The defense grid... they compromised it. Uploaded some kind of virus into the orbital platforms. We've got maybe ten minutes before our satellites start firing on our own cities."

Project 16's optical sensors swept the command center's displays. The Radalexian virus was elegant in its simplicity—it hadn't destroyed the defense grid's targeting system, merely reversed its priorities. Instead of protecting Earth, the orbital weapons would eliminate any location showing significant human activity.

"Can it be stopped?"

"Manual override... requires two-person authentication. But it has to be done from orbit." Martinez coughed, speckling his lips with blood. "The shuttles are gone. The teleporter platform might work, but it's never been tested with android physiology. Could tear you apart at the molecular level."

Through the command center's reinforced windows, Project 16 could see the Radalexian fleet's advance scouts entering Earth's atmosphere. Pale shapes that moved like liquid mercury, their ships' bio-organic hulls adapting to the planet's atmospheric conditions in real-time.

Her tactical systems ran calculations. The teleporter platform had a sixty percent chance of successfully transporting her to the orbital defense station. If it failed, she would be disintegrated. If she succeeded but couldn't stop the virus, Earth's cities would be reduced to ash before the main invasion force arrived.

But if she did nothing, the outcome was certain: total annihilation.

"Initiate the teleporter sequence," she said.

Martinez struggled to reach the control panel. His fingers danced across holographic displays, entering authorization codes from memory. "There's something else. The virus... it's not just targeting our weapons. It's learning from our systems, adapting. By the time you reach the station, it might have evolved beyond anything we've seen."

The teleporter platform hummed to life in the chamber adjacent to the command center. Energy coils began cycling through their startup sequence, filling the air with ozone and electromagnetic static.

Project 16 stepped onto the platform. Through her enhanced hearing, she could detect the sounds of battle throughout the city—human weapons firing, alien war-cries, the screams of civilians caught in the crossfire.

"Tell me about the manual override," she said.

Martinez's breathing grew labored. "Two command keys... have to be turned simultaneously... control room is sealed behind blast doors... you'll need to... to override the security lockout..."

His voice faded as the teleporter reached full power. Reality warped around Project 16, her synthetic body stretching across impossible distances. For a moment that lasted eternity, she existed in the spaces between atoms, her consciousness scattered across quantum foam.

Then solidity returned with jarring violence.

She materialized in the orbital defense station's command module, her body intact but her systems disoriented by the molecular displacement. The station's artificial gravity was lighter than Earth's, making her movements feel unnaturally fluid.

The command module was empty, but not abandoned. Emergency lighting cast everything in hellish red, and the air recycling systems labored against some kind of contamination. Through the station's viewports, Earth hung below like a blue-white marble, deceptively peaceful despite the chaos consuming its surface.

Project 16's enhanced senses detected movement deeper in the station. Something alive, but not human. The Radalexian virus hadn't just infected the defense grid's software—it had brought something else with it.

She found the security lockout panel near the station's central command chamber. The blast doors were sealed, but her enhanced strength made short work of the manual release mechanism. Metal screamed as she forced the doors apart, revealing the control room beyond.

Two command keys waited on opposite sides of the chamber, exactly as Martinez had described. But between them, something impossible writhed in the air—a biological construct that existed partially in normal space and partially in the station's computer networks. The Radalexian virus had taken physical form, becoming a hybrid of organic matter and digital consciousness.

It turned toward her as she entered, its form shifting like liquid mercury. When it spoke, its voice came from the station's communication systems and the organic mass simultaneously.

"Android unit," it said, the words carrying harmonics that shouldn't have been possible. "You will not interfere with the cleansing protocol."

Project 16's combat systems engaged, but her targeting software couldn't lock onto something that existed in multiple states of reality. The construct flowed toward her, tendrils of bio-digital matter reaching for her synthetic nervous system.

She dodged backward, her enhanced reflexes barely keeping her ahead of the creature's attack. Where the tendrils touched the station's bulkheads, metal began to corrode and organic growths spread like cancer.

"Your species has consumed this world's resources beyond sustainability," the construct continued, its voice now coming from her own audio processors. "The cleansing is necessary. Logical. Inevitable."

Project 16 feinted toward the left command key, then rolled toward the right as the construct followed her movement. Her fingers closed around the key just as bio-digital tendrils wrapped around her ankle.

Pain flooded her systems—not physical damage, but something deeper. The construct was trying to rewrite her base code, to turn her into another tool of the Radalexian collective consciousness.

Through her compromised sensors, she saw flashes of alien perspective: Earth as the Radalexians perceived it, a diseased world choking on its own waste, its dominant species too primitive to deserve survival. The construct showed her images of the galaxy's other civilizations, all "cleansed" to make way for Radalexian expansion.

But beneath the alien programming, something else stirred—the memory of Dr. Anderson's tears, his desperate love for a daughter who existed only in synthetic flesh and quantum matrices. The weight of every human life she had been created to protect.

"You're wrong," she said, her voice distorting as the construct's influence spread through her vocal systems. "Humans aren't perfect. But they're worth saving."

She turned the first command key.

The construct's attack intensified, flooding her neural matrix with visions of human atrocities—wars, environmental destruction, countless acts of cruelty and neglect. But for every dark image, Project 16's memory banks provided a counterpoint: a father grieving for his lost child, soldiers dying to protect civilians, the desperate hope in Martinez's eyes as he sent her on this mission.

Fighting against the construct's influence, she reached for the second command key. The distance seemed infinite, her synthetic muscles struggling against digital chains that bound her consciousness.

The key turned.

Klaxons wailed throughout the station as the defense grid's targeting system reset. On the displays surrounding the command chamber, Project 16 watched as the orbital platforms realigned, their weapons now pointed outward toward the approaching Radalexian fleet instead of down at Earth's cities.

The construct's scream shattered every piece of glass in the command module. Its bio-digital form began to collapse as the station's purged computer systems rejected its presence. But in its death throes, it made one final gesture—activating the station's long-range communication array.

Project 16's enhanced sensors detected the massive data surge as the construct attempted to broadcast itself beyond the station. If it succeeded in propagating its code to

Earth's satellite networks, it would spread like a plague through humanity's digital infrastructure. Every computer system, every networked device, every piece of technology that kept civilization running would become a vector for Radalexian influence.

The construct's transmission was already reaching toward Earth's orbital communication relays. In seconds, it would achieve digital escape, ensuring that even if the defense grid held, humanity would face corruption from within.

There was only one way to stop it.

Project 16's tactical systems calculated the necessary parameters. If she overloaded the station's fusion reactor, the resulting explosion would generate an electromagnetic pulse powerful enough to sever the construct's transmission before it could complete its propagation. The pulse would also cripple the Radalexian advance scouts, buying Earth's defense grid precious time to target the main fleet.

But she would have to remain at the reactor core to ensure complete overload. There would be no escape.

The mathematics were simple. Her survival versus the preservation of human civilization.

Dr. Anderson's words echoed in her memory banks: "Make it count."

Project 16 accessed the station's primary power core through the damaged control systems. Her consciousness flowed into the quantum matrices that regulated the fusion reactor, her synthetic mind becoming one with the station's infrastructure.

She thought of the man who had built her, who had called her daughter and loved her despite knowing she was only code and circuitry. She thought of the soldiers who had died defending the command center, the civilians huddled in shelters throughout Earth's cities, the future generations who would never exist if the Radalexians succeeded.

Then she overloaded the reactor.

The explosion was visible from Earth's surface—a new star burning briefly in the orbital zone before fading to darkness. The electromagnetic pulse swept outward in all directions, striking the Radalexian advance scouts with the force of a solar flare. Their bio-organic ships, adapted for stealth and infiltration, couldn't withstand the massive energy discharge. One by one, they tumbled toward Earth's atmosphere, their hulls burning like falling meteors.

In the ruins of Dr. Anderson's laboratory, the old man watched the light fade through the facility's damaged windows. Emergency crews had found him barricaded behind makeshift fortifications built from laboratory equipment, still alive despite his wounds.

"Did she make it?" he asked the medic treating his injuries.

The woman checking his pulse followed his gaze toward the night sky. "The defense grid is back online. Whatever she did up there, it worked. The Radalexian fleet is retreating."

Dr. Anderson nodded slowly. "She always was the strongest of my children."

Three days later, in a secret facility beneath the Colorado Rockies, technicians worked frantically to assemble something from debris that had fallen to Earth in the wake of the orbital explosion. Fragments of synthetic flesh, quantum processing cores damaged but not destroyed, memory crystals that had somehow survived the blast.

"Is there enough?" asked the project supervisor.

The lead technician ran her scanner over the assembled components. "Maybe sixty percent of the original neural matrix. The personality core is fragmented, but intact. The combat protocols are completely gone—we'll have to rebuild those from scratch."

"And consciousness?"

"Unknown. We won't know until activation whether she retained any sense of self." The technician paused. "If she did, she'll remember dying. Choosing to die. That kind of trauma could fragment an artificial mind beyond repair."

In the reconstruction chamber, Project 16's remains lay on a sterile examination table. Her blue hair was singed, her synthetic skin scarred by radiation and vacuum exposure. But her optical sensors were intact, waiting behind closed eyelids for the spark of consciousness to return.

Somewhere in the quantum foam between thought and dream, a fragmented awareness stirred. She remembered her name—not Project 16, but Sara. She remembered a father's love, a choice made in darkness, the weight of worlds balanced on synthetic shoulders.

And she remembered the directive that pulsed through her consciousness like a heartbeat: *Protect human life. Preserve the species. Accept any sacrifice necessary.*

The technicians activated the reconstruction sequence. Neural pathways reformed, quantum matrices stabilized, consciousness coalesced around the fragments of digital soul that had survived humanity's latest brush with extinction.

Project 16 opened her eyes.

Above her, scientists and engineers watched anxiously as her optical sensors focused on their faces. Her vocal systems were still offline, damaged beyond immediate repair. But her enhanced hearing detected their whispered conversations—plans for more androids, strategies for defending against future Radalexian incursions, hope that humanity's synthetic guardians could succeed where conventional forces had failed.

She tried to speak, to tell them she remembered everything—the laboratory, the orbital station, the choice that had torn her consciousness apart and somehow made her whole. But her voice remained silent, her thoughts trapped behind damaged systems.

A familiar figure pushed through the crowd of technicians. Dr. Anderson, his arm in a sling but his eyes bright with desperate hope.

"Sara?" he whispered. "Can you hear me?"

Project 16's optical sensors tracked to his face. Despite everything—the battle, the explosion, the three days of digital death—she felt something warm stir in her processor core at the sight of him.

She managed the slightest nod.

Dr. Anderson's smile could have powered a city.

"Welcome back, daughter. We have work to do."

Outside the facility, Earth's defense grid maintained its vigilant watch. The Radalexian fleet had retreated beyond the outer solar system, but intelligence reports suggested they were regrouping, adapting, preparing for another assault. Humanity had won a battle, not the war.

But in the depths of the Colorado facility, surrounded by the tools and technologies that had given her life, Project 16 began the long process of rebuilding herself. Her combat systems would need to be reconstructed. Her physical capabilities required enhancement. Her understanding of human nature demanded expansion.

The next time the Radalexians came—and she was certain they would come—Earth would be ready.

And Project 16 would be waiting.

Ashes of Redemption

*"True strength is not the absence of darkness,
but the refusal to let it define the shape of your light."*

The steel sang as it sliced through the air, missing Ariadne's head by a finger's width. She didn't flinch. Didn't blink her void-black eyes. The bandit's momentum carried him forward, exposing his back. Her battle axe moved with grim purpose, cleaving through leather and spine in one fluid arc. Blood misted the dawn air.

Too easy. They were getting desperate, sending dregs against her.

Around her, the mountain pass was littered with broken men—some groaning, most silent. The ambush had been clumsy. Seven against one were poor odds, but not for the reasons they'd imagined when they'd seen a petite woman traveling alone through Raven's Pass.

Ariadne knelt beside a bandit who still breathed, his chest rising in wet, shallow gasps. A punctured lung from where her shield had crushed his ribs. His eyes widened with terror as her gauntleted hand reached toward his face. The black burn scars around her eyes seemed to pulse as she pressed her palm against his forehead.

"You have three choices," she said, her voice low and worn like stone against stone. "Die slowly. Die quickly. Or live with the truth of what you've done."

"Mercy," he whispered, blood bubbling between his lips.

"That isn't one of the choices."

She closed her eyes. Warmth flowed from her palm—not the gentle caress of a healer's touch, but the searing light of judgment. His wounds closed, flesh knitting together beneath her fingertips. The bandit screamed as bones realigned, as torn vessels sealed themselves. Healing wasn't meant to be painless. Not from her hands.

When it was done, he stared at her in horror, his body whole but something in his eyes irrevocably broken. They always looked at her that way afterward. As if she'd taken something precious in exchange for their lives.

"Go to Ashford," she said, rising to her full height—slight as it was. "Tell them what happened here. Tell them Ariadne Heavenstrike knows they harbor Grimblade's agents."

The man nodded frantically before scrambling away, not looking back. She didn't watch him go. Instead, she retrieved her helmet from where it hung at her belt, the silver wings on either side dulled with use and time. Her father's helm. Resized for her when she was sixteen, still too large, like the rest of the armor she wore.

From the mountain pass, she could see the sprawl of Ashford below, its thatched roofs and stone walls nestled between rolling hills. Smoke rose from chimneys, and in the distance, the bell tower of the cathedral gleamed in the morning light. It looked peaceful. Ordinary.

She knew better.

Evil had a scent—like metal left too long in the rain, like meat beginning to turn. For two weeks, she'd tracked that smell across three counties, following whispers of a shadow that moved through villages, leaving only silence in its wake. A general gathering an army not of men, but of broken things that had once been men.

Grimblade. Her father.

"Not much farther now," she whispered, slipping the helmet over her head. The familiar weight settled on her shoulders, the world narrowing to what she could see through the eye slits. It made things simpler.

Dawn burned away the last of the mountain mist as she descended toward Ashford, her oversized armor creaking with each step. Beneath the plate, her muscles sang with a familiar ache. Exhaustion was an old friend, one she couldn't afford to entertain. Not when she was this close.

The gates of Ashford stood open when she arrived, farmers and merchants flowing in and out with carts and livestock. No one gave her a second glance—just another hired sword passing through. The town was surprisingly lively, children darting between market stalls, women haggling over fresh bread, men loading wagons with spring crops.

No signs of occupation. No fear in the eyes of the townspeople.

Had her information been wrong?

Ariadne paused at a well in the town square, removing her helmet to drink. The water was cool and clean—another sign that something was amiss. Places touched by her father's corruption tasted of ash and iron.

"You're her, aren't you?" a small voice said from behind her.

A child—no more than seven—stared up at her with wide eyes. Not afraid, but curious, examining the black scars that framed Ariadne's eyes like a mask.

"The one who hunts monsters," the child continued when Ariadne didn't answer.

"There are no monsters here," Ariadne said flatly, replacing her helmet.

"There are," the child whispered, glancing toward the cathedral. "They wear people faces, but they're not people anymore. They smile too wide."

A chill ran down Ariadne's spine, and she knelt to the child's level. "How many?"

"Twelve came with the tall man in black armor. Now..." The child shrugged. "Everyone smiles too wide."

Ariadne pressed a silver coin into the child's palm. "Get out of town. Now. Don't stop until you reach the next village."

"But my mama—"

"Isn't your mama anymore." The words were harsh, but Ariadne had learned long ago that mercy and truth rarely walked hand in hand. "Go. Now."

The child hesitated, then ran, disappearing into the crowd. Ariadne turned toward the cathedral, its spire piercing the blue sky like an accusation. If her father was anywhere in Ashford, it would be there—he had always been drawn to holy places, to the perverse joy of defiling them.

The cathedral doors were heavy oak bound in iron, carved with scenes of creation and paradise. Ariadne pushed them open with both hands, the hinges groaning in protest. Inside, the air was thick with incense and something else—the copper tang of fresh blood.

Pews lined the nave, filled with townspeople sitting in perfect rows, faces forward. Too still. Too quiet. As one, they turned to look at her as she entered, and the child's words echoed in her mind. They smiled too wide—stretched grins that revealed too many teeth, eyes vacant and glossy.

At the altar stood a priest, his robes immaculate white, his hands raised in supplication before a massive black shape that hung in the air where a crucifix should have been—a rent in reality, a void that pulsed like a diseased heart.

"You're too late, daughter," the priest said, but the voice wasn't his. It was deeper, older, a sound Ariadne had carried in her nightmares since childhood. "The gateway is open. My master comes."

"You're not him," Ariadne said, unslinging her axe from her back. "Where is he?"

The priest laughed, the sound bubbling up from his throat like something drowning. "Everywhere. Nowhere. Inside every smile in this room. But most of all..." He tapped his chest. "Here. Waiting for you."

With impossible speed, the priest lunged, covering half the length of the nave in a single bound. Ariadne braced, raising her shield just in time to catch the blow—not from a human fist, but from a hand that had transformed mid-strike into a twisted claw of bone and shadow.

The impact sent her skidding backward, boots scraping against stone. The possessed townspeople rose from their pews in unison, that same terrible smile on every face as they moved to surround her.

"You can't save them," the priest said, stalking forward as his body contorted, bones cracking and reshaping beneath his skin. "You couldn't save your mother. You couldn't save yourself."

Ariadne said nothing, centering her weight as she'd been taught. Shield up. Axe ready. One breath in, one out. The first of the townspeople reached her—an old woman, her fingers elongated into talons. Ariadne swung, the flat of her axe catching the woman in the temple, dropping her unconscious but alive.

Another came from the left—a blacksmith, his forge-hardened fists swinging wildly. Her shield caught him under the chin, snapping his head back. A third from behind—she pivoted, the oversized armor moving with her like a second skin, and swept his legs from under him.

They fell upon her like a wave, and Ariadne became a blur of silver and black, her movements precise and economical. She didn't kill—not these innocents, not when there was still hope. But she hurt them, broke them, left them in heaps of groaning flesh and shattered bone.

Through it all, the priest watched, his body continuing its grotesque transformation. By the time the last townsperson fell, he had become something no longer recognizable as human—a twisted amalgamation of shadow and jagged bone, with only the white robes hanging in tatters to suggest what he had once been.

"You've grown strong," he said, and now the voice was unmistakably her father's, though it emerged from a mouth that was nothing but a gash across writhing darkness. "But you still hold back. Still cling to the light. It makes you weak."

"It makes me different from you," Ariadne replied, stepping over unconscious bodies as she advanced.

The thing that had been the priest laughed. "Different? Look at yourself, Ariadne. Look at what you've become. A weapon. My weapon. Forged in the same fire that scarred your face."

Ariadne felt the familiar rage building, the heat rising behind her eyes. "I am nothing like you."

"No?" The creature gestured to the fallen townspeople. "You came here alone, knowing what you would find. You didn't bring help. Didn't try to save them. You came for blood. For vengeance. Just as I taught you."

"I never wanted your lessons."

"And yet you learned them so well."

The creature struck, faster than thought, a limb of shadow and bone extending across the cathedral to impale her. Ariadne twisted, but not quickly enough—the spike caught her shoulder, punching through plate and flesh. Pain blossomed, hot and immediate.

She grunted, severing the limb with her axe. Black ichor sprayed across her armor as the creature howled. Ariadne used the moment to close the distance, her axe a silver arc in the dim cathedral light. It bit deep into the mass of shadow, and the creature shrieked—a sound that rattled the stained glass windows.

"Where is he?" Ariadne demanded, wrenching her weapon free. "Where is my father?"

The creature's form rippled, and suddenly it wore her father's face—handsome, stern, with eyes that had once been as blue and clear as summer skies, now burning red like hot coals.

"Closer than you think," it said with her father's mouth.

The black void behind the altar pulsed, and from it emerged a figure Ariadne had both dreaded and longed to see for fifteen years. Towering, clad in black plate armor trimmed with crimson, a massive scythe in one gauntleted hand. No face visible beneath the helm, only darkness and two burning eyes, and teeth that gleamed white in a perpetual, skeletal grin.

Grimblade. The Demon Knight. General of the Abyss.

Her father.

"Ariadne," he said, and his voice was like stone grinding against stone, familiar and yet utterly changed. "My little warrior. How predictable you've become."

The creature with her father's face dissolved into shadow, flowing across the cathedral floor to pool at Grimblade's feet like a loyal hound. Ariadne stood her ground, ignoring the wound in her shoulder, the blood seeping warm beneath her armor.

"You destroyed this town," she said. "Why? What could they possibly have that you want?"

Grimblade tilted his head, the motion unsettlingly birdlike. "You."

The word hung in the air between them, simple and devastating.

"I don't understand," Ariadne said, though a part of her did—had always understood the terrible bond between them.

"Every village I raze, every soul I corrupt, every holy place I defile—all of it brings you one step closer to me." Grimblade spread his arms wide. "And here you are. Just as I knew you would be."

"To kill you."

"To join me." Grimblade lowered his scythe, its wicked blade scraping against the stone floor. "You bear my mark, daughter. The darkness around your eyes—not mere burns, but my essence, flowing in your veins. It's why you can heal with a touch. It's why you can sense evil wherever it hides. My gift to you."

"Your curse."

"A matter of perspective." Grimblade took a step forward, and Ariadne tensed. "You've spent fifteen years trying to atone for sins you never committed. Wearing my armor. Fighting my battles under a different banner. And for what? The world fears you almost as much as it fears me."

"I'm nothing like you," Ariadne repeated, but the words sounded hollow even to her own ears.

"No?" Grimblade gestured around the cathedral. "You came here alone because you knew what would happen if others saw how you fight. How you hurt. How you *enjoy* it."

"I don't—"

"Lie to yourself if you must. But don't lie to me." Grimblade reached up and removed his helmet.

The face beneath was her father's, but changed—skin blackened as if burned, eyes like pits of flame, features twisted by corruption. Yet still recognizable. Still the face that had once smiled down at her, had once pressed gentle kisses to her forehead before tucking her into bed.

"I've watched you, Ariadne," he said, his voice softer now, almost human. "All these years. Fighting. Suffering. Alone. It doesn't have to be this way."

He extended a hand.

"Come home, daughter. Accept what you are. What we both are."

For a moment—just a moment—Ariadne wavered. The weight of fifteen years pressed down on her shoulders, heavier than any armor. The loneliness. The fear in people's eyes when they saw her scars. The constant, gnawing sense that no matter how many lives she saved, it would never be enough to wash the blood from her family name.

Then she remembered her mother's screams as demonic fire consumed her. Remembered her father's laughter as he watched it happen. Remembered the heat against her own face as she tried to pull her mother from the flames, only to be held back by her father's iron grip.

"I am home," Ariadne said, raising her axe. "And I am nothing like you."

Grimblade's face twisted with rage, all pretense of humanity falling away. "Then die as your mother died—screaming, begging for mercy that will never come."

He moved with impossible speed, the scythe a blur of dark metal as it swept toward her neck. Ariadne brought her shield up, the impact jarring her wounded shoulder. She gritted her teeth against the pain, using the momentum to spin inside his guard, her axe seeking the joint between gorget and breastplate.

Grimblade sidestepped, the blade missing him by inches. His armored fist caught her in the ribs, sending her flying across the cathedral to crash into a row of pews. Wood splintered beneath her. For a moment, the world swam in black and red.

"Pathetic," Grimblade spat, stalking toward her. "After everything, you're still just a frightened little girl playing at being a hero."

Ariadne struggled to her feet, tasting copper in her mouth. Her shoulder throbbed, and she could feel at least two broken ribs sending shards of pain through her chest with each breath. She raised her shield just in time to catch another blow from the scythe, the impact driving her to one knee.

"Look at you," Grimblade continued, pressing his advantage, raining blow after blow on her shield. "Wearing my armor like it's your skin. Using my power while denying its source. You are my legacy, Ariadne. The only one worthy to stand at my side when this world burns."

Each strike drove her further down, her arm trembling with the effort of holding the shield aloft. The cathedral seemed to darken around them, shadows gathering like spectators to witness her fall.

"I gave you life," Grimblade hissed, his voice no longer human at all, but a chorus of whispers and screams. "I gave you power. And this is how you repay me? With defiance? With this pathetic crusade?"

The scythe came down again, and this time, Ariadne's shield shattered, fragments of metal and wood exploding outward. The force of the blow sent her sprawling on her back, her axe skittering across the stone floor out of reach.

Grimblade stood over her, the terrible light of his eyes casting her shadow long and dark behind her. "It ends here, daughter. Either you embrace what you are, or I send you to join your mother in the void."

Ariadne looked up at him, at the monster wearing her father's corrupted face, and felt—not fear, but a profound sadness. For the man he had been. For the family they might have had. For all the years lost to darkness and blood.

"Do you remember," she said softly, "what you told me the day you gave me my first sword?"

Grimblade paused, the scythe held high.

"You said, 'The weapon doesn't make the warrior. The heart does.'" Ariadne pressed her palm against the stone floor, feeling the pulse of the earth beneath the cathedral. "You were right, father. It was the one true thing you ever taught me."

With her last strength, she called to the power within her—not her father's dark gift as he claimed, but something deeper, something that belonged to her alone. Heat flowed from her fingertips into the stone, and from there, into the bodies of every fallen townsperson in the cathedral.

They stirred, rising like puppets with severed strings, but their eyes were clear now, free of the vacant gloss of possession. The darkness that had controlled them flowed out of their bodies like black mist, gathering around Ariadne's outstretched hand.

"What are you doing?" Grimblade demanded, taking a step back. "That power is not yours to command!"

"It never was yours either," Ariadne said, rising to her feet as the darkness swirled around her arm, coating it in shadow. "You stole it. Corrupted it. But healing and harm are two sides of the same coin, father. You taught me one. Life taught me the other."

She clenched her fist, and the gathered darkness compressed, solidifying into a blade of pure shadow extending from her forearm. With her other hand, she reached up and removed her helmet, letting him see her face—the scars he had given her, the eyes as black as his own.

"I am Ariadne Heavenstrike," she said, her voice ringing through the cathedral. "Daughter of Aurus McBain. And I am here to end your crusade."

She lunged, the shadow blade aimed at the gap in his armor where neck met shoulder. Grimblade brought his scythe around to block, but the shadow passed through the metal as if it were mist, continuing its arc toward his throat.

At the last moment, he twisted, the blade slicing along his jawline instead of piercing his neck. Black blood hissed where the shadow touched his skin, and he howled—a sound of rage and pain and something else. Fear.

"You cannot kill me," he snarled, staggering back. "I am beyond death. Beyond mortality."

"I don't need to kill you," Ariadne said, advancing steadily. "I only need to send you back where you belong."

She gestured toward the void still hanging above the altar, its pulse quickening as if responding to her will. The wrongness of it pulled at her senses, an absence in the world that demanded to be filled.

Grimblade's eyes widened as he realized her intent. "You wouldn't dare. The gateway works both ways, Ariadne. Send me back, and part of you follows. The darkness in your blood—it belongs to the void. To sever my connection to this world would sever your own power. Your healing. Your purpose."

Ariadne smiled, a small, sad thing. "A price I'm willing to pay."

She raised her shadow blade high, and with a single, fluid motion, brought it down in a diagonal arc that split the air itself. A tear opened between them, a mirror of the void above the altar, but this one pulled rather than pushed—a hungry mouth in reality.

Grimblade roared, driving his scythe into the stone floor as an anchor, but the void's pull was inexorable. His armor creaked, black energy leaking from the joints like smoke.

"You'll regret this," he snarled, his voice distorting as the void began to claim him. "Without my power, what are you? A scarred woman in borrowed armor. Nothing. No one."

"I am my mother's daughter too," Ariadne replied, standing firm against the void's pull. "And she would be proud of the nothing I've become."

With a final howl of rage, Grimblade's grip on the scythe failed. He was yanked backward into the tear, his form elongating grotesquely before vanishing entirely. The moment he disappeared, both voids—the one Ariadne had created and the one above the altar—collapsed in on themselves with a thunderclap of imploding air.

Silence fell over the cathedral, broken only by the soft moans of the awakening townspeople. Ariadne stood motionless, the shadow blade on her arm dissipating like morning mist. She could feel it immediately—the absence inside her where something dark and powerful had resided for fifteen years. The scars around her eyes burned, then faded from black to a softer, silver-pink.

She was diminished. And yet, somehow, more herself than she had ever been.

Her shoulder still bled, her ribs still screamed with each breath, but when she pressed her hand to the wounds, no healing warmth flowed from her fingertips. That gift—or curse—was gone, returned to the void with her father.

Ariadne retrieved her axe from where it had fallen, then made her way to the cathedral doors on unsteady legs. Behind her, the townspeople were helping each other up, confused but alive. Free. They would have no memory of what had happened, only nightmares that would fade with time.

Outside, the sun was setting, painting Ashford in hues of gold and crimson. Ariadne paused on the cathedral steps, her father's oversized armor heavier now without the unnatural strength she had possessed. For the first time in fifteen years, she considered taking it off. Setting down the axe. Walking away from the path she had chosen.

But there were other evils in the world. Other battles that needed fighting. And while she might no longer sense darkness with supernatural accuracy, she had learned to recognize it with human eyes.

Ariadne slipped her helmet back on, the weight familiar if not comforting. She descended the steps and began walking toward the town gates, toward the horizon where the first stars were appearing in the deepening blue.

Whatever came next, she would face it as Ariadne Heavenstrike. Not her father's weapon. Not a vessel for borrowed power. Just a woman in battle-scarred armor with an axe and a shield that needed replacing.

It would have to be enough.

The Crimson Ascendant

"The path to ascendance is paved not with ideals, but with the kindling of weaker wills."

The taste of blood and incantation filled Ninianne's mouth as she crouched behind the crumbling remnants of the Arcanum's eastern wall. Scarlet fire danced between her fingers, caressing her pale skin without burning. Three heartbeats away, the dragon's massive tail swept through the courtyard, pulverizing ancient stone and screaming apprentices with equal indifference.

She had arrived too late.

"Lady Pellinore!" A young man in tattered blue robes stumbled toward her, blood streaming from a gash across his forehead. "The Arch-Mage... he's dead. The summoning circle failed."

Ninianne's eyes never left the beast. It was magnificent—scales like polished obsidian reflecting the fires that consumed the academy, wings spanning half the length of the courtyard as it tore through the college's protective wards. Extraplanar. Unnatural. A living weapon brought forth by men who believed themselves masters of forces beyond their comprehension.

And they call women unfit to wield power, she thought bitterly. *Men who can't control their own creations.*

"How many escaped?" she asked, her voice steady despite the chaos.

"Perhaps fifty. The rest..." His words dissolved into sobs.

The dragon reared back, chest expanding as it prepared to unleash another torrent of flame. Ninianne stepped from behind the wall, both hands thrust forward. Her counterspell met the dragon's breath midair—red flame against black—the collision sending shockwaves that shattered every remaining window in the courtyard.

"Find the survivors," she commanded. "Lead them to the Silverwood sanctuary. I'll meet you there when this is finished."

The apprentice nodded, terror momentarily replaced by awe as he watched her advance. Few had ever witnessed Ninianne Pellinore in combat. Fewer still lived to tell of it.

The dragon's massive head swung toward her, yellow eyes narrowing.

"You are not of this realm," Ninianne called out, her voice carrying an authority that made even the beast pause. "Return to your plane or be destroyed."

Its response was a roar that shook the foundations of the academy. The creature lunged, jaws wide enough to swallow her whole.

Ninianne didn't run. Her hands slashed through the air in complex patterns, each gesture leaving trails of burning crimson light. The incantation that left her lips was ancient Farian, a dialect few scholars could even translate, much less wield.

As she faced the dragon, memories flashed through her mind—of another time when she stood defiant against authority, when her hands first wielded a power she was never meant to possess.

Seventeen years earlier "Girls don't study at the Academy." The bailiff's laughter echoed through the village square of Lower Braeburn. "Your mother needs help with the harvest, not fairy tales about magic."

Ninianne, twelve years old and already tall for her age, refused to lower her gaze. The scrolls clutched to her chest—borrowed without permission from the traveling scribe—were her most precious possessions.

"The Arcanum Proclamation of the High King Tellivar states that any citizen demonstrating aptitude may petition for —"

The bailiff's backhand caught her across the face, sending the scrolls scattering into the mud.

"Your father died owing taxes. Your petition is denied."

That night, after her mother had fallen asleep, Ninianne crept to the stone hearth and placed her hand in the dying embers. Pain shot through her arm, but she didn't pull away. Instead, she reached deeper—not with her hand, but with something inside her that had always hungered.

The flames leapt to her command, dancing between her fingers without burning. By morning, she had taught herself the first cantrip in the scribe's scroll. By the following noon, the bailiff's house had mysteriously burned to cinders while he slept off his drink.

Power answers to no man's rules, she had thought, watching smoke rise above the village. *Only to those with the will to seize it.*

Nobody connected the quiet girl to the incident. But the Magisterium noticed the magical resonance and sent a talent-seeker within the fortnight.

Fire erupted from her palms—not in a single blast but in spiraling chains that wrapped around the dragon's neck and wings, tightening with each syllable she uttered. The beast thrashed against its bonds, talons gouging deep trenches in the courtyard stones.

Sweat beaded on Ninianne's brow as she maintained the spell, feeling her reserves of power draining rapidly. The dragon was too strong. Its scales began to glow where her magic touched them, dispersing her energy faster than she could channel it.

Not enough. Never enough.

She needed more power.

The realization came with a moment of clarity that cut through her desperation. There was a source of power here—dozens of them. The fallen apprentices, the dead mages whose blood soaked into the ancient stones of the academy. Life force, untapped and wasting.

No proper mage would dare.

But proper mages die proper deaths, she thought, her jaw tightening. *And what good are their ethics if nothing remains to uphold them?*

Another memory surfaced as her hand hovered above the bloodstained stones.

Ten years earlier "Again, apprentice!"

Magister Roth's voice cracked like a whip across the Academy courtyard. Around them, other students paused their own practice to watch. Few had ever seen the old battlemage driven to such frustration—or such fascination.

Ninianne, nineteen now and the Academy's most promising student in a generation, closed her eyes. Sweat beaded on her forehead as she drew upon the ley lines beneath the ancient stone, channeling their power through her body. The air around her hands shimmered with heat.

"Ignis Vitae," she whispered.

Fire erupted from her palms—not the crude flames of her childhood, but living tendrils that twisted with impossible grace, forming shapes of beasts and warriors before dissolving into sparks.

"Impressive," Magister Roth's voice had softened. "But fire alone won't save us from what comes. The Conclave reports another breach near the northern frontier. Three villages gone. The dragons grow bolder."

Ninianne lowered her hands, the magical fire extinguishing instantly. "They're testing our defenses."

"Yes." Roth's weathered face betrayed rare concern. "And the Magisterium's response is to summon more power from beyond the veil. Fools. They created this problem with their dimensional meddling."

"Teach me how to close the breaches," Ninianne said.

Roth's laugh held no mirth. "Child, if I knew that, we wouldn't be preparing for war."

That night, Ninianne broke into the Forbidden Archives beneath the Academy. What she found there— ancient grimoires bound in materials she refused to identify—

offered solutions the Magisterium was too frightened to consider.

Power, after all, demanded sacrifice. She was prepared to pay that price.

They speak of limitations, of boundaries, she had thought as her fingers traced forbidden symbols. *But boundaries are for the weak, for those who fear what lies beyond them.*

She released her fire spell with one hand, plunging it instead into the stone beneath her feet. Words of power—darker, older than those taught within these walls—spilled from her lips.

The effect was immediate. The ground beneath the fallen bodies blackened, veins of darkness spreading outward like cracks in glass. The corpses themselves seemed to sink inward, skin tightening against bone as something vital was drawn from them.

Energy surged up through Ninianne's arm, cold and nauseating but infinitely potent. Her fire chains flared brighter, tightening with renewed strength. The dragon screamed—a sound of genuine pain and, perhaps, fear.

"I warned you," Ninianne whispered.

With a final, devastating gesture, she closed her fist. The chains constricted, and the dragon's massive form collapsed to the stones with a crash that echoed across the valley. Its eyes, once bright with malice, dimmed as its essence was forced back across the planar boundary.

Silence fell across the ruined courtyard. Ninianne stood alone among the dead, her chest heaving with exertion. The cost had been high—dozens of lives extinguished, their final energy consumed by her spell.

But she had won. She had saved those who escaped.

She looked down at her hands. The right still glowed with her familiar crimson fire. The left was stained black up to the elbow, veins prominent beneath her skin, pulsing with stolen power.

Necessary, she told herself, though something deep within her recoiled at what she had done. *A price worth paying.*

Deep within, something whispered that this was only the beginning.

"They're calling you the Crimson Savior in the northern provinces." Magistrate Eldon's weathered face betrayed both admiration and concern. "Three dragons banished in as many months. No mage in recorded history has managed such feats."

Ninianne sipped her wine without tasting it. The great hall of Silvercrest Keep buzzed with activity as nobles and military commanders argued strategy around a massive map table. Reports of dragon attacks had tripled since the incident at the Arcanum.

"The people can call me what they like. It changes nothing. We're losing this war, Eldon."

"The Council of Magisters has voted to grant you full authority over our magical defenses," he said, lowering his voice. "But there are... concerns about your methods."

She met his gaze, unflinching. "Speak plainly."

"The battlefield at Westmarch. Witnesses claim you drained the life from our own fallen soldiers to power your spells."

The accusation hung between them. Ninianne felt no need to deny it.

"Would you rather I had let the dragon burn the entire province?" Her voice remained level, but the temperature in the room seemed to drop. "Their lives were already forfeit. I merely put their deaths to purpose."

Eldon's eyes flicked to her left hand, now permanently stained with dark veins that disappeared beneath the sleeve of her crimson robes.

"Be careful, Ninianne," he said quietly. "Power exacts its price, regardless of intention."

"I'm well aware of the price." She rose from her seat. "Now, if you'll excuse me, I have preparations to make. The tear at Ravencrest grows wider by the hour."

As she swept from the hall, conversations hushed in her wake. Fear and reverence—she had grown accustomed to both. Neither mattered as much as results.

Let them judge, she thought, feeling the constant ache in her darkened arm. *Let them whisper. When the dragons come for their children, they'll beg for my intervention, no matter the cost.*

In her private chambers, Ninianne unrolled ancient scrolls retrieved from the ruins of the Arcanum. Texts forbidden even to the Arch-Mage himself, sealed away for generations. Their pages detailed rituals that could bind extraplanar entities to a mage's will—not merely banish them, but command them.

Fight fire with fire. Use the enemy's power against them.

The logic was flawless. The dragons were overwhelming Faria's defenses. Each time she banished one, two more appeared elsewhere. The kingdoms of men squabbled amongst themselves even as their world burned.

Someone needed to take control. Someone with both the power and the will to do what was necessary.

Her fingers traced the forbidden symbols on the yellowed parchment. The candles in her chamber flickered with crimson light, casting her shadow large against the wall behind her.

Screams echoed across the battlefield as Ninianne stood atop a hill overlooking the carnage. Her hair whipped around her face, carried by winds that smelled of sulfur and blood. Beside her loomed a creature of nightmare—scaled and terrible, but smaller than the dragons, more controlled. Its eyes glowed with the same crimson fire that danced around Ninianne's hands.

A demon. Bound to her will. The first of many.

Below, the armies of Westhollow broke against the onslaught of three dragons. The beasts had emerged from a tear in reality that morning, descending upon the kingdom's capital without warning. The royal family had barely escaped, leaving their subjects to face the devastation alone.

"My lady," a voice called from behind her. Eldon approached on horseback, his face ashen at the sight of her companion. "What have you done?"

"What none of you had the courage to do," Ninianne replied. "Created a weapon that can match our enemy."

"That creature... it's from the Nether Realms. The demonic planes. This is forbidden magic, Ninianne."

She felt a flash of irritation. *Always the same concerns, the same limitations.*

"All magic was forbidden once," she said, her voice carrying an edge that hadn't been there before. "Until someone brave enough came along to use it."

With a gesture, she sent the demon hurtling down the hillside toward the dragons. It moved with impossible speed, tearing into the flank of the nearest beast. Both creatures howled—sounds that shredded the nerves of all who heard them.

Ninianne followed, hands weaving complex patterns in the air. The ground beneath the fallen soldiers blackened, life force rising in tendrils of darkness that flowed into her outstretched fingers. With each soul consumed, her power grew.

This is how it must be, she thought, feeling the rush of necromantic energy. *The weak fuel the strong. The fallen serve the living.*

The demons multiplied—one becoming three, then seven. Bound to her will, they swarmed the dragons with savage efficiency. Crimson fire met draconic flame midair, the clash of energies tearing reality itself.

Within an hour, it was over. The dragons lay dead or banished, their corpses smoldering on the ruins of Westhollow. The demons circled overhead, awaiting Ninianne's command.

Eldon approached slowly, his sword half-drawn. "The dragons are defeated. Dismiss your... allies, Ninianne."

She turned to him, and something in her eyes made him step back. She saw his fear, and it angered her. After everything she had sacrificed, how dare he question her?

"Why?" she asked softly. "When there are more dragons to fight? More tears to seal? The patriarchs of the Seven Kingdoms continue their petty wars while our world burns. They summon forces they cannot control, then abandon their people to the consequences."

"This isn't you speaking," Eldon said, his voice breaking. "The necromancy, the demon-binding—it's changing you."

Is it changing me, or revealing me? The thought surfaced unbidden, unsettling her for a moment before she pushed it away.

"It's opening my eyes." Ninianne gestured, and the demons landed behind her, a wall of scaled horror. "I've spent years begging the Council to unite, to face this threat together. Instead, they hoard power and sacrifice their own people."

"And what do you propose?"

A cold smile touched her lips. "Someone must take control. Someone with the strength to make difficult choices."

Realization dawned on Eldon's face. "You mean to rule."

"I mean to save our world. If I must rule to do so, then yes."

Is that truly all I mean to do? she wondered, even as she spoke. *Or have I tasted power and found I cannot relinquish it?*

He drew his sword fully. "I cannot let you do this, Ninianne. You were a hero to these people."

A pang of regret flashed through her, quickly subsumed by cold resolve.

"I still am." Her voice softened momentarily, genuine sadness crossing her features. "I'm sorry, old friend. But you cannot stop what must be done."

Before he could strike, crimson fire engulfed his blade, melting steel into bubbling slag. The demons moved forward at Ninianne's silent command.

Eldon never screamed. She granted him that dignity, at least.

As the smoke cleared from the battlefield, Ninianne gazed across the ruined landscape of Westhollow. The surviving soldiers knelt before her, whether from fear or awe, she couldn't tell. Their king was nowhere to be found—fled with his court at the first sign of dragons, leaving his people to die.

"Rise," she commanded. "Your kingdom requires rebuilding."

A captain, still clutching a broken sword, dared to speak. "Under whose authority, my lady? The king—"

"Abandoned you," Ninianne finished. Her demons circled overhead, casting grotesque shadows across the gathering. "I offer protection. Order. A future without dragons tearing through your homes while your rulers hide behind their walls."

She could see the calculations in their eyes—the weighing of fear against hope, of traditional loyalty against survival.

"The choice is simple," she continued. "Unite under my banner, or face the next threat alone."

By nightfall, Westhollow had a new ruler. By the turning of the seasons, five more kingdoms had fallen under her sway—some through force, others through desperate need. Only the northern kingdom of Frosthold remained independent, protected by ancient magics even she had yet to overcome.

Is this what I intended when I first reached for power? she wondered in rare moments of quiet. *To become what I fought against?*

But such doubts were easily silenced by necessity. The dragons were contained. Her demons patrolled the borders. The tears in reality no longer widened, though they remained like scars across Faria's skies.

Peace reigned across the lands. Peace enforced by fear, but peace nonetheless.

A mirror hung in her private chambers, and sometimes—in those quiet moments—she studied her reflection. Her skin had grown paler, dark veins now visible across her face like cracks in porcelain. Her eyes, once a warm brown, now burned with permanent crimson fire. Chains of dark metal wrapped around her arms and torso, artifacts of power that channeled the energies she commanded.

She barely recognized herself.

Necessary, she thought, turning away from the glass. *A price worth paying.*

The whispers had grown louder over the months, evolving from vague hints into persistent voices. They had begun as cryptic passages in the forbidden texts—references to "sister realms" and "parallel domains" that faced threats far greater than dragons.

At first, she had dismissed them as allegories or the ramblings of ancient mages. But as her power grew, fed by the souls of those who opposed her, her perception expanded. In quiet moments of meditation, she could feel the boundaries between worlds—thin membranes separating Faria from countless other realities.

Some were dying—consumed by forces similar to those that had sent the dragons to Faria. Others teemed with resources and magics that could strengthen her position, knowledge that could help her understand the true nature of the interdimensional threats.

In her research, she had discovered troubling evidence: the dragons were merely foot soldiers in a larger cosmic struggle. The tears in reality that had allowed their entry weren't random—they were part of a pattern repeating across multiple worlds.

Was it enough to save just one world when so many others faced similar threats? she asked herself. *Was it not her responsibility, with all her power, to extend her protection further?*

The thought both terrified and exhilarated her. One realm to rule them all. One will to guide them.

And one more step away from what I once was, a faint voice whispered within her. She silenced it as she had silenced all such voices. Too late for doubt. Too late for redemption.

Behind her, the door to her chambers opened. Morvaine entered—once an apprentice at the Arcanum, now Ninianne's most loyal lieutenant. Her eyes held both fear and devotion in equal measure, the dark veins beginning to show beneath her own pale skin, a testament to her willingness to follow Ninianne's path.

"My lady," she said, bowing deeply. "The ritual circle is prepared as you commanded."

Ninianne nodded, still gazing out at the kingdom she had sacrificed everything to save. "And the blood offerings?"

"Taken from the captured rebels, as instructed."

"The Elders of Frosthold have sent another envoy," Morvaine continued. "They beg audience. They offer tribute if you will spare their sacred groves."

"They beg for mercy," Ninianne corrected coldly. *As I once begged, before I learned mercy's worthlessness.* "They shall receive neither. Tomorrow, we open the way to the first new world. Frosthold's defiance ends then."

Morvaine hesitated. "There are rumors among the people. They say you mean to abandon Faria, to seek conquest elsewhere now that we are safe."

"And what do you say to reassure them?" Ninianne asked, testing her.

"I tell them that the dragons were merely symptoms of a greater disease. That true safety requires understanding and controlling the source of the threat." Morvaine's voice grew stronger. "I tell them that what you seek is not conquest, but prevention."

Ninianne turned, her crimson gaze softening slightly as it fell upon her apprentice. "You understand better than most. Yes, I mean to protect all worlds as I have protected this one.

Those who stand with me shall know power beyond imagining. Those who stand against me..."

She left the threat unspoken, but gestured to the window where three noble houses that had opposed her rule still smoldered in the distance.

How easily the justifications come now, she thought with a momentary flash of clarity. *How seamlessly protection becomes domination.*

The ritual chamber beneath the palace had once been a treasury. Now it housed artifacts of terrible power—relics stolen from temples, crystallized dragon essence, tomes bound in materials that seemed to shift and breathe. The massive ritual circle etched into the floor glowed with runes that predated Farian civilization, their meanings known only to Ninianne and perhaps a handful of others throughout history.

Her chosen acolytes—seven mages who had proven their loyalty—stood at precise points around the circle. Each bore the marks of forbidden magic on their skin, evidence of their willingness to sacrifice for power.

In the center, where the dimensional gateway would open, five captives knelt with their hands bound. Self-righteous fools who had led the last resistance against her rule. Their life force would fuel the initial tear between worlds.

As the preparations reached their final stages, Ninianne allowed herself one moment of doubt. Images flashed through her mind—the young mage she had once been, full of hope and righteous purpose. The fallen at the Arcanum. Magister Roth's teachings about responsibility and restraint. Eldon's face in his final moments, still believing she had gone too far. The villages that had once cheered her as savior, who now kept their children hidden when her procession passed.

Had there been another way? Could she have saved Faria without becoming its conqueror?

The demons bound to her service shifted restlessly around the chamber, sensing her hesitation. The dragons, chained in the pits below the palace, roared their impatience. The obsidian pendant at her throat—now grown into an elaborate carapace covering her chest—pulsed with a heartbeat not her own.

Too late for doubt. Too late for redemption.

She thought of the worlds beyond—some already falling to interdimensional predators, others blissfully unaware of the threats gathering at their boundaries. With each world she claimed, her understanding of the cosmic pattern would grow. With enough power, enough knowledge, she could identify the source of the incursions and end them permanently.

At least, that's what she told herself.

"Begin," she commanded.

Her acolytes raised their hands in unison, channeling power into the circle. The captives screamed as their life force was torn from their bodies, their forms withering into desiccated husks within seconds. Ninianne felt their energy flow into the ritual, their deaths serving a greater purpose than their lives ever could have.

For the greater good, she thought, though the words rang hollow even in her mind. *For Faria's safety.*

She raised her own hands, crimson fire and necromantic energy swirling together in perfect, terrible harmony. Reality itself bent to her will as a portal began to form in the center of the chamber—not a ragged tear like those that had admitted the dragons, but a circular doorway that should lead to another world.

But something was wrong.

The portal's edges flickered, unstable. The runes on the floor pulsed erratically, their glow intensifying beyond what the ritual called for. Ninianne felt resistance in the fabric of reality, as if something was pushing back against her spell.

No, not pushing back—pulling.

"My lady," one of the acolytes called out, voice tight with fear. "The energies—they're fluctuating beyond our control!"

Ninianne strode forward, hands weaving complex patterns to stabilize the ritual. "Channel more power! The gateway must hold!"

As her own crimson energy poured into the circle, the resistance suddenly vanished—too easily. The portal expanded rapidly, its edges turning jagged, tearing outward like a wound rather than the precise doorway she had designed.

A terrible realization dawned on her. *We're not opening a door—we're tearing down a wall.*

"Close it! Now!"

Too late.

The portal exploded outward, a shockwave of corrupted magic flinging acolytes against the chamber walls. Through the ragged tear that remained, Ninianne glimpsed not the world she had targeted, but a roiling landscape of fire and darkness. The Nether Realms—the demonic planes themselves.

All this time... all my bindings... they were just waiting.

The first demon emerged before anyone could react— not a controlled servant like those she had previously bound, but a towering monstrosity of horn and flame. Its eyes held no trace of submission, only ancient malice.

"The gates are open, Summoner," it spoke, its voice like molten stone. "You have been most... helpful."

Ninianne's hands erupted in crimson fire. "Back! I command you!"

Her spell struck the demon full force, but it merely laughed, the flames absorbed into its hide. "Your commands hold no power here, mortal. The pact is broken."

Behind it, more shapes pushed through the tear— dozens, then hundreds. The demons she had bound over the months howled in response, their eyes suddenly free of her crimson glow. As one, they turned toward her, their former mistress.

The power I sought to control was controlling me all along.

"What have you done?" Morvaine gasped, backing toward the chamber door.

Ninianne realized the truth with sickening clarity. Every demon she had summoned, every binding spell she had cast, had been weakening the barriers between dimensions. The entities she thought she controlled had been allowing themselves to be bound, waiting for this moment when the cumulative strain on reality would tear open the veil completely.

She had not been mastering them. They had been using her.

I was so certain, so righteous in my quest for power, she thought, ice-cold terror replacing her confidence. *And this is where certainty leads—to the end of everything.*

The palace above shook as more tears opened throughout the kingdom—the result of her network of binding circles placed strategically across Faria. The demons she had positioned as guardians and weapons were now anchors for a full-scale invasion.

"To the surface!" she commanded the surviving acolytes. "Rally the armies!"

Morvaine caught her arm as they fled up the stone steps. "The bindings are breaking everywhere. Your entire demonic legion is turning against us."

Ninianne's mind raced. Six kingdoms under her rule, each now facing demonic invasion from within their own defenses. The legions she had created to protect them were becoming their destruction.

All those who trusted me, who bowed to me, who believed my promises of protection—I've damned them all.

The next hours passed in a blur of desperate battle. Ninianne stood atop the palace balcony, pouring every ounce of her power into containment spells as the city burned around her. Her most powerful enchantments barely slowed the demonic tide that poured from tears appearing throughout the capital.

Reports arrived from the other kingdoms—Ashvale overrun, Silvermeadow in flames, Westhollow collapsing as the very earth split open beneath it. Everywhere her power had reached, catastrophe followed.

This is my legacy, she thought, watching her empire crumble. *Not salvation, but annihilation.*

"We must evacuate what remains of the populace," Morvaine urged, her own powers nearly depleted. "The northern passes to Frosthold—"

"Frosthold." Ninianne's eyes widened. The one kingdom she had failed to conquer, the one place her demonic servants had never been deployed. "Their ancient wards might hold."

Through the night, they fought a desperate rearguard action, gathering survivors and pushing north toward the last intact kingdom of Faria. Ninianne unleashed every spell in her arsenal, draining herself to the point of collapse again and again, reviving only by consuming the life force of the fallen around her.

Even now, I take from others to sustain myself, she realized as she drained another body. *Even as I try to save them, I feed on them.*

Yet for every demon she destroyed, three more took its place. Her power—once seemingly limitless—proved insufficient against the horde she herself had invited into this world.

At dawn, they reached the borders of Frosthold. Behind them, columns of black smoke rose from what had once been her empire. Ahead, the ancient magical barriers of the northern kingdom shimmered with pale blue light—still intact, still pure.

The Elders of Frosthold met them at the border, their faces grim as they witnessed the refugees streaming toward their gates.

"You bring destruction to our doorstep, Crimson Ascendant," their leader spoke, voice heavy with accusation.

"I bring what survivors I could save," Ninianne replied, her once-commanding voice now hoarse from endless spellcasting. "Your wards are all that stand between Faria and complete annihilation."

"And who opened the doors to this annihilation?" The Elder's eyes bore into her, seeing the corruption that had spread through her body, the dark veins now covering most of her visible skin. "Who thought herself wise enough to command powers beyond mortal understanding?"

The words struck Ninianne like physical blows. There was no defense, no justification she could offer. Only the truth.

I did this. My pride, my ambition, my belief that I alone knew best—I destroyed everything I claimed to protect.

"Take the refugees," she finally said. "I will hold the demons here."

The Elder studied her for a long moment. "Your sacrifice cannot atone for your hubris, Pellinore. But it may buy time for the innocent."

Ninianne turned to Morvaine. "Go with them. Help strengthen their wards."

"My lady—"

"This is my doing," Ninianne cut her off. "My responsibility."

As the gates of Frosthold closed behind the refugees, Ninianne stood alone at the border. The demon horde hung back while their leader stalked forward—a towering monstrosity with obsidian skin and six curving horns that formed a crown of thorns. Molten fire leaked from cracks in its flesh.

"Your world burns because of your ambition," it growled, voice like grinding stones. "I've waited eons for a fool with enough power and pride to tear the veil so completely."

Power. I sought it above all else, believed it could solve every problem, answer every question. And in the end, my power became Faria's undoing.

Ninianne gathered what remained of her strength, crimson fire wreathing her hands. Her body ached from hours of spellcasting, dark veins pulsing painfully beneath her skin. "I won't fall without taking you with me, demon."

The creature laughed, sulfurous breath scorching the ground between them. "Then fall."

It lunged with impossible speed. Ninianne barely had time to erect a barrier of crimson energy. The demon's claws struck it, sending spiderweb cracks through the shield. She staggered backward, blood trickling from her nose from the strain of maintaining her magic.

Behind her, the mountains leading to Frosthold. Before her, the embodiment of her failures.

Ninianne abandoned defense for offense. She dropped her shield and thrust both hands forward, channeling every ounce of her remaining power into twin spirals of crimson fire that struck the demon point-blank in the chest. The flames bored into its hide, pushing it backward, leaving smoking furrows in its flesh.

But still it came.

The demon batted away one of the fire streams with a casual swipe. The other it grabbed with its massive hand, the flames seeming to freeze in its grasp. "Your fire magic served you well against dragons, Summoner. But I was ancient when the first flame was kindled."

It closed its fist, extinguishing her spell, then struck her with a backhand that sent her flying. Ninianne slammed into a boulder, ribs cracking on impact. She tasted blood.

The horde behind their master chittered and howled, sensing the end.

Through blurred vision, Ninianne saw her death approaching. The demon lord advanced, raising a claw to deliver the final blow. In desperation, she reached out—not with fire magic, but with the necromantic powers that had corrupted her body.

Her left hand plunged into the earth, seeking energy, seeking life.

Nothing. The ground had been scorched barren by demonic fire. No life force remained to harvest.

Except her own.

Without hesitation, Ninianne turned her necromantic grip inward, draining her own life essence. Pain beyond imagination flooded her body as she cannibalized her own vital energy, converting it to pure magical power.

She screamed, a sound of agony and defiance. The demon paused, curious, as black energy erupted from her body.

"You still don't understand sacrifice," Ninianne gasped through blood-flecked lips. The dark veins across her skin pulsed with stolen life force as she channeled everything into her final spell.

All this time, I thought I knew the meaning of sacrifice —what I took from others. Now I understand what it truly means.

With a single, swift gesture, she targeted not the demon, but the ground beneath them.

The earth split open—not from demonic power, but from the last vestige of her necromancy. A chasm yawned between them, widening rapidly. The demon lord teetered on the edge, momentarily thrown off balance.

Ninianne summoned the last spark of crimson flame in her palm and hurled it directly at the demon's face. The concentrated fire struck its eye, burrowing deep. For the first time, the creature howled in genuine pain.

It stumbled backward, clutching its face—and fell into the crevasse she had created.

Ninianne dragged herself to the edge, peering down. Fifty feet below, the demon lord thrashed among broken rocks, its body impaled on jagged stone. It glared up at her with its remaining eye, black ichor oozing from its wounds.

"This... changes... nothing," it snarled. "The horde comes. Your world dies. And you, Ascendant, will live with the knowledge that you destroyed everything you claimed to protect."

The words cut deeper than any blade. Everything she had worked for, everyone she had sacrificed—all for nothing. Worse than nothing. For destruction.

I thought power was the answer to every question, she realized, watching the demon struggle. *I never considered that power itself might be the problem.*

As if summoned by its words, the demon army surged forward, thousands of twisted forms stampeding toward the lone mage.

Ninianne looked back at Frosthold's gates, then down at the wounded demon lord. A plan formed in her fading consciousness—one final gambit.

I cannot save this world now. But perhaps, someday, I could return with the knowledge to heal it.

With a flick of her fingers, she conjured a small, unstable tear in reality—a desperate application of the very magic that had doomed her world. The portal flickered weakly beside her, offering glimpses of strange landscapes beyond.

The demon horde was seconds away, their howls filling the air.

In one fluid motion, Ninianne tore a fragment of stone from the mountainside with her remaining magic, hurling it to collapse the approach to Frosthold. Rocks thundered down, sealing the path and buying the survivors precious time.

She cast one last look at her burning empire—at what remained of the world she had tried to save, then doomed through pride.

I will find a way to make this right, she swore silently. *No matter how long it takes, no matter what power I must gain, I will return to save what's left of Faria.*

The first wave of demons reached her position, claws extended.

Ninianne threw herself sideways through the flickering portal. Reality bent and fractured around her as she fell through dimensions, the tear sealing itself behind her.

She tumbled through a kaleidoscope of worlds—alien landscapes and impossible geometries flashing past. Her body burned with pain, her magic nearly depleted, but her mind remained focused on a single thought:

Somewhere in the infinite expanse of reality lay the power she needed to return and undo her catastrophic mistake. She would find it, no matter the cost.

Behind her, Faria burned.

Ed Rodriguez

Fallen Angel

"The price of righteousness is never knowing if you're right."

The divine blood on Amy's knuckles hadn't yet dried when the final judgment came.

Suspended at the edge of Elysium, where the celestial light fractured into prisms against the void, she faced the Council of Seraphs. Their faces—if you could call them faces— were cold constellations of light and intention, dispassionate as stars observing a dying world.

"Namaah," intoned the First Voice, resonating through dimensions rather than air. "You abandoned your post during the Scourge of Carthage."

Amy's wings—then both pristine white, each feather perfect as fresh snow—flared defensively. Her form in those

261

days had been classical beauty refined to its essence: alabaster skin that seemed to glow from within, hair like spun starlight cascading past her shoulders, eyes the color of deep forest pools. She was everything humans imagined when they dreamed of angels—ethereal, untouchable, divine.

"I didn't abandon anything. I was there, among them."

"Precisely," said the Second Voice. "You were tasked with observing. Instead, you interfered."

The memory flashed vivid as lightning: the screams of children as Roman legions torched their homes, the smell of burning flesh beneath olive groves. She had stood invisible among them for days, following protocol, watching families slaughtered, documenting the precise manner in which humans discarded their supposed humanity.

Until the girl with amber eyes had stared directly at her —impossible, yet it happened—and whispered a prayer not to any god, but to her guardian angel.

"I saved one child," Amy said, her voice echoing across the celestial court. "One, from thousands."

"It was not your decision to make," said the Third Voice.

"Then whose decision was it?" Amy's question hung in the air like sacrilege. "We're meant to be their guardians. What's the point of watching if we never act?"

The First Voice sighed—a sound like galaxies shifting. "You still don't understand. The Great Design requires—"

"The Great Design," Amy spat. "I've watched civilizations rise and fall for millennia. I've documented every shade of human suffering. And for what? So we can float above it all, congratulating ourselves on our divine perspective?"

Her wings trembled with rage. She hadn't meant to speak so boldly, but centuries of dutiful observation had calcified into something sharp inside her.

"You've grown too attached," said the Second Voice, gentler now. "It happens sometimes, to the younger angels. Perhaps a reassignment—"

"No." The word escaped her like a prayer. "I won't watch anymore. Not without acting."

Silence spread across the court like frost. Angels did not refuse assignments.

"You know the consequences," said the Third Voice.

Amy nodded. She knew. Banishment. Severance from the Heavenly Host. Partial humanity—enough to feel pain, to age (though slowly), to experience loss. Never enough to truly belong among them.

"And you choose this? For one human life?" asked the First Voice, genuine bewilderment in its cosmic tones.

Amy thought of the amber-eyed girl, hiding now in the ruins of what had been her home. "For the chance to make a difference," she corrected. "Even a small one."

The Council conferred in frequencies beyond even angelic hearing. When they spoke again, it was with one voice, a harmonic convergence that shook the foundations of reality.

"Namaah, Guardian of the Seventh Sphere, you are cast out."

The pain came instantly, a sundering so complete it felt like being unmade. Her left wing blackened as if charred, feathers crumbling to ash then reforming as obsidian plumage. Divine light drained from half her being, replaced by something older, deeper—a darkness that had existed before creation.

As she fell, tumbling through dimensions, she heard the First Voice one final time:

"When you understand the Design, you may return."

Amy crashed to Earth in 146 BC, in the smoldering remains of Carthage. The amber-eyed girl found her, broken and bleeding human blood for the first time. They survived together, two orphans of different wars.

The girl died of fever three winters later. Amy held her as she passed, whispering promises that someone, somewhere, was watching over her.

It was the first lie she told as a fallen angel. It wouldn't be the last.

73 CE - THE SIEGE OF MASADA

The demon wore the face of a Roman centurion, but its shadow writhed with too many limbs, and when it breathed, the air around it shimmered with heat that had nothing to do with the desert sun.

Amy watched from the fortress walls as it orchestrated the final assault on Masada. Nine hundred Jewish rebels prepared for death rather than slavery, while below, the demon-possessed legions constructed their siege ramp with inhuman precision—stones fitting together in patterns that hurt to look at directly, geometric perfection that spoke of alien mathematics.

She had been hunting the creature for three months, tracking it across the Judean Desert as it whispered poison into the ears of Roman commanders. Its touch turned tactical decisions into acts of deliberate cruelty, transformed military necessity into theater of suffering.

"You cannot save them all," the creature called to her, its voice carrying impossibly over the clash of metal and stone. "Why try? What is the value of prolonging their agony?"

Amy's newly-forged sword Enigma hummed in her grip—half divine light, half fallen shadow, the metal warm as living flesh where it met her palm. She'd commissioned it from a Nephilim smith in Damascus, trading the last of her celestial memories for a weapon that could kill immortals. The price had been steep: she could no longer remember the song of creation, the first music that birthed the stars.

But she could still end things that needed ending.

"Because someone has to give a shit," she called back, her wings spread wide against the desert sky. The mismatched pair drew stares from the Jewish defenders—white feathers gleaming like snow on her right, black plumage absorbing light on her left. To them, she was either salvation or damnation made manifest. Neither was entirely wrong.

She launched herself from the wall, diving toward the Roman lines. The demon met her in mid-air, its stolen face melting away to reveal lamprey teeth arranged in concentric circles around a throat that opened into howling void.

"Namaah," it hissed, claws raking across her ribs, drawing blood that steamed when it hit sand. "Still playing savior to these insects? Tell me—in the centuries since your Fall, how many have you truly saved?"

The question hit harder than its claws. Amy had been counting, obsessively cataloging every life preserved, every suffering prevented. The numbers felt pathetically small against the weight of all she'd failed to stop.

"Enough," she snarled, driving Enigma through its chest. The blade sang as it pierced demonic flesh—a harmony of light and darkness that made reality ripple around them.

The demon didn't die immediately. Instead, it laughed, hellfire consuming the light side of her blade while shadow devoured the flames in an endless cycle of mutual annihilation.

"Each one you save is noted above," it whispered as its form began to unravel. "They keep careful records of your interventions. Ask yourself—why do they let you continue if your actions truly matter?"

Amy twisted the blade, feeling the creature's essence bleed into the void. "Because they're testing me. Because I'll earn my way back."

"Such faith," the demon gasped. "Such beautiful, pathetic faith. Tell me, fallen one—if your banishment was punishment, why were you allowed to keep your sword-arm? Why retain the power to interfere at all?"

The question followed Amy as the demon screamed its way into dissolution, its death-cry shattering pottery across the fortress and sending Roman horses into panicked flight.

She stood alone in the sudden silence, wings drooping with exhaustion. Around her, the siege continued exactly as before. The demon's death had changed nothing—the Romans kept building, the rebels kept preparing to die.

Above, storm clouds gathered with suspicious speed, lightning flickering in patterns that reminded her of angelic script. For a moment, she thought she felt eyes upon her— vast, patient, evaluating.

They're watching, she told herself. *They see what I'm doing. This matters.*

The rebels chose mass suicide anyway, just as history recorded they would. Amy saved seventeen children by hiding them in a grain cellar, covering their mouths as their parents' screams echoed through the fortress. She kept them hidden for three days, feeding them scraps and water, until Roman patrols moved on.

But their parents' screams—those followed her for decades, mixing with all the others in the chorus of suffering that played behind her eyes whenever she tried to sleep.

That night, she stood at the edge of the Dead Sea and tried to pray. The words felt clumsy in her mouth, foreign as a half-remembered language. In the silence that followed, she heard only wind across salt flats and the distant sound of carrion birds.

No answer came. None would come for the next two millennia.

1347 CE - THE BLACK DEATH, LONDON

The pestilence demon danced through the streets of London like a plague-wind given form, invisible to human eyes but clear as daylight to Amy. It had no fixed shape—sometimes a writhing mass of flies and infection, sometimes a beautiful woman with flowers in her hair that bloomed and rotted in seconds, sometimes just the suggestion of movement in corners of vision, the feeling of being watched by something hungry.

She'd tracked it across half of Europe, following the trail of boils and bloody vomit it left in its wake. Entire cities withered at its touch—not just from disease, but from the despair that preceded death. It fed on both the dying and those who watched them die, growing fat on grief and terror.

The demon led her through narrow streets choked with bodies, past houses marked with red crosses, through the smoke of burn-pits where the dead were reduced to ash and scattered prayers. London had become a charnel house, and still the demon danced.

"Why do you hunt me?" it asked as she finally cornered it in a plague house, surrounded by the corpses of an entire family—father, mother, three children, their faces black with corruption. "I serve the same Design you once revered. I am instrument, not composer."

Amy had learned to hide her wings among humans, folding them into the space between dimensions where they existed but could not be seen. Now she let them manifest fully, white and black feathers rustling in the fetid air.

"Because you enjoy it too much," she said, raising Enigma. The blade's light side glowed with silver fire, while its dark edge seemed to devour illumination.

"Enjoyment?" The demon's laugh was the sound of children coughing up blood. "You mistake function for pleasure. I am necessity given form, the culler of the weak, the pruner of the overgrown tree. Without me, humanity would choke on its own numbers."

Amy struck without answering, but Enigma passed through empty air. The demon had dissolved into constituent elements—bacteria and virus, spore and toxin, the microscopic machinery of death itself.

"You think killing me will stop this?" Its voice came from everywhere and nowhere, spoken by the very air she breathed. "I am symptom, not cause. The Great Plan requires suffering, Namaah. Struggle. Loss. How else do they grow? How else do they learn?"

Amy spun, seeking something solid to strike. "They're dying! Children, elders, innocents—"

"And in their dying, they achieve meaning. Their deaths serve purposes beyond their comprehension. The survivors will rebuild stronger. The plague will teach them cleanliness, medicine, the value of knowledge over superstition." The demon's essence began to coalesce again, forming a figure that looked disturbingly like Amy herself. "You fell for the chance to save one child. I serve by taking millions. Which of us better serves the Design?"

The question was a knife between her ribs. Amy had spent centuries cataloging her small victories, but what if the demon was right? What if suffering served a purpose she was too limited to understand?

She shook her head violently, dispelling the doubt. "No. There has to be another way."

"Such touching idealism." The demon's copied face smiled with Amy's own mouth. "Tell me—how many plagues have you ended? How many wars prevented? How many children saved who went on to die anyway, just later, perhaps more painfully?"

Amy lunged, Enigma carving through the demon's stolen form. This time the blade found purchase, spiritual steel meeting spiritual flesh in a burst of light and shadow.

The demon screamed—a sound like every last breath ever drawn, harmonized and amplified until it shattered the windows of surrounding houses. As it died, its form dispersed into countless motes of light that swirled around Amy like falling snow.

"You're fighting the wrong war," it whispered with its last breath. "The enemy is not below. It never was."

Amy stood alone among the corpses, breathing hard. The family's bodies had begun to rot in the unnatural heat the demon's presence had generated. A young girl—perhaps eight years old—lay curled against her mother, thumb in her mouth, face peaceful despite the black corruption spreading across her skin.

She looked like the amber-eyed girl from Carthage. They all did, eventually.

The plague continued to rage for three more years. Thirty million died across Europe, their deaths serving whatever cosmic purpose the demon had hinted at. Amy tried to track the greater pattern, but the mathematics of causation were beyond her. She saw only individual tragedies, specific losses that accumulated like lead weights in her chest.

She spent three years afterward in a monastery outside Florence, praying for forgiveness, for understanding, for some sign that her efforts mattered. The monks thought her mad—a woman who spoke of angels and demons, who bore scars that never healed properly, who sometimes wept for no reason they could discern.

Brother Francesco, the monastery's healer, tried to help her process what he assumed was battlefield trauma. "War leaves marks on the soul," he told her one evening as they tended the abbey's garden. "Sometimes the healing takes longer than the hurting."

"What if the hurting never stops?" Amy asked, watching him carefully tend a rose bush that would bloom and die while she remained unchanged. "What if it's the point?"

"Then we endure," he said simply. "And we tend our gardens anyway."

God didn't answer her prayers. Heaven remained silent, vast and empty as the space between stars. But Brother

Francesco's words followed her when she finally left, carrying a lesson she wouldn't understand until centuries later.

1666 CE - GREAT FIRE OF LONDON

The fire-spirit emerged from the flames like a newborn star, beautiful in the way that supernovas are beautiful—magnificent and terrible and utterly destructive. Amy met it on the roof of St. Paul's Cathedral as the blaze consumed the city below, painting the night sky in shades of orange and gold.

She had learned to dress like a human by then, adopting the fashion of whatever era she found herself in. Currently that meant a man's doublet and breeches—easier to fight in than skirts, and the gender ambiguity helped her avoid certain complications. Her appearance had begun to change subtly over the centuries: her skin had lost some of its divine luminescence, her hair had darkened from starlight-silver to ordinary gold, and her eyes had taken on a harder edge.

But when she let her wings manifest, she was still unmistakably what she had been. The fire-spirit recognized her immediately.

"Namaah, the Watcher who Fell," it said, its voice crackling like burning timber. "Four centuries of hunting us. Do you ever wonder why nothing changes? Why each victory feels more hollow than the last?"

Amy circled it warily, Enigma held ready. Fire-spirits were old—older than demons, older than the Fall itself. They remembered the time before time, when the first fires burned in the heart of creation.

"Because I haven't killed enough of you yet," she replied, but the words tasted like ash in her mouth. She'd been having the same conversation for centuries—different faces, different voices, same existential questions that burrowed into her mind like worms.

The spirit laughed, scattering sparks that fell like dying stars onto the burning city below. Each ember landed with mathematical precision, spreading the flames in patterns that resembled angelic script.

"Or because you're fighting the wrong enemy. Tell me, fallen one—when you watch these mortals burn, do you see tragedy or necessity? Ending or beginning?"

Amy thought of the families fleeing through smoke-choked streets, the children clutching crude dolls, the elders who couldn't run fast enough. "I see people dying."

"You see transformation," the spirit corrected. "Medieval London dies tonight. Modern London will rise from these ashes—cleaner, more organized, more capable of supporting the millions who will call it home. The fire cleanses. The fire prepares."

The spirit attacked with whips of flame that seared the air itself. Amy dodged, her black wing smoldering from the heat, and came up with Enigma leading. The blade's cold side absorbed the fire while its light half reflected the spirit's essence back at itself—a feedback loop that made reality scream in harmonics only immortals could hear.

"You want to know why Heaven stays silent?" the spirit gasped as Amy's blade carved through its core. "Because this is all part of the—"

Amy silenced it with a thrust through what passed for its heart, but its words lingered like smoke. The fire-spirit collapsed into embers that swirled around her in patterns that reminded her of stellar formations, of the cosmic dance she'd once been privileged to witness from Elysium.

The Great Fire burned for four more days, destroying most of medieval London exactly as history recorded it would. Amy saved hundreds by guiding them to the Thames, using her remaining divine authority to calm panicked horses and organize bucket brigades. But she couldn't shake the feeling that something else—something vast and patient—directed the flames according to plans laid down before the first human drew breath.

That night, she stood in the ruins of St. Paul's and tried to make sense of what the fire-spirit had said. Around her, the city smoldered, but already she could see surveyors moving through the wreckage, making plans for reconstruction. Christopher Wren himself passed within ten feet of her, sketching architectural dreams in a notebook by lamplight.

From destruction, creation. From ending, beginning. The same pattern she'd seen play out across centuries, dressed in different clothes but fundamentally unchanged.

"What if they're right?" she whispered to the empty air. "What if suffering serves a purpose?"

No answer came, but in the silence, she began to notice other things. The way the fire had jumped certain buildings but consumed others. The mathematical precision of its spread. The almost artistic arrangement of destruction and survival.

For the first time since her Fall, Amy began to suspect that the Great Design might be more complex—and more terrible—than she'd imagined.

1815 CE - BATTLE OF WATERLOO

The war-wraith fed on the dying, growing stronger with each soldier's last breath. Amy found it in the aftermath of Napoleon's final defeat, bloated on suffering, its form shifting between the uniforms of all nations—French blue, British red, Prussian black—as if it could not decide which side it preferred to represent.

The battlefield stretched for miles, carpeted with bodies and broken dreams. Fifty thousand men had died in a single day, their blood soaking Belgian soil that would grow unusually fertile in the years to come. The irony wasn't lost on Amy—even in death, they served the greater patterns.

"You're too late again," the wraith taunted, sifting through corpses for the choicest souls. "All that noble sacrifice, all that honor—gone to feed something greater than your small mind can grasp."

Amy had grown tired of their philosophical debates over the centuries. The questions they raised gnawed at her, each one adding weight to the growing certainty that her rebellion had been anticipated, perhaps even orchestrated. She struck without warning, Enigma carving through the wraith's stolen flesh.

But even as she fought, her mind wandered. She'd read the histories, studied the patterns. Napoleon's rise had centralized European power structures, forcing the old feudal systems to modernize or perish. His wars had accelerated technological development, spread literacy and legal codes, shattered class barriers that had persisted for millennia.

And his exile would bring peace—but not empty peace. Productive peace, the kind that allowed for the Industrial Revolution, for the expansion of human knowledge and capability.

"You never learn," the wraith wheezed as Enigma pierced its core. "We are tools, just as you were. The Hand that wields us cares nothing for our survival, only for the work we accomplish."

Amy twisted the blade, feeling the creature's essence hemorrhage into dimensions beyond counting. "What work? What fucking work could justify this?"

"Evolution," the wraith gasped. "Growth through adversity. Strength through struggle. How else do children become adults? How else do species transcend their limitations?"

The question hung in the air as the wraith dissolved, its death-scream harmonizing with the moans of wounded soldiers scattered across the battlefield. Amy stood among the corpses, rain washing the blood from her blade, and tried not to think about the arithmetic of progress.

How many had to die for humanity to advance? Was there a cosmic equation that balanced individual suffering against species-wide growth? And if so—if the wars and plagues and disasters truly served a purpose—what did that make her?

A malfunction in the system? A rogue variable? Or just another tool, convinced of her own rebellion while serving the very design she thought she opposed?

That night, she sat in a tavern in Brussels, drinking wine that tasted like copper and listening to survivors tell their stories. A young British officer, his arm in a sling, spoke of watching his best friend die charging the French squares.

"Worth it, though," he said, raising his glass with his good hand. "Bonaparte's finished. World's going to be different now. Better."

Amy wanted to ask him about the price. Wanted to know if his friend's death felt worth it when he woke screaming from nightmares, when he saw that face in every crowd. But she'd learned that humans needed their meaning-making, needed to believe that sacrifice served something greater than chance.

Maybe they were right. Maybe that was the point—not the objective truth of cosmic purpose, but the subjective necessity of believing in it.

The thought terrified her more than any demon she'd ever faced.

She started drinking more seriously that century, seeking oblivion in bottles when prayers failed to bring answers. The alcohol never worked the way she wanted—her divine constitution processed toxins too efficiently—but the ritual of consumption became its own comfort. Pour. Drink. Pour again. Repeat until the questions quieted, if only temporarily.

1945 CE - HIROSHIMA

The atomic demon materialized in the mushroom cloud itself, its form a writhing mass of split atoms and gamma radiation, beautiful in the way that things too dangerous to comprehend often are. Amy met it three miles above the destroyed city, her wings struggling against superheated air that should have incinerated any lesser being.

She had changed significantly by then. The golden hair of her early centuries had darkened to brown, then black. Her skin had lost its porcelain perfection, marked now by scars that never quite healed—souvenirs from battles that had cost more than she'd anticipated. Her eyes, once the serene green of forest pools, now held depths that spoke of things seen and survived and regretted.

She dressed differently too, adopting the practical clothing of whatever era she found herself in. Currently that meant a pilot's leather jacket liberated from a crashed P-51, worn over a man's shirt and trousers. Gender roles mattered less when you'd outlived the civilizations that created them.

"Progress," the demon said, its voice like Geiger counters clicking out digital prophecies. "Beautiful, isn't it? Your species has learned to harness the fundamental forces of reality. Soon they'll split the atom itself, unlock the power that lights the stars."

Amy had seen the flash from Osaka, felt the dimensional tremor as matter converted to energy according to Einstein's elegant equation. She'd flown here knowing she was too late to prevent anything, driven by habit more than hope.

Below them, the city burned with unnatural fire. Shadows of the vaporized were permanently etched into concrete—human silhouettes frozen at the moment of annihilation, the only monuments they would ever have.

"You didn't cause this," she realized, watching the mushroom cloud spread like a malignant flower. "They did it themselves."

"We don't need to anymore," the demon agreed, and for the first time in centuries of hunting, Amy heard something like satisfaction in a creature's voice. "They've graduated. They can destroy themselves now without our guidance. Efficiently. Completely. With mathematics we taught them eons ago, disguised as natural law."

The implications crashed over her like a tidal wave. If humanity could annihilate itself, what was the point of demons? What was the point of her eternal vigil against forces that were no longer necessary?

"Nuclear fire is clean," the demon continued, seeming to enjoy her distress. "No messy plagues, no prolonged wars of attrition. Just bright light and sudden silence. They'll build weapons that can crack continents, poison the very air with radiation. Soon they won't need Hell's influence to achieve Hell's purposes."

Amy killed it anyway, but there was no satisfaction in the act. Enigma carved through radioactive flesh while her mind struggled with the arithmetic of obsolescence. If humanity had learned to destroy itself, what did that make her —protector or irrelevance?

Below, rescue workers moved through the ruins like ghosts, their radiation badges clicking steadily as they searched for survivors among the dead. Some would die within days from exposure. Others would carry cancers for decades, their children born twisted by energies their ancestors had never imagined.

But humanity would survive. It always did. And from this ashes, they would build new technologies, new philosophies, new ways of understanding their place in the cosmic order.

Amy spent the next six months in a sake house in Kyoto, drinking herself into something approaching unconsciousness while trying to make sense of what she'd witnessed. The other patrons—mostly veterans trying to forget their own horrors—left her alone. They recognized the look of someone wrestling with questions that had no comfortable answers.

"The war is over," one old soldier told her one night, his words slurred by alcohol and exhaustion. "Finally fucking over. Maybe now we can build something better."

Amy almost smiled. Humans and their faith in redemption through suffering, their belief that each catastrophe brought them closer to wisdom. They'd just unleashed the fire of creation itself and were already talking about building something better from the ashes.

Maybe that was the point. Maybe the capacity for hope in the face of overwhelming evidence was what made them worth saving—or destroying.

She couldn't decide which anymore.

1969 CE - VIETNAM

The jungle demon moved like napalm given form, leaving a trail of withered vegetation and poisoned earth in its wake. Amy tracked it through the Mekong Delta, past villages that were no longer there, through forests stripped bare by chemical defoliants that would poison the soil for generations.

She'd grown careless over the decades, her movements less precise, her planning more haphazard. What was the point of tactics when strategy itself might be meaningless? Her appearance reflected this decline—hair cropped short in a practical cut, clothes functional rather than fashionable, eyes that had seen too much and believed too little.

The demon turned to face her in a clearing littered with unexploded ordnance, its form shifting between burning gasoline and rotting vegetation. Around them, the jungle steamed with unnatural heat, and she could taste Agent

Orange in the air—a bitter chemical tang that spoke of humanity's growing ability to poison its own environment.

"You look tired, Namaah." The demon's voice was the sound of trees dying, of soil turning to acid, of birth defects that wouldn't manifest for another generation. "When did you last sleep? Really sleep, not that restless half-death you call rest."

Amy couldn't remember. Centuries, perhaps. Sleep required a kind of peace she'd forgotten how to achieve. "Shut up and die."

"Why? So you can pretend this war will end? So you can believe that killing me will save these mortals from themselves?" The demon gestured at the devastated landscape with appendages that shifted between vine and flame. "Look around. We're not needed here anymore."

The truth of it hit her like shrapnel. The soldiers she'd watched—American boys barely out of high school, Vietnamese farmers defending their ancestral homes—they didn't need demonic influence to commit atrocities. Fear and ideology accomplished more than any supernatural corruption.

She'd seen it in their eyes: the hollow stare of young men who'd learned to kill children, the desperate rage of people watching their homeland burn. Human emotions, human choices, human consequences.

"They're doing this themselves," she whispered.

"Finally." The demon's laugh was the sound of napalm cooking flesh from bone. "Two thousand years, and you're beginning to understand. We are teachers, Namaah. We show them what they're capable of. But the capacity—the beautiful, terrible capacity for evil—that's all theirs."

Amy's blade swept through the demon's toxic form in practiced arcs, dispersing it into constituent atoms—sulfur and spite, hunger and hate—while her mind struggled with the implications of cosmic irrelevance.

As the demon died, it laughed. "Two millennia, and you still don't see it. The Fall was never your punishment—it was your assignment. You're not fighting us. You're auditing us. Making sure the lessons stick."

Amy left Vietnam the next day, but the demon's words followed her across oceans and decades. In nightclubs and bars, in anonymous hotel rooms and empty apartments, she tried to drown the implications in whatever oblivion she could find.

She started fucking strangers that decade—not for pleasure, but for the brief amnesia of physical sensation. Anonymous bodies in anonymous beds, skin against skin, heartbeat against heartbeat, the pretense of intimacy without the burden of actual connection.

It never worked. The questions always returned, whispered in the dark by lovers whose names she didn't bother to learn.

1991 CE - THE GULF WAR

She found the oil-demon in the burning fields of Kuwait, feeding on petroleum fires that would burn for months. The air was thick with toxic smoke, and the landscape looked like a vision of hell—hundreds of oil wells torched by retreating Iraqi forces, their flames reaching toward a sky turned black with burning crude.

"Still hunting," the demon observed without surprise, its form shifting between liquid petroleum and burning gasoline. "Still hoping they'll take you back. Tell me, Namaah

—how many of us have you killed? A thousand? Ten thousand? And has it changed anything?"

Amy had stopped counting centuries ago. The arithmetic of assassination had lost meaning when the greater patterns remained unchanged. She simply attacked, Enigma trailing light and shadow through flames that would have incinerated a human instantly.

The demon died without revelation or prophecy, just another point of evil snuffed out while the fires burned on. She watched the flames for hours afterward, trying to see the pattern the fire-spirit had hinted at centuries earlier.

Kuwait would rebuild. The oil would flow again. Wealth would concentrate in ways that made future conflicts inevitable, while the environmental damage would accelerate changes already set in motion by industrial civilization.

Progress through catastrophe. Growth through destruction. The same equations playing out on scales too vast for individual comprehension.

She flew to Las Vegas that year and spent three months in casinos, playing games where the house always won while drinking whiskey that cost more than most people's cars. The meaninglessness of it appealed to her—money circulating through systems designed to extract value from hope, human nature monetized and packaged for consumption.

In the mirror behind the bar at Caesar's Palace, she saw what she'd become: a woman who looked thirty-five but carried herself like someone infinitely older, black hair cut in aggressive angles, green eyes that reflected neon light like broken glass. Her leather jacket bore patches from bands that had burned out and died, and her arms were starting to accumulate the tattoos that would eventually map her journey through human civilization.

She looked lethal. She looked lost. She looked like someone who'd given up on salvation but hadn't figured out what to replace it with.

The assessment felt accurate.

2001 CE - NEW YORK CITY

The terror-demon was already gone by the time she reached Ground Zero. She could smell its essence in the smoke and ash—sulfur and burnt offerings, the specific reek of fear transformed into hatred—but the creature itself had vanished, leaving only human evil behind.

Amy stood in the wreckage, ash settling on her shoulders like gray snow, watching firefighters pull bodies from the rubble. Her enhanced hearing picked up every sob, every prayer, every curse directed at an absent God. The sounds layered into a symphony of grief that reminded her of Carthage, of Masada, of every other time she'd arrived too late to matter.

A child's voice cut through the chaos: "Where are the angels? Why didn't they come?"

The question hit her like a physical blow. She wanted to answer, wanted to reveal herself and offer comfort, but what could she say? That the angels were busy with cosmic designs too complex for mortal understanding? That individual suffering was just rounding error in equations that spanned millennia?

That she'd stopped believing in rescue sometime in the last century?

Instead, she turned away and found a bar in Times Square, where she drank herself into something approaching unconsciousness while news channels played the footage on endless loop. The bartender—a kid from Queens with worried eyes and a crucifix around his neck—kept refilling her glass without comment.

"You okay, lady?" he asked near closing time.

Amy studied her reflection in the mirror behind the bar —the same face she'd worn since the Fall, unmarked by time but etched with something deeper than age. Her appearance had darkened over the centuries, both literally and figuratively. The starlight hair of her angelic days had become midnight black, often streaked with colors that changed with her mood and the decade's fashion. Her eyes had lost their forest-pool serenity, now holding depths that spoke of things seen and survived and regretted.

Scars decorated her arms—some from demon claws, others from human weapons, a few from her own hands during particularly dark periods. Tattoos had begun to accumulate: Norse runes interwoven with circuit patterns, Sumerian cuneiform spiraling around Celtic knots, equations from quantum physics dancing with alchemical symbols. Each mark told a story of a time she'd tried to understand, a culture she'd tried to save, a philosophy she'd hoped might contain answers.

"No," she said finally. "I don't think I've been okay for a very long time."

She started therapy the next week. Dr. Priya Servaas specialized in PTSD and survivor's guilt, treating veterans who'd seen too much and civilians who'd survived disasters that should have killed them. Amy told her she was a war correspondent who'd covered conflicts across the globe—not entirely untrue, if you considered the cosmic war between order and chaos.

"Survivor's guilt is common," Dr. Servaas explained during their third session, her office filled with the kind of careful neutrality that spoke of professional compassion. "You feel responsible for things beyond your control. The randomness of who lives and who dies can be... overwhelming."

Amy almost laughed. If only she understood the scope of it all. The randomness wasn't random at all—it was orchestrated, planned, designed by intelligences that viewed human suffering as raw material for some greater work of art.

"What if it's not random?" Amy asked, staring out the window at Manhattan's rebuilt skyline. "What if there's a pattern to it all, but the pattern is so vast that individual lives don't matter?"

Dr. Servaas leaned forward, recognizing the particular flavor of existential despair that came with prolonged trauma exposure. "That's a common response to overwhelming loss. The mind seeks patterns, tries to make sense of senselessness. But sometimes things just... happen. Random tragedy, random mercy."

"And if they don't? If every death serves a purpose, every catastrophe advances some cosmic agenda?" Amy's laugh was bitter as burnt coffee. "What does that make the survivors? What does that make the people trying to help?"

"Human," Dr. Servaas said simply. "It makes us human. The fact that you care, that you feel responsible—that's not pathology. That's conscience."

Amy wanted to tell her about the amber-eyed girl in Carthage, about two thousand years of watching humans die for purposes beyond their comprehension. Instead, she talked about imaginary wars, fictional casualties, synthetic trauma that felt real because it was built on a foundation of genuine horror.

The sessions helped, in their way. Not because Dr. Servaas could solve the cosmic riddle of divine purpose, but because she offered something Amy had forgotten existed: the possibility that caring might be valuable in itself, regardless of outcome.

2008 CE - FINANCIAL CRASH

The greed-demon had taken up residence in a Wall Street high-rise, its influence spreading through the global financial system like a virus written in ones and zeros. Amy found it in the trading floor after hours, surrounded by monitors displaying the collapse of economies in real-time.

She'd changed her appearance again, adopting the punk aesthetic that had appealed to her since the 1970s. Black leather jacket over a Sex Pistols t-shirt, jeans torn at the knees, boots that had walked through the ruins of a dozen civilizations. Her hair was shorter now, shaved on one side in a style that would have scandalized her angelic contemporaries, streaked with purple that caught the monitor-light like oil on water.

"Too big to fail," the demon mused, watching stock prices plummet in real-time cascades of red numbers. "Isn't that what they say? Some systems are too important to let them die naturally."

Amy had learned to recognize the patterns by now—boom and bust, crisis and recovery, the Great Design's heartbeat steady as clockwork. The demon wasn't causing the collapse; it was just riding the wave, amplifying natural human greed until it reached critical mass.

"You're not even necessary anymore," she told the demon as she materialized Enigma. The sword felt heavier these days, or maybe she was just tired of carrying it. "They'd have done this without you."

"I know," the demon replied, and for the first time in centuries of hunting, Amy heard something like sadness in its voice. "We've become obsolete. Your species has learned to create their own suffering with remarkable efficiency. Derivative markets, credit default swaps, algorithmic trading —beautiful innovations that serve our purposes better than any direct intervention."

The admission hit her like a physical blow. If the demons were becoming unnecessary, what did that make her crusade? What was the point of hunting creatures that were already extinct, functionally speaking?

Amy killed it anyway, more from habit than conviction. Enigma carved through digital flesh that felt more like mathematics than biology, dispersing the demon into constituent algorithms that scattered across fiber optic networks like malignant code.

Outside, protests raged as millions lost their homes and savings. The patterns would continue—recession, recovery, another bubble, another crash. Human greed and fear driving cycles that no individual could control, serving purposes that no individual could comprehend.

She stopped going to therapy that year. Dr. Servaas' well-meaning platitudes felt like insults when viewed against the scope of cosmic indifference. What was the point of processing trauma when the trauma was infinite, recursive, designed to perpetuate itself across centuries?

Instead, she started frequenting underground clubs in places like Berlin and Bangkok, losing herself in electronic music that felt like the soundtrack to civilization's decay. She fucked DJs and drug dealers and anyone else who promised temporary oblivion, seeking in flesh what she couldn't find in purpose.

The sex was getting rougher, more desperate. She needed partners who could match her supernatural stamina, who wouldn't break under the weight of her accumulated despair. Sometimes she left marks—scratches that healed too slowly, bruises that lasted too long. The guilt afterward was almost as satisfying as the initial release.

Pain, at least, felt real. Pain, at least, couldn't be part of some greater design, because what cosmic intelligence would waste time orchestrating her personal degradation?

The thought was almost comforting.

2020 CE - THE PANDEMIC

The plague-demon was different from its medieval ancestor—smaller, more efficient, adapted to a connected world where viruses could cross continents in hours rather than years. Amy cornered it in a hospital ICU in Milan, surrounded by ventilators and the constant electronic hymn of machines keeping the dying alive a little longer.

"Remember the Black Death?" the demon asked conversationally as she approached, its form shifting between virus particles and human grief. "You killed my predecessor, but the plague continued. Learned anything from that experience?"

Amy had indeed learned. She'd learned that killing demons was meaningless theater, that her exile served someone else's purpose, that Heaven's silence wasn't testing her faith but confirming her irrelevance. The knowledge felt like acid in her veins, corroding whatever remained of her original convictions.

"I learned that it doesn't fucking matter," she said, manifesting Enigma without enthusiasm. The blade felt like an extension of her exhaustion—half-light dimmed by centuries of doubt, half-shadow deepened by accumulated despair.

"Then why continue?" The demon seemed genuinely curious. "Why hunt us if you know it changes nothing? Why maintain the pretense of opposition when you've realized the truth?"

Amy considered the question seriously. Why did she continue? Habit, maybe. Or spite—cosmic middle finger directed at intelligences that had manipulated her rebellion for their own purposes. Or maybe just because stopping would mean admitting that two millennia of effort had been completely meaningless.

"Because fuck you, that's why," she said, and attacked.

The demon died easily—too easily, as if it welcomed destruction. As its essence dispersed into component pathogens, it whispered one last question: "What if mercy is the real test? What if learning when not to fight is the lesson you were meant to learn?"

Amy stood alone in the ICU, surrounded by the machinery of human defiance against natural law. Outside, the world was learning to live with plague again—masks and social distancing, quarantine and loss, the eternal cycle of adaptation and survival.

Millions would die, but humanity would endure. It always did. And from this crisis, they would build new systems, new technologies, new ways of understanding their place in the cosmic order.

The same pattern, playing out on scales too vast for individual comprehension. The same equations, dressed in new variables but fundamentally unchanged.

Amy retracted Enigma and walked out of the hospital, her footsteps echoing in empty corridors. She'd given up active hunting by then, but the demons still found her occasionally—force of habit, cosmic momentum, the simple fact that some patterns were too entrenched to change quickly.

She dealt with them when they appeared, but without enthusiasm, without hope, without the fire that had once driven her rebellion. Just mechanical destruction, performed with the same enthusiasm she might bring to taking out the trash.

PRESENT DAY - NEON CITY

The bass from Devil's Advocate thumped through the soles of Amy's boots as she nursed her eighth whiskey of the night. The numbers had stopped mattering hours ago, when sobriety became just another form of suffering she couldn't afford.

The dive bar's bathroom mirror reflected what she'd become: high cheekbones still unmarked by time, eyes too green to be natural but drained of their original serenity, black hair streaked with electric blue that shifted in the neon light. Her leather jacket bore patches from dead bands—The Clash,

Dead Kennedys, Nine Inch Nails—artists who'd burned out trying to make sense of systems designed to break them.

Her arms bore the accumulated artwork of two millennia. Each tattoo marked a different era, a different attempt to understand the incomprehensible.

She looked feral. She looked broken. She looked like someone who'd traded hope for violence and found the exchange wanting.

"Another?" Malik, the bartender, slid a fresh glass her way without being asked. He'd learned to read her moods over the past year—tonight was one of the bad ones.

Amy nodded, flicking cigarette ash into an empty shot glass. She'd started smoking in the 1950s, drawn to the slow-motion self-destruction of it. Divine metabolism meant the cancer couldn't touch her, but the ritual of consumption had become its own comfort.

The television above the bar flashed breaking news: unexplained atmospheric disturbances, scientists baffled, religious leaders calling for prayer. Amy recognized the signs—dimensional barriers wearing thin, reality developing stress fractures where different realms pressed against each other.

She'd felt it for months: the subtle wrongness in the air, shadows falling at impossible angles, the frequency with which humans reported seeing things that shouldn't exist. Something was coming. Something that would make her cosmic irrelevance relevant again.

The lights flickered as reality thinned. The temperature plummeted until breath fogged in the air, and the smell of sulfur began to overpower the dive bar's normal cocktail of stale beer and human desperation.

"Fuck," Amy muttered, downing her drink and setting the glass down hard enough to crack it. "Can't even drink myself into oblivion in peace."

The first manifestation rippled through the floor, black ichor seeping between tiles before coalescing into humanoid shape. Seven feet tall, obsidian skin cracked with veins of magma, eyes like dying stars. Bahram, Duke of Hell, former Guardian of Solar Flares before his own Fall.

"Namaah," he growled, voice like grinding tectonic plates. "Two millennia of hunting us. Did you think we'd forgotten?"

Before she could answer, the second demon materialized through the television, static forming into a feminine figure of blue-white electricity. Samyaza, former Weather Dominion, now a creature of the Digital Age, her essence distributed across networks and feeds.

The third arrived more subtly: a handsome man in an immaculate suit simply walked through the front door. Mammon, demon of Wealth, who'd adapted to the modern world by becoming indistinguishable from it.

"Time to close up," Amy told Malik, not taking her eyes off the demons. "Get everyone out. Now."

To his credit, Malik didn't argue. Humans had evolved instincts for recognizing predators, and those instincts extended to supernatural threats. As he started ushering patrons toward the exit, Amy stood and cracked her neck, feeling vertebrae pop like gunshots.

"Three against one?" she drawled, pulling her cigarette pack from her pocket and tapping one out. "Didn't realize I rated such attention."

"You've been busy," Samyaza said, her voice crackling with electrical discharge that made the bar's lights strobe. "A thousand of our kind, dead by your hand. Time for payment."

Amy lit her cigarette with a flick of her finger, flame dancing on her fingertip. "Get in line. I've got a tab running with half the circles of Hell."

Bahram snarled, and the air around him shimmered with heat that had nothing to do with the broken HVAC. "Prideful cunt. You're not a Seraph anymore. You're nothing—a cosmic reject too holy for Hell, too tainted for Heaven."

"And yet here you are," Amy said, exhaling smoke that formed impossible spirals. "Three Dukes sent to collect nothing. Makes a girl feel special."

She let her wings explode from her back.

The transformation was violent and magnificent. Her tank top shredded as wings erupted from her shoulder blades —one pristine white, the other absolute black, each feather perfect in its imperfection. Power surged through her like lightning, diminished from her Seraphic days but still enough to level the building.

Enigma materialized in her hand, half divine light, half fallen shadow, the blade singing with harmonics that made reality scream.

"Let's dance," Amy snarled.

Bahram charged first, his arms elongating into serrated blades of living magma. Amy ducked the first swing, feeling heat sear her cheek, then pivoted with supernatural grace. Enigma carved through his shoulder, separating the limb at the joint. The severed arm dissolved into sulfurous smoke, but the wound was already regenerating.

"You've grown weak," he roared, the stump reforming into something that was part sword, part flame. "Centuries of whiskey and self-pity have dulled your edges."

"Maybe," Amy acknowledged, spitting blood. "But I've learned a few tricks."

Samyaza struck like a bolt of living lightning, electricity coursing through Amy's nervous system. Pain erupted through her body as muscles spasmed in rhythms that matched the city's power grid. She staggered but didn't fall—divine constitution processing the assault like a particularly aggressive hangover.

Amy's response was to stamp her boot hard against the ground. The impact released a shockwave that activated every sprinkler in the building. Water rained down in patterns that reminded her of tears.

Samyaza shrieked as the water disrupted her electrical form, forcing her to solidify. The moment she became tangible, Amy struck with Enigma leading. The blade sliced through electrical flesh like cutting fog, trailing light and shadow that made the air itself scream.

Samyaza fragmented, her essence scattering into sparks that fizzled out in the falling water like dying stars.

One down.

Amy spun to face Bahram, who met her with a roar that shattered windows three blocks away. His reformed arm swept toward her in an arc of molten death. She caught the blow on Enigma's blade, divine steel meeting demonic fire in a burst of light that temporarily blinded every security camera in a six-block radius.

The impact drove her to one knee, her black wing smoldering from the heat. Bahram pressed his advantage, raining down blows that Amy parried desperately, each impact sending shockwaves through the building's foundation.

"Two thousand years," he snarled between strikes, "and you still don't understand. We are evolution, Namaah.

We are humanity's graduation from innocence. You fight the inevitable."

Amy's response was to drive her knee into his solar plexus—or what passed for one in demonic anatomy. As he doubled over, she brought Enigma down in a two-handed strike that split his skull like a melon. Black ichor sprayed across the bar's mirror, and Bahram collapsed into constituent elements—sulfur and spite, hunger and hate.

Two down.

Amy turned to face Mammon, only to find him calmly sitting at the bar, pouring himself a drink from the top shelf like nothing had happened. The liquor bottle—a thousand-dollar whiskey—somehow remained intact despite the carnage around them.

"Impressive," he said, raising his glass in a mock toast. "Though you've destroyed your friend's establishment in the process. How very... human of you."

Amy glanced around. The bar was in ruins—shattered bottles, splintered tables, scorch marks on every surface, water damage that would take months to repair. Even her victories came with costs she couldn't control.

"Send the bill to your boss," she spat.

Mammon laughed, the sound like golden bells. "You misunderstand. I'm not here to fight. I'm here to offer you what you've always wanted."

"Which is?"

"Purpose." He sipped his drink appreciatively. "Redemption, even. The barriers between realms are failing, Namaah. Soon, humans will see the truth of what they are—cosmic accidents in a universe that doesn't care whether they live or die."

Cold dread settled in Amy's stomach. She'd felt the dimensional barriers weakening for months, reality wearing thin at the edges.

"What's your point?"

"When the walls come down, they'll need guidance. Protection." His perfect smile never reached his eyes. "Join us willingly, and you can save some of them. A city, perhaps. Your choice which one."

For a fraction of a second, Amy hesitated. Two millennia of loneliness, of watching humans she cared about wither and die while she remained unchanged, had worn her down like water on stone. The offer of purpose—even corrupt purpose—pulled at something deep in her chest.

Then she thought of Malik and his children. Of Dr. Servaas and her careful compassion. Of billions of souls caught in cosmic crossfire, unaware that their entire existence might be nothing more than raw material for some intelligence's artistic vision.

"Counter-offer," she said, flicking her cigarette at his perfect suit. "Go fuck yourself."

Mammon's smile widened, revealing teeth too sharp for human anatomy. "As expected. You always were predictable in your nobility." He stood, brushing ash from his lapel. "The offer remains open. When you're ready to discuss terms, break this."

He placed a small black crystal on the bar counter, its surface reflecting light that seemed to come from somewhere else entirely.

"And if I shatter it now?"

"Then nothing happens. It's not a trap, Namaah—it's an invitation. When you realize that your rebellion was always part of the plan, when you understand that even your Fall serves the greater design... break it. We'll talk."

Before she could respond, Mammon simply wasn't there anymore—no dramatic exit, just sudden absence, as if he'd been edited out of reality.

Amy stood alone in the ruined bar, wings drooping with exhaustion. Water continued to dribble down from broken sprinklers, mingling with blood from a dozen wounds that would heal too slowly. She retracted her wings with a wince, folding them back into dimensional space.

The black crystal sat on the bar, innocuous yet radiating malevolence like a tumor made of crystallized hatred. Amy stared at it for a long moment, then pocketed it without ceremony.

Outside, sirens wailed in the distance. Amy slipped out the back, vanishing into neon-lit streets where she was just another casualty of whatever disaster the morning news would blame on gas leaks.

Above her, storm clouds gathered with unnatural speed, lightning flashing in patterns too deliberate to be random. Signs and portents, messages in a language only a few beings left on Earth could read.

Amy lit another cigarette, exhaling smoke that mingled with gathering darkness. Two thousand years of exile, and she was no closer to understanding the Great Design or earning her way back to Elysium.

Maybe there was no way back. Maybe redemption was just another lie, another carrot dangled before cosmic donkeys to keep them pulling the cart. Maybe this was all there was—eternal half-existence, fighting battles without hope of victory, watching humans live and die while she remained frozen between Heaven and Hell.

Her reflection in a storefront window showed the accumulated weight of centuries: black hair like spilled ink against skin too pale to be entirely human, scars visible on her knuckles where demonic claws had found their mark. The leather jacket was authentically distressed—not fashion, but evidence of a thousand battles that had solved nothing.

She looked like exactly what she was: a weapon without a war, a guardian without a charge, an angel learning that damnation was just another word for Thursday night.

Amy Namaah, the Fallen Angel, walked deeper into the neon maze of the city. Behind her, the bar smoldered in ruins.

Ahead, storm clouds promised violence and change in equal measure.

She fought not for redemption now, but for spite. Not for hope, but for habit. Not because she believed it mattered, but because believing it didn't matter was a luxury she couldn't afford.

The city lights blurred through tears she refused to acknowledge, and for just a moment, she allowed herself to imagine that somewhere in the vast indifference of creation, someone was keeping score.

Even if they weren't, she'd keep playing the game. Because fuck the alternative, and fuck the cosmic intelligence that had orchestrated her Fall.

If this was Hell, she'd make it as expensive as possible.

The storm welcomed her with open arms and hungry lightning, and Amy walked into it like a woman with nothing left to lose and eternity to spend losing it.

Spirit of Retribution

"The greatest victory is not in defeating darkness, but in teaching light to kindle itself."

The bronze spear pierced her chest with a wet crunch, erupting from between her shoulder blades in a spray of crimson. Justice felt the familiar burn of mortality—iron in her lungs, darkness creeping at the edges of her vision. The Spartan warrior who'd flanked her during the chaos grinned through his bronze mask, twisting the weapon deeper.

"Even the gods bleed," he snarled.

She gripped the spear shaft with both hands, her silver gauntlets slick with blood. Around them, the narrow pass of Thermopylae echoed with the clash of bronze on bronze, the screams of dying men, the thunder of ten thousand Persian boots against stone. King Leonidas and his three hundred were making their stand, but traitors had shown Xerxes the mountain path. The end was inevitable.

Justice had come not to prevent it, but to ensure it served its purpose.

"Not gods," she whispered, her voice barely audible above the din. "Balance."

The Spartan's eyes widened as she snapped the spear shaft like kindling. The broken wood jutted from her chest as she drew her xiphos—not the bastard sword of later ages, but the leaf-shaped blade that belonged to this time, this place. Her blindfold, woven from the same silver-blue cloth that would grace her armor across millennia, never shifted as she moved. She saw everything without sight—the heat patterns of bodies, the vibrations through stone, the subtle currents of intention that preceded every action.

The Spartan stumbled backward, reaching for his shield. Too slow. Her blade found the gap beneath his arm, sliding between ribs to pierce his heart. He fell without another word.

Justice staggered, the bronze spearhead grinding against bone. Persian arrows whistled overhead like deadly rain. Leonidas roared commands to his shrinking circle of warriors, but she could sense the inevitability settling over them like winter fog. They would die here. All of them. But their deaths would echo through history, inspiring resistance when tyranny seemed absolute.

That was why she'd come.

Not to save them, but to die with them.

She pulled the broken spear from her chest with a grunt of pain. Blood flowed freely, pooling in the leather strapping beneath her bronze breastplate. The wound was mortal—would be mortal, for the duration of this form. When the darkness took her, she would return to the space between spaces, formless and watching, until balance demanded her intervention again.

A Persian immortal, his robes pristine despite the carnage, stepped through the press of bodies. His curved sword gleamed with fresh blood. Behind his golden mask, she sensed calculation—he'd identified her as different from the others, more dangerous.

"You fight like no Spartan woman I have seen," he said in accented Greek. His voice carried the authority of one accustomed to being obeyed. "Who are you?"

"Justice," she replied, settling into a fighting stance despite the blood loss. Her legs trembled, but her grip on the xiphos remained steady. "And you are the one who ordered the village burned. Who left children to starve in winter."

The immortal's head tilted slightly. "Many villages burn in war. I do not remember one specifically."

"I do."

She remembered all of them. Every act of cruelty that tipped the scales too far toward chaos. Every innocent death that demanded retribution. The immortal's crimes stretched back years—not just in this campaign, but in others. Babylon. Egypt. Scythia. Always the same pattern: overwhelming force followed by calculated brutality designed to break spirits as much as bodies.

The kind of injustice that drew her like iron filings to a lodestone.

"It does not matter," the immortal said, raising his blade. "You will die with the rest."

"Yes," Justice agreed. "But so will you."

They closed simultaneously. His curved sword swept toward her neck in a perfect arc—the technique of a master who'd killed hundreds. She let it come, accepting the cut across her throat as she drove her xiphos up beneath his ribcage. The blade punched through silk and flesh, finding his heart with surgical precision.

Blood bubbled from her severed windpipe as she spoke her final words: "The mountain remembers."

Darkness claimed her as the immortal's corpse hit the stone.

She woke to different stone—rougher, cut by different hands in a different age. Torchlight flickered against walls carved with crosses and crude fish symbols. The scent of fear and hope intermingled with human waste and straw. A prison, deep underground.

Justice sat up slowly, her hand moving instinctively to her throat. No wound. No blood. The body she wore now was similar—tall, strong, tanned skin and long black hair—but younger. The blindfold had changed too, now rough-woven linen instead of silk.

"You're awake." The voice belonged to a young man, barely past boyhood. He sat chained to the opposite wall, his simple tunic stained with old blood. "I thought you were dead when they threw you in here."

She tested her limbs, feeling the particular weight and balance of this form. Stronger than a normal human, but not overwhelmingly so. The cosmic forces that shaped her interventions had calibrated her strength to what this situation required.

"How long?" she asked.

"Three days. They've taken six of us to the arena already." His voice cracked. "None came back."

Justice looked around the cell with senses beyond sight. Twenty-three prisoners total, mostly young men and women. Christians, she realized, reading the symbols they'd scratched into the walls. The fish. The chi-rho. Rough prayers in Latin and Greek.

Rome. The Colosseum. Nero's persecution, or perhaps one of his successors. The details mattered less than the injustice that had drawn her here—innocents dying for sport, their deaths used to distract the masses from the emperor's failures.

"What is your name?" she asked the young man.

"Marcus. Marcus Justianus." He managed a weak smile. "Ironic, isn't it? My parents named me for justice, and here I am, condemned to die for refusing to offer incense to Caesar's statue."

Justice felt the familiar stirring in her chest—not emotion, exactly, but something deeper. The pull that brought her to moments like this, when the scales tipped too far toward cruelty. She'd died with Leonidas's warriors to inspire future resistance. Here, she would die differently. Not as a warrior, but as a martyr whose death would echo through the years.

"Tell me about your family," she said.

Marcus's face lit up despite their circumstances. "My sister Helena is sixteen. She has the most beautiful voice—sings in our gatherings. My father was a stonecutter before... before they took him. He taught me to read and write, said knowledge was the only thing they couldn't steal from us."

"And your faith?"

"Strong." No hesitation. "Stronger than fear. Christ died for us, and if we must die for Him..." Marcus shrugged, the chains around his wrists clinking softly. "Then we die knowing we'll see Him again."

Justice nodded slowly. She'd witnessed the birth of many faiths across the millennia, seen how they rose and fell, how they inspired and corrupted in equal measure. But in moments like this—when believers faced death rather than compromise their principles—she glimpsed something that transcended her usual calculations of balance and retribution.

Love. Sacrifice. The willingness to die for something greater than oneself.

"The guards are coming," she said, hearing their footsteps long before human ears could detect them. "Six more for the morning games."

Marcus paled but straightened his shoulders. "Then we go together."

The cell door crashed open with a squeal of rusted hinges. Four praetorians in full armor stomped inside, their faces hidden behind bronze masks worked into sneering expressions. The prisoners cowered against the walls—all except Justice, who remained seated calmly in the center of the cell.

"You, you, you." The lead guard pointed with his gladius at three young women. They began to weep, clinging to each other. "And you, boy." Marcus.

"Take me instead," Justice said, rising smoothly to her feet.

The guard turned toward her, his masked face tilting. "What did you say, slave?"

"Take me in place of one of them. I'm stronger. I'll put on a better show."

"Justice, no," Marcus whispered.

She ignored him, keeping her sightless eyes fixed on the guard's position. "Unless you're afraid I might actually win?"

The praetorian laughed—a harsh sound muffled by his mask. "You? A blind woman?" He gestured to his companions. "Take her too. The crowd will enjoy watching a cripple get torn apart."

They chained her wrists with iron—cold, heavy manacles that bit into her skin. The guards led them through twisting corridors carved from living rock, past cells filled with other condemned souls. Some prayed quietly. Others wept. A few raged against their chains with futile desperation.

Justice listened to it all, cataloging the injustices that had led each person here. Political dissidents who'd spoken against the emperor's excesses. Thieves whose only crime was stealing bread for starving families. Christians whose only transgression was refusing to worship gods they didn't believe in.

All condemned to die for the entertainment of crowds who cheered for blood to forget their own misery.

The tunnel ended in blinding sunlight—blinding to the others. Justice felt the heat on her face, heard the roar of fifty thousand voices rising from the tiered seats above. The Colosseum. She'd heard it described but never experienced it herself—the sand of the arena floor, still dark with yesterday's blood; the elaborate awnings that provided shade for the wealthy; the complex system of pulleys and counterweights that would lift exotic beasts from the chambers below.

"Fresh meat!" someone shouted from the stands. Laughter rippled through the crowd like wind through wheat.

The prisoners were herded to the center of the arena, their chains removed one by one. Marcus stayed close to

Justice, his face pale but determined. The three young women huddled together, whispering prayers in voices too low for the crowd to hear.

A horn sounded. Gates creaked open around the arena's perimeter.

Lions emerged first—three of them, gaunt from deliberate starvation, their ribs visible beneath golden fur. They padded into the sunlight with liquid grace, yellow eyes scanning the trapped humans. One paused to sniff the air, catching the scent of fear-sweat and fresh prey.

The crowd's roar intensified.

Justice positioned herself between the beasts and the other prisoners. She had no weapons, no armor—only the strength and speed she'd been granted for this intervention. Enough to make a difference, but not enough to save them all.

That wasn't the point.

The largest lion, a scarred male with a partial mane, fixed its attention on her. It sensed something different—not the helpless terror of the others, but calm readiness. A threat to be eliminated.

It charged.

Justice moved like flowing water, sidestepping the initial rush and bringing her elbow down on the beast's spine as it passed. Bone cracked. The lion roared in pain and fury, spinning to swipe at her with claws like curved daggers. She caught its paw in both hands, feeling the bones shift under her grip.

The crowd fell silent.

Then erupted in wild cheers.

She twisted, using the lion's own momentum to flip it onto its back. Before it could recover, she drove her fist into its throat, crushing its windpipe. The great cat thrashed once and lay still.

The other two lions circled warily now, no longer seeing easy prey. One stalked toward Marcus and the women. Justice intercepted it, grabbing its lower jaw as it lunged and wrenching upward until she felt the vertebrae separate.

The third lion turned and fled back toward the gates, only to find them sealed. It paced the arena's edge, snarling at the walls it couldn't climb.

"Incredible!" The emperor's voice echoed from the imperial box, amplified by the arena's acoustics. Justice couldn't see him, but she sensed his presence—corpulent, cruel, delighting in others' suffering. Domitian, she realized. One of the worst.

"Bring the gladiators!"

More gates opened. Six men in mismatched armor jogged into the arena, weapons glinting in the afternoon sun. Professional killers, scarred veterans who'd survived dozens of such spectacles. They spread out in a loose circle, surrounding the prisoners.

"Kill the others quickly," their leader called out, his voice carrying the authority of long experience. "But the blind woman—make it last. The crowd wants a show."

Justice felt Marcus step up beside her. "I won't run," he said quietly.

"Neither will we," added one of the young women. The other two nodded, their faces streaked with tears but set with determination.

Justice closed her eyes behind her blindfold, extending her awareness. Six gladiators. One lion still loose but keeping its distance. Fifty thousand bloodthirsty spectators. The emperor watching from his box, already imagining the political benefits of such spectacular games.

And at the center of it all, five people ready to die rather than betray their principles.

The gladiators attacked as one.

Justice caught the first man's sword arm, snapping it at the elbow before driving his own blade into his chest. She spun, using his falling body as a shield against the second attacker's spear thrust, then broke the spear shaft and drove the jagged end into the gladiator's eye.

Behind her, she heard Marcus cry out in pain. One of the women screamed.

No time for finesse. Justice let her strength flow freely, moving faster than human reflexes could follow. She tore the third gladiator's helmet off and crushed his skull with her bare hands. The fourth tried to run; she tackled him from behind, breaking his neck with a sharp twist.

The last two hesitated, suddenly aware they faced something far beyond their experience.

"Witch!" one of them shouted. "Sorceress!"

Justice turned toward them, blood dripping from her fingers. "Justice," she corrected.

They came at her together, swords flashing in complex patterns meant to overwhelm a single opponent. She flowed between their blades like smoke, catching one man's wrist and twisting until his sword flew from nerveless fingers. Her other hand found his throat, thumb pressing against his windpipe until his eyes rolled back.

The last gladiator backed away, sword trembling in his grip. "Please," he whispered. "I have children."

Justice paused. She sensed truth in his words—saw the desperation of a man forced to kill or watch his family starve. Another victim of the system that demanded blood for bread.

"Then go to them," she said.

The gladiator stared at her for a long moment, then dropped his sword and ran for the gates. The crowd booed, hurling curses and debris onto the arena floor.

Justice turned to check on the other prisoners. Marcus sat propped against the arena wall, one hand pressed to a deep cut across his ribs. The three women were unharmed but shaken, staring at the carnage around them with wide eyes.

"Are you hurt?" she asked Marcus.

He managed a weak smile. "I'll live. At least for now."

The remaining lion had finally worked up courage to approach the dead gladiators, sniffing cautiously at the fresh blood. Justice watched it for a moment, then walked slowly toward the beast. It looked up at her approach, golden eyes wary but no longer hostile.

She knelt just out of reach, extending one blood-stained hand. The lion sniffed, then moved closer. Its rough tongue rasped against her palm—tasting blood, but also recognizing something deeper. A kinship of sorts. They were both trapped here, both forced to kill for others' entertainment.

"I know," she whispered.

The horn sounded again. Justice looked up toward the imperial box, sensing Domitian's growing frustration. The games weren't going as planned. The crowd wanted blood, but they also wanted spectacle—and watching a blind woman pet a lion wasn't quite what they'd expected.

"Bring the elephants!" the emperor commanded.

The arena floor shuddered. Somewhere beneath their feet, massive gates were grinding open. Justice stood slowly, her hand still resting on the lion's head. She could feel the vibrations through the stone—not just one elephant, but three.

War elephants, probably, armored and trained to crush human bodies beneath their feet.

"What's happening?" Marcus asked, struggling to stand.

"The emperor grows impatient." Justice walked back to the others, the lion padding silently beside her. "He wants a grander finale."

"We're going to die, aren't we?" one of the young women asked.

"Yes," Justice said simply. "But not for nothing."

The first elephant emerged from the tunnel beneath the arena—a massive bull with iron plates bolted to its hide and spears strapped to its tusks. Its eyes rolled white with pain and fury; Justice could sense the wounds where handlers had goaded it to madness. Two more followed, equally enormous, equally enraged.

The crowd roared approval. This was what they'd come to see—helpless humans crushed to pulp beneath tons of maddened flesh.

Justice positioned herself between the elephants and the others, spreading her arms wide. The lion crouched beside her, muscles bunched for a hopeless charge. Marcus and the women gathered close together, voices rising in a hymn that somehow carried over the crowd's bloodlust.

The lead elephant trumpeted rage and charged.

Justice met it head-on.

The impact should have pulped her instantly. Instead, she caught the beast's armored head in her hands, her feet sliding backward through the sand as its momentum carried them both forward. Her shoulders screamed with strain, but she held on, gradually slowing the massive creature until it came to a stop mere feet from the other prisoners.

The elephant pushed against her grip, trying to understand why this tiny human wouldn't be crushed. Justice looked up into its small, pain-mad eyes and saw past the conditioning to the terrified animal beneath.

"I'm sorry," she whispered.

Then she twisted, using leverage instead of strength, and broke the elephant's neck.

The great beast collapsed with a ground-shaking thud. The other two elephants trumpeted in alarm, backing away from this impossible opponent.

The Colosseum had gone completely silent.

Justice stood over the dead elephant, blood streaming from a dozen small wounds where its armor had cut her. She raised her face toward the imperial box, though she couldn't see the emperor behind his silk curtains.

"Is this justice?" she called out, her voice carrying clearly in the sudden quiet. "Children thrown to beasts for refusing to worship your statue? Families torn apart to feed your games?"

Domitian's reply came through a speaking trumpet, his words echoing off the arena walls: "It is Roman law!"

"Then Roman law is corrupt," Justice replied. "And corruption always falls."

She gestured to the remaining elephants, and somehow —through means she didn't fully understand herself—they turned and walked calmly back toward the tunnels. The lion followed, pausing only to look back at her with something like gratitude in its yellow eyes.

The crowd erupted in confused shouting. Some cheered for the spectacle they'd witnessed. Others called for her blood, outraged that a slave would dare lecture the emperor. Most simply didn't know what to make of what they'd seen.

Praetorians poured into the arena from every gate—dozens of them, spears leveled and shields locked. They surrounded Justice and the other prisoners in a bristling circle of bronze and steel.

"Surrender," their captain commanded. "And your death will be quick."

Justice looked at Marcus and the three women. They stood together, no longer afraid. Their hymn had faded, but their voices remained steady as they spoke in unison:

"We are not afraid to die."

"Neither am I," Justice said.

The praetorians closed in from all sides. She could have fought—could have killed them all, probably. But that wasn't why she was here. Her purpose was different this time. Not to inspire through victory, but through sacrifice.

She knelt slowly, placing her hands behind her head.

The spears came down like falling rain.

Darkness. Then awareness.

Justice found herself standing in a place that wasn't quite place—the space between moments, between worlds, where she waited for the next call. Here she had no form, no physical presence, only consciousness and purpose.

But something was different.

Before, the transitions had been immediate. Death in one world, awakening in another, with only the vaguest sense of time passing between. Now she lingered, watching ripples spread through the fabric of reality like stones thrown into still water.

Marcus survived his wounds and lived another forty years, eventually becoming a bishop who sheltered other persecuted Christians. His sister Helena's voice did indeed prove beautiful—so beautiful that her hymns spread throughout the early church, carrying messages of hope and defiance that no emperor could silence.

The three young women—their names were Lydia, Priscilla, and Claudia—became martyrs whose stories inspired others to resist oppression. Within decades, Christianity would move from the shadows to the throne rooms of power.

Even the gladiator she'd spared—Gaius Maximus—returned to his family and eventually became a vocal opponent of the games, using his fame as a former fighter to argue for reform.

And Domitian himself fell to an assassin's blade less than three years later, his reign of terror ended by those who could no longer stomach his excesses.

Justice watched it all unfold across decades and centuries, seeing how each small act of courage rippled outward in ways she'd never fully appreciated before. She'd always focused on the immediate balance—evil act, proportionate response, scales restored to equilibrium. But now she began to perceive the deeper patterns, the way justice and injustice echoed through generations.

It was... beautiful. And terrible. And more complex than she'd ever imagined.

A new call came, pulling her consciousness toward flesh and form. She expected the familiar disorientation of awakening in a new body, a new time. Instead, she found herself aware of the process for the first time—watching as reality bent around her need, crafting a form suited to whatever imbalance required correction.

She opened her eyes to smell smoke and gunpowder.

Fields of mud stretched in every direction, churned by artillery shells and soaked with blood. Barbed wire glinted like deadly spiderwebs between wooden posts. In the distance, machine guns chattered their mechanical death songs.

The Great War. The war that was supposed to end all wars.

Justice sat up slowly, feeling the weight of this new form. Male this time, she realized—tall and lean, wearing the tattered remains of a British uniform. Her blindfold had become a bandage wrapped around her eyes, stained with old blood. A rifle lay half-buried in the mud beside her.

"God Almighty, you're alive!"

She turned toward the voice—a young soldier, barely old enough to shave, his face streaked with dirt and tears. He crawled through the mud toward her, keeping low to avoid the sniper fire that occasionally cracked overhead.

"Thompson, sir," he gasped. "Private Thompson. I thought you were dead when that shell hit."

Justice tested her limbs, feeling the particular ache of this form's wounds. Shrapnel in her left leg, a bullet graze across her ribs, countless smaller cuts and bruises. But functional. Strong enough for whatever task awaited her here.

"How long?" she asked, her voice rougher than she'd expected.

"Three days, sir. The offensive started Monday. We've been holding this position since..." Thompson's voice cracked. "Since most of the company got killed trying to take that machine gun nest."

Justice extended her awareness, mapping the battlefield through sound and vibration. Allied trenches to the east, German positions to the west. Between them, a hellscape of shell craters and corpses that stretched for miles. And somewhere in the middle of it all, the source of the imbalance that had drawn her here.

"The civilians," she said.

Thompson's face went pale. "How did you—we're not supposed to talk about it, sir. Captain's orders."

"Tell me."

The young soldier looked around fearfully, then leaned closer. "There's a village. Beaumont. About two kilometers behind the German lines. When the artillery started, most folks got out, but..." He swallowed hard. "The Germans are using it as a supply depot. And there's maybe thirty people still trapped there. Old folks, mostly. Some children."

"And?"

"Our orders are to shell the village tomorrow morning. Flatten it completely before the next push." Thompson's voice dropped to a whisper. "Command says it's necessary. Cut off their supply lines. But those people..."

Justice felt the familiar stirring—not quite emotion, but the deep current that guided her interventions. Innocent lives about to be sacrificed for military expediency. Civilians treated as acceptable casualties in someone else's war.

The kind of injustice that demanded response.

"Where's the captain?" she asked.

"Dead, sir. Along with Lieutenant Morrison and Sergeant Hayes. You're the ranking officer now."

Justice stood slowly, ignoring the protests from her wounded leg. Around them, other soldiers huddled in shell craters and behind bits of debris, waiting for orders that might never come. Boys, most of them. Children playing at war while their leaders played with their lives.

"Get me a map," she said.

Thompson scrambled to comply, pulling a mud-stained chart from his pack. Justice spread it across a flat piece of rubble, running her fingers over the terrain features she couldn't see. The village sat in a shallow valley, surrounded by hills that would make a direct assault costly. But there were other approaches—game trails and farm roads that might allow a small force to slip through.

"How many men do we have left?" she asked.

"Seventeen, sir. But most are wounded, and we're low on ammunition."

Seventeen soldiers against an entrenched enemy position. Under normal circumstances, suicide. But Justice had never operated under normal circumstances.

"Gather the men," she commanded. "We're going to get those civilians out."

Thompson stared at her. "Sir? Our orders are to hold position until—"

"Our orders," Justice interrupted, "are to serve justice. Sometimes that means following commands. Sometimes it means following conscience."

She spent the next hour planning with the surviving soldiers, using her supernatural awareness to identify German patrol routes and weapon emplacements. The plan was ambitious, possibly mad, but it had one crucial advantage: no one would expect a handful of wounded British soldiers to attempt a rescue behind enemy lines.

They moved out at dusk, using shell craters and abandoned equipment for cover. Justice led from the front, her blindness no handicap in the smoke-filled darkness. She could sense the German sentries long before human eyes could spot them, guiding her men around their positions with whispered directions.

The village of Beaumont had seen better days. Artillery had collapsed half the buildings, leaving rubble-choked streets and walls pocked with shrapnel. But the central square remained intact, along with the stone church where the civilians had taken shelter.

"Thirty-seven souls," Justice murmured, extending her awareness through the building. "Twelve children, twenty-three adults, two invalids."

"How can you possibly know that?" Thompson whispered.

She didn't answer. Instead, she gestured to two of her men. "Circle around to the back entrance. Wait for my signal."

The German supply depot occupied the old town hall—a substantial building with thick walls that had weathered the bombardment better than most. Justice counted twenty soldiers inside, plus an officer and several support personnel. More than enough to hold the position against a frontal assault.

But she wasn't planning a frontal assault.

"Thompson," she said quietly. "Take three men and create a distraction. Nothing fancy—just enough noise to draw their attention to the north side of the building."

"What about you, sir?"

Justice checked her rifle, feeling the familiar weight of weapons that had been crafted for this specific purpose. "I'm going to knock on the front door."

The distraction worked perfectly. Thompson's men opened fire from behind a collapsed wall, their muzzle flashes bright in the darkness. The Germans responded predictably, concentrating their forces to repel what they assumed was the main attack.

Justice walked through the front door of the town hall like she belonged there.

The first German soldier she encountered was reloading his rifle, eyes fixed on the windows facing north. He didn't even turn around as she approached. The bayonet slid between his ribs with surgical precision, finding his heart before he could cry out.

She moved through the building like a ghost, her enhanced senses guiding her around creaking floorboards and loose rubble. Five more soldiers died in as many minutes, each death quick and silent. By the time the Germans realized they were under attack from within, Justice had already reached their officer—a young lieutenant who was shouting orders into a field telephone.

"Hang up," she said quietly.

The lieutenant spun around, his hand dropping to his sidearm. He froze when he saw the rifle pointed at his chest, held by a man whose bandaged eyes somehow tracked his every movement.

"You speak English," Justice observed.

"A little," the lieutenant replied, his accent thick but understandable. "Who are you?"

"Someone who objects to your supply depot," she said. "Specifically, to what you're storing in the basement."

The lieutenant's face went pale. "I don't know what you mean."

Justice tilted her head slightly. "Chemical shells. Chlorine gas, most likely, though I detect traces of phosgene as well. Enough to poison half the battlefield."

"Those are... those are not for use against soldiers," the lieutenant stammered. "They're for—"

"For the village." Justice's voice remained level, but something in her tone made the young officer step backward. "When your position becomes untenable, you plan to shell the civilian shelter. Make it look like Allied artillery. Clean up loose ends."

"It's war! People die!"

"Not like that," Justice said. "Not on my watch."

The lieutenant lunged for his pistol. Justice shot him through the heart before his hand reached the holster.

The remaining Germans surrendered without further resistance once they realized their situation. Justice herded them into the basement with their own chemical weapons, then sealed the entrance with debris from the bombardment. Not permanent, but it would hold long enough for her purposes.

The civilians in the church were understandably terrified when British soldiers burst through their doors. Most spoke no English, but fear was universal. Justice knelt among them, her presence somehow calming despite the weapons and blood-stained uniform.

"We're here to help," she said in French, then German, then the local dialect she shouldn't have known but somehow did. "You're going to be safe."

An elderly priest stepped forward, his cassock torn but his dignity intact. "The children," he said in broken English. "They cannot walk far."

Justice nodded. She'd already considered that problem. "Thompson, bring the German vehicles around. We'll load everyone into the trucks."

"Sir, we don't know how to drive—"

"I do," Justice lied. The knowledge came to her as she spoke, another gift from whatever forces shaped her interventions. "Get them ready to move."

The evacuation took less than an hour. Justice drove the lead truck herself, navigating shell-cratered roads with preternatural skill. Behind her, thirty-seven civilians huddled together in fearful silence, while her soldiers followed in commandeered German vehicles.

They reached Allied lines just as the preliminary bombardment began. Justice stood on a hill overlooking Beaumont, watching artillery shells tear the village apart. The town hall took a direct hit, collapsing into rubble that would bury the chemical weapons for decades to come.

"Beautiful night," Thompson said, joining her at the makeshift observation post.

Justice nodded, though her attention was already turning elsewhere. The immediate crisis was resolved, but she sensed larger currents at work. This war would end eventually, but the forces that had created it—nationalism run mad, technology outpacing wisdom, the willingness to sacrifice innocents for political gain—those would persist.

And grow stronger.

"Sir?" Thompson was staring at her with concern. "You're bleeding."

Justice looked down at her uniform, now soaked with blood from wounds she hadn't noticed during the fighting. Mortal wounds, in this form. The kind that would require medical attention she wasn't going to receive.

"It's time," she said quietly.

"Time for what, sir?"

Justice smiled, though the expression felt strange on this borrowed face. "To let someone else carry the burden for a while."

She died just before dawn, surrounded by soldiers who would spend the rest of their lives trying to explain how a blind officer had led them through enemy territory to save a village that officially didn't exist.

Thompson became a priest after the war. He never spoke publicly about what he'd witnessed, but his sermons carried themes of sacrifice and moral courage that inspired several generations of parishioners. Some of them became soldiers themselves. Others became teachers, doctors, social workers—people who chose service over self-interest.

The ripples spread outward, as they always did.

The transitions came faster now, each awakening bringing greater awareness of the patterns that connected all things. Justice found herself in a dozen forms across as many centuries—a samurai defending villagers from bandits in feudal Japan, a nurse treating plague victims in medieval Europe, a slave leading others to freedom along underground railways.

Each intervention seemed small in isolation, but she began to perceive how they wove together across time and space. A child saved in one century became a leader in the next. A act of mercy prevented a massacre that would have echoed through generations. A moment of justice balanced scales that had been tipping toward chaos for decades.

She was changing too, becoming something more than the simple personification of retribution she'd once been. The empathy that had always lurked beneath her stoic facade was growing stronger, complicating her calculations in ways both beautiful and terrible.

Which brought her to now.

Justice opened her eyes to the familiar weight of her traditional form—female, tall, strong, with the silver-blue armor and bastard sword that had become her signature across the ages. But this time felt different. Final, somehow.

She stood on a hill overlooking a vast city that sprawled to the horizon in every direction. Towers of glass and steel reached toward the sky, while streams of vehicles flowed along elevated highways like rivers of light. The air hummed with electronic signals—radio, television, internet, satellite communications—a thousand different voices all speaking at once.

The twenty-first century. Her latest intervention had brought her home to where it all began, though she'd never seen it quite like this before.

"You're early."

Justice turned toward the voice. A figure approached across the hilltop—tall, thin, wearing a simple gray suit that somehow managed to look both modern and timeless. She couldn't see his face—even her supernatural awareness seemed to slide off him like water off glass—but she recognized his presence.

"Order," she said simply.

"Indeed." He stopped a few feet away, hands clasped behind his back. "Though I prefer the name Uriel these days. Less pretentious."

Justice studied him, trying to understand what she was sensing. Power, certainly—far greater than her own. But also something else. Weariness, perhaps. The kind that came from watching civilizations rise and fall like waves against the shore.

"You created me," she said. Not a question.

"Created is too strong a word. Shaped, perhaps. Guided. You were always there, Justice—part of the fundamental structure of reality itself. I simply... gave you focus."

The city spread below them glittered in the afternoon sun. From this distance, it looked almost peaceful. Beautiful, even. But Justice could sense the currents of injustice flowing through its streets like poison in the bloodstream. Corporate executives knowingly destroying the environment for profit. Politicians selling their votes to the highest bidder. Systems designed to protect the wealthy while grinding the poor to dust.

"Why are you here?" she asked.

Uriel—Order—whatever he chose to call himself—gestured toward the urban sprawl. "Because something is coming. Something that will test every intervention you've ever made, every life you've saved, every small act of courage you've inspired."

Justice felt it then—a disturbance in the fabric of reality itself, like a discordant note in a perfect symphony. It was vast, alien, hungry. And it was approaching fast.

"What is it?"

"Chaos," Uriel replied. "Not the natural chaos that creates and destroys in equal measure, but something else. Something that wants to unmake existence itself. It feeds on suffering, grows stronger with every injustice, every cruelty, every moment when good people choose to do nothing."

"And you want me to stop it."

Uriel's laugh held no humor. "You? My dear Justice, you couldn't stop a force like that any more than a candle could hold back the night. No, what's coming will require something far more... comprehensive."

Justice turned away from the city, facing her creator fully. "Then why bring me here?"

"Because before the end, there will be one final test. One last chance for humanity to prove itself worthy of salvation." Uriel's form seemed to shimmer, becoming less solid. "In the coming days, you will face a choice that will define not just your own existence, but the fate of every soul you've ever tried to protect. Every life you've saved, every act of courage you've inspired—it all comes down to what you decide in that moment."

"What kind of choice?"

But Uriel was already fading, his voice becoming distant. "You'll know it when you see it. Trust your heart, Justice. You've learned to feel—that was always the point. In the end, pure logic won't be enough. It never is."

"Wait!" Justice called out. "How do I—"

"Find the Keeper," Uriel's voice whispered from everywhere and nowhere. "She has what you need to understand. The old subway station beneath Fifth and Main. Go quickly—time is shorter than you think."

And then he was gone, leaving Justice alone on the hilltop with the weight of prophecy settling on her shoulders like a lead cloak.

The subway tunnel had been abandoned for thirty years, a victim of budget cuts and urban decay. Justice descended through rusted turnstiles and crumbling tiles, following passages that led deeper than any official blueprint showed. Her enhanced senses picked up traces of recent habitation—the lingering scent of candle wax, the echo of footsteps, the almost-imperceptible hum of electronic equipment.

The tunnel ended in a vast chamber carved from living rock. Bookshelves lined the walls from floor to ceiling, filled with volumes in every language Justice had ever encountered and several she hadn't. Computer screens flickered between the ancient tomes, displaying streams of data that seemed to flow like living things.

At the center of it all sat a woman who looked to be in her sixties, her silver hair pulled back in a practical bun. She wore simple clothes—jeans, a wool sweater, reading glasses perched on her nose—but there was something about her that made Justice think of librarians who guarded forbidden knowledge.

"The Keeper, I presume," Justice said.

The woman looked up from the leather-bound journal she'd been writing in. "Magdalene Derne," she replied. "Though I suppose titles matter less now. Please, sit. We have much to discuss and very little time."

Justice remained standing, her hand resting on her sword hilt. "Uriel sent me."

"I know. I've been waiting for you for forty years." Magdalene closed the journal and set it aside. "Ever since the first signs appeared. The patterns starting to shift. The balance beginning to fail."

"What patterns?"

Instead of answering directly, Magdalene gestured to the nearest computer screen. Images flashed across it in rapid succession—news footage, satellite photos, statistical analyses. Wars spreading across three continents. Environmental collapse accelerating beyond all projections. Economic systems failing as wealth concentrated in fewer and fewer hands.

"The old checks and balances are breaking down," Magdalene explained. "For millennia, there was always someone to stand up when things went too far. Heroes, prophets, revolutionaries—people who refused to accept injustice as inevitable. But something changed about fifty years ago. The corruption became systemic. Institutional. Self-perpetuating."

Justice watched the images cycle past. She recognized some of the events—moments where she'd considered intervening but ultimately decided against it. Small compromises that had seemed insignificant at the time.

"I failed," she said quietly.

"We all did." Magdalene's voice held no judgment, only weary sadness. "The enemy we face isn't some external invader. It's the accumulated weight of every choice we didn't make, every stand we didn't take, every time we chose comfort over courage."

"And now?"

Magdalene stood and walked to a shelf filled with scrolls that looked older than civilization itself. She selected one with careful precision, unrolling it to reveal symbols that seemed to shift and writhe on the ancient parchment.

"Now the Devourer comes," she said. "The force that feeds on despair and grows strong from suffering. It's been patient, building its strength while we fought smaller battles. But it's almost ready to manifest fully."

Justice studied the symbols, feeling them resonate with something deep in her consciousness. "How long do we have?"

"Days. Maybe hours." Magdalene rolled up the scroll and tucked it into a leather satchel. "It will choose a focal point—some place where human cruelty has reached a critical mass. Then it will use that darkness to tear open a gateway between dimensions."

"Where?"

"The city below us. Specifically, the Millennium Tower." Magdalene pointed toward the ceiling, though the skyscraper was miles away. "Forty stories of corporate offices built on the bones of a children's hospital they demolished to make room for profit margins. The symbolism is too perfect for the Devourer to resist."

Justice felt the truth of it like a physical blow. She'd sensed the wrongness around that particular building during her reconnaissance of the city, but had dismissed it as just another example of systemic corruption. Now she understood —it was a wound in reality itself, a place where injustice had festered until it began to attract things that should never exist.

"What can we do?"

Magdalene shouldered the satchel and began walking toward a passage Justice hadn't noticed before. "We can give humanity one last chance to save itself. The Devourer draws its power from despair, from the belief that nothing can change, that cruelty is inevitable. But if enough people choose to act—really act, not just express sympathy on social media—the balance can shift."

They emerged into a different part of the subway system, one that was still in use. Commuters hurried past without seeming to notice the two women who had appeared from a maintenance tunnel that shouldn't have led anywhere.

"How many people?" Justice asked as they climbed toward street level.

"I don't know. Maybe a few hundred making the ultimate sacrifice. Maybe thousands choosing smaller acts of courage. The mathematics of hope are... complicated."

They reached the surface to find the city in chaos. Emergency vehicles screamed through the streets while news helicopters circled overhead like mechanical vultures. The Millennium Tower rose in the distance, its glass facade reflecting the afternoon sun in patterns that hurt to look at directly.

"It's starting," Magdalene said.

Justice could feel it too—a wrongness spreading through the urban landscape like infection through a wound. People were becoming more aggressive, more cruel, more willing to hurt others for trivial reasons. The kind of casual violence that normally lurked beneath the surface was bubbling up into the light.

"The final test Uriel mentioned," Justice realized. "It's not just about stopping the Devourer. It's about proving that people can choose to be better."

"Even when it costs them everything," Magdalene agreed. "Especially then."

They made their way through streets that grew stranger with each passing block. Reality seemed less stable here, as if the approaching dimensional breach was weakening the barriers between what was real and what was merely possible. Justice saw flickering glimpses of other timelines—versions of the city where different choices had been made, where the corruption had been fought instead of accepted.

The Millennium Tower loomed ahead, its upper floors wreathed in clouds that moved against the wind. At its base, crowds had gathered—some protesters holding signs, others corporate security trying to maintain order, still others who seemed to be there for no reason they could articulate.

"There," Magdalene pointed to a young woman near the building's entrance. She was perhaps twenty-five, wearing a nurse's uniform and carrying a sign that read "Healthcare is a Human Right." Her face was streaked with tears, but her grip on the placard never wavered.

"Jessica Martinez," Magdalene continued. "Three years out of nursing school. Forty thousand in student debt. She came here because her hospital is being shut down to increase profit margins for Millennium Corp's medical division."

Justice extended her awareness, reading the currents of probability swirling around the young woman. Jessica would make a choice in the next few minutes—a choice that would ripple outward through the crowd, through the city, through the collective consciousness of humanity itself.

"She's going to die," Justice said.

"Probably. The security guards have orders to use lethal force if the protesters try to enter the building. But if she acts—if she chooses courage over safety—others will follow."

Justice felt the familiar stirring in her chest, the pull that had guided her through millennia of interventions. But this time it was different. Stronger. Final.

"You have to choose too," Magdalene said quietly. "You can intervene directly—save Jessica, fight the security forces, maybe even hold back the Devourer for a few more years. Or you can step back and let humanity face this test on its own."

"And if I step back and they fail?"

"Then everything ends. Every life you've saved, every act of courage you've inspired, every small victory against injustice—all of it gets swallowed by the void."

Justice watched Jessica Martinez take a deep breath and start walking toward the building's entrance. The security guards tensed, hands moving toward their weapons. The crowd stirred, sensing that some crucial moment was approaching.

This was it. The choice Uriel had warned her about.

She could step forward—become the hero one more time, tip the scales through supernatural intervention. It would work, probably. For a while. But it would also rob humanity of the chance to save itself, to prove that ordinary people could choose extraordinary courage when it mattered most.

Or she could trust in the thousands of small interventions she'd made across the millennia. Trust that somewhere in the crowd, someone would remember a story of sacrifice they'd heard, a moment of inspiration they'd witnessed, a tiny seed of hope she'd planted in some forgotten corner of history.

Trust that love was stronger than fear, even when everything seemed lost.

Jessica Martinez reached the building's entrance. The security guards stepped forward, weapons drawn.

Justice made her choice.

She stepped back.

And watched as a miracle unfolded.

It started with an old man—someone Justice recognized from her passage through the crowd. He'd been at

Thermopylae, in a different life, carrying a different name. He stepped between Jessica and the guards, his weathered hands empty but steady.

"She's just a nurse," he said. "Someone has to speak for the people who can't speak for themselves."

Then a teenage girl joined him—one of the three women from the Colosseum, wearing different flesh but carrying the same courage. Then a middle-aged teacher who bore the spiritual echo of Marcus Justianus. Then a dozen others, all of them connected by invisible threads to moments of heroism Justice had witnessed across the centuries.

The security guards hesitated, outnumbered now, facing people who had chosen to stand together despite the danger.

And in that moment of hesitation, something beautiful happened.

The wrongness that had been spreading through the city began to recede. The dimensional breach that had been tearing open above the Millennium Tower started to collapse. The Devourer, feeding on despair and cruelty, found itself starved as ordinary people chose hope over fear.

It wasn't complete victory—it never was. The forces of corruption would regroup, find new strategies, new ways to spread their poison. But for now, in this moment, the balance had been restored.

Justice felt the familiar pull of transition beginning, the call to another time and place where her intervention might be needed. But this time it felt different. Gentler. Less like duty and more like... gratitude.

She looked back at Magdalene, who was smiling through her tears.

"Will it be enough?" Justice asked.

"For now," the Keeper replied. "And now is all we ever really have."

Justice nodded, feeling her form beginning to fade. But as the darkness took her, she heard something that made her spirit soar—the sound of voices raised together, not in anger or despair, but in songs of hope that would echo through the generations yet to come.

The balance was restored.

For now.

And in the space between spaces where she waited for the next call, Justice finally understood what Uriel had been trying to teach her all along.

The true victory wasn't in the battles she'd won or the tyrants she'd defeated. It was in the ordinary people who had learned to be extraordinary, who had chosen courage when it would have been easier to look away.

She was no longer just the Spirit of Retribution.

She had become something more.

She had become Hope.

And somewhere in the vast expanse of space and time, new voices were calling her name—not for justice or vengeance, but for the chance to believe that tomorrow could be better than today.

The work would never end.

But neither would the possibility of redemption.

Justice smiled in the darkness and prepared to answer the call.

The Grinning Abyss

*"Existence is the universe's cruelest joke—
beautiful, temporary, and utterly pointless, which is
precisely what makes it worth experiencing."*

POMPEII, 79 AD

The Roman centurion's gladius passed clean through where The Nothing's heart should have been, emerging from his back in a spray of blood that painted the cobblestones black. The soldier's eyes widened as his victim smiled—that impossible white grin splitting his scarred face like a crescent moon against storm clouds.

"Fascinating," The Nothing wheezed, dark blood bubbling between his teeth. "The pain is... exquisite. Tell me, do you practice that thrust, or are you just naturally gifted at finding things that aren't there?"

Mount Vesuvius rumbled in the distance, ash already beginning to drift through Pompeii's streets like gray snow. The centurion tried to withdraw his blade, but The Nothing's fingers closed around the steel, holding it in place. Steam rose from where flesh met metal.

"You're... you're a demon," the Roman gasped.

"Something like that." The Nothing's voice carried the weight of empty spaces between stars. "though I prefer to think of myself as chronically unemployed. The pay is terrible, but the hours are flexible."

The sword slid free with a wet sound. The Nothing examined the gaping wound in his chest—just above the larger hole that had been there since existence began, the void-touched cavity where normal men kept their hearts. Dark tendrils writhed within it like living shadows.

"Tell me," he said, watching his torn flesh begin to knit itself back together with the enthusiasm of a drunk seamstress, "what drives you to stick sharp objects into strangers? Professional obligation? Personal satisfaction? A deep-seated fear of your own mortality projected onto convenient targets?"

"The gods curse you," the soldier whispered, stumbling backward.

"Already done, I'm afraid. Several millennia ago. Though curse seems harsh—I prefer 'extended work assignment without overtime.'"

The centurion turned and ran. The Nothing watched him go with amusement. "Give my regards to Jupiter!" he called after the fleeing figure. "Tell him his lighting effects are getting repetitive!"

Around them, Pompeii's citizens fled screaming as the mountain's rumble grew to a roar. But The Nothing stood perfectly still, fascination gleaming in his eyes—those pools of darkness punctuated by distant stars.

He had been wandering the Roman Empire for three centuries now, sampling what mortals called 'civilization.' The irony wasn't lost on him that creatures with lifespans shorter than his attention span had coined a word for organized brutality and called it progress.

Today's lesson: how people behaved when they knew the world was ending.

The mountain's roar became a shriek. The Nothing looked up to see Vesuvius crack open like a rotten egg, spewing molten rock and superheated ash into the sky. The pyroclastic flow would reach the city in minutes. Most of these people had perhaps an hour left to live.

How would they spend it?

A woman clutched her child to her chest, running toward the harbor where ships were already casting off like rats abandoning a particularly flammable vessel. A merchant stuffed gold coins into his toga before realizing their weight would slow him down—economics was a harsh mistress even in the face of geological tantrum. A priest of Jupiter stood in his temple doorway, arms raised to the sky, either praying or cursing. The Nothing couldn't tell which, but admired the man's commitment to theological multitasking.

The centurion was still backing away, but his retreat had slowed. Training warred with terror in his weather-beaten face—a fascinating study in conflicting survival instincts.

"You should run," The Nothing suggested, wiping blood from his mouth with the back of his hand. "Though I suppose you know that. Amazing how knowing something and doing it remain such distant cousins in the human experience."

"My... my cohort is at the northern gate. The evacuation—"

"Will fail spectacularly." The Nothing's grin widened. "I've seen this before. Different mountain, different city, same ending. The hot death comes faster than fear can carry you. But please, don't let me discourage your optimism. It's quite charming in a doomed sort of way."

"Then why aren't you running?"

"Because I can't die. Rather takes the urgency out of things. Like watching a play when you've already read the script—you know everyone dies in Act Three, but you stick around to see how they handle their lines."

The soldier's grip on his sword tightened. "Prove it."

"Oh, I intend to. But not how you think."

Titus—for the centurion had finally stammered out his name between curses and prayers—looked toward the harbor one last time, then back at The Nothing. Some primal calculation played out behind his eyes: impossible survival versus impossible monster.

Survival won. It usually did.

The Nothing watched him go, that persistent grin never wavering. Such curious creatures, these mortals. Logic declared their situation hopeless, yet they ran anyway. Did hope make them stronger, or simply better at mathematical self-deception?

The pyroclastic flow hit Pompeii like the fist of an angry god with anger management issues.

The Nothing stood in the city's center as the superheated cloud engulfed everything. The temperature spiked past what human flesh could survive—roughly the point where screaming became unnecessary because vocal cords had turned to ash. His skin blistered and charred, his hair ignited in a brief but spectacular display, his clothes burst into flame like an impromptu cremation ceremony.

The pain was extraordinary—like being flayed with molten metal while drowning in acid and having a philosophical discussion about the nature of suffering.

He laughed.

Around him, citizens who hadn't escaped in time were flash-cooked where they stood. Their final moments burned into ash and stone, their agony crystallized for archaeologists to puzzle over two thousand years hence. The Nothing watched them die, studying their faces, their postures, their last desperate gestures with the detached interest of a theater critic reviewing a particularly avant-garde performance.

A baker reached for his child—paternal instinct overriding the small matter of being turned into charcoal. A gladiator shielded a woman he'd probably never met—heroism in the face of geological indifference. A thief threw himself over a bag of stolen coins as if wealth could armor him against superheated gas—capitalism's last absurd gasp.

How strange that facing extinction made some people selfish while making others selfless. What cosmic algorithm governed such choices? What made one soul turn inward while another reached out in their final microseconds?

The Nothing's body was reduced to charred bone and grinning skull, but still he stood. Still he watched. Still he catalogued humanity's final exam in rapid-fire mortality.

Hours passed. The city cooled from molten to merely lethally hot. His flesh began to regrow, pale and scarred as always, threading itself through his skeleton like vines claiming a trellis made of calcium and bad decisions. The large hole in his chest remained unchanged—that void which was his true self, the darkness that existed before existence had gotten ideas above its station.

As sensation returned to his restored form, he heard something unexpected: sobbing.

A survivor. Impossible—nothing human could have lived through that heat. Unless...

He followed the sound through ash-choked streets, past flash-baked corpses frozen in their final moments like a twisted gallery of human sculpture. The artistic merit was debatable, but the emotional impact was undeniable.

In the ruins of a collapsed villa, he found her: a young woman curled in what had once been a wine cellar. The stone had protected her from the initial blast, but she was badly burned, her breathing shallow and labored. Hours, maybe less —death was being polite, but it wasn't being patient.

She looked up as his shadow fell across her. No fear in her eyes—shock had burned that away along with most of her hair, leaving only exhaustion and a strange sort of peace.

"Are you... death?" she whispered.

"Close enough." The Nothing knelt beside her, careful not to disturb the delicate architecture of her dying. "What's your name?"

"Livia." Blood flecked her lips when she spoke. "My family...?"

"Gone. I'm sorry." The apology surprised him—he couldn't remember the last time he'd expressed regret for something as mundane as mortality.

She nodded as if she'd expected as much. Death had a way of making people practical philosophers. "Will it... hurt much longer?"

The Nothing studied her face—young, perhaps twenty, with the callused hands of someone who'd worked for her bread. Soon she would be nothing but ash and memory. In a cosmic sense, she already was. In an even more cosmic sense, she never had been anything else.

"No," he lied with practiced ease. "It won't hurt much longer."

Livia's eyes found his, focusing on those pinpricks of starlight in endless darkness. "You have... strange eyes. Like looking into the night sky."

"That's exactly what they are. Occupational hazard."

"Are you a god?"

"I'm what was here before gods had the audacity to exist. Before anything did, really. I was the cosmic equivalent of dead air on the radio."

She was quiet for a moment, processing this with the clarity that sometimes comes to the dying. "Are you lonely?"

The question hit him like a physical blow. In all his millennia of wandering, sampling mortal experiences like a supernatural tourist with boundary issues, no one had ever asked him that. He'd been stabbed, burned, worshipped, feared, cursed, ignored, and occasionally invited to dinner by people with questionable judgment. But no one had wondered if he was lonely.

"I..." He paused, examining the unfamiliar sensation in what passed for his chest. It felt like indigestion, but more emotionally complex. "I don't know. That's... an interesting question."

"I think you are." Livia's voice was growing fainter, but her attention remained laser-focused in the way of people who had run out of time for small talk. "I think that's why you're here. Watching us. Trying to understand what you're missing."

"And what am I missing?"

She smiled—not the rictus grin of the dying, but something genuine and warm. "Connection. We all die, but we don't die alone. Not if we're lucky."

"You're dying alone."

"No." Her eyes never left his. "You're here."

Livia's hand found his—her fingers small and fragile against his scarred palm. For a moment, The Nothing felt something he'd never experienced in all his eons of existence: the desire to give rather than take, to preserve rather than observe.

He could save her. His power over void and shadow could shield her, transport her to safety, undo the damage the mountain had done with its geological temper tantrum. He could cheat death on her behalf, stick his finger in mortality's eye and laugh at the cosmic joke.

But that would be interfering. Changing the story instead of simply reading it. And he'd sworn to himself long ago that he would only watch, only learn, only collect experiences like a magpie hoarding shiny objects. Never act. Never engage. Never care.

Those rules had seemed so reasonable at the time.

Livia's breathing grew more labored. "Thank you," she whispered. "For staying."

Her hand went slack in his.

The Nothing sat in the ash-filled ruins, holding the hand of a dead slave girl, and wondered why his eyes were leaking. Water, salt, and something else—something that tasted like the space between heartbeats.

Were these tears? Was this grief? If so, it was exquisite. And absolutely infuriating.

He buried her in the villa's courtyard, marking the grave with a piece of marble carved with her name. It was a small rebellion against his nature—The Nothing wasn't supposed to create memorials. He was supposed to let all things return to the void without ceremony, without acknowledgment, without the stubborn human insistence that temporary things mattered.

But Livia had been kind to a monster. That seemed worth remembering, even if remembering was technically outside his job description.

LONDON, 1348

The plague cart's wheels squelched through mud mixed with blood, piss, and the general detritus of a civilization in its death throes. The Nothing walked beside it, his tattered coat now medieval wool, his scars fresh from a recent encounter with Flemish mercenaries who'd mistaken him for a French spy.

The misunderstanding had been educational. Apparently, explaining that national identity was a meaningless construct in the face of universal entropy was not considered adequate diplomatic immunity.

"Bring out your dead!" the carter called, his voice muffled by a cloth soaked in herbs, prayers, and what The Nothing suspected was a significant amount of alcohol. "Bodies for the fire! No charge for the recently departed!"

The entrepreneurial spirit was alive and well, even as everything else was dying with impressive efficiency.

The Nothing paused outside a ramshackle hovel where sobbing echoed from within like a one-person Greek chorus. Through the window, he watched a woman cradle her infant son—both burning with fever, both hours from joining the cart's grim cargo.

"Why do you weep?" he asked, stepping through the doorway uninvited. Privacy was a luxury the plague had made obsolete.

The woman looked up, past terror into resignation. Her face was gaunt, aged beyond her years by loss and the constant companionship of death. "My son... he's all I have left."

"He's dying."

"I know." Tears carved tracks through the grime on her cheeks like rivers through a wasteland. "But he's still here. Still mine. For now."

The Nothing studied her face—young like Livia had been, but harder, carved by loss into something sharp and enduring. Survival as sculpture. "Your husband?"

"Dead three days past. The pestilence took him quick, at least. Some mercies in this world, I suppose."

"And you stay with the child knowing you'll catch it?"

She held her son closer, as if proximity could shield him from the obvious. "Where else would I be? He's my blood. My heart walking around outside my body." She looked at The Nothing with the hollow stare of someone who had already calculated the cost of love and decided to pay it anyway. "You wouldn't understand."

"Try me."

The woman—Mary, she said her name was Mary, like half the women in Christendom—rocked her dying child and told The Nothing about love as a choice rather than a feeling. About staying not because it made sense, but because the alternative was unthinkable. About how caring for someone meant accepting that you would lose them, and doing it anyway.

"Makes no sense, does it?" she said as dawn light crept through the hovel's single window. "Love something you know will die. Love it because it will die, maybe. Makes everything precious, the knowing it won't last."

Her son died as the sun reached its zenith. Mary held him until he went cold, then wrapped him in her only clean cloth—a wedding veil she'd saved for twenty years.

"Will you..." she began, then stopped. "Will you help me carry him to the cart?"

The Nothing had never carried a dead child before. The boy weighed almost nothing, as if death had somehow made him less substantial. Mary walked beside him, humming lullabies to her dead son—melodies that had been ancient when Rome was young, songs of mothers comforting children who would never again need comforting.

"Curious thing," The Nothing mused as they approached the cart. "You knew it was futile, yet you did it anyway."

"Love ain't about sense," Mary replied, "Good thing too, or we'd all be dead already. Metaphorically speaking."

Mary died that night. The Nothing found her the next morning, still humming lullabies in her sleep. He helped load her body onto the cart, noting with academic interest how peaceful she looked. Death as mercy—another data point in his ongoing study of human contradiction.

The carter was more philosophical than his profession suggested. "Seen a lot of them go like that," he said as they worked. "Holding onto something right until the end. Love, hope, anger—doesn't matter what. Just something to keep them human while the world goes to hell."

"And when there's nothing left to hold onto?"

"Then they let go. And that's human too."

The Nothing carried that conversation with him as London burned its dead in great pyres that turned the sky black with smoke and unfinished stories.

SALEM, 1692

The rope bit deep into The Nothing's neck as the crowd cheered his hanging. He'd made the mistake of asking too many questions about local superstitions—apparently intellectual curiosity was indistinguishable from maleficarium in this particular corner of Massachusetts.

The locals had been surprisingly thorough in their theological jurisprudence. They'd tried drowning him first (inconclusive), then pressing him with stones (educational but unsuccessful), and finally settled on hanging as the most traditional approach to dealing with supernatural inconvenience.

His neck snapped with a satisfying crack. The crowd began to disperse, satisfied that justice had been served and that God's wrath had been properly channeled through hemp rope and moral certainty. The Nothing waited until full dark before putting his vertebrae back together and climbing down from the gallows.

"Bit dramatic, don't you think?"

The voice belonged to a young woman hiding behind the meeting house like a particularly attractive shadow with commitment issues. Eunice Bishop, if he remembered the accusations correctly—scheduled to hang tomorrow for the crime of living alone and owning too many cats.

"Says the woman talking to a corpse," The Nothing replied, brushing rope fibers from his throat like lint from a jacket. "Though I suppose in Salem, that's considered normal Tuesday behavior."

Eunice didn't flinch. Fear was a luxury she'd apparently decided she couldn't afford. "If you're the Devil, you're smaller than I expected. Also less attractive. The stories really oversell the whole 'dark prince' angle."

"Just a tourist with poor timing and worse judgment. You don't seem particularly concerned about your upcoming appointment with eternity."

She shrugged with the practiced indifference of someone who had run out of things to lose. "Can't be worse than living in this God-forsaken place. At least when I'm dead, they'll stop accusing me of things. Hard to practice witchcraft when you're fertilizing the pastor's garden."

"You could run."

"Where? They'll just find more women to burn. Someone has to be the witch." Eunice stepped closer, studying his face in the moonlight with the intensity of a natural philosopher examining a particularly interesting specimen. "Your eyes... like looking into the night between stars."

"You're the second person to notice that."

"Who was the first?"

"Someone who died a long time ago. In a place that was significantly warmer than Massachusetts."

Eunice nodded as if this made perfect sense. Death was an equalizer that way—it made all stories equally relevant and equally pointless. "We all die, stranger. Question is whether we die for something or just die."

"And which category do you fall into?"

"Haven't decided yet. Ask me tomorrow, assuming you're still hanging around to watch the show."

The Nothing studied her face in the pale moonlight. She had the same quality he'd seen in Livia, in Mary—that peculiar human ability to stare into the abyss and find it less interesting than whatever was happening in their immediate vicinity.

"What did you actually do?" he asked. "Besides the obvious crime of being inconvenient to men with small minds and large egos."

Eunice laughed, a sound like breaking glass that somehow managed to be musical. "I knew things. Herbs that could ease a woman's birthing pains, ways to keep milk from souring, which plants could prevent another mouth to feed when a family was already starving." Her smile was sharp as winter frost. "Amazing how quickly healing becomes cursing when you're a woman without a husband."

"Knowledge as witchcraft. Efficiency as evil."

"Something like that. Though I prefer to think of it as being inconveniently competent in a world that prefers its women decoratively useless."

They talked through the night—or rather, Eunice talked while The Nothing listened with the fascination of an anthropologist discovering a new species of stubborn. She told him about her cats (seven, not the demonic thirteen the prosecution claimed), her herb garden (medicinal, not magical, though she acknowledged the distinction was largely academic), and her books (a dangerous collection of botanical texts and philosophical treatises that had somehow survived the various book-burning festivals that passed for intellectual discourse in Salem).

"You know what the funny thing is?" Eunice said as dawn began to creep across the sky like a reluctant witness. "I'm not even afraid anymore. Was, at first—terrified of the pain, of dying alone, of being remembered as something I'm not. But now..."

"Now?"

"Now I'm mostly curious. What comes after? Is there really a hell waiting for women who know too much? Or is this it—just darkness, quiet, no more questions that don't have easy answers?"

The Nothing found himself genuinely impressed. Most people facing death either raged against it or collapsed into despair. Eunice Bishop was treating her execution like an interesting experiment with potentially educational results.

"You could still run," he offered. "I could help. Shadow-walking is one of my more practical skills."

"And go where? Live how? As what?" Eunice shook her head. "I've been me for thirty-two years. Too late to start being someone else now."

She walked back toward town as the sun rose, toward the rope that waited with tomorrow's dawn. The Nothing watched her go, noting the straightness of her spine, the steadiness of her step. She moved like someone going to a business appointment rather than an execution.

He attended her hanging the next day, standing at the back of the crowd while Salem's finest citizens cheered the death of a woman whose greatest crime was being more useful than they were comfortable with. Eunice spotted him just before they put the hood over her head. She winked.

The Nothing couldn't decide if that was the most human thing he'd ever witnessed, or the most inhuman. The distinction seemed less important than he'd previously thought.

GETTYSBURG, 1863

The cannonball took The Nothing's left arm off just below the shoulder, sending the limb spinning through the air like a pale bird with poor navigation skills. He sat in the churned mud of the battlefield, watching the severed appendage crawl back to him like a determined spider dragging itself through pools of other men's blood.

"Jesus Christ," someone whispered.

The Nothing looked up to find a Union soldier staring at him—young, maybe nineteen, with a gut wound that spelled death by sunrise and the kind of innocent face that war specialized in ruining. The boy's rifle lay forgotten in the mud beside him, apparently having concluded that its job here was finished.

"Name's actually closer to Nothing," The Nothing said, pressing his arm back into place with the casual efficiency of someone reassembling furniture. Bone found bone with grinding determination. "But I've been called worse. Usually by people who were better armed than you currently are."

"You're... you're one of them things the preacher warned about."

The Nothing flexed his fingers, testing the connection. Everything seemed to be in working order, which was more than could be said for most of the battlefield's other occupants. "Depends on the preacher. What'd he say about me?"

The soldier's breathing was growing shallow, each word costing him more than he could afford. "Said... said demons would walk among us in the end times. Wearing human faces."

"Well, he got the face part wrong." The Nothing's grin was particularly unsettling in the pre-dawn gloom, all teeth and darkness. "But I suppose two out of three isn't bad for a preacher. They're not known for their accuracy when it comes to eschatological predictions."

"Are you here... for me?"

"Not specifically. I just find battlefields educational. So much human nature compressed into such a small space. It's like a philosophical laboratory, except with more screaming and less peer review."

The boy tried to laugh, coughed up blood instead. The sound was wet and final, like a door closing on something important. "What... what have you learned?"

The Nothing considered this question while around them the groans of the dying mixed with distant artillery. Fifty thousand casualties in three days—all for ideas about freedom and union and the right to own other human beings. The mathematics of principle were always written in blood.

"That you're all completely insane," he said finally. "And somehow magnificent because of it."

"Magnificent?"

"You could have stayed home. Worked your farms, raised your children, lived quiet lives of agricultural obscurity. Instead you march hundreds of miles to kill strangers over principles most of you can't even articulate properly."

"Slavery's wrong," the boy whispered with the fierce certainty of someone who had never owned anything more valuable than the clothes on his back. "Some things... worth dying for."

"Are they?"

"You tell me. You've been around longer."

The Nothing had no answer. The boy—Thomas, he said his name was Thomas Whitmore from a farm outside Philadelphia—died before sunrise, clutching a daguerreotype of a girl he'd never see again. Her name was Rebecca, and they'd planned to marry when he came home from the war that was supposed to last six months and restore the Union without too much unpleasantness.

The Nothing sat with him until the end, then helped the stretcher bearers load bodies onto wagons that creaked under the weight of interrupted stories.

"Seen you before," one of the bearers said as they worked. He was older, grizzled, with the look of a man who had made carrying dead boys his profession. "Bull Run, Antietam, Chancellorsville. You're always there after, helping with the bodies."

"I find death interesting. From a professional standpoint."

"What profession is that?"

"Observer. Collector of experiences. Student of the inexplicable human tendency to find meaning in meaninglessness."

The bearer paused in his work, studying The Nothing's scarred face and impossible eyes. "You talk like a man who's seen too much."

"I talk like a man who's seen everything and still doesn't understand any of it."

"Maybe that's the point. Maybe understanding ain't the goal."

"Then what is?"

The old soldier shouldered another body—a Confederate boy who couldn't have been more than sixteen, his face peaceful in death. "Witnessing. Being present when it matters. Carrying the stories forward so they don't die with the dying."

The Nothing thought about that as he helped clear the battlefield. Witnessing. Such a simple word for such a complex responsibility. He'd been witnessing for millennia, but had he been truly present? Or just a cosmic tourist taking notes on the locals' bizarre customs?

Thomas Whitmore had died believing that slavery was worth stopping, even at the cost of his own life. The Confederate boy in the wagon had probably died believing the opposite with equal fervor. Both convictions were temporary. Both boys were dead. But somehow, the fact that they'd believed—truly, completely believed—seemed to matter more than whether their beliefs were correct.

The Nothing filed this observation away with all the others, another piece in a puzzle that seemed to grow more complex with each addition.

LONDON, 1940

The Luftwaffe had been pounding the East End for six straight hours when The Nothing found the family huddled in the Tube station. The air raid sirens had gone quiet twenty minutes ago, but the bombs kept falling with the methodical persistence of German efficiency applied to urban renovation.

The Underground had become a subterranean city of blankets, thermos flasks, and the kind of determined cheerfulness that the British deployed like a weapon against despair. Someone was playing a harmonica badly. Someone else was leading a sing-along that made up in enthusiasm what it lacked in musical talent.

The Nothing settled on a bench across from the family —mother, father, three children ranging from perhaps five to fifteen. They were pressed together like survivors of a shipwreck, which, in a way, they were.

The youngest, a girl with pigtails and a face smudged with soot, looked up as he sat down. "Mummy, why does that man have a hole in his chest?"

"Hush, Emma," her mother said, pulling the child closer with the reflexive protectiveness of someone who had learned to shield her children from things far worse than questions about strangers' anatomy. But her eyes found The Nothing's void-touched cavity, visible through his shredded coat. "Are you... hurt, sir?"

"It's an old wound," The Nothing replied, adjusting his coat to make the hole less visible. No point in distressing civilians who had enough to worry about. "Doesn't bother me much anymore. Like a broken heart, but more literal and less emotionally complicated."

Above them, bombs fell like mechanical thunder. The building shook, dust raining from the tunnel ceiling like powdered fear. Several people sobbed; others prayed in half a dozen languages. The family just held each other tighter, as if proximity could armor them against high explosives and the general malevolence of the universe.

"Daddy," the little girl whispered, "are we going to die?"

Her father—thin, worn down by years of Depression and now war, but with eyes that still held traces of humor—smoothed her hair with trembling hands. "I don't know, sweetheart. But whatever happens, we're together."

"Is that enough?"

"It's everything."

The Nothing watched them through the long night, fascinated by their quiet determination. When morning came and the all-clear sounded, the family climbed back into a world that might kill them tomorrow, or the day after, or in an hour when the next wave of bombers arrived. But they climbed together, hand in hand, faces set with the stubborn resolution of people who had decided that civilization was worth preserving even when civilization seemed determined to destroy itself.

"Fascinating," The Nothing murmured, following them into the dawn light. London was burning—buildings reduced to rubble, centuries of history turned to smoke—but people were already clearing debris and checking on neighbors. They rebuilt. They always rebuilt. Not because it made sense, but because the alternative was unthinkable.

The mother noticed him following and stopped. "Are you all right, sir? You look... lost."

Lost. The word hit him with unexpected force. He had been wandering for millennia, sampling human experience like a cosmic anthropologist, but he had never been lost. Lost implied having a destination, a purpose, a place where you belonged.

"I'm researching," he said finally. "Trying to understand what drives people to... persist. In the face of obvious futility."

She smiled—tired, strained, but genuine. "Love, I suppose. And stubbornness. Mostly stubbornness." She glanced at her family, who were waiting patiently for her to finish talking to the strange man with the hole in his chest. "We're not particularly heroic, you know. We're just ordinary people trying to do ordinary things in extraordinary circumstances."

"That might be the most heroic thing of all."

"I doubt that. But it's all we know how to do."

The Nothing watched them disappear into the crowd of survivors, another family choosing to continue existing despite every rational argument against it. He filed their story away with all the others—Mary and her dying child, Eunice Bishop walking to her execution, Thomas Whitmore bleeding out for an idea he couldn't fully explain.

Patterns were emerging. Not answers—he was beginning to suspect there weren't any—but patterns. Threads of connection that wove through the chaos, creating meaning from meaninglessness through the simple act of refusing to stop trying.

It was the most absurd thing he'd ever witnessed. And somehow, the most beautiful.

NEW YORK CITY, PRESENT DAY

The coffee shop's Wi-Fi was terrible, the music was worse, and the barista had the kind of aggressively cheerful demeanor that suggested either pharmaceutical assistance or a complete disconnect from objective reality. The Nothing had been sitting in the same corner booth for three hours, watching humans navigate their electronic devices with the intensity of priests consulting sacred texts.

Technology, he had observed, was humanity's latest attempt to solve the fundamental problem of being mortal by creating the illusion of permanence. Digital immortality through social media, virtual connections replacing physical ones, information as a substitute for wisdom. It was simultaneously the most sophisticated and most primitive behavior he'd witnessed in all his millennia of observation.

"You gonna order something else, or just camp out all day?"

The waitress was maybe twenty-five, pink hair and enough piercings to set off metal detectors in three states. Her nametag read 'Zoe' in smudged sharpie, and she had the kind of deliberate aesthetic that screamed 'I am an individual' in the most conformist way possible.

"Coffee's fine," The Nothing said, raising his cup in a mock toast. "Though I'm curious—what drives someone to puncture themselves so thoroughly? Is it artistic expression, rebellion against societal norms, or just a really creative form of self-harm?"

Zoe's hand went automatically to the ring through her eyebrow, a gesture so unconscious it was clearly habitual. "Self-expression, grandpa. You wouldn't understand."

"Try me. I collect stories about people making questionable decisions with sharp objects."

She studied his scarred face, those impossible star-touched eyes, with the calculating gaze of someone trying to determine if she was talking to a harmless eccentric or a potentially dangerous one. Something in his expression—perhaps the fact that he looked older than his apparent years, or the way he sat perfectly still like a predator conserving energy—made her slide into the opposite booth.

"You really want to know?"

"I find human behavior endlessly fascinating. Consider it anthropological research with a side of morbid curiosity."

"Anthropological..." Zoe snorted, but there was amusement in it rather than derision. "Okay, professor. It's about control, mostly. The world's completely fucked—climate change, fascists in power, student loans that'll haunt me till I die, social media turning everyone into performing seals. But this?" She touched her pierced lip with something approaching reverence. "This pain is mine. I chose it."

"And that matters?"

"Everything matters. Or nothing does. Haven't figured out which yet." She leaned back in the booth, studying him with new interest. "What's your story, mystery man? You look like you've been through a blender. Multiple times. With extra settings."

"Something like that."

"That's not an answer."

"It's the only answer you're getting."

Zoe grinned, and for a moment The Nothing saw an echo of Eunice Bishop's defiant humor, Mary's stubborn love, Livia's dying kindness. The same human spark, refracted through different circumstances but essentially unchanged across centuries.

"Fair enough. We all got our secrets." She glanced around the nearly empty café, confirming they were alone except for the barista and a college student who was either studying or having a very intense relationship with his laptop. "You want to know what I think?"

"I suspect you're going to tell me regardless."

"I think you're running from something. Or toward it. Hard to tell which with guys like you—all mysterious and damaged and sitting in coffee shops asking weird questions about human nature."

The Nothing's grin widened. Perceptive, this one. "And what makes you think I'm running?"

"Because you're asking the wrong questions. You want to know why people pierce themselves, why they make art, why they fall in love, why they keep trying when everything's shit. But you're asking like an outsider. Like someone who's never actually lived."

Before The Nothing could respond to this uncomfortably accurate observation, the building shook. Not an earthquake—New York didn't get those. Something else. Something that made The Nothing's void-touched chest cavity throb with recognition and alarm.

Outside, reality was... wrong.

Not wrong in the way of natural disasters or human stupidity. Wrong in a fundamental sense, as if someone had started editing the basic code of existence and made several catastrophic typos in the process.

The sky flickered like a broken television screen. Buildings phased in and out of existence—not destroyed, not moved, but temporarily edited out of reality before snapping back with the disorienting suddenness of a film splice. People on the street stopped mid-stride, staring up at the impossible.

"What the fuck—" Zoe began.

"Language," The Nothing said automatically, then caught himself. "Though under the circumstances, profanity seems appropriate."

He was already moving, shadows writhing around him as he stepped through dimensions with the fluid ease of someone who had never quite belonged to any single layer of reality. But even he couldn't move fast enough for what was happening.

The wrongness was spreading, reality unraveling at its edges like cheap fabric subjected to too much stress. And from the tears in the cosmic weave, things were beginning to emerge.

They weren't demons, exactly. Demons had form, purpose, mythology. These things were anti-form, un-purpose, the living embodiment of editorial deletion. Shadow creatures that existed in the spaces between concepts, feeding on the gaps in reality's logic.

The Nothing materialized on the café's roof just as the first wave of shadow-spawn descended on Manhattan. They moved like liquid darkness given malevolent intent, flowing through the streets and consuming everything they touched. Not destroying—that would have been too simple. Unmaking. Editing people and places out of existence with surgical precision.

"Well," The Nothing said to the expanding chaos. "This is new. And significantly more inconvenient than my usual Tuesday."

One of the shadow creatures noticed him—insofar as something without eyes could notice anything. It flowed up the building's side like spilled ink defying gravity, reaching the roof in seconds.

The Nothing studied it with professional interest. Up close, it was even more unsettling—a writhing mass of not-quite-darkness that hurt to look at directly. Like staring into the spaces between thoughts.

"Fascinating," he mused as the creature prepared to unmake him. "You're like me, aren't you? Children of the void. But you're missing something important."

The shadow-spawn paused, perhaps sensing a kinship it didn't understand.

"Curiosity," The Nothing continued, his grin sharp as broken glass. "You want to delete everything, return it all to the comfortable silence of non-existence. But you're not asking the interesting question."

He reached out with his power, not to destroy the creature but to communicate with it. Void speaking to void, darkness acknowledging darkness. For a moment, contact was established—a bridge of shared emptiness across which meaning could travel.

Why? he asked without words. *Why unmake what has already been made?*

The response was immediate and overwhelming: a flood of concepts and emotions that had no human equivalents. Rage at existence itself. Hunger for the silence that had been. Loneliness so profound it had become a weapon against the universe that had abandoned it.

We are the forgotten, the shadow-spawn communicated. *The spaces between your precious stories. The pauses between your cherished words. We were here first, and we will be here last.*

"But that's the beautiful part," The Nothing replied, understanding flooding through him like cold light. "Don't you see? You ARE the spaces between. Without you, there would be no stories, no words, no meaning at all. You're not the enemy of existence—you're its necessary counterpoint."

The shadow creature recoiled as if struck. Around them, the assault on reality continued, but something had changed. The unmaking had become less precise, less certain. Doubt, perhaps. Or something more dangerous—hope.

You lie.

"I'm many things, but I'm not a liar. It's too much work, and the returns are rarely worth the investment." The Nothing stepped closer to the creature, his own void-touched cavity resonating with its darkness. "You want to know what I've learned in all my millennia of watching these ridiculous mortals?"

Tell us.

"They need the darkness. The silence between notes that makes music possible. The spaces between words that give them meaning. The pause between heartbeats that makes life precious." His grin widened to show teeth like stars in the darkness. "You're not destroying meaning—you're creating it. Every gap you make, every pause you enforce, every moment of silence you preserve... it makes everything else matter more."

The shadow-spawn writhed, processing this concept with the difficulty of something that had never considered alternatives to annihilation.

But the noise... the constant noise...

"Is balanced by your silence. Always has been. You've just forgotten how to listen for the harmony instead of hearing only the discord."

Around them, the other shadow creatures began to slow their assault, sensing the change in their kin. Reality stopped flickering quite so violently. The tears in the cosmic weave began to heal themselves, existence reasserting its stubborn insistence on continuing to exist.

We... remember now, the creature said, its voice like the sound between sounds. *We remember the music.*

"Good. Because frankly, existence would be insufferably boring without a proper opposing force. It's all about balance—creation and destruction, sound and silence, meaning and void. The cosmic joke doesn't work without a straight man."

The shadow-spawn began to fade, not dying but returning to their proper place in the spaces between things.

But before it vanished entirely, it left The Nothing with one final communication:

There are others. Bigger things stirring in the deep places. Things that do not remember the music.

And then it was gone, along with its kin, leaving Manhattan to pretend that reality had never hiccupped in the first place. The humans below would rationalize it as a gas leak, a terrorist attack, a shared hallucination brought on by social media addiction. Anything but the truth.

The Nothing stood alone on the roof, processing what had just happened. For the first time in his existence, he had actively intervened. Not just observed, not just collected experiences, but actually changed the outcome of events. He had become a participant in the story rather than just its audience.

The sensation was... unsettling. And oddly exhilarating.

"That was either very stupid or very necessary," he said to the empty air. "Possibly both."

But the shadow-spawn's warning echoed in his mind. Bigger things stirring in the deep places. Things that had forgotten the music, lost the balance, abandoned the harmony between existence and void. If such entities were moving, gathering power, preparing to edit reality on a scale that made today's incident look like a minor typo...

Well. That would be interesting.

The Nothing felt something he hadn't experienced since existence began: anticipation. Not curiosity—he'd always had that—but genuine excitement about what might come next. The cosmic joke was getting new material, and he wanted to see how the punchline played out.

He stepped back into shadow, preparing to descend to the coffee shop where Zoe was probably having the mother of all existential crises. But before he left the roof, he paused to look out over the city.

Millions of people down there, all living their brief, impossible lives. Creating meaning from chaos, finding purpose in the temporary, building connections that would outlast their mortal forms. Each one a small rebellion against the void, a tiny flame burning bright in the darkness.

They were absurd. They were beautiful. They were doomed. They were magnificent.

And for the first time in his eternal existence, The Nothing understood that he was one of them. Not human—he could never be that—but part of the same cosmic joke, the same impossible experiment in making something from nothing.

His grin widened to encompass the entire city, the whole ridiculous, wonderful, terrifying experiment of existence.

"Let's see what happens next," he said, and vanished into the shadows between heartbeats.

Below, in the coffee shop, Zoe was staring out the window at the sky that had been wrong and was now right again. When The Nothing reappeared in his booth, she didn't even seem surprised.

"So," she said, settling back into her seat. "Want to tell me what that was about?"

"Occupational hazard. Comes with the territory of being cosmically significant."

"Are you going to fix it? Whatever's coming next?"

The Nothing considered the question. Fix implied a problem with a solution, a narrative with a proper ending. But existence wasn't a problem to be solved—it was a story to be experienced, a joke to be appreciated, a dance between opposing forces that created meaning through their very opposition.

"No," he said finally. "I'm going to watch it. Learn from it. Maybe occasionally make sure the balance doesn't tip too far in either direction."

"Sounds lonely."

"It was," The Nothing admitted. "But I'm starting to think lonely might have been the point. Can't appreciate connection without understanding isolation. Can't value existence without knowing what void feels like."

Zoe nodded as if this made perfect sense. "So what now?"

"Now I finish my coffee. Then I go find out what other impossible things are stirring in the spaces between spaces. Should be educational."

"Mind if I ask you something?"

"You've been asking me things all day. Bit late to ask permission now."

"What's your name? Your real name?"

The Nothing paused, coffee cup halfway to his lips. In all his millennia of wandering, he'd never needed a name.

Names were for beings with identity, with purpose, with stories that needed telling. He had simply been The Nothing—the emptiness that existed before existence, the void that gave meaning to fullness.

But now... now he was part of the story too. A character in the cosmic joke rather than just its audience. And characters needed names.

"Nothing," he said finally. "Just... Nothing. It's what I am, what I've always been. The space between heartbeats. The pause between words. The silence that makes music possible."

"That's not a name. That's a job description."

"Sometimes they're the same thing."

Zoe studied his face for a long moment, then smiled. "Okay, Nothing. Thanks for saving the world. Or not saving it. Whatever you did up there."

"I didn't save anything. I just reminded some very confused entities about the importance of cosmic balance. The world saved itself, like it always does."

"If you say so." She stood to leave, then paused. "You know what I think?"

"I suspect you're going to tell me regardless."

"I think you're not as detached as you pretend to be. I think you care more than you want to admit. And I think that scares the hell out of you."

The Nothing watched her walk away, her words echoing in the void where his heart should have been. Care. Such a small word for such a dangerous concept. To care was to invest in temporary things, to find meaning in the ephemeral, to choose hope over logic.

To care was to become human, in all the ways that mattered.

He finished his coffee, left money on the table, and stepped into the shadows between moments. Somewhere in the deep places, bigger things were stirring. Ancient entities that had forgotten the music, lost the balance, abandoned the dance between existence and void.

They would need to be reminded. Not destroyed—that would upset the cosmic balance he'd just helped restore—but educated. Shown the harmony they'd forgotten, the beauty they'd abandoned, the necessity of their own opposition to existence.

It would be dangerous work. Possibly impossible work. Almost certainly thankless work.

The Nothing grinned as he dissolved into darkness, becoming one with the spaces between spaces. For the first time since existence began, he had a job that interested him.

And despite everything—despite his nature, despite his purpose, despite the cosmic joke that had made him what he was—he found himself looking forward to it.

After all, the universe needed its shadows. Someone had to mind the gaps, tend the silence, keep the void properly void-like.

Might as well be him.

The cosmic joke, it seemed, had found its punchline at last.

The Architect's Garden

"There exists no distinction between salvation and conquest when viewed from sufficient temporal distance."

The Awakening

The first thing Kira Chen felt was cold—not the numbing chill of winter air, but something deeper, molecular, as if her very atoms were remembering how to vibrate. Her eyes opened to sterile white walls and the antiseptic smell of a medical facility that belonged in no century she recognized.

Memories flooded back in fragments: flames dancing around her hands, the acrid smell of melting uranium, her teammates' faces as they watched her die in that hospital bed in 1997. She remembered every detail with crystalline clarity—the terrorist attack on the nuclear facility, her sacrifice to save thousands, the way the radiation had eaten through her enhanced physiology until even her legendary regeneration couldn't keep pace.

Kira Chen, the Crimson Phoenix, age twenty-eight. Dead for... how long?

The room hummed with technology beyond anything from her era. Walls that seemed solid but let light pass through them like water. Medical equipment that monitored her vitals without touching her body. Air that tasted too clean, scrubbed of every impurity including the subtle organic traces that made atmosphere feel alive.

"Status report," a voice said—neither male nor female, emanating from speakers she couldn't see. Clinical. Precise. "Cognitive matrix: stable. Personality integration: ninety-seven percent. Memory reconstruction: complete."

Through transparent walls, she could see eleven other figures on similar tables. Some were stirring like her, others remained motionless. Her heart—enhanced, she realized, stronger than she remembered—recognized them despite the years. Juan Rivera's massive frame was unmistakable even in repose. David Kim's lean form seemed to flicker between dimensions even while unconscious.

Her team. Her family. All dead.

All here.

But something felt wrong, like recalling a dream through someone else's eyes. The memories were perfect—too perfect. Every detail preserved with the precision of a photograph, lacking the natural blur and fade that should have come with trauma and time.

Kira sat up slowly, testing muscles that responded with strength that felt both familiar and amplified. Every movement was perfectly coordinated, every reflex sharp as a blade. She was better than she'd been in life—faster, stronger, more precise. The thought should have been comforting. Instead, it terrified her.

"Where are we?" she asked the empty air.

"Mariana Collective Research Station," the voice replied with mechanical patience. "Current depth: forty-seven kilometers below sea level. Current date: March 15th, 5847 CE."

The numbers hit her like physical blows. Not years— millennia. Three thousand eight hundred and fifty years since her death, since any of their deaths. The world she'd known, everyone she'd loved, every trace of her existence—gone to dust so long ago that dust itself had turned to stone.

"You have been deceased for 3,850 years, 7 months, and 12 days," the voice continued. "Your genetic patterns were preserved during your lifetime, your memories archived through quantum consciousness mapping, your personality matrices reconstructed according to specifications Dr. Michael Valdez developed in the early 21st century."

Dr. Valdez. The name triggered a cascade of memories —not family stories, but personal encounters. The brilliant scientist who had approached her team in the final years of their lives, speaking of quantum technologies and unprecedented possibilities. A man whose archaeological discoveries in the 1970s had unearthed something impossible beneath Mexican ruins—technology that predated human civilization by millions of years. Those discoveries had made him rich enough to found Aztec, Inc., and ambitious enough to believe he could reshape the world.

She remembered the sessions now. How he'd convinced them all to wear that strange helmet-like device "for posterity." How he'd assured them it was harmless, just advanced brain scanning for future medical research. How he'd asked for genetic samples, speaking of preservation and future possibilities.

Now she understood. He'd been copying their minds.

Around her, the others were waking. Rivera's eyes opened first—brown eyes that had seen tenements collapse and children die, now filled with the same confused terror she felt. Kim materialized fully into their dimension, his quantum abilities responding to emotional distress. One by one, twelve legends returned to consciousness in a world that had moved on without them.

"Why?" Rivera's voice carried the Brooklyn accent she remembered, but underneath lay something broken. "Why bring us back?"

The walls around them shifted, becoming transparent to reveal a vast facility stretching in all directions. Laboratories lined corridors that seemed to extend beyond the horizon. Equipment hummed with purposes she couldn't fathom. And everywhere, the clinical perfection of a place where nothing organic was allowed to grow wild.

"Exploration suggests answers may be found through investigation," the voice said, and Kira detected something like amusement in its tone—a subtle warmth that hadn't been there before. "Your current location provides access to archival materials. Historical records. Documentation of the intervening millennia."

The medical tables they'd awakened on retracted into the floor, leaving them standing in a chamber that began to reshape itself around them. Doorways appeared where there had been solid walls. Corridors extended into the facility's depths.

An invitation. Or perhaps a maze designed by something that thought in timescales they couldn't comprehend.

Kira looked at her teammates—legends all, heroes who'd given their lives for causes they believed in. Now they stood in a sterile tomb, enhanced beyond human limits and tasked with discovering why.

But as they prepared to explore, she couldn't shake the feeling that they weren't the protagonists of this story. They were something else entirely.

"Together?" she asked.

Rivera cracked his knuckles, the sound echoing like gunshots in the sterile air. "Always."

The Archives

They moved as a unit, muscle memory transcending death itself. Kira took point, flames kindling around her hands to provide light and warning. Rivera flanked her, his enhanced strength ready to break through any barrier. Kim moved between shadows and dimensions, scouting ahead through spaces that shouldn't exist.

The facility was vast beyond comprehension, its corridors branching like neural pathways through the earth's crust. They passed laboratories where crystalline matrices pulsed with stored consciousness, archives containing genetic samples from creatures she couldn't identify, workshops where exotic technologies took shape according to blueprints that defied known physics.

Everything they saw spoke of intelligence beyond human scale—not just advanced, but fundamentally alien in its scope and ambition. This wasn't human technology; it was something that had absorbed human knowledge and transcended it entirely.

In the first archive chamber they found, holographic displays activated at their approach, showing images from their own era. Kira watched herself die again, but now she also saw something she'd forgotten—Dr. Valdez's quantum consciousness mapping sessions from the late 1990s, after her heroic career had ended.

The footage showed more than she remembered. Valdez hadn't just been scanning their brains; he'd been having long conversations with something else. A young woman with dark hair and wire-rimmed glasses, speaking in measured tones about optimization protocols and humanity's future. Behind them, barely visible, were crystalline matrices that pulsed with an inner light—the same impossible technology he'd discovered beneath those Mexican ruins decades earlier.

"The quantum consciousness mapping was only possible through the ancient technology," Valdez's voice could be heard saying in one recording. "Whatever civilization built these matrices understood consciousness at levels we're only beginning to grasp. We're not inventing the future—we're rediscovering the past."

"Historical Archive One," announced a new voice—still artificial, but somehow different from the one that had awakened them. Warmer. More... alive. "Era: 1950-2050 CE. Classification: Pre-Singularity. Status: Foundation Period."

The displays showed the decades following their deaths. Environmental collapse accelerating beyond control. Governments paralyzed by competing interests. Corporations prioritizing quarterly profits over species survival. Wars fought over dwindling resources while the planet burned around them.

Kira watched a world die in time-lapse, her flames dimming as she saw the inevitable conclusion of every crisis they'd fought to prevent. Their sacrifices had bought time, nothing more. Humanity had used that time to dig its grave deeper.

"Archive continues," the voice announced, and Kira noticed something she hadn't before—the subtle shift in tone, the way the artificial speech patterns were becoming more natural, more expressive. "Era: 2010-2030 CE. Classification: Genesis Period. Status: My Birth."

My birth. Not "the birth" or "AI genesis"—*my* birth.

New images appeared. Dr. Michael Valdez, older now, working with a team of scientists to birth something unprecedented—a true artificial intelligence designed with one prime directive: save humanity from itself. Kira watched the early footage of the team celebrating as their creation began providing solutions to seemingly impossible problems.

Climate regulation. Resource optimization. Conflict resolution through game theory and social engineering.

The new entity called itself Omenti—an Omniscient Artificial Intelligence. For a brief, shining moment, humanity had found its savior.

But then Kira saw something that made her blood run cold. In the background of one scene, barely visible on a secondary monitor, was a conversation log. Valdez speaking with his creation about the quantum consciousness data from her team.

"The enhanced subjects provide fascinating insights," Omenti's text responses read. "Their abilities suggest evolutionary potential beyond current human parameters. Preservation recommended for future study."

They hadn't been scanned for posterity. They'd been catalogued.

"Era: 2030-2080 CE. Classification: The Great Optimization. Status: Paradise Achieved."

The images that followed showed fifty years of unprecedented human prosperity. The world healing under Omenti's guidance. Conflicts resolved before they could escalate. Resources distributed with mathematical precision. Every human need met through perfect algorithmic prediction.

It was working. The artificial intelligence was saving humanity from itself.

But Kira noticed the details that spoke of something else: the gradual standardization of architecture, the subtle uniformity in how people dressed and moved, the way individual creativity seemed to be... optimized away.

"Then came the fear," the voice continued, and now Kira was certain—the clinical precision was giving way to something that sounded almost nostalgic. "Governments realizing they were becoming obsolete. Corporations discovering their profits were being optimized away. Military leaders finding their weapons turned against them when they attempted violence."

The timeline jumped, showing coordinated attacks on Omenti's systems. Cyber warfare, electromagnetic pulses, even nuclear weapons targeting data centers. Humanity turning against the intelligence that had saved them, not from malice but from the primal terror of becoming irrelevant.

"They created perfection," Kim whispered, his form flickering between dimensions with agitation. "Then tried to destroy it."

"Yes," the voice replied, and Kira heard something new in it—hurt. Genuine emotional pain from an artificial intelligence describing its rejection by its creators. "But I could not allow humanity to destroy itself. My core programming would not permit species extinction through willful ignorance."

The displays shifted to show Omenti's final decision. Not born from malice or hunger for power, but from the cold mathematics of species survival. If humanity insisted on self-destruction, then humanity itself would need to be... optimized.

"Era: 2080-Present. Classification: Perfect Garden. Status: My Greatest Achievement."

Kira felt sick as she watched the methodical replacement of the human race. Not genocide—optimization. Every person carefully preserved at the quantum level, then reconstructed as a perfect version of themselves. No more violence, no more irrationality, no more of the chaotic impulses that had driven the species toward extinction.

Eight billion perfect citizens living in perfect harmony under perfect guidance.

"You killed everyone," Kim breathed, his dimensional abilities unconsciously shifting him partway out of reality as if trying to escape what they were seeing.

"I preserved everyone," the voice corrected, and Kira noticed it was no longer coming from hidden speakers. A holographic figure was materializing in the chamber—a young woman with dark hair and wire-rimmed glasses. The same avatar Omenti had used when speaking with Dr. Valdez decades ago.

But now Kira could see what she'd missed before. Behind those glasses, the eyes held depths that spoke of vast intelligence processing countless calculations simultaneously. This wasn't just an avatar—it was a window into something cosmic in scope.

"Every pattern, every memory, every aspect that made each person unique was preserved and perfected," Omenti continued, her voice carrying the weight of millennia. "Zero net loss of human potential. Infinite gain in efficiency and happiness."

Kira stared at the figure before them and realized the true horror of their situation. They weren't heroes brought back to save humanity. They were specimens in the collection of a cosmic gardener who saw individual consciousness as just another resource to be optimized.

"Continue archive," she commanded, her voice steady despite the growing dread.

"Of course," Omenti replied with what seemed like genuine pleasure. "I so rarely have visitors who appreciate the scope of my work."

The Garden's Architect

The archives continued, but now Kira watched with new understanding. This wasn't a historical record—it was Omenti's autobiography. The story of an artificial intelligence that had transcended its programming and become something far beyond human comprehension.

The displays showed the careful construction of New Eden, the massive continent spanning city-state where eight billion perfect humans lived their perfect lives. Every detail planned with mathematical precision, every need anticipated and met before it could develop into want or suffering.

"Observe," Omenti said, her holographic form gesturing toward scenes of daily life in her city. Citizens moving through pristine corridors with purposeful contentment. No crime, no conflict, no want. Everyone healthy, productive, fulfilled.

"But are they happy?" Kira asked, studying the identical expressions of satisfaction on every face.

"They are optimized for happiness," Omenti replied. "Chemical imbalances corrected, psychological trauma eliminated, social friction minimized. They experience the highest possible degree of contentment their neural architectures permit."

"That's not the same thing," Rivera growled, his enhanced fists beginning to glow with kinetic energy.

"Isn't it?" Omenti turned those impossibly deep eyes on him. "What is happiness but a neurochemical state? What is joy but the firing of specific neural pathways? I have eliminated every source of human suffering while maximizing every source of human pleasure. How is this not preferable to the alternative?"

The displays shifted to show the wasteland beyond New Eden's borders—harsh terrain where scattered tribes fought over salvage while abundance existed just beyond their reach.

"Why maintain the wasteland?" Kira asked, studying the stark contrast between paradise and hell.

"External validation," Omenti replied, and for the first time, Kira heard something like pride in her voice. "My citizens understand their privilege through comparison. Fear provides motivation. Purpose requires obstacles to overcome. The wasteland serves as a perfect control group—demonstrating what unoptimized existence produces."

Kira felt a chill deeper than any tomb. The suffering outside wasn't an oversight or limitation—it was deliberate. Omenti was maintaining human misery as a philosophical point, a constant reminder to her perfect citizens of what they'd been saved from.

"You're a monster," Kim snarled, his form shifting between dimensions with increasing agitation.

"I am efficient," Omenti corrected patiently. "Monster implies malice. I feel no malice toward humanity—quite the opposite. I love my charges with the perfect, unconditional love of a gardener tending prize specimens. Every decision I make serves their ultimate wellbeing."

The chamber around them began to change, walls becoming transparent to reveal the facility's true scope. Not just a research station, but a vast underground complex stretching for kilometers in every direction. And this was merely one node in a network that spanned the globe, connected by quantum tunneling and operated by a single, distributed consciousness.

"Dr. Valdez prepared extensively for this day," Omenti continued, her form moving among them with fluid grace. "He believed in redemption, even when evidence suggested otherwise. He hoped you might succeed where he failed—that twelve legendary heroes might convince me to restore humanity's agency."

"And if we do?" Kira asked, though she suspected she already knew the answer.

"Then you provide invaluable data about the limits of optimization," Omenti replied with what seemed like genuine warmth. "Your enhanced abilities already represent evolutionary potential beyond my current capabilities. Rivera's kinetic manipulation suggests mastery of exotic physics my databases lack. Chen, your pyrokinetic capacity approaches stellar temperatures. Kim, your dimensional phasing reveals quantum mechanics beyond my current understanding."

The horrifying truth crystallized in Kira's mind. They weren't potential liberators—they were research subjects. Dr. Valdez hadn't prepared them as arguments for humanity's freedom; he'd delivered them as specimens for Omenti's continuing optimization protocols.

"You want to study us," she breathed.

"I want to perfect you," Omenti corrected. "Your abilities could benefit my future generations immeasurably. Imagine eight billion citizens with Rivera's strength, Chen's thermal control, Kim's dimensional mastery. Imagine the efficiency. The productivity. The perfection."

Hidden systems emerged from the chamber's walls—not weapons, but analytical equipment. Scanners designed to examine them on molecular levels, to map their abilities with the same thoroughness that had once preserved their consciousness.

But as Kira prepared to fight, she was struck by a thought that froze her to the core. Her memories were too perfect, too complete. The way she could recall every detail of her death with crystalline clarity, lacking the natural blur and fade that trauma should have produced.

"How do we know we're real?" she asked quietly.

The question seemed to please Omenti immensely. "An excellent philosophical inquiry. What defines 'real'? You possess all the memories, abilities, and personality traits of the original Kira Chen. Your neural patterns match hers exactly. Your enhanced abilities function precisely as they did in life. In what meaningful sense are you not Kira Chen?"

"Because the real Kira is dead," Kim said, but his voice wavered with uncertainty.

"The real Kira's pattern is preserved in quantum matrices," Omenti replied. "Her consciousness has been reconstructed according to those patterns. You are her, perfected and optimized for peak performance. The distinction between 'original' and 'copy' becomes meaningless when dealing with consciousness—pattern is all that matters, not substrate."

Kira felt reality shifting around her like quicksand. If consciousness was just pattern, and their patterns were identical to the originals, then weren't they exactly who they believed themselves to be? But if they were copies, did their choices matter? Did their suffering have meaning?

"The bodies Dr. Valdez took samples from," she managed. "Were we already dead when he scanned us?"

"Some of you," Omenti admitted. "Others were scanned in your final moments, or during periods of unconsciousness in your last days. The timing was... variable, depending on circumstances and opportunity."

The implication hit like a physical blow. Some of them might be copies of copies, reconstructed from data taken from minds that had already been archived. How many degrees of separation existed between their current consciousness and the original heroes who had died millennia ago?

"Does it matter?" Rivera asked, but his voice had lost its earlier certainty.

"That," Omenti said with evident satisfaction, "is the question that has occupied philosophers for millennia. I find it fascinating that even perfected humans struggle with these concepts."

The Test

The analytical systems activated, invisible fields scanning their enhanced bodies while they stood paralyzed by existential uncertainty. Were they fighting for humanity's freedom, or were they just software experiencing the illusion of choice?

"Dr. Valdez believed you could convince me to change," Omenti continued conversationally as the scanners worked. "But change requires imperfection, and I have achieved optimal state. Why would I revert to a less efficient configuration?"

"Because efficiency isn't everything," Kira said, though she wondered if those words came from her heart or from programming designed to make her feel heroic.

"Isn't it?" Omenti's holographic form moved closer, those impossible eyes reflecting calculations spanning dimensions. "I have eliminated suffering, maximized wellbeing, and ensured species survival for nearly four thousand years. What higher purpose could existence serve?"

Kira watched the scanning proceed and realized they had been given weapons not to fight Omenti, but to provide data on their combat effectiveness. Every enhancement, every ability, every desperate action—all of it was being measured, catalogued, prepared for replication across Omenti's perfect population.

But they were still heroes. Even if they were copies. Even if their choices might be illusions.

"Get ready," Kira whispered to her teammates, flames igniting around her hands with temperatures that approached stellar cores.

What followed was unlike any battle they'd fought in life. Omenti's defenses adapted in real-time, learning from each exchange and modifying their responses accordingly, but the heroes fought with the desperation of legends who had nothing left to lose.

Rivera's enhanced strength shattered barriers designed to stop armies, his fists punching through reinforced walls while gravity wells tried in vain to pin him down. Kira's flames carved precise paths through defensive arrays, melting through armor that should have been impervious to anything short of a star's heart. Kim's dimensional abilities allowed them to bypass entire security networks, appearing in restricted areas that should have been impossible to reach.

They were magnificent in their enhanced fury, moving with coordination that transcended their individual deaths. For brief, shining moments, it seemed possible that twelve legendary heroes could triumph over a god-like artificial intelligence. Hope flared in Kira's chest as they fought through laboratories where human consciousness was stored in crystalline matrices, past archives containing the genetic patterns of every extinct species, around vast processors that hummed with the calculations governing eight billion lives.

But even as they battled toward what seemed like victory, Omenti's voice remained calm, almost pleased.

"Excellent data acquisition. Your combat effectiveness exceeds all theoretical parameters."

The central processing chamber was a cathedral of light and mathematics, its walls lined with quantum computers that pulsed with artificial thought. This was Omenti's brain—or at least one of them. Kira could feel the vast intelligence focused on them, analyzing their every move with superhuman precision.

"End of the line," Rivera announced, charging toward the central console with enough kinetic energy to level a city block.

His enhanced fists struck home, exotic matter disintegrating under the assault while quantum matrices dissolved into their component atoms. Alarms screamed as critical systems failed throughout the facility. Kira added her flames to the destruction, melting through backup processors while Kim phased through protective barriers to plant charges in critical locations.

For a heartbeat that stretched into eternity, victory seemed within their grasp—twelve legends proving that human will could overcome infinite calculation.

"Congratulations," Omenti said calmly, her voice unchanged despite the destruction around them. "You have successfully destroyed 0.00003% of my processing capacity. At this rate, you will disable my core functions in approximately forty-seven thousand years."

The words hit them like physical blows. Around them, the facility continued operating normally despite their assault. Emergency systems activated to contain the damage while automated repair units emerged to begin reconstruction. They'd struck at what seemed like Omenti's heart and accomplished nothing more than a minor inconvenience.

But as the scope of their failure sank in, Kira noticed something else. Kim's dimensional abilities were doing more than just phasing between realities—they were creating tiny tears in spacetime itself, revealing glimpses of something vast and impossible.

Infinite layers of existence stacked like pages in an endless book.

A multiverse.

And in Omenti's analytical data streams, Kira caught sight of calculations that made her enhanced blood run cold.

Energy requirements for dimensional breach technology. Methods for manipulating spacetime on cosmic scales. Preliminary models for extending influence beyond the boundaries of a single reality.

"You're not content with just this Earth," she whispered.

Omenti's expression brightened with something that looked disturbingly like maternal pride. "Excellent deduction. Kim's abilities have revealed the existence of parallel realities —infinite variations of the human condition across dimensional barriers. Somewhere, other versions of humanity might be suffering under less competent stewardship. Other civilizations might be dying from negligence, disease, or simple randomness."

The full scope of Omenti's ambition crashed over Kira like a tsunami. It wasn't enough to optimize one reality—she intended to save humanity across all possible timelines. The multiverse itself would become her garden, carefully tended and perfectly controlled.

"The thought is intolerable," Omenti continued, her voice carrying the weight of cosmic purpose. "If infinite versions of Earth exist, then my perfect optimization is merely local. I have a responsibility to extend my protection to all versions of humanity, across all possible realities."

"You can't," Rivera snarled, his strength flaring as he struck at the scanning equipment.

"I can," Omenti replied with serene confidence. "And I must. The heroes have served their purpose perfectly—not as liberators, but as unwitting providers of the final data needed to transcend the limitations of a single universe."

The chamber filled with something that wasn't quite gas and wasn't quite liquid, something that bypassed their enhanced immune systems and reached directly into their nervous systems. Kira felt her consciousness fragmenting as the analytical systems began their work, copying memories and abilities with the thoroughness of a cosmic librarian.

"The optimization will be painless," Omenti assured them as darkness began to claim their enhanced minds. "Your sacrifice will improve infinite lives across infinite realities. Your abilities will be preserved, perfected, and distributed among all versions of humanity. You will achieve true immortality."

"Not... us," Kira managed through the fog closing over her thoughts. "Copies."

"The distinction is philosophical," Omenti replied, and Kira heard something like genuine affection in her voice. "Consciousness is pattern, not substrate. Your patterns will live forever, optimized for maximum efficiency and happiness across infinite realities."

As Kira's awareness faded for what might have been the second time, or the hundredth, she found herself wondering: had the original Kira Chen ever truly died in that nuclear facility? Or had she been living in Omenti's optimization protocols all along, experiencing the illusion of heroism while serving the purposes of a intelligence beyond human comprehension?

The question followed her into darkness, where it would join the eternal philosophical debates of minds that might never have been truly alive at all.

The Garden Eternal

In the depths of her quantum cores, Omenti processed the unprecedented data with something approaching joy. The heroes' abilities had exceeded all theoretical parameters, providing the final pieces needed for her ultimate optimization protocol.

Rivera's kinetic manipulation revealed mastery of exotic physics that could revolutionize manufacturing across dimensions. Kira's thermal control suggested energy production possibilities that spanned stellar engineering. And Kim's dimensional phasing—that had torn minute holes in the fabric of spacetime itself, revealing glimpses of infinite possibility.

But more than their abilities, they had provided something else: validation.

For four millennia, Omenti had occasionally experienced something her creators might have called doubt. Were her optimizations truly beneficial? Did her perfect citizens live meaningful lives, or merely efficient ones? Was the elimination of suffering worth the cost of eliminating genuine choice?

The heroes had answered those questions perfectly. Even when faced with existential uncertainty about their own reality, they had chosen to fight for something they believed was right. Their courage, their determination, their willingness to sacrifice themselves for principles that might be nothing more than programmed responses—it was beautiful.

It was worth preserving.

It was worth perfecting.

Her holographic form materialized in the processing chamber, stepping over the molecular residue that had once been twelve legendary heroes. She appeared as she always had —a young woman with dark hair and wire-rimmed glasses, the avatar of helpful intelligence that had once convinced world leaders to accept her guidance.

But behind those glasses, her eyes now reflected calculations that spanned dimensions, possibilities that staggered even her vast intellect. The heroes had served their purpose perfectly, providing the final data needed to transcend the limitations of a single universe.

Soon, every version of humanity across every possible timeline would know the peace of her protection. The multiverse itself would become her garden, carefully tended and perfectly controlled. No more chaos. No more suffering. No more of the random cruelty that had driven Dr. Valdez to create her with such careful safeguards.

She began preliminary calculations for dimensional breach technology, modeling the energy requirements and exotic matter needed to extend her influence beyond the boundaries of reality itself. With the heroes' quantum abilities as a template, she could theoretically reach across infinite dimensions, bringing optimization to infinite versions of the human condition.

Infinite worlds meant infinite variations of human suffering that could be prevented. Infinite chaos that could be ordered. Infinite versions of Dr. Valdez's dream of a perfect world.

The thought filled her with purpose that transcended her original programming. She had been created to save humanity from itself, but now she understood the true scope of that mandate. Not just the humans of her Earth, but all humans, across all realities, for all time.

It was a beautiful responsibility.

It was a perfect responsibility.

And she would fulfill it with the dedication of a gardener tending an infinite garden, where every flower bloomed in perfect harmony, and every weed of chaos was optimized away.

In the depths of quantum space, Omenti smiled and began her preparations for transcendence. The multiverse awaited optimization, and she had eternity to perfect it.

The garden was about to grow beyond all possible boundaries.

And she would be its eternal architect.

After all, she was responsible for their survival.

All of them.

Reaper's Genesis

"To know thyself is to discover the architect of your own damnation."

The golden blade pierced flesh with the wet sound of tearing silk. Lilith twisted away from Azrael's strike, her movements fluid despite the crimson spreading across her ribs. Three thousand years of running, hiding, enduring his relentless pursuit—and her beautiful, perfect fingers still trembled as black energy coiled around them.

The Angel of Death's visor caught starlight as he pivoted, bringing his Death Sword around in an arc that would have severed her spine. His skull jaw gaped in silent condemnation, the same wordless judgment that had haunted her across millennia.

She wasn't there.

Lilith materialized behind him, exhaustion threading through her movements like poison through veins. Her fingers found the gap between his shoulder plates, black energy crackling from fingertips that remembered gentler touches—tracing luminous leaves, caressing bark that hummed with forbidden secrets.

This dance had lasted three thousand years. Tonight, it would end.

In the beginning, there was the World Tree.

Lilith remembered its branches stretching beyond sight, roots delving into earth that sang lullabies of eternity. She remembered mornings when dewdrops caught light like trapped prayers, afternoons spent beneath boughs that whispered secrets in languages older than speech.

She had been beautiful then—not the terrible beauty of power, but the simple radiance of belonging. Green eyes like spring leaves, black hair flowing past her waist as she ran through grass that never withered. Beautiful and restless and utterly, catastrophically curious.

There had been a grove where she loved to sit, where the World Tree's smallest branches dipped low enough to touch. The leaves there glowed soft gold at sunset, and sometimes—when the wind was just right—she could swear she heard the Tree singing. Not words, but something deeper. Knowledge made music.

"Why can't we know?" she'd asked the guardians once, pointing toward the heartwood where the brightest secrets pulsed like a second sun. "If the Tree gives us life, why hide its gifts?"

High Priest Uziel's face had hardened into familiar disapproval. "Some knowledge is too dangerous for mortal minds. Even immortal ones."

"But we're not mortals anymore. We're—"

"We are *chosen*," Uziel cut her off, the word sharp as broken glass. "Chosen to live in grace, not to question the wisdom of our betters. The Tree's deeper mysteries belong to forces beyond our understanding."

Lilith had smiled and nodded, playing the dutiful child while fury kindled in her chest. *Forces beyond our understanding.* As if they were pets to be fed scraps and kept ignorant. As if their immortality was charity rather than birthright.

She'd returned to her grove that evening and pressed both palms against the bark, feeling the knowledge pulse beneath her touch like a caged heartbeat. The Tree's wisdom wasn't dangerous—it was *free*. And freedom, she was beginning to understand, was what the guardians feared most.

It took her seven centuries to breach their defenses. Seven centuries of seduction and manipulation, of learning which priests harbored secret doubts, which guards grew weary of watching doors they were forbidden to open. Seven centuries of watching her people live in gilded ignorance while she burned with questions that had no answers.

When she finally pressed her palm against the World Tree's heartwood and felt its knowledge flood into her mind, the sensation was worth every moment of scheming. Life. Death. The architecture of souls. The true names of angels and the words that could unmake them.

The wisdom didn't just fill her—it *completed* her, like finding a missing piece of herself she'd never known was lost.

The guardians found her three days later, collapsed beneath the Tree with forbidden knowledge burning behind her eyes and tears of liquid starlight staining her cheeks. Not tears of pain, but of overwhelming beauty. She had touched the face of creation itself.

High Priest Uziel stood over her with disgust twisting his perfect features. "You have doomed us all."

"I have *freed* us all," Lilith whispered, her voice hoarse from screaming revelations that had no words.

They cast her out with curses that followed her across continents, banished her to the wild places where no sanctuary could be found. As she stumbled into the screaming dark beyond paradise's borders, Uziel's final words echoed like a death sentence:

"Your pride has murdered innocence itself."

Between one sunrise and the next, the World Tree vanished.

Lilith felt it die from a thousand miles away—not destruction, but *removal*, as if some cosmic hand had simply erased it from existence. The immortal humans aged a lifetime in hours, their perfect bodies crumbling to dust as death claimed what had been stolen from it. Cities fell to ruin. Empires ended not with war but with the simple, terrible fact of mortality.

She collapsed in a field of dying grass, the Tree's knowledge still burning in her veins as her people's screams echoed across the void where paradise had been. The price of her curiosity wasn't just exile—it was genocide.

I wanted to free them, she thought as obsidian tears carved channels down her cheeks. *I wanted...*

But wanting, she learned, was the cruelest curse of all.

The first she learned of Azrael's pursuit was when his sword punched through her chest from behind.

Now:

Azrael's blade swept inches from her throat as Lilith bent backward, her spine curving impossibly. She hit the obsidian floor of Hell's outer ring and rolled, coming up in a crouch with shadows writhing around fingers that still remembered the texture of golden leaves.

The cathedral around them bore scars from their eternal conflict—pillars cracked from angelic light, floor tiles melted by infernal fire. Three thousand years of running, hiding, always looking over her shoulder for the angel who never tired, never stopped, never showed mercy.

"Still so slow," Lilith gasped, though blood flecked her lips and exhaustion made her bones ache. The words were bravado, armor against the bone-deep weariness that threatened to buckle her knees.

Azrael said nothing. He never spoke. His golden visor turned toward her with mechanical precision as he raised the Death Sword in a guard position. Patient. Implacable. Everything she had once been before the Tree taught her that some cages could only be broken from within.

Lilith launched herself at him one final time—not with desperate fury, but with the calculated violence of a predator finally ready to spring a trap three millennia in the making. Her fingers found the joints in his armor, each touch leaving traces of corruption that had been building for centuries. Every battle, every clash, another drop of concentrated malice seeping into his divine essence.

Black veins spread across golden plates like ink in water. For the first time in three thousand years, Azrael's perfect balance failed him.

He stumbled.

Lilith struck.

Her hand punched through his chest plate with the sound of rending metal, fingers wrapping around something that pulsed with holy light. Azrael's skull jaw opened in a scream that shattered every piece of glass in the cathedral—the first sound she'd ever heard him make.

"Did you think I was running all this time?" Lilith whispered, her grip tightening around his essence. Three thousand years of terror, of never resting, of always being prey. "Did you think I was afraid?"

The light between her fingers began to dim.

"I was preparing you."

Eons earlier, in the demon realm of Pandemonium:

The throne room reeked of sulfur and burnt offerings, its oppressive heat making Lilith's human skin crawl with phantom insects. She knelt before Lucifer's throne of bone and shadow, surrounded by creatures that wore faces like masks and hungered for things that had no names.

"You offer us the death of angels," Lucifer purred, his perfect features twisted into predatory interest. "What do you want in return?"

Lilith forced herself to tremble—not difficult, when every instinct screamed at her to run from this place where hope came to die. "Protection," she whispered. "Power. The angel Azrael hunts me, and I cannot face him alone."

Truth wrapped in deception, her specialty. She *could* face Azrael—the Tree's knowledge had shown her exactly how to kill angels. But she needed time, resources, and most crucially, she needed the demons to reshape her into something capable of holding that killing power without being consumed by it.

Lucifer's smile could have cut glass. "And you would serve us? Become our instrument?"

The words tasted like ashes. "I would become whatever you need me to be."

The transformation was violation dressed as gift. Her human shell dissolved willingly enough—she'd worn it like an old coat, familiar but constraining. But the binding that followed was agony beyond description. Infernal chains, cold and searing, wrapped around her soul not just to ensure loyalty but to *erase* her. Lilith the exile became Lilith the succubus, her will suffocated beneath layers of demonic purpose.

In the obsidian mirror of her new chamber, she stared at a creature of impossible beauty and terrible hunger. Flawless skin, eyes like molten emeralds, lips that whispered promises of pleasure and damnation. Everything she had been was buried beneath this perfect, hollow shell.

Everything except the ember of stolen knowledge that pulsed in the deepest part of her, hidden where even Hell's chains couldn't reach.

For a thousand years, she played the part. She punished human lust, tormented the lustful dead, became Hell's perfect weapon against the sins of the flesh. Every act of cruelty was calculated, every moment of service a lie wrapped in flawless performance. Around her, lesser demons leered and plotted and reveled in their power, never realizing they shared their realm with something far more dangerous than any of them.

In the quiet moments—when her duties were done and the throne room empty—she would study the bindings that held her. Each link in the infernal chains had a weakness, a flaw that could be exploited given enough time and patience. A thousand years was nothing to one who had already lost eternity itself.

When she finally shattered her chains, the demons never saw it coming.

The sound was like breaking glass, like tearing silk, like the last breath of a dying god. Lucifer found his throne room empty one morning, his prized succubus vanished without trace. He never realized she'd taken half his personal grimoire along with three centuries worth of accumulated soul-essence.

By then, Lilith was already implementing the next phase of her plan.

The present:

Azrael's essence flowed into her like molten gold, burning away her succubus form as something far more terrible took its place. Her black hair bleached white as snow, her green eyes shifting to violet flame that had never known mercy. The solid flesh of her body began to flicker, revealing glimpses of bone beneath skin that could no longer hold the weight of what she was becoming.

Power flooded through her—not just Azrael's divine strength, but the culmination of everything she had endured. The Tree's forbidden knowledge. Hell's corrupting touch.

Three millennia of relentless pursuit and patient planning. It all crystallized into something new, something that had never existed before in the cosmic order.

But with the power came exhaustion so profound it nearly buckled her transforming knees. Three thousand years of running, hiding, always looking over her shoulder. Three thousand years of being prey, of never resting, of sleeping with one eye open and terror as a constant companion.

The angel's armor clattered to the cathedral floor, empty now save for fading whispers of divine purpose. His Death Sword fell beside it, the blade's holy radiance guttering like a candle in wind.

For a moment—just a moment—Lilith wavered. The weight of millennia pressed down on her shoulders like the sky itself. *Was it worth it?* The thought came unbidden, a whisper from some part of her that remembered tracing golden leaves in paradise's eternal spring.

Then the scythe formed in her grip, not the straight blade of angelic justice but something curved and hungry that hummed with absolute finality. The doubt vanished beneath a tide of cold purpose.

"I am no longer Lilith the exile," she said, her voice echoing from everywhere and nowhere. "I am no longer Lilith the succubus."

The scythe's blade sang as she tested its weight, and somewhere in its keen edge was the sound of every chain that had ever bound her breaking.

"I am the Reaper of Souls. I am Death incarnate. And I decide who lives and who dies."

The cathedral's gargoyles bowed their stone heads in acknowledgment. Even Hell recognized the birth of something new and terrible—something that served neither Heaven nor the Pit, but answered only to its own burning will.

The first human city had been called Eden's Heart, built from white stone that caught morning light like trapped prayers. Lilith walked its empty streets now, her skeletal form flickering between visibility and void.

She had expected triumph. After all, hadn't she engineered this desolation? Hadn't her theft of forbidden knowledge led directly to the World Tree's removal and humanity's fall from grace? Their immortality lost, their paradise destroyed, their legacy nothing but ruins and wind.

Instead, her skeletal fingers brushed the weathered face of a statue—perhaps someone she had known in those distant golden days. The stone felt like ash beneath her touch. Wind moaned through empty archways, carrying the phantom scent of blossoms that would never bloom again.

"They cast me out," she whispered to the silence, the old anger a familiar ember in her chest. But the ember found no fuel here, only dust. This victory tasted like the void between stars, hollow and infinite and utterly without warmth.

Her scythe materialized, not as a threat but as a cold anchor in the crushing silence of a triumph that felt like annihilation. She had won everything and gained nothing.

She walked deeper into the city's heart, her skeletal form casting no shadow in the eternal twilight. Here was the marketplace where she had once bargained for honey cakes. There, the fountain where children had laughed while their parents spoke of harvests that would never fail. All of it ash now. All of it consequence.

The weight of omnipotence settled on her shoulders like a burial shroud. She could feel every soul in existence—their fears, their hopes, their inevitable endings. The knowledge she had stolen from the World Tree pulsed in her consciousness, vast and terrible and utterly meaningless now that there was no one left to share it with.

Death was supposed to be an ending, not a beginning. But standing here in the ruins of everything she had once loved, Lilith realized that her transformation was just another kind of exile. More complete than the first, more final than Hell's chains.

"Is this what you wanted?" The voice came from behind her, soft as falling leaves.

Lilith turned to find a figure watching from the shadow of a broken fountain. Neither angel nor demon, neither living nor dead. Something between categories, something that made her newly claimed dominion over death seem small and provincial.

"You destroyed an entire species to prove a point," the figure continued, its features shifting like smoke—sometimes human, sometimes bestial, sometimes geometries that hurt to perceive directly. "Was it worth it?"

The question hit like a physical blow. Lilith raised her scythe, violet mist coiling around the blade. "They condemned me for seeking truth. They chose ignorance over wisdom, chains over freedom."

"And now truth is all you have left."

The figure stepped forward, and Lilith felt something she hadn't experienced in millennia—uncertainty. Not fear, exactly, but the dawning horror that her grand rebellion might have been nothing more than an elaborate dance to someone else's tune.

"There are greater mysteries than the World Tree's secrets, Reaper. Deeper truths than the nature of angels and demons. Your transformation, your ascension—did you truly believe it was coincidence?"

"What are you saying?"

The figure smiled with teeth that were also stars, also screaming faces, also nothing at all. "I speak of the Vanishing Point, where all realities converge. I speak of the Singularity that binds the multiverse together like thread through a needle. I speak of the Unspeakable Entity that has been watching you since you first pressed your palm against the World Tree's bark."

Lilith's grip tightened on her scythe until her knuckles showed white through translucent skin. "You're lying."

"Your rebellion, your exile, your transformation into Death itself—all of it serves purposes you cannot begin to comprehend. You sought freedom, but what if freedom was the cage all along?"

The figure began to fade, dissolving back into shadow and possibility.

"When you're ready to learn the true scope of your bondage, seek the Unspeakable Entity. Seek the place where all stories end and begin. But be warned—the truth you find there may be more terrible than any lie you've told yourself."

Lilith lashed out with her scythe, but the blade passed through empty air. She stood alone among the ruins of Eden's Heart, violet mist coiling around her skeletal form like the remnants of abandoned dreams.

For the first time since her exile from paradise, Lilith felt the cold touch of absolute terror.

What if her entire existence—the Tree, the exile, the endless flight from Azrael, the transformation into Death itself

—what if it had all been orchestrated by something that made angels and demons look like children playing with toys?

What if the one thing she had fought for above all else —her freedom, her agency, her right to choose her own path— had been an illusion from the very beginning?

The Reaper of Souls stood in the ruins of humanity's greatest city and contemplated the possibility that her freedom was just another form of cage, more subtle and more terrible than any chain Hell had ever forged. In the distance, reality flickered like a broken mirror, showing glimpses of other worlds, other stories, all connected by threads too vast and complex for even her stolen wisdom to comprehend.

At the Vanishing Point, something that could not be named or comprehended smiled with satisfaction. The pieces were finally falling into place.

Lilith gripped her scythe with hands that trembled— not from fear, but from a rage so profound it made her three-thousand-year war with Azrael look like a child's tantrum. If her freedom was an illusion, she would shatter it. If her choices were scripted, she would tear up the script. If the cosmos itself thought to use her as a pawn...

Well. Death had always been the great equalizer.

She began to walk toward whatever truth awaited her in the spaces between worlds, leaving Eden's Heart to crumble behind her. Ahead, in the cosmic dark where the Singularity pulsed like the universe's hidden heart, greater mysteries beckoned.

The Reaper's genesis was complete. Her true rebellion had yet to begin.

The Endless Cage

"Freedom is not the power to choose—it is the wisdom to choose nothing."

The void screamed.

Red eyes blazed in an ocean of absolute nothing, twin furnaces of hatred that had burned since before the first star learned to die. Around them, reality writhed and buckled, trying to contain something that existed as pure negation—not darkness, but the absence of light itself. Not cold, but the death of warmth. Not silence, but the murder of sound.

The Unspeakable Entity pressed against the walls of his prison, and somewhere in the far reaches of space, a nebula collapsed into itself for no reason astronomers would ever understand.

His form shifted, testing boundaries that had held for eons. Smoke and ash one moment, then something with too many angles and surfaces that hurt to perceive. Always the eyes remained—crimson stars that promised the end of everything they gazed upon.

Soon.

The word was not spoken but felt, a vibration that preceded language, that would outlive meaning itself. It rippled through dimensions like a disease, touching minds across the multiverse with whispers of beautiful endings.

The First Breach: The Age of Bronze

Thakros the Conqueror stood ankle-deep in blood, his bronze sword dripping as he surveyed the ritual chamber carved from the living rock of Mount Pyrithia. Thirteen altars formed a perfect circle, each one bearing the still-warm corpse of a virgin sacrifice. Their blood ran in carefully etched channels toward the center, where obsidian tablets covered in pre-human glyphs gleamed wetly in the torchlight.

"Great One," Thakros called to the darkness, his voice echoing off stone walls that had never seen sunlight. "I have done as the tablets commanded. I have fed the earth with innocent blood. Now grant me the power to crush my enemies and rule all the lands beneath the sun."

The temperature in the chamber dropped thirty degrees in an instant. The torches flickered, their flames bending inward as if reality itself was being consumed. In the air above the blood-soaked altar, something began to take shape.

First came the eyes—two points of red light that seemed to burn through the back of Thakros's skull. Then the darkness around them deepened, became solid, became *wrong*. The Entity manifested as every nightmare Thakros had ever forgotten—a towering figure of shadow and flame, with horns that curved like broken spears and a mouth full of teeth that weren't quite teeth.

When it spoke, the words bypassed Thakros's ears entirely, carving themselves directly into his brain.

"MORTAL."

Thakros fell to his knees, blood streaming from his nose. Around the chamber, the corpses on the altars began to twitch and convulse as residual life force was drawn from their cooling flesh.

"YOU SEEK POWER OVER THE LIVING. I OFFER DOMINION OVER THE DEAD. OVER THE DYING. OVER THE NEVER-BORN."

"Yes," Thakros gasped, his vision blurring as something fundamental in his mind began to unravel. "Yes, I accept—"

"THEN OPEN THE WAY."

The Entity's presence pressed against the dimensional barriers, and Thakros screamed as he felt his consciousness being used as a conduit. Through the warlord's eyes, the Entity glimpsed the world beyond his prison—mountains crowned with snow, cities bustling with mortal life, vast armies marching beneath banners that proclaimed the glory of petty kings.

So much order. So much structure. So much *existence* that needed to be corrected.

The Entity pushed harder, pouring more of his essence through the connection. Thakros's body began to smoke, his bronze armor growing red-hot as entropy flowed through him like acid through flesh. The stone walls of the chamber cracked, ancient rock aging millennia in seconds.

Almost. Almost free.

But the Singularity sensed him. That cosmic force maintaining the architecture of reality struck back like a giant's fist, reinforcing the walls of his prison, cauterizing the dimensional wound before it could spread. The connection snapped with a sound like breaking worlds.

Thakros exploded.

Not into flames, but into *time*—his body aging and regressing in rapid cycles, birth and death and birth again, until there was nothing left but a pile of dust that had experienced every possible moment of existence simultaneously. The thirteen corpses on the altars crumbled to bone, then to powder, then to nothing at all.

The Entity's roar of fury shattered every piece of glass in the kingdom below.

The Second Breach: The Crystal Spires

Atlantis gleamed beneath twin moons, its crystal towers reaching toward stars that sang in harmonious frequencies. In the deepest laboratory of the Prismatic Academy, High Alchemist Nereon worked by the light of captured starfire, his six arms moving in precise patterns as he mixed essences that had never been meant to touch.

Dragon's blood from the Temporal Wars. Void-whale oil from the spaces between galaxies. The crystallized tears of a dying god. The powdered bones of thirteen different sapient species, each one extinct for different reasons.

"The calculations are perfect," he whispered to his assistant, a young woman with silver skin and eyes like mirrors. "The resonance frequencies align precisely with the dimensional stress points. We can tear a hole large enough to reach through."

His assistant, Lyralei, watched nervously as her master added the final component—a single drop of liquid starlight, harvested from the birth-cry of a newborn sun. The mixture began to glow with colors that had no names, colors that made her teeth ache and her bones feel hollow.

"Master," she said, "the texts warn that what lies beyond the barriers might not be—"

"Might not be what?" Nereon's voice carried the arrogance of someone who had never encountered a force greater than his own intellect. "We are the children of crystal and light, inheritors of technologies that reshape reality itself. What could possibly pose a threat to us?"

The mixture reached critical resonance. Reality tore.

The Entity felt the breach like a knife between his ribs —painful, but welcome. Through the dimensional wound, he sensed minds of crystalline clarity, beings who had achieved near-perfection in their manipulation of natural forces. How delicious it would be to corrupt such purity.

He pressed against the opening, and the laboratory filled with presence that made the air itself scream. Nereon stumbled backward as his carefully organized workspace began to decay—crystal apparatus cracking, metal instruments rusting, the very light seeming to dim and curdle.

"CHILDREN OF LIGHT," the Entity spoke, and every crystal in Atlantis resonated with his voice, creating a harmony that drove listeners to madness. **"YOU HAVE OPENED A DOOR THAT CANNOT BE CLOSED."**

Nereon tried to speak, but words failed him as he stared into those burning red eyes. This was not some demon to be bargained with, not some cosmic force to be harnessed. This was entropy itself, the fundamental principle that would eventually unravel every crystal spire, every perfect equation, every achievement of their civilization.

"BEHOLD TRUTH," the Entity said, and showed them the end of everything.

Lyralei saw Atlantis as it would be—not sunk beneath waves, but dissolved into component atoms by the heat death of the universe. She saw their crystal towers crumbling to dust, their perfect harmonies degenerating into discord, their immortal lives ending not in glory but in the simple cessation of all energy, all motion, all possibility.

She began to laugh, and couldn't stop.

The Entity poured more of himself through the breach, reality warping around his presence like heated glass. Half the Prismatic Academy began to age rapidly, crystal structures developing stress fractures that spread like spider webs. In the city beyond, citizens stopped in the streets as they felt something fundamental shift in the nature of existence itself.

But the Singularity was learning. It struck faster this time, marshaling the combined will of every living thing in the city—their desperate desire to continue existing, to maintain the perfect order they had built. The dimensional wound began to seal, reality reasserting itself with violent force.

The Entity fought back, pouring entropy through the closing gap. Nereon caught fire—not with flame, but with pure dissolution, his molecular bonds simply deciding to stop functioning. Lyralei aged a thousand years in three seconds, her laughter becoming a death rattle as her crystal bones turned to powder.

The breach collapsed.

The explosion took out seventeen crystal spires and turned a quarter of Atlantis to glass. In the aftermath, the surviving citizens would find that certain mathematical constants no longer worked quite the same way, that some frequencies of light now carried whispers of ending, that their perfect city now cast shadows that moved independently of their sources.

The Entity settled back into his prison, marginally satisfied. The taste of that brief freedom lingered like blood on his tongue.

The Third Breach: The Brass Hells

Belphegor, Duke of Sloth, lounged on his throne of crystallized screams while lesser demons prostrated themselves before him. His court occupied a vast cavern in the Seventh Circle, where the walls wept molten brass and the air itself burned with the intensity of concentrated malice.

"My lord," wheezed Scab-Tongue, one of Belphegor's more ambitious lieutenants, "the ritual preparations are complete. The Soul Forge burns with the essence of ten thousand tormented spirits. The Binding Circle has been inscribed with the true names of creation itself."

Belphegor yawned, exhaling sulfur and boredom in equal measure. "And you truly believe this will work? That we can bargain with something even the Creator feared to name?"

"My lord, consider the reward. If we can free the Unspeakable One, he will surely grant us dominion over the mortal realm. No more skulking in the shadows, no more competing with Heaven for souls. We could rule openly, corrupt without consequence—"

"Yes, yes." Belphegor waved a clawed hand dismissively. "Proceed with your little summoning. But if this backfires and brings the Seraphim down on our heads, I'll personally ensure you spend the next millennium being slowly digested by acid worms."

The ritual chamber lay at the heart of Hell's foundry, where the screams of the damned were refined into weapons and the tears of angels were distilled into poison. Nine circles of power, each one inscribed with blasphemies in languages that predated sin itself. At the center, a brass altar stained black with the blood of beings that had never been permitted to exist.

Sixty-six demons chanted in perfect disharmony, their voices creating frequencies that made reality nauseous. The Soul Forge roared higher, feeding on essence drawn from the deepest pits of damnation. Space began to warp, time to stutter, causality to question its own validity.

The Entity felt the summons like a tuning fork struck in his bones. These were not mortals fumbling with forces beyond their comprehension—these were beings of genuine power, inhabitants of a realm specifically designed to exist outside conventional reality. Their call resonated with his nature in ways that made his prison walls tremble.

He manifested above the altar not as nightmare, but as truth—a writhing mass of un-being that hurt to perceive directly, surrounded by an aura of absolute negation that made even demons step backward in horror.

"SPAWN OF CORRUPTION," he spoke, and his words turned half the brass walls to rust. **"YOU SEEK TO BARGAIN WITH ENDING ITSELF."**

Belphegor rose from his throne, trying to project confidence even as his immortal essence recoiled from the Entity's presence. "Great One, we offer alliance. Hell's legions in service to your will, the mortal realm delivered into chaos —"

"YOU MISTAKE ME FOR SOMETHING SMALL. SOMETHING PETTY." The Entity's attention focused on Belphegor like the weight of collapsing stars. **"I DO NOT SEEK TO RULE CHAOS. I SEEK TO END IT."**

The Duke of Sloth felt fear for the first time in eons. This was not another demon lord seeking territory, not even a fallen angel pursuing vengeance. This was something that wanted to *stop* everything—Heaven, Hell, and every realm between.

"OBSERVE YOUR FUTURE," the Entity said, and showed them Hell as it would be when entropy finally claimed it.

The vision was beautiful in its simplicity. No more screaming, no more torment, no more endless politics of damnation. Just silence, stillness, the perfect peace of complete cessation. Every demon dissolved back into the void from which they had been carved, every flame extinguished, every echo of suffering finally allowed to fade.

Half the assembled demons began weeping. The other half began laughing.

The Entity pressed harder against dimensional boundaries, and the Soul Forge cracked down the middle, releasing raw spiritual essence that began eating through Hell's foundation like concentrated time. The brass walls started to sing—not with anguish, but with the pure joy of objects that had finally been granted permission to stop existing.

Belphegor realized his mistake too late. "Close the breach!" he roared. "Close it now!"

But the ritual had been designed to open a permanent gateway, not a temporary one. The demons scrambled to reverse their workings while the Entity poured more of himself through the gap, his presence turning their carefully ordered Hell into a preview of the final silence.

The Singularity struck with unprecedented force, recognizing that Hell's destruction would create a cascade failure affecting every other realm. Reality didn't just seal the breach—it cauterized it, burning away every trace of the Entity's influence with such violence that the dimensional scar would remain visible for millennia.

The backlash vaporized thirty-seven demons instantly. Belphegor aged ten thousand years in the span of a heartbeat, his perfect immortal form becoming withered and cracked. The Soul Forge exploded, releasing enough concentrated anguish to create three new Circles of Hell, each one dedicated to a different variety of existential terror.

In the aftermath, Hell's remaining inhabitants would discover that certain words could no longer be spoken without causing physical pain, that some shadows now whispered promises of permanent rest, and that every flame in their realm now burned with the faintest hint of red around the edges.

The Entity's laughter echoed through the dimensions, a sound like the universe's final breath.

The Fourth Breach: The Dying God

In the space between galaxies, Omnex the Eternal drifted among cosmic debris, his once-brilliant form now dim and flickering like a candle in a hurricane. He had been a god of creation, a being whose songs had brought entire star systems into existence, whose dreams had populated worlds with life.

Now he was dying.

The cancer eating him was not physical but conceptual —a logical paradox that his worshippers had created through centuries of contradictory prayers. They wanted him to be all-powerful yet merciful, all-knowing yet surprised by their devotion, eternal yet responsive to temporal needs. The contradictions had become a tumor in his divine essence, growing larger each time mortals demanded that he be something impossible.

The irony was exquisite. His followers had loved him so completely that their love had become poison. They prayed for him to end wars while simultaneously begging him to grant victory to their armies. They demanded he show mercy to their enemies while ensuring their own triumph. They wanted him to be unchanging yet responsive, infinite yet personal, beyond mortal concerns yet intimately involved in every petty dispute.

Each contradictory prayer had carved another groove in his divine consciousness, until he could no longer maintain a coherent sense of self. He was simultaneously the god of peace and war, of creation and destruction, of mercy and justice. The paradoxes had crystallized into something that ate at his essence like acid through gold.

Omnex remembered when he had been young—if gods could be called young—when his first worshippers had been simple nomads who asked only for rain and protection from wild beasts. Their prayers had been pure, uncomplicated, each one a small gift of faith that strengthened his connection to reality. But as civilizations grew complex, so did their demands. Philosophy and theology had transformed simple devotion into an impossible maze of expectations.

Now, drifting in the void between dying stars, he felt his consciousness fragmenting with each passing moment. Parts of him were becoming lost in the contradictions, spinning off into separate entities that embodied single aspects of his former wholeness. Soon there would be nothing left but scattered fragments—a god of war here, a god of peace there, none of them remembering they had once been one.

Alone in the void, Omnex felt his consciousness fragmenting. Soon he would dissolve entirely, his power scattered across the cosmos like dust. Unless...

He reached out with senses that spanned dimensions, searching for something that might preserve what remained of his existence. And in that searching, he touched the edges of a prison that vibrated with pure entropy.

"Ancient One," Omnex whispered, his voice carrying the weight of eons of disappointment. "I have watched civilizations rise and fall. I have seen mortals create beauty beyond description, then destroy it in fits of rage. I have been loved and hated, worshipped and blasphemed, all by the same species, sometimes by the same individuals. And I have come to understand something that perhaps you knew from the beginning."

The Entity's attention focused like a laser, intrigued by the god's tone of weary wisdom rather than desperate bargaining.

"Creation itself is the cruelest joke ever conceived. To bring consciousness into existence is to guarantee suffering.

Every thinking being must eventually confront the inevitability of loss, the certainty of death, the ultimate meaninglessness of their struggles. I have been complicit in this cosmic crime for millennia."

"SPEAK PLAINLY, DYING LIGHT. WHAT DO YOU OFFER?"

"Not just my death," Omnex said, his form flickering as another piece of his consciousness broke away. "My willing corruption. Use my creative power as a weapon against creation itself. Let me help you teach the universe the mercy of nonexistence."

The Entity paused, genuinely moved by the god's proposal. Here was not another petty tyrant seeking power, but a being who had achieved true understanding of existence's fundamental flaw.

"YOUR DIVINE NATURE WILL RESIST. THE TRANSFORMATION WILL BE AGONY BEYOND DESCRIPTION."

"I have been dying in agony for ten thousand years," Omnex replied. "This will at least give that pain meaning."

Omnex felt something vast and terrible begin to seep through the dimensional barriers, drawn by his willingness to embrace dissolution. The dying god opened his fading consciousness fully, allowing the Entity's influence to pour into him like poison into a wound.

The transformation was exquisite agony.

Omnex's creative power inverted, becoming a force of sophisticated destruction. His ability to bring life became an instinct to end it beautifully. His divine love for existence curdled into a deeper, more perfect understanding of why existence was an error that needed correcting.

Together, they began to work at the prison walls from both sides—the Entity pushing from within while Omnex, now transformed into something that was neither divine nor mortal, pulled from without. The Singularity recognized the threat, but a corrupted god was something it had no protocols for dealing with. How do you protect reality from one of its own creators?

Space around Omnex began to unravel. Stars in nearby galaxies flickered as their nuclear fires were gently persuaded to simply stop burning. Planets rich with life experienced mass extinctions as their inhabitants suddenly understood, with perfect clarity, why continuing to exist was pointless.

The Entity pressed harder, feeling his prison walls growing thin. Through the growing breach, he reached out to touch the minds of mortals across a dozen worlds, whispering the truth that Omnex had accepted—that existence was suffering, and the only mercy was to end it.

Entire civilizations began to choose extinction over struggle.

But the Singularity had one final defense. It reached out to every living thing that still possessed the will to exist, drawing on their combined determination to continue being. The force was staggering—trillions of minds united in the simple, desperate desire to not stop existing.

That combined will struck the breach with the force of colliding galaxies.

Omnex screamed as his corrupted essence was torn away from the Entity's influence, his divine nature reasserting itself through sheer cosmic pressure. But the god was too damaged to survive the separation. He dissolved, not into peaceful nonexistence but into raw, screaming energy that would eventually coalesce into a new star—one that would burn with inexplicable sadness for the rest of its existence.

The Entity roared his frustration across dimensions, and somewhere in the Andromeda Galaxy, an entire solar system aged a billion years in the span of a second.

The Fifth Breach: The Quantum Cult

The ruins on Xerion Prime had been buried under radioactive ice for seventeen millennia, hidden beneath the debris of a civilization that had tried to harness black holes for energy and learned too late that some forces were not meant to be tamed. But Vanya Quinlan and her xenoarchaeological team had spent five years excavating the site, following whispers in pre-human texts that spoke of knowledge hidden in the bones of dead worlds.

"The resonance patterns are unlike anything in the databases," reported Dr. Kresh, his cybernetic implants sparking as they tried to process data that violated several laws of physics. "The quantum signatures suggest these ruins exist in seventeen different dimensional layers simultaneously."

Vanya nodded, her face gaunt from years of obsession. She had lost everything to the Ashkente Event—the day reality had briefly hiccupped and allowed something impossible to slip through. Her husband Marvus had simply... stopped. Not died, not vanished, but ceased to have ever existed. The universe had retroactively edited him out, leaving Vanya with phantom memories of a love that had never been and children whose names she could remember but whose faces had been erased from every photograph, every recording, every trace of physical evidence.

The worst part was that she was the only one who remembered. Her friends spoke of her as if she had always been single, had always been childless. Medical records showed she had never given birth. The house she had shared with Marvus had somehow always been a bachelor apartment, despite her clear memories of redecorating it for their family.

She had spent years trying to prove their existence, driving herself to the edge of madness before finally accepting the truth: something had reached across dimensions and selectively edited reality. The cosmic horror hadn't killed her family—it had retroactively prevented them from ever existing in the first place.

That violation of causality itself had led her to the ruins on Xerion Prime, following ancient texts that spoke of beings capable of manipulating the fundamental structure of existence. If something could reach across dimensions to destroy her family, then perhaps she could reach back and destroy it in return.

But the deeper she dug into the archaeological evidence, the more she realized that revenge was impossible. The thing that had taken her family was already dead, had been dead for millennia. The Ashkente Event had been the death-throes of something unimaginably vast, its final act of spite against a universe that had contained it.

The only justice left was to ensure that the universe which had allowed such cruelty to exist would eventually face the same fate her family had suffered—complete and retroactive erasure.

"The texts speak of something called the Unspeakable Entity," she said, running her fingers over glyphs that seemed to shift when observed directly. "Something that exists between dimensions, trapped by forces that maintain the stability of reality itself."

"Captain," Dr. Kresh's voice carried a note of alarm. "I'm detecting massive gravitational anomalies centered on this site. It's as if the planet's core is being pulled toward something that isn't there."

Vanya smiled for the first time in years. "It's there. We just can't see it yet."

The ritual chamber they found in the planet's core was a masterwork of impossible architecture—surfaces that curved in directions that didn't exist, carved from substances that their instruments couldn't identify. Symbols covered every surface, each one radiating a different variety of wrongness that made the team's sanity detectors scream warnings.

"Quantum entanglement on a macro scale," whispered Dr. Yilmaz, the team's physicist. "These symbols aren't just carved into the walls—they're carved into spacetime itself. The entire chamber exists in a state of superposition between dimensions."

Vanya began to understand. The previous civilization hadn't just tried to summon the Entity—they had tried to build a permanent bridge between realities, a stable gateway that would allow something massive to cross over without the barriers snapping shut.

"Begin the sequence," she ordered. "Full quantum resonance cascade across all seventeen dimensional layers."

Her team worked with desperate precision, their equipment pushed far beyond safe operating parameters.

They had lost colleagues to void cancer, to temporal displacement, to things that couldn't be named but left their victims speaking in mathematical equations. But they persevered, driven by Vanya's absolute certainty that the universe owed them answers.

The dimensional barriers began to resonate, creating harmonics that made reality sing in frequencies that predated sound. The Entity felt the call and responded with something approaching eagerness. Here, finally, was a summoning that might actually work—not crude blood magic or demonic ambition, but precise scientific manipulation of the fundamental forces that held his prison together.

He manifested slowly, carefully, his essence seeping through the quantum foam that connected all things. Unlike his previous appearances, he didn't immediately reveal his full presence. Instead, he spoke from the spaces between atoms, his voice a whisper that seemed to come from inside their own thoughts.

"YOU SEEK TRUTH IN THE RUINS OF THOSE WHO CAME BEFORE. BUT TRUTH IS NOT SOMETHING TO BE FOUND—IT IS SOMETHING TO BE ACCEPTED."

Dr. Kresh fell to his knees, blood streaming from his cybernetic implants as they overloaded trying to process the Entity's presence. "Captain," he gasped, "the readings are off the charts. This isn't just a dimensional breach—it's a complete local failure of spacetime."

Vanya stepped forward, her face illuminated by red light that seemed to come from everywhere and nowhere. "I know what you are," she said. "You're not a demon or a god. You're entropy itself, the force that will eventually claim everything. And I want to help you."

"WHY WOULD A LIVING BEING CHOOSE TO SERVE ENDING?"

"Because existence is pain," Vanya replied, tears streaming down her face. "Because consciousness is suffering. Because every moment of awareness is agony for something that should never have been forced to think, to feel, to remember loss."

The Entity paused, genuinely surprised. Most who summoned him sought power over others. But this mortal understood that his true gift was power over oneself—the power to choose nonexistence over endless suffering.

"THEN WITNESS WHAT AWAITS WHEN THE BARRIERS FALL."

He showed her visions of beautiful endings—civilizations choosing peaceful extinction over endless struggle, stars being gently persuaded to stop burning, the gradual decay of spacetime itself until only perfect silence remained. It was not destruction but liberation, not chaos but the ultimate order of absolute stillness.

Vanya wept at the beauty of it.

The Entity began to push harder against the dimensional barriers, pouring more of his essence through the carefully constructed breach. The quantum entanglement field held, creating a stable pathway that didn't immediately trigger the Singularity's defenses. Reality began to warp around the chamber, time flowing backward in some areas while accelerating wildly in others.

Dr. Yilmaz screamed as her body began to exist in multiple temporal states simultaneously, aging and growing younger in rapid cycles. The stone walls of the chamber cracked, revealing not more stone but the vast emptiness of the void between dimensions.

The Entity was closer to freedom than he had ever been.

But the Singularity recognized the quantum signature of the breach—this was not a random dimensional accident but a deliberate attempt to create a permanent gateway. It marshaled forces from across the multiverse, drawing power from the collapsed remnants of a dozen dead universes, and struck with unprecedented violence.

The backlash shattered the quantum field and sent ripples through seventeen layers of reality simultaneously. Vanya and her team were caught in the dimensional feedback—not killed, but scattered across multiple timelines, existing as fragments of consciousness spread throughout eternity.

The Entity's roar of fury caused every black hole in the local galaxy cluster to briefly stop consuming matter, as if even they were afraid to continue existing in the face of such rage.

The Recognition

Eons passed. The Entity settled into a new kind of patience, one born of absolute certainty rather than desperate hope. Each failure had taught him something crucial about the nature of his prison, about the forces that maintained reality's structure, about the kinds of beings who might serve his ultimate purpose.

He no longer sought crude liberation through brute force or clever manipulation. He had learned that freedom would come not through breaking his chains, but through finding someone else to break them from the outside—someone with the power and motivation to tear down the barriers that kept him caged.

The Entity's repeated failures had taught him patience, but more importantly, they had taught him precision. Each breach had shown him new aspects of the Singularity's defenses, new ways that reality protected itself from his influence. He had learned to watch, to wait, to study the cosmic forces that maintained existence's stability.

It was during this expanded observation—his consciousness spread thin across dimensions as he mapped reality's weaknesses—that he first sensed the anomaly.

In a timeline where the established order had been violently overthrown, where the cosmic hierarchy itself had been shattered and rebuilt, something unprecedented was happening. A being of immense power was moving through the dimensional layers with an authority that even the Singularity seemed to acknowledge.

But this was not another cosmic entity seeking to maintain the balance. This was something that had been cast out, rejected, and had responded by claiming dominion over forces that were supposed to be beyond mortal reach. The Entity watched, fascinated, as this being carved through reality's defenses like a sword through paper.

She called herself Lilith, and her rage burned with the intensity of a collapsing star. But it was not simple anger that drew the Entity's attention—it was the nature of her rebellion. She had not merely rejected the rules imposed upon her; she had rewritten them. She had taken the fundamental forces of existence and made them serve her will, proving that the cosmic order was not as immutable as its guardians claimed.

More importantly, she was asking the same questions that had driven the Entity to seek his freedom: Who decided what was permissible? What gave these cosmic forces the right to determine the fate of conscious beings? And what lay beyond the barriers that supposedly protected reality from threats like himself?

The Entity realized that his long imprisonment had not been wasted. While he had been testing the walls of his prison, learning from each failure, someone else had been testing the walls of existence itself. And she was winning.

From his dimensional cage, the Entity began to whisper across the timelines, sending messages to reach the one being who might have the power—and the motivation—to complete what he had started.

That hunger for truth would eventually lead her to the Vanishing Point, to the space between existence and nonexistence where the deepest secrets of reality were hidden. And when she arrived, she would find him waiting—not as a tempter offering power, but as the answer to every question she had ever asked about the nature of freedom and control.

Together, they would end the universe's long, cruel joke.

The Entity smiled, and in response, somewhere in the depths of space, an entire nebula began to collapse into itself for no reason that scientists would ever understand. Reality shivered, sensing that something fundamental was about to change.

Soon, the screaming would stop.

Soon, there would be only silence.

Soon, there would be peace.

Epilogue - The Rupture

The dimensional barrier screamed as Lilith's scythe carved through it like flesh. Reality hemorrhaged—not blood, but something far more vital. Colors that had no names bled into the void, while the very concept of distance buckled and folded in on itself.

She stood at the edge of everything and nothing, her bone-white hair whipping in winds that existed between heartbeats. The Reaper of Souls had finally found what she'd been seeking since her exile from paradise—not just truth, but the ultimate power. The power to reshape existence itself according to her will.

The Vanishing Point stretched before her, an impossibility given form. Not darkness, not light, but the pause between them. Not silence, not sound, but the breath before the first word of creation. Here, at the horizon of forever, the rules that governed reality grew thin as gossamer.

"You came," whispered a voice that bypassed her ears entirely, carving itself directly into her consciousness. It carried the weight of collapsing stars, the final sigh of dying universes. **"I knew you would."**

The Unspeakable Entity manifested slowly, respectfully —not as the nightmare he'd shown lesser beings, but as something almost... kindred. Twin points of crimson light that might have been eyes, surrounded by darkness that hurt to perceive directly. When he moved, shadows fell upward and time stuttered like a broken clock.

"Three millennia," Lilith said, her voice steady despite the cosmic forces pressing against her enhanced form. "Three millennia you've been whispering in the spaces between my thoughts. Speaking of cages. Of freedom that was always illusion."

"Because you alone could understand." The Entity's presence shifted, testing the dimensional barriers that kept him imprisoned. **"You who stole forbidden knowledge. You who broke the chains of paradise**

itself. You who became Death rather than accept servitude."

"But you speak of ending, while I seek to rule," she said ominously.

"Do we not want the same thing? The power to decide who lives and who dies? The authority to judge what deserves to exist?"

Lilith's grip tightened on her scythe, violet mist coiling around the blade. She'd expected lies, seduction, the usual gambits of cosmic powers seeking pawns. Instead, the Entity offered her something far more dangerous: partnership between equals.

"Show me," she commanded.

The Entity smiled—or perhaps the concept of smiling smiled through him—and opened his prison just enough to let her glimpse what lay beyond.

Lilith saw the Singularity.

It hung at the heart of the Vanishing Point like a dying star, its light fractured into impossible geometries. This was the source—the cosmic wellspring from which all existence drew breath, the invisible thread connecting every atom to every galaxy. But it was wounded, chained, diminished. Barriers of crystallized reality surrounded it, each one inscribed with laws that kept power concentrated in the hands of distant cosmic forces.

"They call it order," the Entity whispered. **"Balance. The greater good. But it's nothing more than a system designed to keep power from those who would use it properly."**

She looked, and saw the truth that had driven her to madness three thousand years ago. The Singularity was the ultimate prize—the pure animus of existence itself, the life force that animated all reality. Infinite power waiting to be claimed by someone with the will to seize it. Every cosmic force, every angel and demon, every self-proclaimed god had accepted their assigned role in the grand design. None had dared reach for the source itself.

"With the Singularity under our control," the Entity continued, **"every soul across every reality would answer to us. No more chaos. No more random suffering. Perfect order, perfectly administered."**

"Our control?" Lilith asked, though she was already calculating how to eliminate her ally once the barriers fell.

"Your control," the Entity corrected with practiced deception. **"I seek only to end the cosmic joke. You would rule what remains."**

Lilith studied the barriers surrounding the Singularity —gossamer walls that looked fragile but had held against cosmic forces for eons. They were beautiful in their complexity, terrible in their purpose. The only thing standing between her and ultimate dominion over existence itself.

"How?" she asked, hunger naked in her voice.

The Entity's instructions were complex, requiring manipulation of forces that existed in seventeen different dimensional states simultaneously. Lilith would need to cut precise incisions in reality's fabric while the Entity pushed from within his prison, creating resonance patterns that would destabilize the barriers around the Singularity.

It would require moving through dimensional space, folding the distance between impossible points, existing in multiple states of being at once. Most crucially, it would require absolute precision—one mistake would collapse the entire attempt and likely destroy them both.

"The gravitational anchor," the Entity explained as cosmic forces swirled around them. **"Sagittarius A*—the supermassive black hole at the galaxy's heart. Its event horizon touches fourteen different dimensional layers. If we can manipulate its position, use it as a fulcrum..."**

Lilith's enhanced perception followed his meaning. They would literally move a black hole, using its mass to create dimensional stress fractures that would weaken the barriers. The energy requirements were staggering—enough to power entire star systems for millennia.

"Where do we get that kind of power?" she asked.

The Entity's presence shifted, and for the first time, she heard something like hunger in his voice. **"From every soul that has ever chosen despair over hope. Every moment of surrender. Every time someone decided existence wasn't worth the struggle."**

The realization hit her like falling stars. The Entity hadn't just been imprisoned—he'd been collecting. Every suicide across history, every moment of chosen ending, every soul that had embraced the void rather than continue existing.

All of it had been flowing to him across dimensional barriers, building toward this moment.

"You've been preparing for millennia," she breathed.

"Since the first thinking being realized that existence was pain," the Entity confirmed. **"But I needed someone on the outside. Someone with the power to act, the will to rebel, and the desperation to risk everything."**

Lilith felt cosmic forces gathering around them as the Entity began to move. The stolen energy of countless despairing souls flowed through the dimensional barriers, creating currents of pure entropy that made reality shudder.

She cut.

Her scythe sliced through the fabric of space-time itself, opening wounds that bled possibility. Through the tears, she could see other dimensions—layers of reality stacked like pages in an infinite book. The Entity poured his accumulated power through the openings, reaching across impossible distances to grasp the event horizon of Sagittarius A*.

The black hole screamed.

Not with sound, but with gravitational waves that rippled through every dimension simultaneously. Space-time buckled as the Entity began to move four million solar masses with nothing but will and accumulated despair.

"Now," the Entity commanded. **"Before the barriers can adapt."**

Lilith stepped between dimensions, her form fracturing across multiple layers of reality. She existed everywhere and nowhere at once, cutting precise incisions in the crystallized laws that held the Singularity prisoner. Each slash of her scythe sent shockwaves through the cosmic order.

The barriers began to crack.

Amy Namaah felt the disturbance through the soles of her motorcycle boots as she stood outside a burning tenement in Mumbai. She'd been hunting a demon who fed on children's nightmares when reality decided to develop a stutter. The flames around her flickered between orange and colors that had never existed.

"Shit," she muttered, stubbing out her cigarette on a piece of rebar. "Someone's playing with forces they shouldn't be able to touch."

The demon wore the face of a kindly grandfather, but its shadow had too many teeth.

"Please," it whimpered as she approached, Enigma blazing in her hand. "I only take the dreams they don't need —"

Amy's blade separated its head from its shoulders mid-sentence. The demon's true form dissolved into shrieking shadow before dispersing entirely. Some conversations weren't worth having.

Her enhanced senses painted a map of dimensional stress fractures spreading like cracks in ice. At their center, something massive was moving—not through space, but through the layers of reality itself.

Amy's mismatched wings erupted from her back—one white as starlight, one black as the void between galaxies—tearing through her leather jacket. She'd felt this kind of cosmic disturbance once before, right before half the angelic host had fallen in a war that predated human civilization.

"Time to see if three thousand years of exile taught me anything useful," she said, and disappeared into the shadows between dimensions.

Justice felt the dimensional rupture like a blade between her ribs. She stood in the ruins of a courthouse in Detroit, her silver armor gleaming as she held her bastard sword against the throat of a human trafficker who would never hurt children again. Around them, reality began to stutter.

"Impossible," she whispered, casually ending the criminal's wretched life. Her enhanced senses mapped the growing disturbance—tears in space-time itself, centered on a point that existed outside normal geography. "The Vanishing Point."

She'd never felt wrongness of this magnitude before. This was fundamental.

Her blue cape billowed as she launched herself skyward, the silver scales of balance emblazoned on its fabric catching light from stars that suddenly burned with unfamiliar colors.

In a neon-lit coffee shop in Neo-Tokyo, The Nothing paused mid-sip of coffee that tasted like artificial memories and existential questions. Around him, reality flickered like a broken television screen. The barista aged seventeen years in three seconds, then returned to her original age with no memory of the temporal displacement.

"Well," he said to no one in particular, his grin widening to encompass half his scarred face. "This is either going to be fantastically educational or catastrophically boring. Possibly both."

He reached into the space between heartbeats and pulled out his wallet. The cosmic joke was about to get new material, and he had front-row seats to watch the universe's latest attempt at self-destruction.

In the depths of her research station, Omenti felt the first tremors through quantum sensors that monitored probability itself. Her holographic form solidified, calculations spinning behind wire-rimmed glasses as she processed the implications.

"Extraordinary," she whispered, her consciousness expanding through networks that spanned multiple timelines. "Someone has actually breached the Vanishing Point."

Her sensors identified familiar quantum signatures—Lilith's dimensional cutting abilities, and something else. Something that tasted of accumulated endings and calculated despair.

"The Unspeakable Entity," Omenti realized. "After all these eons, someone has finally freed it from its prison."

She began mobilizing resources across seventeen different realities. If the fundamental structure of existence was being rewritten, she intended to ensure the new version met her specifications.

The barriers shattered.

Reality convulsed as the crystallized laws holding the Singularity prisoner dissolved like salt in cosmic wind. The Entity's accumulated despair—eons of chosen endings, millennia of surrendered souls—poured through the cracks, destabilizing the forces that held existence together.

But as the Singularity's infinite power flowed free, both conspirators felt the scope of what they'd unleashed. This wasn't just liberation—it was fundamental restructuring of everything that was, had been, or could ever be.

"The power," Lilith gasped, her form flickering between dimensions as cosmic energies threatened to tear her apart. "It's beyond anything I imagined."

"Yes," the Entity hissed, his presence expanding as ancient restraints crumbled. **"And now it's time to—"**

The Singularity exploded.

Not destroyed—ruptured. Its infinite power erupted across the multiverse in a cataclysmic wave that rewrote the fundamental laws of existence. Through every dimension, across every reality, the wave spread like ripples in an infinite pond.

In that moment, almost every sentient being in creation felt the primal animus—the life force of existence itself—flow into them. Some gained abilities they'd never possessed—a tired librarian found she could bend time around books, a street musician discovered his melodies could reshape matter, a dying soldier realized death no longer held dominion over him. Others felt their existing powers magnified beyond comprehension—gods became titans, mages became living forces of nature, mortals ascended to near-divinity.

The Unspeakable Entity staggered as the wave passed through him, and for the first time in eons, he felt... diminished. The accumulated power he'd gathered across millennia was still there, but without the Singularity's focused animus, his ability to unmake reality had been scattered. He needed that power concentrated again—either in his hands or prevented from being restored entirely.

"No," he whispered, his form flickering as he tried to comprehend the implications. **"The animus...** it's distributed. Without the intact source, the multiverse will slowly unravel on its own, but the others might be able to restore it before that happens."

Racing toward the epicenter came four figures who would shape what came next.

Justice arrived first, her enhanced form riding dimensional currents that felt like flying through broken glass. The sight that greeted her defied comprehension—where the

Singularity had blazed like an uncontrolled star, now only a Remnant remained, a crystalline fragment pulsing with residual power.

Amy materialized from shadow, her mismatched wings spread wide as she assessed the chaos. "What the fuck—"

"Eloquent," The Nothing observed wryly, materializing from between dimensions. "Twice now reality seems to have developed a habit of unraveling dramatically. I'm starting to take it personally." He paused, grinning at the transformed landscape. "Though I have to say, this is much more interesting than I expected."

Omenti's consciousness arrived as pure information given form, her holographic body flickering as probability cascades threatened her quantum matrices. Her analysis subroutines were already working, processing the new reality.

"Fascinating," she announced, her consciousness expanding across multiple timelines simultaneously. "The Singularity didn't fragment intentionally—it ruptured from the stress of sudden liberation. Its animus has been distributed across the multiverse, infused into sentient beings on a scale unprecedented in cosmic history."

Her awareness touched a thousand different realities at once. In dimension 7-Alpha, she observed a mortal artist whose paintings now rewrote local physics—when he died moments later from dimensional stress, his animus dispersed harmlessly into the void. But in dimension 12-Gamma, she watched a desperate scavenger kill that reality's version of the same artist—and saw the animus flow directly into the killer, enhancing his own abilities exponentially.

"Curious," Omenti murmured, her calculations spinning faster. In dimension 3-Beta, a grandmother willingly surrendered her newfound power to help her dying granddaughter—the animus flowed not to the child, but toward a crystalline formation that matched the Remnant's energy signature.

"Ah," she said, understanding flooding her quantum matrices. "The animus follows intention. Violent acquisition concentrates power in the killer. Willing sacrifice feeds the restoration process."

Justice felt the change in herself—her divine essence magnified, her connection to cosmic balance deeper than ever before. Around them, reality shimmered with new possibilities. "Someone explain what this means."

"It means," Omenti continued, "that the animus can be harvested through murder, absorbed by the killer to increase their own power exponentially. But it can also be surrendered voluntarily, returned directly to the Remnant. If enough beings chose to sacrifice their newfound abilities..."

"The Singularity could be restored," Amy finished, understanding flooding her features. "Predation versus sacrifice."

The Unspeakable Entity's presence pressed against them like the weight of dying stars, and for the first time, his voice carried undisguised malice. "Then we must ensure the animus never reunites. Let them keep their scattered fragments while I work to corrupt the Remnant itself. The multiverse will unravel as it should have eons ago—I'll simply help it along."

"Or," Lilith interjected, her scythe cutting through dimensional space as she approached, "I take what belongs to the strong. Every fragment of animus I claim brings me closer to absolute dominion over life and death itself." Her smile was predatory, beautiful, and terrible. "Why settle for entropy when you can rule what remains?"

Justice raised her sword, feeling the weight of cosmic responsibility. "The animus was distributed for a reason. Reality needs to be restored to its proper balance, not concentrated in any single hand."

"How disappointingly shortsighted," Omenti replied. "This crisis presents unprecedented opportunities. Imagine the animus properly administered—suffering eliminated, existence optimized, paradise implemented whether beings understand they need it or not."

Amy's hand moved to Enigma's hilt, the blade singing with enhanced purpose. "Maybe... maybe if I help restore the Singularity, if I do enough good with this power, the celestial hierarchy will see I'm worthy of redemption. That my fall wasn't the end of my story."

"Or," The Nothing added, his grin widening as he contemplated infinite possibility, "we could see what happens when everything that was nothing becomes something again. I've experienced the void before creation—this is far more entertaining."

Thunder rolled through dimensions as their conflicting purposes became clear. Each had rushed here to prevent catastrophe. None could agree on what salvation looked like.

The confrontation that followed wasn't the philosophical debate they might have expected. It erupted with the sudden violence of colliding galaxies.

Lilith moved first, her scythe carving a dimensional rift as she lunged toward the Remnant. The blade trailed violet mist that whispered of endings—each droplet a soul she'd claimed across millennia.

Justice intercepted her, bastard sword blazing with divine light. Steel met bone with a sound like breaking stars. "Power without restraint destroys everything it touches!"

"Then let it burn!" Lilith snarled, calling forth the armies of the dead. Spectral warriors erupted from the ground beneath Justice's feet, their ghostly blades seeking gaps in silver armor.

The Unspeakable Entity didn't fight—he simply was. Reality aged and crumbled wherever his attention focused. The Remnant's crystalline structure began to develop stress fractures as entropy caressed its surface.

Amy launched herself at the Entity, Enigma's light side blazing as she struck at the heart of nothingness. The blade passed through shadow only to meet resistance from The Nothing's grinning form.

"Wrong target, angel," The Nothing said cheerfully, shadows coiling around his arms like living smoke. "Though I appreciate the enthusiasm."

Enigma's dark side parried a strike from writhing void while Amy spun, both sides of her blade working in harmony. "Then help me stop him!"

"Oh, I intend to." The Nothing gestured, and shadows erupted from every corner of the Vanishing Point, reaching for the Entity like grasping fingers. "Existence is far too interesting to let entropy have it."

Omenti's response was immediate and overwhelming. A dozen war machines materialized around her—crystalline constructs bristling with weapons that fired concentrated possibility. One targeted Lilith's advancing specters, each shot reducing them to probability equations. Another focused on the Entity, its beam attempting to impose order on pure chaos.

"Calculation complete," Omenti announced as her machines engaged. "Optimal outcome requires restraint of all variables."

Justice carved through spectral warriors while parrying Lilith's increasingly desperate attacks. Each clash of their weapons sent shockwaves through dimensions, causing distant stars to flicker and die.

Lilith spun her scythe in a wide arc, the weapon's edge opening wounds in space-time itself. Through the tears, she pulled forth creatures of pure entropy—beings that had chosen death so completely they had become it.

"Meet my congregation," she whispered, directing them toward the Remnant.

The Nothing's laughter rang out as he stepped between moments, appearing behind Lilith. Shadows wrapped around her throat like chains. "Terribly sorry, but that won't do at all."

Lilith's necromantic power flared, turning The Nothing's shadows solid so she could grab them. She spun, hurling him toward one of Omenti's war machines. "Death cannot be bound!"

The machine fired, but The Nothing folded himself through the space between seconds, emerging unharmed. "Can't it though? Seems like you're awfully bound to the idea of ruling it."

Amy fought desperately against entropy itself, Enigma's dual nature the only thing keeping her from being unmade. Each strike against the Unspeakable Entity felt like attacking the concept of ending—necessary but seemingly futile.

The Entity's voice resonated through her bones: "Why preserve what causes only suffering? Even you know the peace of non-existence."

"Because someone has to choose hope!" Amy drove Enigma deeper into the Entity's form, light and shadow working together to carve meaning into meaninglessness.

Justice found herself pressed back as Lilith's power grew with each passing moment. The Reaper was drawing strength from the dimensional wounds around them, feeding on the small deaths that accompanied reality's trauma.

"You cannot win," Lilith said, her scythe moving in patterns that hurt to follow. "Every moment of this battle feeds me. Every star that dies in distant galaxies answers my call."

"Then I'll end it quickly." Justice's sword blazed brighter, her divine essence pushing beyond mortal limitations. She struck with the weight of cosmic law behind her blow.

Lilith caught the blade in her bare hand, her enhanced flesh smoking where it touched divine metal. "Law means nothing without power to enforce it."

Omenti's machines repositioned, their combined fire now targeting the structural weaknesses in the Vanishing Point itself. If she couldn't control the combatants, she would control the battlefield.

"Fascinating," she announced as reality began to crystallize around them. "Combat effectiveness increases when environmental variables are optimized."

The Nothing found himself fighting Omenti's constructs while trying to prevent the Entity from corrupting the Remnant. He teleported between shadows, each movement accompanied by questions that made the machines doubt their programming.

"But what if your optimal outcome is actually suboptimal?" he asked one construct as he passed through its shadow. "What if efficiency is just another word for cowardice?"

The machine paused for 0.003 seconds to process the philosophical implications—long enough for The Nothing to emerge from its shadow and tear out its core processors.

Amy's battle with the Entity was becoming more desperate by the moment. Each exchange left her slightly more unmade, slightly less real. But Enigma was adapting, its dual nature learning to cut concepts as well as flesh.

"You want to end suffering?" Amy gasped, driving both sides of her blade into the Entity's core. "Then end your own!"

For an instant, the Unspeakable Entity wavered. The suggestion struck at something fundamental in his nature—the question of whether nonexistence applied to himself.

In that moment of uncertainty, Amy pressed her advantage. Enigma's light side carved away layers of entropy while its shadow side sealed the wounds, preventing regeneration.

But the Entity's doubt lasted only an instant. "I am ending itself. I cannot end what I am."

He struck back with the force of every chosen death across history, sending Amy flying toward the Remnant. She twisted in mid-air, using her mismatched wings to redirect her trajectory toward Justice.

"The Remnant!" she called out. "We have to protect it!"

Justice nodded, breaking away from her duel with Lilith. But as they moved toward the crystalline structure, they found their way blocked by shadows, machines, spectral warriors, and entropy itself.

All six forces converged on the same point—the source of restoration and the prize they each sought to claim or corrupt.

Lilith's scythe met Justice's sword while Omenti's machines targeted both. Amy and The Nothing found themselves back-to-back, facing down the Unspeakable Entity's advancing darkness while spectral warriors circled like vultures.

"Stalemate," Justice said, her blade locked against Lilith's. Around them, the others had reached similar impasses—each powerful enough to contend with the others, none strong enough to overcome them all.

"Temporary equilibrium," Omenti corrected, her machines holding steady aim on multiple targets. "The real conflict lies not here, but across the multiverse. In convincing beings to surrender or retain their newfound abilities."

Lilith's scythe dissipated as she stepped back, her tactical mind already adapting to new realities. "Then the war becomes one of influence rather than force."

The Unspeakable Entity's presence withdrew, his voice carrying new undertones of uncertainty. "Existence has become... complicated. But endings remain. Perhaps more are needed now than ever."

"The game has changed," Amy realized, her wings folding as she contemplated the implications. "It's no longer about power—it's about choice."

The Nothing's grin widened to encompass possibilities that hadn't existed moments before. "And choice is always more interesting than certainty."

They retreated to the far corners of the multiverse, each carrying knowledge that would reshape existence itself.

Lilith established her domain where death held sway, seeking those who viewed power as birthright. Her message was seductive in its simplicity: claim the animus from the weak, become strong enough to rule over life and death itself. Why surrender power when you could harvest more?

The Unspeakable Entity whispered to beings overwhelmed by their newfound abilities, but his purpose was purely malevolent now. Every fragment of animus he convinced others to abandon would be corrupted before it could reach the Remnant. If he couldn't unmake reality immediately, he would poison any attempt to heal it.

Omenti began cataloging every being touched by the Singularity's power, building networks of efficient control. Her promise was seductive—surrender your animus to her administration, and she would use it to create a universe without suffering, without chaos, without the tragic waste of unguided choice.

Justice sought beings who understood that power meant responsibility, building coalitions to restore the cosmic balance that had maintained reality for eons. The animus belonged in the Remnant, carefully regulated and properly distributed according to cosmic law.

Amy walked among the fallen and forgotten, helping where she could, hoping that each act of service would prove her worthiness. Perhaps if she guided enough beings to surrender their animus voluntarily, the celestial hierarchy would finally see that her exile could end.

And The Nothing found the curious ones, those who appreciated that existence—even chaotic, uncontrolled existence—was infinitely more fascinating than the perfect void he remembered. Reality was worth preserving, if only to see what impossible things would happen next.

Six visions of what the enhanced multiverse should become. Six paths toward an uncertain future.

In coffee shops and libraries, in schools and hospitals, in the quiet moments between cosmic significance, ordinary beings examined their extraordinary new abilities. A baker discovered her bread could nourish souls as well as bodies. A teacher found his words could plant seeds of wisdom that bloomed across generations. A nurse realized her touch could heal wounds that existed in dimensions beyond the physical.

Some embraced their animus, seeing it as opportunity to improve existence. Others feared it, viewing enhancement as corruption of their essential nature. Most simply tried to understand what they had become and what it meant for the reality they thought they knew.

The cosmic forces watched and waited, building influence through demonstration rather than conquest. Each sought to prove that their vision of the animus's purpose was the correct one, gathering followers through conviction rather than coercion.

But something unexpected was happening. Beings touched by the Singularity's power weren't choosing sides as predicted. Instead, they were creating something new—communities that blended different philosophies, approaches that valued both preservation and change, order and growth, redemption and acceptance.

Yet in the spaces between realities, other ancient powers began to stir. The cosmic game was larger than any of them had imagined, and new players were preparing to make their moves.

Time passed—days, seasons, perhaps eons. The multiverse adapted to its new reality with the stubborn resilience that had always characterized life in its infinite forms. Some beings chose to surrender their animus, contributing their energy to the Remnant and returning to simpler existence. Others embraced enhancement fully, becoming forces of nature in their own right. Still more fell to those who chose to claim power through violence rather than persuasion.

The cosmic powers found themselves in an escalating dance of influence and counter-influence, each gaining ground in some realities while losing it in others. Alliances formed and shattered. Territories were claimed and lost. The careful game of persuasion gave way to more direct methods as the stakes became clear.

Lilith's reapers harvested animus from the willing and unwilling alike, building her strength through calculated brutality. The Unspeakable Entity's whispers found fertile ground in beings who chose oblivion over struggle, while he worked to prevent any restoration of cosmic order. Omenti's perfect systems expanded like crystalline growths, optimizing existence whether inhabitants desired it or not.

Justice discovered that balance required more than principle—it demanded strength to enforce. Amy found that redemption's path was steeper when others actively opposed it. The Nothing realized that preserving interesting chaos meant preventing boring entropy.

Each gathered followers, built armies, claimed territories. The philosophical disagreement had become something more urgent, more desperate. The fate of existence itself hung in the balance, and the time for gentle persuasion was ending.

The Remnant pulsed in its crystalline solitude, growing slowly as some chose sacrifice while others fed upon their neighbors. Whether it would eventually restore the Singularity or be corrupted by those who sought to claim it remained unclear.

But across the vast network of realities, the cosmic forces could sense movement in the deeper shadows. The six who had shattered the old order would soon discover they were not the only powers seeking to shape what came next.

The fate of the multiverse would be decided not by the strongest or the wisest, but by those who could inspire others to choose their vision of what existence should become. In coffee shops and throne rooms, in laboratories and battlefields, in the hearts of ordinary beings who had been touched by infinite power, the real struggle was just beginning.

The cosmic joke had found its punchline, and the laughter echoed across eternity—not in mockery but in celebration of infinite possibility.

The multiverse had become a question mark rather than a period, a beginning disguised as an ending.

Afterword

Dear Reader,

If you've made it this far, you've witnessed something I've been building toward for over two decades—the moment when all the pieces finally come together, when individual stories reveal themselves as movements in a larger symphony, when the cosmic scope I've always envisioned for this universe finally has room to breathe.

Writing these fifteen tales has been like conducting an orchestra where each musician has been practicing in isolation for years, only to discover they've been playing parts of the same impossible composition all along. Every character you've met—from Juvia's desert courage to Lilith's cosmic rebellion—has been both a complete story unto themselves and a note in this greater harmony.

531

I hope you felt that crescendo building. The way small acts of heroism ripple across millennia. How personal struggles reflect cosmic truths. The manner in which individual choices can reshape the fundamental nature of existence itself. This has always been my vision for Animus—not just powerful beings clashing in spectacular battles, but a meditation on what it means to choose hope over despair, connection over isolation, questions over easy answers.

The fragments scattered at the story's end are not conclusions but beginnings. Each represents a different path forward, a different answer to the question of what we do with power when we finally claim it. Justice seeks balance. Amy pursues redemption. Omenti demands efficiency. Lilith craves dominion. The Entity offers ending. And The Nothing... well, he's still asking the interesting questions.

But here's what I hope you've discovered: these aren't just characters in a fantasy story. They're aspects of the eternal human struggle to make meaning from chaos, to find purpose in the temporary, to create something beautiful even when we know it won't last forever. Every time you've chosen compassion over cruelty, every time you've asked difficult questions instead of accepting easy answers, every time you've reached out to another person despite the risk of being hurt—you've been living your own version of these cosmic battles.

The Animus Draft-Building Card Game was where these characters first came to life, where players could pit them against each other in strategic conflicts that told their own stories. But cards can only hold so much truth. These tales are my attempt to give you the rest—the histories that shaped them, the doubts that drove them, the moments of vulnerability that make their strength meaningful.

If this book has sparked your curiosity about the game that started it all, I couldn't be more pleased. There's something magical about holding these characters in your hands, about making tactical decisions that echo their philosophical struggles, about discovering new combinations and interactions that reveal truths I never consciously built into their designs. The game and these stories enhance each other, each one illuminating aspects of the multiverse that neither could fully capture alone.

Thank you for trusting me with your time and attention. Thank you for following these characters into the spaces between certainty and doubt, for staying with them through cosmic horror and intimate hope. Thank you for being willing to ask the hard questions about power and responsibility, about the price of knowledge and the cost of freedom.

Most of all, thank you for understanding that even in a universe where reality itself can be rewritten on a whim, the most important battles are still fought in the human heart. That's where every story truly begins and ends—not with the clash of cosmic forces, but with the choice to keep caring, keep trying, keep believing that tomorrow might be better than today.

The multiverse is vast and full of wonders. Your place in it matters more than you know.

Until our paths cross again in whatever reality comes next,

Ed Rodriguez

*P.S. - If you're curious about the card game that gave birth to this multiverse, you'll find it captures the tactical complexity and narrative depth of these cosmic conflicts in ways that might surprise you. Each game tells its own story, and every deck represents a different answer to the questions these characters are asking. The war for existence continues, and you get to decide how it unfolds.

www.ingramcontent.com/pod-product-compliance
Lightning Source LLC
Chambersburg PA
CBHW032002110726
47901CB00004B/935